Two~~Tw~~worlds

The Art of ~~Dying~~ Lôve

R.B. Anderson

Published by Neue Cadence

ISBN 978-0-9963613-0-9

Printed in the United States

Editor: Burton Mitchell, Author of The End Justifies The Means, (T.E.J.T.M.,)

Electronic Publishing: Terri Rose-Anderson, VisionServer

Cover Illustration: RB Anderson

Hawk photo on cover courtesy Jon Lutz, birdsofcolorado.com

ACKNOWLEDGMENTS

I would like to express my gratitude to the many people who
assisted and provided support, in making this book a reality:

Louise Ann Parrish Anderson–Allison Ross,
a remarkable lady, who viewed life as a great adventure.
Without her wisdom, insight, courage and constant passion to explore,
this book would not have been possible.

Fellow author, editor and friend Burton Mitchell
whose compassion and unrelenting attention to detail
helped keep me on track.

Nancy Lofholm who befriended Louise and chronicled her recollections
of life and expectations about her death, through a series of articles
published in the Grand Junction Daily Sentinel.

Terri Rose-Anderson, my soul-mate, for her love, understanding
and encouragement.

As Louise wrote in her notebooks:
"To my 'Vigilantes' Family Don and Jill along with my Hospice family
Shirley Roe, Linda Gifford, Tom Trumball who wield their own form
of radiation treatment–Awareness, Concern and Caring.… I feel honor
bound to share some of my most secret self awarenesses with you."

INTRODUCTION

Louise Anderson saw her diagnosis of six months to live as her 'Greatest Adventure.'

This book is a collaboration, with many insights and wisdom from a series of notebooks written by Louise Ann Parrish Anderson, pen name Allison Ross, documenting her process of dying. Louise recorded conversations she had with Soul entities she referred to as GA's. These GA's have lived many lifetimes.

Louise called her Soul friends GA's, or Guiding Angels, not Guardian Angels, as many call them. She would always say, "Because they do not guard, they guide a person along life's path." This is a unique collaboration of the GA on the other side, Louise between dimensions and myself living in the here and now. We'll attempt to bring light to this dim dimension of the in-between.

This introduction has an excerpt from a series of articles published in the Daily Sentinel, written by Nancy Lofholm, as she chronicled Louise's recollections of her life and expectations about her death.

Louise wrote her notebooks with the intention of three parts:

1. Etiquette of Dying–code of behavior.

2. Art of Dying

3. Ethics of Dying

GA's instructed, "The sections of your Dying Books–you have mis-named 'The Etiquette, Ethics and Art of Dying.' It is invalid, since there is no death– the three section are to be titled: 'The Etiquette, Art and Ethics of LOVE.' The decorum, creative application and moral principles, the fundamental Truth."

Louise stated, "I do not want to be drugged and dragged across the border–but to go with awareness and appreciation. — A Soul search with as much honesty and courage as one infinitesimal earthling can muster for its beginning cosmic awareness."

"This book is no empty pretentiousness, but comes from a long lifetime of commitment to searching for hints to Truths. From early childhood experiencing death at the turn of the century during the grim Victorian-Edwardian era of black-veiled women, black-windowed hearses, drawn by black horses."

"At the age of thirteen I lay awake nights puzzling over the mystery– What is time? Why? How come they say it's this way? When something inside me suspects... no one knows there's more to this mystery than anyone here and now even suspects."

"Then decades later, being a Gray Lady with the Red Cross at the V.A. hospital after WWII. Then studying for seven years with a very advanced psychologist... Dr. Boroff– never ceasing and re-searching for glimmers of answers."

"I hope and trust that the doctors who attend me in these last months will be interested in, or at least honor the passionate commitment of one minuscule person's search along the borderline. A search for a few more shards that humankind has found broken, over the ages, for some basic and ultimate Truth."

"I suppose I never really 'belonged' on planet earth... but merely took this life on as a project for examination or exploration. But of course that's what it really is, for all of us humans. Only most people don't bother to consider the basic whys and wherefores of our sojourn here. Hence the arrogant dictatorial assumptions of our sundry societies self-designated 'Wise Ones,' not content merely to argue among themselves. They must stir up their followers into frenzies of little loyalties and enormous destructive hatreds, until poor old planet earth, which would nourish all, becomes the target–the enemy, marked for destruction. Well, well now! So here are my diatribes."

Nancy Lofholm - Daily Sentinel wrote, "So Much To Do, So Little Time."

"With an I-give-up toss of her hands, Louise tips back in her favorite easy chair and laughs like a school girl over the prospect of dying. 'It's going to be the greatest adventure of my life, but I don't know how in the world I'm going to get everything done before my time comes. There is so much to do and so little time. Where do you start when you have six months to live?' True to character, Louise started with a flurry of tea parties, it's not possible to visit without an invitation for tea. When not socializing she was busy marking her possessions to divvy up among her family and friends, and looking for answers to questions on her journey toward understanding death."

Author's Note–Following are excerpts directly from Louise's notebooks. Nothing was changed, other than to type the hand-scribbled notes, in order to give the reader a feeling for the communication between Louise and her Guiding Angels (GA).

These are the first passages in the many notebooks written during the last six years of her adventure on this planet–in the body many knew, and loved as Louise. Let's take an inside-out view from one of earth's grand explorers.

GA: " Few have ever dared explore the In-Between...

Come! Come

with us now!"

"If the language of these dictations seems deliberate, its because we are not 'hep' to your current ever changing language."

"I see you are looking up the word amanuensis –stenographer, copyist, secretary–well yes that is as good a word as any for what you are doing".

Louise: "It occurs to me that one reason for my continued, or renewed, remission–may be that my GA's needs to train another amanuensis... and that I am still in the midst of translation.

HAIKU

Twilight or Dawn? This

Dialogue in Darkness by

the not-yet Dead..."

GA: "Well now! This is what you earth persons might say: 'Is one for the book!'"

GA: "It's not often that we hear Earth persons complaining that what they had assumed was their death schedule has been postponed... with no definite time set."

Louise: "How come me? I'm not a psychic!"

GA: "No but you're available, and willing."

Louise (bluntly): "I'm curious, I seem always to be exploring the edges,

You'd think I'd be to playful for work as serious as this."

GA: "Oh no! We always prefer a blithe spirit to a doleful one. But the blithe are as you USA Westerners might say, some what harder to corral."

Louise: "I have a feeling it's my 'blithe' spirited mother who got me into this!"

GA: "Possibly. But you know there is a whole coterie of blithe Spirits on both sides of the borders."

Louise: "How do you select your symbols for us?"

GA: "We use the materials at hand."

Louise: "Why do our insights come so late in life?"

GA: "Not always late in life, but when insights are truly looked for, and listened for in silence."

Louise: "Why all these ridiculous dogmatisms of our infinitesimal human species?"

GA: "Remembering is not enough. Re-experiencing is necessary for Soul growth."

Louise: "Puzzling over the horrendous task of moving me and my possessions to a new place and thinking of what must be mind-boggling traffic from here to higher realms."

GA: "But of course you must know that Souls have no such heavy paraphernalia. The sooner the Earth Soul learns to strip itself of possessions—possessions that are the possessors... the freer is the Soul for all its new adventures."

Louise: "If this book is to be an honest investigation of Dying... then I must investigate and experience all aspects, the dark as well as the Light."

GA: "You have no real way of interpreting Death here, because when you experience it you are already on the other side."

February 23, 1993 - 6:00 am

Louise: "Now entering the second month of my 87th year, I dedicate this beautiful gift of book, of waiting white pages to the last stages of my this-earth-time transition toward the next-stage of ongoing Soul evolution. May a few more incites lighten, brighten–not only my own darkening way but also the inevitable way of a few others who may read herein. Guidance from Light to bright for our mortal eyes to see... I pray now only for glimmerings."

"It is evidently not enough to theorize. I started this project with a sort of blithe carelessness. Well if I'm going through a process that has generally been examined only by outsiders, why not discover how it really works? On all levels, physical, mental, emotional, and spiritual, but the only true participator. Who but the experiencer can really know?"

"A year later I find myself in the midst of a script being written, read, and performed... a sort of half glorious, half nightmarish, half enlightening happening, or rather happenings. I am honor-bound to follow through to the end... whatever, however that "end" may be. Obviously I, as a karmic being expect this dying process to reveal itself as merely another bridge in the whole series of crossings... so for now... to be continued."

February 26, 1993

GA: "The Cosmic Creator is never as some earth people think repetitious. Always innovative, always relevant creations of meaningful variations. Patterns that seem, to the untrained mind, to be the childish scribblings it-itself might have produced, are of course, so far beyond even the higher levels, that all lower levels can only be expanded into awe."

Louise: "How am I to know what is authentic in these bits of wisdom?"

GA: "You may never know here, but inadequate as your here and now is, receive the glimmers of Light with as much wisdom and gratitude as your ever-growing Soul can muster."

March 6, 1993 - 2:30 am

GA: "On Going Home. You've been in our dimensions far more often and far longer than your brief assignments of explorations to planet Earth."

June 29, 1993 -3:00 am

Louise: "I must be extremely cautious, that I do not let my dreams get mixed up in this experiment. Yet at the same time be aware of some significant symbols in dreams that may have a valid importance in this inter-dimensional awareness research."

"One wonderful thing about living a long life, is that it gives you a chance to discover patterns. To perceive how that long-ago incident repeats itself in this—a slightly different way, but never a random way, all to form a meaningful event and enlightening an ever-growing significant pattern of holiness."

June 30, 1993 - 6:00 am

GA: "This in-between world does indeed need its own codes of etiquette, art and ethics..."

Louise: "Life's greatest miracle is ours every day, and we do not even perceive it, much less appreciate it: That every meal we eat to nourish our own uniqueness we partake of the world, the whole earth's bounty. From the seas of foreign lands to the range of our own little home lands these crumbs of the planet's bounty are miraclized to become energetic, thinking, creative you and me. The miracle not only of uniqueness, but the Cosmic given the ability to perceive and foster our own uniqueness, as our particular way of contributing to the evolution of our own little world."

July 4, 2002

RB Anderson: It's ironic, that Louise took six years to finish her notes, and here I am, taking steps on a journey that started six years ago when my wife and I sat at the bedside of my dying grandmother Louise Parrish Anderson. "Rusty," my grandmother always called me by the all-but-forgotten family nickname, "Rusty, I don't have the strength to finish this. Would you take my notebooks and bring them to completion, would you finish it for me after I go on?"

I anxiously agreed. After all, she and I had talked and written each other on many occasions during the last years of her life. It shouldn't be that difficult. Ha, who was I kidding? She has been writing about the process of dying–death is a tough one to tackle. And it has taken me many years to write this story of "Two Worlds."

Louise is a remarkable lady, seeing cancer as her greatest adventure, her next grand step.

It's all in that first step. The first steps of life's journey; the first step into the egg of life, then leaving your mother's womb, your first cry, the awkward first time you walk, first- kiss, love, job, marriage, child–on and on to that first step after leaving our body into the vast unknown...

This novel is a fiction based on Louise and her GA's insights. Though the plot is fictitious, the underlying story is based on universal truths. You determine what is fiction and what is real. As in life–the line is quite blurred.

You did it, Louise. You made it.

We all knew how this chapter of your story was going to end. But this is not a story about the end, but about the in-between and the beginning.

This is a Love story.

Louise Ann Parish Anderson

CHAPTER 1
Finding the End of the World

Friday, December 21, was the end of the world. At least for some of us. But not as we would have expected. The Mayan calendar had predicted the end of the world this year, which didn't happen for most people, though in a way our world ended that weekend.

A jaguar, waterfall, ancient cliff dwellings, high desert landscapes, an Inca Sun God and my grandmother Louise– the subject matter in my paintings had changed in the months leading to that serendipitous weekend. What little I can remember from my dreams, was finding its way in paint, to materialize on these recent canvases. Little did I know that these new paintings were an omen of things to come.

It began when we left the road, literally, and took a path less traveled. That path took us to a place and time we never realized existed, though it was right under our noses. Through the following day this new reality slowly became apparent to my wife Celeste and me.

The end of December was abnormally hot, so we decided to take a short camping trip, and be home for Christmas. That trip ended the world as we knew it. I'll try to explain: I am Steele Brandon, an artist, kind of burned out from 40 years in advertising design. I wear my somewhat shaggy gray hair long enough to cover the top of my ears and like to think of myself as fit, though truth be known–I am 40 pounds overweight. As a young man I was considered handsome–today I hear distinguished a lot. Whatever that means. My beautiful wife Celeste, the love of my life has wonderful natural white-blond shoulder-length hair and a smile that melted me from the time I first saw her. Our two dogs, Isis and Maya, like to camp with us as often as we can find time. So we decided to explore a new area–one that turns out had been pulling at us from our dreams.

"Funny," Celeste said as we traveled along the back roads off Highway 12. "This area is strangely familiar." We were somewhere around the four corners area in Utah. I had a primordial feeling similar to Celeste, kind of a déjà vu. I instinctively turned off the road and started up a dry sandy ravine, surrounded by tall desert crested wheat grass and sage brush.

For some reason I was headed for a distant familiar peak. "Steele, where are you going?" Celeste asked.

"Don't know, I just had a sensation and decided to explore. Trust me, it will be great," I replied.

Twisting and turning our way up a dry, sandy riverbed, it slowly became a small stream. The altitude changed as we followed the creek, eventually leaving the grass along the creek bank behind. We now traveled across smooth sandstone, headed toward a box canyon. Peculiar rock pillars, like those in Bryce Canyon, seemed to grow from the canyon walls becoming more and more prevalent. Inching along the tight trail, my peripheral vision glimpsed impression of structures, built into the rocks. But when I looked directly, I discovered they were just my imagination. Only a play of the shadows from the strong afternoon sun?

I maneuvered around a particularly sharp corner and came to a stop at the base of a huge rock structure, where two walls of the canyon we had been following converged.

"We have arrived," I stated.

"Where, hun?"

"Beats me," I told Celeste. A large totem-shaped rock structure, known as a Hoodoo, blocked us from driving any further. I pulled our Xterra to a wide spot and parked. We could see a trail winding up the mountain beside an ancient stone sentinel, that stood as if guarding unknown secrets. Working our way around the stone guard, we found the entrance to a mysteriously inviting hiking trail.

We pulled out our backpacking gear and started up the trail. Celeste, our two dogs–Isis, a regal Smooth Collie, and Maya, our little party-colored Cocker Spaniel and we began a hike, that will turn out to be the hike of our lives.

The path looked tough, yet as we walked, there was little strain on any of us. Gravity seemed to be our friend this day. Strolling along this ancient path we had a sense of family. Like we were walking with a gathering, yet at any moment it was only the four of us. We climbed higher along this rocky trail and out of my peripheral vision I again saw habitable structures along the canyon walls, but of course they weren't there, couldn't be, just my imagination. Negative shapes created by shadows like before.

We followed the tight, winding trail around the side of a waterfall where we were forced to climb single file through steep rocky formations in the cliffs.

As we topped the plateau, we gazed across a flat terrain. The same river that plunged from these heights was now a lazy creek meandering like a snake through clear pools in the sandstone. Ponderosa pine and mesquite trees grew along beautiful inlets. A short walk later we came to a cove that was so inviting.

"This is a good spot for camp," I said.

"No, let's look a little further, just around that corner," Celeste replied.

We found more inlets, some fed by small springs flowing from cracks in the stone that trickled along sponge-like moss where tiny flowers grew in recesses that looked carved by eons of flowing water.

"This is the place." Sculpted into the rock walls by an invisible hand were cave-like rooms that supplied better shelter than any tent. As our little family explored, it became apparent there was something in the vicinity. We were not alone. We explored lair after lair, then turned through a room and the creek materialized again. WOW, a mountain lion stood lapping from a clear pool of water.

"Turn around slowly," Celeste said. The dogs followed us as we left. Thankfully the lion ignored us.

We went on to explore other alcoves. Walking around another rock wall we stopped. A bear sat in the waning sun peeking across the top of a sandstone arch. It was illuminated in the last rays of light, just enjoying himself like a wild actor, in nature's theater.

"Do not move too suddenly, and you will all be fine. Benard is friendly enough. We believe you met the mountain lion earlier, her name is Maverick."

Startled, we looked back to see who was speaking to us. A young man and woman were standing behind us. Their voices were so calm that none of us were concerned. Generally when approached off-guard like that, Isis and Maya would have come out of their skin. The hair on Isis' back would stand up and their voices would bark out a warning. Come to think of it, they both would usually raise their chorus of growls and barks in furious unity, when coming across any of the wildlife we just happened across. Odd?

"You like our place?" the young lady asked. She was tall and attractive with the dark complexion of an Inca princess. Her long black hair reflected a purple hint that framed her face, emphasizing beautiful obsidian eyes giving the appearance of not having pupils. She wore a silver tiara with tiny pearl beads threaded through her long hair. A green jewel was delicately linked to the tiara and dangled at the center of her forehead. "We have been preparing and waiting for you. You're the first to arrive. Let us show you around," she exclaimed.

"Excuse us. We have not introduced ourselves: I am Ix Ek' Naa - of the former Kaan kingdom in Campeche, daughter of Lady Bakab, wife of the King Tuun K'ab' Hix. You can call me Star. This is Yuknoom Yich'aak K'ahk', of the previous Kaan kingdom. It is easier to refer to him as Jaguar." Jaguar stood well over six feet with a strong build and chiseled features. His short black hair framed an ageless clean-cut face, punctuated by the same polished obsidian eyes.

Star and Jaguar led us out through an opening in the rock a few paces away. We all emerged on an open patio overlooking the canyon we had climbed earlier. About three feet below a natural retaining wall was a beautiful pond, that briefly lived there before it cascaded from this lofty palace's balcony, falling between sculpted earth pillars. The canyon walls breathed the sun's warmth. The sun was setting, producing wonderful hues of crimson and gold that glimmered across the water, sending refractions dancing throughout the natural alcove holding the pool at our feet. It felt as if we had been transported to heaven. The only thing missing were some harps.

"Welcome to our home," Star pronounced. "We affectionately call it the Falls. But you must be tired. That is quite a climb up the canyon. We have prepared a room for you, make yourselves at home, and we can talk in the morning. You are safe here. Everything is in harmony now that you are flowing with the earth's natural energy. Enjoy your dreams."

Flowing with earth's natural energy? That cipher put my mind into an inquisitive posture, which was quickly dissolved by the beauty surrounding us and the millions of stars glinting from the Milky Way overhead. "Thank you, we could use a place to stay for the night. It is going to be cold and we didn't feel like pitching a tent," came Celeste's appreciative response.

Celeste, Isis, Maya and I followed Star as she led the way through a door, that I swear was not in that rock wall when we entered the overlook.

"Good night," Star said.

'Saying thank you is surface etiquette,

 feeling thank you is from the heart,

 living thank you is from the soul.'

We truly thank you for coming."

There was something familiar to Star's 'thank you' haiku. Pondering the poem, I drifted to sleep.

I dreamed of Louise, my poetic grandmother... Louise and Star becoming one as my grandmother was standing in this unique place reciting the thank-you parable.

Eggs, rosemary, strawberries, pine trees, am I still dreaming? The aroma of the morning wafted through my senses as I slowly opened my eyes.

"You hungry?" Celeste asked, cuddled against my chest. We were wrapped in a warmth coming from the soft bed of natural fibers, as we stirred from the night's wonderfully relaxing sleep.

"I can't remember such a restful night. I feel like a new person. And yes, I'm starving," was my reply.

"Glad you are awake. Perfect timing, breakfast is just being served. You have a visitor I believe you will like to see again. Come out to the balcony when you are up," Star pronounced.

I splashed my face with cold water from the spring flowing out of the nearby rock wall and pulled a shirt on over my head. Celeste followed, cleaning in the clear water. Isis and Maya drank from the basin the spring created before it disappeared back into the rock.

I was bewildered at what was happening, wondering if we were somehow dreaming all of this.

"Muffins, I smell muffins. But where could you find an oven up here to bake them?"

"Are you ready to eat, hun?" Celeste asked, pulling me by the arm. We followed the aroma of fresh baked wonders when...

"There you are, I was told you finally made it," came the familiar voice from behind me.

"Louise!" Celeste exclaimed.

I spun around and there she stood. It was my grandmother Louise, though she was much younger, appearing to be in her mid-40's. "Can't be!" I exclaimed... "You are, ah, well, you passed away over 18 years ago."

"Good term. 'Passed away,' or maybe it should be 'moved on.' That is what I did. I moved on," Louise explained. "I believe you already understand esoterically that the life we all live, is a plane of existence, one of many. There comes a time when certain beings have learned enough to advance to another spiritual zone, like graduating in school. The way you and mankind have existed is a certain grade or class in the ever-evolving spirit that lives in all of us."

"Let's eat. We do not want breakfast to get cold," came Star's voice from the balcony.

Louise must have heard my stomach growling so she said, "We'll finish catching up over breakfast."

We all headed for the balcony and there in the morning light waited an omelet with a garnish of rosemary, strawberries and blueberries with cream in small cups, and steaming golden-brown muffins. Their aroma rose in a delicate steam drifting in the cool morning air.

We enjoyed this wonderful bounty, sitting in silence with our new companions gazing over the canyon. Soft beams of morning light crept over the ridge bringing warmth and a new day's life. None of us wanted to break the moment.

As Celeste took in all of the surrounding beauty, she finally exclaimed, "This is like having an early Christmas, it is all so magical, or rather a miracle."

"It is much like Christmas, dear, though here we celebrate during what you call Easter, because that is when we got Jesus back. Jaguar, would you explain the difference between magic and miracles?" Louise asked.

Jaguar sipped his coffee then told us. "Magic is manipulation by people clever enough to have studied and discovered some earthly laws beyond the crowd's understanding. A Miracle is an utterly different category: miracles are a glimpse of cosmic forces, a brief touch from spirit to help awaken our earthly souls to their potential. Much like many of the accomplishments, or miracles attributed to Jesus."

"Then this is truly a miracle," Celeste returned. "Thank you all."

Star went on to explain. "In essence what has happened and is happening to you since yesterday, when you turned off Highway 12, seems like magic. Magic, because you do not fully understand the earthly or cosmic laws in play. Everything since yesterday has been slowly evolving into this dimension, called Gaia."

"It started when you recognized the vortex and acted on it. You turned into the outer fringe of this dimension and as you traveled, your consciousness allowed you to continue through–going deeper until you became part of this plane of existence. It took time, you slowly became more integrated as you climbed the trail. You started to become aware of the people and their homes around you. So right now, none of you exist in your dimension."

"Wow, you mean we are dead?" I asked.

"No, well, yes in a way," Jaguar continued. "Dead is a relative term. If you mean you do not exist in your dimension, then the answer would be yes, at this specific moment. But in a more esoteric sense, no. You are not dead because for a while you can return, and you have only been missing from your world, as far as anyone is concerned."

Louise walked around the breakfast table and rested a hand on my shoulder, to give me some reassurance. "Do not worry, Steele. Actually, death as well as love are all an inextricable part of Soul learning."

Celeste leaned over to me and whispered, "This is all getting to be too much. I'm getting frightened."

I had to agree, I was feeling like we were going insane. "I don't understand. What do you mean we are not dead because for a while you can return? And yesterday when we first met you told us we were the first to arrive."

Louise smiled. "Please do not be afraid. I will explain what I can. You and Celeste are the first to come across the veil at this spot without actually passing away. This makes you both uniquely capable individuals. Though you should not be alone."

"Due to arcane celestial alignments, Earth is in a quantum shift, which aligns the planet with its destined position in the cosmos–its perfected state as a planet. This will allow a planetary shift into an evolved cycle of life. What this means is, the veil between dimensions is thin enough that people, having learned enough from Earth's dimension of existence, can graduate and move to a higher grade of learning without passing away. This is necessary for Earth-Gaia to remain in this advanced cycle of life. You, I, all humanity, along with our planet, are in this together."

Louise smiled, "Congratulations on your graduation."

Jaguar saw that we were not convinced. "Let me put it in scientific terms. Graduation is generated when a person expands awareness, and realizes their true self, which connects them with elevated potentials of consciousness. That restores access and memory of the infinite possibilities of our being. Scientists such as Feynman and Hawking have explained this world as multi-universes. Or the many-worlds interpretation of quantum theory, and Superstring theory as directions in space and time. This interpretation is quite accurate, with only one thing missing: the higher vibration at which those universes and our bodies must resonate in order to make the transition–to graduate.”

“To better understand, think of this in the form of light waves. We can only see a small part of the spectrum of light. In much the same way, we can only see certain vibrations of energy. So as energy vibrates at a higher speed, it disappears from our awareness. That does not mean it ceases to exist. What you experience as death is the body giving out before the higher vibration is attained. When that happens the consciousness or spirit leaves the body and finds a new body as the physical form in a new-born baby.”

As Jaguar explained, I noticed other dwellings materialize in the rocky cliffs up and down the canyon.

“What is happening? There are other homes becoming visible throughout the canyon walls?”

Jaguar looked concerned. “We must hurry then. Louise, tell them more about why Celeste and Steele were selected, while Star and I make preparations.”

Louise went on. “Let me back track so I can fill you in. Before I passed away, I gave you the journals I had been writing about the process of dying. Do you remember the discussions we had when I gave those to you? I explained that I received help from my ‘Guiding Angels’. Star and Jaguar are what at that time I thought were those angels.”

“When I passed from our dimension, they were here to help me further understand what was happening. We can talk more about that later, when we have more time. We all keep referring to time, because when a new person comes across as you both did, you have a limited period where you can return across the veil, before the transition becomes solid or more permanent.”

“How much time do we have?” Celeste and I both blurted out in trepidation.

Louise smiled. “That depends on how quickly you assimilate your surroundings. You both seem to be learning quite quickly, so we must hurry."

I'm sure I looked concerned. "Louise, what did Jaguar mean when he said we were selected?"

She took my hand reassuringly. "Let's find Jaguar so he can explain." After a moment's pause, Louise continued. "What I can tell you is that you two have the spirit of warriors or you would not have come this far."

Jaguar and Star walked in. "You have both been inundated with so much. You are taking it very well. Let us tell you why you were selected to visit us, and please allow us to ask for your help. You are both unique for a number of reasons, not the least of which is your constant search for truth, along with your understanding and persistence to show others that fear, struggle and war are not a path forward."

"For those reasons, along with many others, we are asking you to be on the forefront of the graduation process. Many people are ready to move to this level. However, most are stuck, for numerous reasons. We are confident you both have the talent and ability to help some of them realize what is happening and to aid in their graduation."

"Time is short, so we will tell you more as we walk down the trail with you," Star said, obviously concerned. "Here are your packs. We hope you do not mind, we packed your things while you spoke with Louise. We must start down the canyon before it is too late."

For a moment the quiet between us was deafening as we began the journey down the trail back to our world. The only sounds came from the canyon as it seemed to be telling us goodbye. The birds, waterfall, even the rocky canyon walls seemed alive with a natural symphony. We felt in harmony with them all.

Jaguar broke the silence. "As you know there is much fear, anger and hatred in your world. These emotions are keeping many people that have a deep understanding, from reaching the vibration which enables them to understand where the veil is thin enough to cross. Even those that perceive the veil are often too frightened to venture further, so they write-off any unusual feeling or vision as imagination. As soon as you do not believe, that moment's quintessence is lost."

As I listened, there were so many questions. "How on earth are we expected to assist these people to believe when what they are seeing vanishes so quickly?"

Star thought for a second then proceeded. "You are not alone. There have been many teachers throughout history. Find them, and together you will succeed. We are all interconnected. Our lives are tied invisibly to those whose destinies connect with one another. Your task is to blend science, spirituality and emotion in a way that helps people understand and connect."

"You have heard of 'Six degrees of separation;' that everyone is six or fewer steps, by way of introduction, from any other person in the world. That chain of 'a friend of a friend' can be made to connect any two people in six steps. Use that concept. You have friends that have similar beliefs as your own. So also do they, and so on. It only takes three to become many. To further our collaboration between our worlds, we have included a few items in your packs that will facilitate the process–should you choose to help."

Jaguar and Louise were talking and they both looked uneasy. "Before you decide to work with us, we have to warn you. There are many who, for their own reason, or a group's agenda, do not want any of this to succeed. Governments, political parties, and religions in particular."

Louise persisted. "Work quietly and do not draw any unnecessary attention to yourselves. Some of these people feel very threatened by losing control of their fear-based authority."

Jaguar suddenly had a blank stare, as a wet spot spread across his chest. He crumpled to the dusty path at our feet. An echo reverberated through the canyon. We all became deathly aware that it was a distant gun shot. It had to have been a high-powered rifle, to hit him from the obvious distance the sound conveyed. A remote sound of a truck's engine receded into a whisper. The hush was deafening. It had been only seconds, before I caught my breath and became aware of the screams and sudden frenzy.

Some of those screams were mine.

"RUN!" shouted Star. "We have healers to attend him, you must get beyond the veil before it is too late. And remember–be careful. We will contact you soon."

❯ ❯ ❯

CHAPTER 2
Jump Technology

'It's an exciting time to be alive–I guess?' James thought. 'Not sure I'll ever get used to 3-dimensional printers, talking books, and this Jump technology. Sounds like it belongs in a science fiction story. It's not right. Or is it?'

Something in the back of his mind liked it. James thought the technology was on to something. But what? Virtual reality wasn't enough; that scared the shit out of him. 'Then some smart-ass geek, my son of all people, had to take you, body and soul, into another dimension to play a game. Wonder where your body actually goes when you Jump? It can't be safe.'

He heard on the news the other day that the police were looking for a kid. 'What was his name? Bingo? No, that wasn't it.' The police think they had linked the kid's disappearance to a Jump Portal.

'Damn! I wish my wife Heather was here. I should have been able to protect her. God help me.'

"Sir… hello, Mr. Knecht. We have arrived at Stamford Plaza, about five minutes from the Sydney Airport."

"Ah. Oh, yes, next to the Kingsford Smith International Airport. Thank you, Potters," James stammered.

"You have a meeting with Mr. Bradbury at 1:30 p.m. in the Kingsford Room at the Plaza, then the plane to Los Angeles leaves from terminal 1, US Airways at 3:20 pm. You are on a 747, as you like. In Los Angeles, you will have a connecting flight to Denver. It is all in the itinerary I uploaded to your phone, sir."

"Yes, good work, Potters."

James abruptly realized that his daydream had taken him somewhere else during the limo ride to the airport. Everything from getting in the limo, and the drive to the airport didn't seem to have happened. The last thing he clearly remembered was coffee and Danish, and…oh, that article in the paper about Jump technology.

The meeting was a bore, same political bullshit with everyone trying to position themselves to come out on top. At least he was able to handle Mr. Bradbury. 'Bradbury won't be spewing his save-the-world shit anymore,' James thought.

'Why on earth is Australia so damn far from everything? Thirteen and a half hours to LA, that's a long way to come for a one-hour job.'

Somehow on the flight from Sydney to LA, James was able to sleep. Sometime during the movie after dinner, when the hostess with her trained smile made, or rather manufactured, with the intention of serving customers, put that almost edible meal in front of him.

James had strange dreams...floating in another dimension, feeling alone, cold, two of his three children and wife floating along with him just out of reach. A red globe, looking like an old hanging lamp or light fixture from his mother's house. A retro 60's lampshade on it. Huge, ugly. He hated that thing! This enormous globe shattered into millions of small fragments.

As James woke he remembered thinking, 'I only have one child, Ian, and my wife is gone. The dream doesn't make any sense. But when do they?'

The flight from LA to Denver was nondescript, same manufactured smiles and bad food. He couldn't bring himself to eat, though a couple of cocktails helped relieve the cramped legs, but even first class gets tight after so many hours.

Before she left him, his former girlfriend had called him a shallow, self-absorbed, social hermit, among other things that probably shouldn't be repeated. But he doesn't see himself that way at all. A little gray at 60, he still sees a handsome man in the mirror who is proud of keeping in good shape. James represents a special interest group, lobbying for Academi, formerly known as Blackwater. It is the largest mercenary group in the world, with strong connections to the Roman Catholic Church. So James always figured he has God on his side.

James didn't have time for many personal relationships. He likes his life organized and familiar. He takes pleasure from the finer things in life–a good wine, say 2006 Bourgogne Pinot Noir and Steak Kobe at Soho's in New York. Complement that with a sexy, beautiful young lady or two and, well, what more could a man need?

Ian picked James up at Denver International Airport. James' back was to Ian as he stood watching the multi-colored packages spin around the luggage carousel.

"Dad, is that you? I hardly recognized you, it's been so long! How was your trip? Jasmine and the kids can't wait to meet you."

Ian is his estranged son. James always thought of Ian as a brilliant kid. Of course he is no longer a kid, but he will always think of him that way. Maybe that's part of the underlying problem between them. That, and of course, Ian blaming James for his mother's death. That's what James always used as an excuse for the problems between them.

Ian wore his hair very short. He always had a great smile. In his thirties, he's a technology wizard. He grew up with the burden of being known world-wide for graduating with a major in mathematics and computer science from MIT, at the age of twelve.

Ian was currently under contract, tearing apart software for God only knows who. He also sits in on major court hearings, as a leading computer forensic expert. He makes outrageous money, but other than a few techno-toys, doesn't seem to care or flaunt it.

Ian, his wife Jasmine, and two children live a seemingly ordinary life, on an acre of land in a western suburb of Denver, on Black Widow Drive, in the foothills of Shadow Mountain, a prelude to the Rocky Mountains. It always sounded like something out of a spy novel to James. Their two wonderful kids were grandkids James had never met.

After a drive from the Denver airport, Ian pulled into his three-car garage, and they took the luggage into the festively-decorated home. James was there for Christmas.

"Dad, this is my lovely wife Jasmine." Jasmine is a striking, natural beauty. She has a relaxed appearance with blue eyes, shoulder-length layered blond hair and natural pink lips.

"Nice to meet you, Jasmine," James said, with a bow. "Thank you for inviting me for Christmas dinner."

Ian excused themselves to show James his computer room. It was not a Dickens surrounding at all. The room looked like a control center in the Pentagon's war command. Computer screens floating in the air like ghosts: words, lights, pictures and symbols flashing like apparitions, coming to life on one of his many computer screens at a touch, or voice command.

Ian was always listening to news. As they talked there came a newsflash: "Australia's Handon Bradbury has been assassinated. Mr. Bradbury was well-respected in government circles and was expected to become a member of the Australian House of Representatives in the coming election. He was known for his stance against the escalation of international wars. Mr. Bradbury was running as a green candidate because of his alliance with Greenpeace and the Australian Conservation Fund."

"Dad, the other day I heard that your company had some contract or affiliation with Bradbury, so did you know him?"

James looked at Ian, with a surprised look. "No... no, I didn't."

Ian seemed saddened. "His death is going to really hurt the environmental struggle to fix the problems with our eco-system. I'm sorry to hear the news."

Ian changed the subject. "Glad you're here, dad, you told me you have been wanting to know about the Portal and Jumping. It's really exciting, and a strange sensation. But since when did you start caring about technology?"

James shrugged, and just smiled.

"Anyway, when you first enter the Portal opening, you feel disoriented, almost as if you stepped into a dream. All of your surroundings change, everything that is not made of organic material or a natural part of the earth is gone. You have a brief impression of weightlessness. A bright white light surrounds you, forming a tunnel encircling your consciousness, then everything becomes still."

"Sounds nauseating," James exclaimed.

Ian continued, "I guess, at first, but you get used to it and it becomes spellbinding, intriguing, thrilling!"

"I'll have to take your word for that. Doesn't sound like anything I want to experience, especially after a Christmas dinner." James winked at his son—with a hint, hint gesture.

"Ha! Yes, that's coming soon, I hope. Jasmine, can I help with dinner?" he called out.

A resounding response came from the other room. "No babe, I have everything covered."

"Jasmine seems like a great catch, son."

"Yeh, I am the luckiest guy in the world, really lucky!"

James continued with his questions. "Physically, what do you feel like? Is it painful? Is your imagined body solid? Can you take anything with you?"

"Let me explain. Your body is not imagined; it is your real body.

It's difficult to explain since it is more than an appearance, more of an awareness, like nothing you have ever experienced. Yes, you can take something with you as long as you have direct contact with it during the Jump. And no, it does not hurt."

"You can see for yourself. But before you can enter the Portal, we have to sequence your DNA. Once the computer has your DNA imprint, it marries it with your mental signature and you are set. Next, we program your destination on the computer interface, and you are ready to go. When you enter the Portal, you are literally transported–mind, body and soul, in a manner of speaking–into this new world. As you go through a Portal, you become 'You' within the other world. Your actual appearance is somewhat ghostlike, semi-transparent, as are all the other people you encounter in that world."

As Ian explained, James noticed the Portal door, that looked ordinary enough at first glance. On closer inspection, he saw an odd-looking transparent neon tube around the door's architrave, with a strange reflection on a mirror-like strip on the floor. A soft alternating glow emanated just out of sequence from top to bottom of the opening. It was hypnotizing. Staring into the doorway the very air liquefied, then wavered like gelatin. It moved gently with a warm, dreamlike invitation. "What's the door about, Ian?"

Turning from the computer screen he was preparing to show James, Ian squinted his left eye with a nervous tic. "Oh, that's the Jump Portal, but it's older technology." He opened the drawer of a spotlessly clean desk and showed his dad a cylindrical polished metal object about seven inches long. It looked like the handle of a light saber, from the Star Wars movies.

"This will revolutionize everything!" Ian held up the Wand. "Something that started out as a game, can now be considered a teleportation Wand. Now we can travel anywhere in the world in seconds!" He slid a button forward with his thumb, and lights began to swirl around him. "This is a portable version of the Portal door. I just designed it." With a proud tilt of his chin, he opened his mouth to explain further...and a song began to play. Ian turned the portable device off and put it back in the drawer.

Resonating musical chimes filled the house with a techno reverberation. James looked inquisitively at Ian. "Sounds like electronic dance music I remember hearing from the late 80's in Eastern Europe."

"The door bell," Ian said.

"Dinner is ready," called Jasmine.

James caught the scent in Ian's control center, as the aroma of roast turkey dinner wafted in from the kitchen. He hadn't eaten anything since the dull taste of cardboard served on the plane from Australia, about seven hours ago. "I'm starving!" James said.

"Ian, have you seen the credit card? Please pay the delivery person for the special pies I ordered while I finish setting the table," Jasmine said from the kitchen. "Call Alek, and Kristen, would you please?"

Doors started slamming and the sound of James' two grandkids came bouncing off the balusters of the stairs, Alek taking two or three in a stride, followed by his little sister, Kristen. Alek could be a professional basketball player someday. Where did he get his height at 12 years old?

Ian caught Alek as he tried to race by. "Kids, come meet your granddad. He is going to have dinner with us for Christmas." Alek shook James' hand. "Glad to meet you, sir." Kristen hid behind her dad and peeked out. "Hello, are you my daddy's daddy?"

"Yes, honey," Ian smiled. "Anyone hungry?"

CHAPTER 3
Louise's Notebooks

[Eighteen years earlier...]

There she was…with a smile as her final testament of understanding. Louise left behind the earth-bound space suit she inhabited for her 86-year pilgrimage. Louise Parrish Anderson (Allison Ross, as she was known to many that read her books and poetry) crossed the great divide after submission of her final thesis: "The Etiquette, Ethics and Art of Dying". No—she had replaced 'dying' with "The Art of Love."

[Six years before her death...]

"I have some bad news, Louise," the very words she was afraid she would hear from her doctor. "Louise, there is no easy way to say this, you should sit down."

"Doctor, I know. How long do I have to live?"

This was the question Louise really came to the doctor to find out. "I'd say six months, maybe one year." There it was, in the light of day, no longer hidden in the recesses of her fears.

"Well, then. Is this not a grand new adventure?" Louise exclaimed, to her doctor's amazement.

'But come to think of it, that is what I would expect to hear from this exceptional person,' the doctor thought. Louise was always looking at life from a different perspective. One of amazement and hope. "God bless you, Louise, let me know if there is anything I can do," replied Dr. Elizabeth.

That evening, Louise decided she would write one final book. A book about this ultimate new adventure. A book about death, about crossing over. What could she learn from this passage? Could she find something that would help others understand this unknown frontier? Maybe a glimmer, some understanding from the path betwixt life and death that would serve as a beacon of hope to whomever might read her book.

That was the impetus that began a six-year adventure of life, death and love. To the edge, of an understood reality, and beyond to the ultimate understanding. That reality is not what we think. Louise went on to fill 19 notebooks with amazing insights, and secrets to this dimension we call death.

* * *

[Current Days...]

Steele and Celeste stopped for the night. The car's brakes were soft, kind of squishy. Steele didn't want to maneuver the sharp, tight turns, coming out of the back country, knowing it would be dark soon. So they found a small flat spot to camp, hoping the person that shot Jaguar was long gone. Together they pitched the tent, both suspiciously looking over their shoulders.

Steele started a small fire, then reached into his backpack and pulled out a notebook to read. The notebook was one of the volumes Louise had given him that documented the final chapter of her life.

As he read, his thoughts drifted. 'What on earth had happened the last couple of days? I used to feel like I controlled my life. Didn't realize I was so disconnected.' These were but a few thoughts and questions finding refuge in his mind. So many questions that only lead to more questions. 'Will the uncertainty ever end?'

"Oh, great, another question," he said.

Celeste stood beside him, warming herself by the campfire. She saw the concern in his eyes. "It was really great to see Louise again, babe. Not quite the dolphin, out playing in the ocean with her new friends. Like she always said she would, before she passed. Let's get some sleep, Steele, are you all right?"

He shook his head, clearing his mind before replying. "Yeh, I was just thinking about Louise. What a day, I am so tired. Do you believe everything that happened the last two days? After Jaguar was shot, everything became a blur. I can barely remember you and me running down the canyon with our girls bounding ahead of us as if we were playing a game. Do you think he is dead? If you die in that dimension, in Gaia, where do you go? What are we going to do?"

Celeste looked into his eyes. "Shush, just relax, things will become clearer after we have some sleep. In the morning we can fix the Xterra and get back on the road."

He put an arm around Celeste, pulled her close and gave her a gentle kiss. "How was I ever so lucky to find you?" They settled back in one another's arms and watched the fire.

The flames danced along the wood, so hypnotizing and serene. As they stared at the intricate dance, Maya and Isis began to stir, then growl.

They looked up from nature's theater and Louise was sitting across the other side of the fire pit with a gentle smile.

"Do not worry, children, everything will work out. There is so much I want to tell you. First, Jaguar will be fine, after some rest. We were all between the two dimensions when he was shot from such a great distance, so the bullet didn't penetrate his heart."

She walked around the fire, sat between them and took each of them by the hand. "I have some advice that will help you for now. Learn to understand and manipulate your dreams. Dreams are a bridge to help you understand this new dimension. When you learn to consciously use your dreams, we will be able to visit and communicate any time you want. Until that time this will help."

She reached into their backpack behind her, pulling out a crystal pendant then handed it to Celeste. "If you run into any problems, or have questions, use the crystal we gave you at the Falls. Wear it around your neck, hanging over your heart. Still your minds, and think of who you would like to speak with, as you meditate or fall to sleep. This will help you be aware in your dreams, and be able to communicate between our worlds. The crystal will not be necessary, once you become more in tune with your dreams. With understanding, the dream state will no longer be necessary."

Louise continued. "Before I go, I would like to tell you about your loved ones that have crossed. This might put your minds to rest and possibly answer some questions you may be having."

She looked into Steele's eyes. "Your grandfather, my husband Daddy-Bob, passed years ago. He was reborn in Washington, still a strikingly handsome man, if I may say so. He's in his late 30's now. In the lumber industry again. Something about the outdoors and lumber is in his being. I have tried to communicate with him, from time to time, though he is not hearing me. Do not know if he will make it across this lifetime. But I will wait. I am sure we will be together again, one of these lifetimes."

"Your mother, Van Emery, spends time in and out of Gaia. She is on the border between our worlds. From what I am told, she used to visit Gaia when she was younger. This dimension scared her, like it does many who are not ready. As you know, she is battling Alzheimer's. She is in Gaia as often as not - though she does not remember when on Earth."

"Your stepfather Frank has another life on earth helping someone close to cross over. He is truly a Saint. James has made it his mission to help as many families as possible. Your family was a challenging mission during his previous life on Earth."

"Steele, your mother's parents, the Burton's, are back in Oklahoma. They are married again, now in their 40's. Their daughter, Abby, was your great-grandmother Burton previously. That family is tight, living another similar lifetime together. A few twists in their relationships, but very similar. Funny how some of us kind of get stuck in a loop. I believe something there has to be learned before they are comfortable moving on."

Louise turned to Celeste. "Celeste, I speak to your mother in her dreams from time to time. You never knew Betty and I were close friends, before her lifetime as your mother in Ohio. I have a feeling she might just make it to Gaia this lifetime. Seems to enjoy our visits. She is living a wealthy life, in New York as a sophisticated lady. Happy with her ties to the theater. She supports a young playwright. He is attempting to bring a story about reincarnation to the theater. The playwright was her grandson, your nephew John, who passed, falling from a bridge in Arizona. He spends a great deal of time here, and tells me that he will not cross to Gaia, until he helps Betty across. That is the driving force behind his current work."

Louise looked saddened. "I lost track of both of your fathers. They are lost in anger, I pray they find paths away from that emotion. That is one of the most crippling emotions someone can get lost in."

"Remember, love is always the answer. I love you both and will see you again soon. We'll have tea." With that she vanished.

Steele and Celeste retired to the tent, unsure what to think about their future.

The night was cold and they all struggled for a share of the blankets. Celeste and Steele rolled and tossed the entire night. Isis sleeping horizontally gave their legs little room. When the morning finally came Steele was relieved.

Unzipping the tent, the girls were the first to spring from the opening. They were greeted by crisp morning air, along with a pastel orange and pink sunrise, streaking into an azure sky that became darker the higher it climbed. A birch moon with Jupiter scarcely visible hung above the sparse multi-colored clouds.

Stretching stiff muscles from the night's unrest, Steele started coffee on the old Coleman then headed straight to the SUV to see what the problem was. A large wet spot was visible having soaked into the sandy soil beneath the front tire on the driver's side. He pinched the wet soil between his thumb and first two fingers. The smell told him it was brake fluid.

Steele mumbled to himself. "Must have kicked up a rock and broken the brake line. Damn."

"What?" Celeste asked as she stretched next to the tent.

"We lost all of our brake fluid, must be a broken line–damn," he repeated in disgust. "I'll take a day-pack with a few things and walk to the highway and get help. You relax, be back before you know it."

Celeste put some cheese, apples and water in the pack. Steele's imagination was lucid that morning. He envisioned standing at the highway flagging down a tow truck. The truck was an old white Ford with a gold logo on the side. Behind the wheel was a lady driver–it was all so clear he thought, 'Did I dream this last night?'

"Thanks, baby." Throwing the pack over his shoulder he called Isis and started down the dusty road. "It must be ten miles to the highway. This is going to be a long walk, may be late before I'm back. Maya, stay with Celeste."

Not two miles down the road they came to a curve, with a rock formation blocking the view of their path. As they cleared the formation, Steele couldn't believe his eyes. There at a fork in the road sat the very tow truck he saw in his earlier vision, with a woman driver sitting on the hood. 'What a coincidence,' he thought.

She stood as they approached. She was wearing dirty coveralls with 'Vicky' stitched in red above the logo. Her blond hair was pulled back and she wore a grease-stained ball cap, the brim tilted backwards. "I'm here, just as you asked last night."

"We didn't speak last night?" came Steele's puzzled reply.

She smiled, "Well, no, you didn't say much. It was your grandmother who did all the talking. Louise, I believe she said her name was. I'm amazed at all she knows about the 2008 Xterra. Front driver's side brake line, right."

The confused expression on Steele's face made her question, "Are you all right? You're pale. Sit down here on this rock, steady yourself and have a drink of water." After he had a short rest she asked, "Which way to your vehicle? I need to get back before dad gets mad."

Returning to the camp in the tow truck, the three surprised Celeste. "That was fast, you couldn't have gone to the highway. What is happening?"

Steele just shrugged his shoulders, "Not sure. This is Vicky."

Vicky made short work of replacing the part. When she finished she showed them the replaced brake line. "Odd, looks like the line was cut. How do you suppose that happened?"

Again, all Steele could manage was a shrug of his shoulders. "Don't know. Maybe it was a sharp rock. How much do I owe you?"

"You don't remember? You gave me your credit card number last night to cover the trip and the parts. You'll get an invoice in the mail. Should be around $275. Have a safe trip home." With that, she turned and said over her shoulder, "Give my best to Louise, she is really something."

"Thank you so much," Celeste said, then thought, 'You don't know how special she really is.'

* * *

"Jasmine, that was a wonderful dinner!" James said, licking his lips. "I can't remember the last home-cooked meal I enjoyed this much. But I should get over to my hotel before they give my room away."

She gave a concerned look to Ian. "Please stay, we have the guest room made up and would love for you to spend the night. We can all get to know one another, and the kids need to know their granddad."

James looked to Ian for a sign of his thoughts, Ian smiled. "Yes. Stay, we can all play a game before Alek and Kristen's bedtime."

The kids both argued, "Daaaad, it's Christmas Eve, we want to stay up."

"You know Santa can't come while you are awake," was Jasmine's counter.

Alek looked doubtful. "Mom, you know that Santa isn't..."

"Alek!" Ian's stout command stopped Alek mid-word.

"OK, dad," Alek pouted.

Ian pulled a Chutes and Ladders game from the closet. "I haven't seen that game since you were about Kristen's age," James said. "That brings back memories. Ian, do you remember playing that when you were small?"

"Dad, this is the same game. It is one of the only good memories I have from childhood. We used to play it sitting at your mom's house. On that old dining table she had, under that ugly old red globe light she was so proud of. What ever happened to that ugly lamp? I don't remember ever seeing it again after..." His thoughts seemed to drift away, like he was looking through his memories for something. "....after, mmm...well, I can't seem to remember."

"Anyway," Ian continued, "it's the same game, beat up old box, missing pieces and all. Look."

He handed James the game and memories came flooding back. "That old lamp, yeh, it was ugly. Seems like it shattered, I can't remember either. Who wants to make the first move?"

That was the best Christmas Eve that James could remember. They all laughed, played and visited for hours. His grandkids were such a delight! Far past bedtime, among protests, Ian told the kids to get to bed. Of course, that was after they left cookies and milk on the hearth of their fireplace.

"Ian, Jasmine, thank you for a wonderful evening," James complimented. "You have both done a wonderful job raising Alek and Kristen."

"No thanks to you, dad." Ian looked at his father with contempt.

"Ian!" Jasmine shouted.

James was obviously hurt. "No. It's okay, Jasmine. I deserve that, I haven't been there for any of you. Please let me say good night to the kids, and then I'll take my leave. I have obviously out-stayed my welcome."

"No, dad, I'm sorry that just slipped out. We have presents to open tomorrow and the kids would be crushed if you weren't here in the morning. Please stay."

"Are you sure? I would like to see them open their gifts, nothing like children and Christmas." James smiled.

"Stay," Ian and Jasmine both said.

"Well, all right. Thank you. Maybe you could tell me more about your remote Portal device. That looks very interesting."

Jasmine looked relieved. "I'll clean up, you two go talk."

"Would you like a drink, dad? Scotch, right?"

James was surprised. "How do you know?"

"An article about you in Newsweek, talked about your lifestyle and your connection to that horrible company, Academi, or uh, Blackwater. You still work for them?"

"Not much anymore," James lied, as he took the glass of Scotch and changed the subject. "How does that Portal magic wand work?"

Ian frowned. "It's not a magic wand, dad! Magic is only manipulation, by people clever enough to have discovered some scientific laws beyond our understanding. This is science and technology. Here, look." He reached into his desk drawer, and pulled out the Wand. "This button slides forward, and the dimensional shift starts, when the alternating florescent blue and white Portal lights start flashing in rotation. As you can see, the lights continue to grow and spiral outward until they consume whomever is holding the Portal handle. But I must caution. If the person with the handle has not been sequenced and their DNA profile is not established, it can be deadly!"

As he said that, Ian seemed to slip away, fading ghostlike then becoming invisible. Suddenly he was standing behind his father.

"Wow–you startled me. Where did you go?" James asked.

"I didn't physically go anywhere," Ian answered. "Until I program the Jump to another place. Otherwise a Jump only moves me through another dimension, where I become invisible to you, and I simply walked around you. Everything natural, such as rocks, trees and earth remain the same, only clearer, like looking at things through a magnifying glass. But a person cannot remain in that dimension for too long."

James was excited, this could be exactly what he needed. "I would like to make a Jump. What would it take to sequence my DNA? Do you have the capability here, or would we have to go somewhere?"

"Slow down, dad. You sound like Alek when he gets excited. I can sequence your DNA here. It will be easier than usual, because we are blood relatives and our DNA is similar."

"How long will it take?" James asked.

Ian had an inquisitive look. "I can draw some blood and by morning you could make your first Jump. But it has to be short, so you can acclimate to the other side. Roll up your sleeve, I'll get a blood kit."

When finished, they found Jasmine in the living room meditating to soft music, and the sound of a creek. She was sitting in lotus position in front of a photo of a waterfall running over sandstone. The smooth rock had multicolored varnished streaks of red and orange, with a majestic lone pine in the foreground.

"Beautiful picture," James commented, as they entered the room. Ian said they had taken the photo while on vacation in Utah.

"You should enter it in a contest–it is really an award winner. Very magical," James replied. "Looks like it's time to turn in. I could use some sleep. It has been a very long day of travel. Thank you for everything, I'll see you in the morning."

The morning erupted with all the excitement a five and twelve-year old bring to Christmas. The noise forced their granddad's eyes open. He pulled himself to the window and looked out across the back yard. The sunrise appeared to concede to Alek and Kristen's screams, forcing the night sky to relinquish its grip on darkness.

Surrendering as well, James slipped into his clothes and headed downstairs. The aroma of spices drifted from the kitchen, where Jasmine was pulling delicious-looking cinnamon rolls with a maple glaze from the oven. The kids were bouncing around, pestering their mother to let them open 'Just One' gift. Across the open kitchen he saw Ian starting a fire in the living room fireplace. "Morning, dad, would you like some coffee?"

"Alek, Kristen–STOP pestering your mom. Get in here and help me find what Santa left under the tree for you." James couldn't believe kids could move so fast–they were across the room, instantly appearing under the tree rummaging around for gifts.

"Mine" - "No, that's mine! This is yours." "Oh, here is one for grandpa."

"OK," Jasmine announced as she entered the room. Wrapping paper abruptly started flying through the air. The new-found family munched on cinnamon rolls as the gifts were opened. After the last present appeared from its hiding place, Kristen and Alek headed away to play with their new toys.

"Thank you!" "Yeh, thanks," could barely be heard as they raced away. Ian followed Jasmine into the kitchen with an armful of glasses and plates.

"Dad, after I help with the dishes, we'll go see if your sequencing is finished, so you can take your first Jump."

"Can I help?" James asked.

"You could put the wrapping paper in that trash bag on the couch, if you wouldn't mind," Jasmine replied.

A few minutes later, Ian looked at one of the computer screens in his office. "The algorithm is complete. Dad, look, this is you in numeric form. Your digital DNA signature. We enter your numeric signature into the portable device here." Ian held the Wand so James could see him enter the numbers. "Or, of course, I could use the wireless network and transfer the signature, but the person using this Portal may not have a computer with them, that's why we can enter it manually. Then we enter a destination." He pressed 'Destination' on a small touch screen and entered the number '1'.

"This destination is pre-programmed. Or you can enter the latitude and longitude of a location. However, this must be done carefully, or you could reappear in a rock wall."

"Before you make this Jump, I need to tell you something. This will be your only Jump. I'm shutting down this project. I didn't realize how dangerous this would become. It all started as a game, but has gone too far! Some people using the other two test Portals I have produced are disappearing! They don't come back from the other side. Not only that, but I have been approached to use this as a weapon for war!"

A sad expression appeared in Ian's eyes as they began to tear. "I will not stand for that! This could be a wonderful application, if there wasn't so much hatred and greed in the world. After tonight, I am destroying the Portals and erasing all data so it can't be recreated. At least not easily."

With great concern, James asked. "Do I have to worry about this Jump?"

Ian smiled as he wiped away a tear. "No, just push this green button after you have crossed over. The only reason two people have been lost over there, is they can't find the Portal door's location. They were not sequenced properly, or they stay too long. You will be all right, just look around a little while, then push the green button and you will return just fine."

Ian handed his dad the Wand, and with a deep breath, James pushed the button and was gone. There is no explanation for the experience–one second James was in Ian's office, the next he was looking at his son's house from a small park down the street. Everything was brighter, more defined, and he could actually feel the space he occupied. Like he was somehow connected to it all!

Suddenly there was a disturbance. Something like standing on a street corner when a large truck passes by, only there was pressure, but no wind. What was it? James didn't want to find out so he immediately pressed the green button and appeared in Ian's office.

"What was that?" No sooner had the words left his mouth, than an arm reached around James from behind and snatched the Portal Wand from his grip. He turned quickly, seeing the back of a large bald man vanish! James was stunned, his mouth wide open in amazement. He didn't know what to do. Looking over to Ian, he saw his son run through the Portal door in his office–only to return within seconds. He ran to a computer, pressed some keys, then dove back through the Portal without a word.

Jasmine unsuspectingly walked in. "What do you think of your first Jump? Where is Ian?"

James did his best to explain what had just taken place. Her demeanor took on a tinge of anger, mixed with rage. Her words, "Watch the kids," faded as she ran through the Portal door after her husband.

Laughter, along with sounds of excitement and joy brought James' attention back from stunned silence, as the dancing lights around the Portal door faded. At least the kids were all right.

'What should I tell them?' He thought – 'I'll leave well enough alone for now.' Listening to the kids play, his thoughts ran wild. 'What am I going to tell Alek and Kristen, if their parents don't return? Where are their parents, and what am I going to do if they don't come back?'

It was only minutes, but it seemed like hours before Ian ran back through the door...a step ahead of an explosion that ripped through the Portal hurling him across the room, knocking James from his feet.

As smoke cleared, Ian pushed himself to his feet, excruciatingly slowly and brushed himself off. He didn't find anything broken. "Dad, are you all right? Damn, he blew up the Portal Door and stole the Wand! He must have Jumped here through one of the other Doors I created. Did you recognize the guy that took the Wand?"

"I didn't get a good look at him, son. He was bald and a big man, but all I saw was the back of his head."

Ian called to his wife. When she didn't reply, he looked confused. "Where is Jasmine, are the kids all right?"

James attempted to hide his confused feelings. "The kids are fine, they're playing in the other room. But Ian, Jasmine followed you through the Portal, she was right behind you." Ian's startled look turned to panic. "Please tell me she programmed a destination first."

"Didn't have time to, she was chasing you."

"Shit, she knows better!" Ian shouted in frustration. "She could be anywhere!" Ian slumped into his desk chair, hands covering his face. "They must have her...and I can't do anything about it. My Portal door has been destroyed, and the Wand has been stolen!"

❯ ❯ ❯

CHAPTER 4
Lost and Alone

"Hello... Hello, can anyone hear me!" Jasmine called out, frightened, dazed and confused. 'Where am I?' she thought. 'This all looks so familiar, but how did I get here?' Jasmine had been wandering through this new landscape a good part of the day. The sun had moved halfway across the sky. 'I must have been out here five hours, at least. It will be dark soon and I'm cold.' She decided to find shelter and gather some firewood, then realized she didn't have any matches or a lighter. "Hello. Help... can anyone hear me!"

"Are you all right? I heard you calling," answered a tall young lady, coming down the trail.

"Oh, thank God!" she sighed in relief. "Can you help me? I'm lost and it's getting cold."

"Certainly, relax. I'm Star, we have shelter just up the trail, above that waterfall. Here, take my jacket, I'll be fine in this sweater. Tell me, how did you find yourself up here without any supplies?"

"Very happy to meet you, my name is Jasmine. About how I got here... ah, well... I'm not sure. It's a strange story, not sure you would believe me. Actually I don't really understand it myself," Jasmine replied, feeling very dumbfounded.

Star realized how inconsiderate she was being. "Your explanation can wait. Let's get you water, some food and proper clothing, then we can talk." Within a short walk they approached the wondrous home where Star and Jaguar lived.

Jasmine's eyes widened in amazement. "How is all of this possible? This looks like something out of a fairy tale."

"I'll explain in time," said Star, handing Jasmine some water and cheese. "Have a drink, eat something and then you can tell me how you became lost up here."

"Thank you so much." Jasmine took a long drink and a few bites of cheese. "Well, where can I begin? You will not believe me. My husband has invented this new technology. It started as a game, that would take a player into a virtual reality. Only the virtual became more of a real experience. Anyway, my husband was in some kind of trouble and went into the Portal. I went in after him, thinking I would follow him to his destination. I forgot– you need to program the destination for each Jump separately. I don't know how I ended up here."

"Funny though, he always told me that if you see anyone else while in the Portal's alternate reality, they would appear faint, almost transparent. You look very solid to me."

"That is a strange story. Are you sure you're feeling all right?" Star was concerned. "You look rather pale." Star didn't want to alarm her, but Jasmine looked exactly like she had explained, almost transparent. 'What on earth is going on?' Star thought. 'This is something I've never seen. I'll ask Jaguar and Louise to join us.'

A few moments later, Louise walked into the room. "What is happening? I just received your thoughts and..." Louise saw Jasmine and realized what Star was thinking. "Oh... Hello, young lady. I am Louise, a friend of Star and Jaguar. But you haven't met Jaguar, that is his nickname, he should be along soon. When he gets here we can decide what we can do to help you."

"Excuse us for just a minute, make yourself at home. Louise, can I talk to you in the other room?" Star pulled Louise along.

"I've never experienced anything like this before," Star said quietly. "She appears as though she has crossed over without reaching the correct vibration to stay in this dimension, yet here she is. Do you have any idea how we can help her, Louise?"

Just then Jaguar walked in. "What are you thinking? I couldn't quite make out your thoughts. Something about a young lady being stuck, and her husband's technology?" Louise and Star just looked at him and said at the same time, "Follow us."

Star led the way. "Jasmine, this is Jaguar, he will be able to help you." 'I hope,' she thought to herself.

Jasmine picked up on the uneasiness of the group. "Nice to meet you as well. What seems to be wrong? We can't be too far from a road or your vehicles. I would be happy to pay one of you to take me to a phone in the morning, so I can call my husband. That is if it's all right for me to spend the night."

Jaguar smiled. "You are welcome to spend the night, but we may have a problem getting you to a phone."

"I'm not sure how to explain," Star intervened. "But let me try. The technology your husband invented must move you through another dimension in order to transport you to a different location."

Jasmine looked at Star inquisitively. "Yes, that is the way he explained it to me."

"Well," Star continued. "You seem to have...um...well, somehow become stuck in this different dimension. And in this dimension you appear to us, as the diaphanous people you described, when you told me about meeting someone else in the Portal."

"NO! That can't be, you all look perfectly normal."

Louise attempted to ease Jasmine's obvious discomfort. "I'm sure everything will be fine. We just have to put our minds together and figure out a solution. You see, we live in this dimension, and have been visited by others from your world. However, this world is a natural evolution for mankind when a person reaches a certain level of consciousness. Do you follow me?"

Jasmine was more uneasy than ever! "You mean like when a guru becomes enlightened, is that what you are saying?"

"Yes, you are understanding. The thing is, none of us have ever met anyone like you before. You are here, but not completely here, so we need to think of some way to send you back to your world. Let us backtrack to see if we can figure out how you got here in the first place. What was the last thing you remember thinking about before you entered the Portal behind your husband? Maybe that has something to do with it."

Looking somewhat relieved, Jasmine answered, "That's it. I was meditating in front of my favorite photo, a picture I took while on vacation in Utah. That is why this waterfall looks so familiar. This is where I took that photo! Good, all we have to do is tell my husband where we are and he can come through the Portal and get me."

"It is not going to be quite that easy," Jaguar said. "We do not have phones here. In fact, even if we did, we can't just call another dimension. But wait... I know how we can contact your husband. What is his name, and where do you live? We just recently met Louise's grandson and his wife, who had crossed over and then returned. We should be able to contact them. They went back to your world before their evolution became permanent. Louise has a blood tie to her grandson so she should be able to make contact."

"Good idea," said Louise. "Though they are now a long way from here and I may not be able to reach that far across the veil, until they use the crystal we gave them to amplify the communication. However, I am sure they will have questions and want to contact me soon. Wait a minute–I know I can reach Akira though. She is my mentor and lives in their world from time to time. She can contact them and give them the information to reach your husband."

Star nodded to Louise. "You send a thought to Akira, and I'll get us something for dinner, then we can get some sleep. Jasmine, you must be worn out after the day you have had."

* * *

After Steele and Celeste's odd encounter with Vicky fixing the brakes, the drive back to Durango was ordinary, though their ill-ease was evident, from constant suspicious looks over shoulders at every passing car. Especially the large black SUV they passed a short time back. "Baby, we've been watching too many movies."

Celeste smiled, "Yeh, cue the spy music. Speaking of spy movies–do you think someone really cut our brake line?" Celeste asked.

He had been wondering the same thing. "Could be just a sharp rock. Right?" He changed the subject. "Who would ever have guessed our short camping trip would turn out finding Louise in another dimension called Gaia?"

"Yeh, especially in human form," she laughed. "Louise always insisted she would come back as a dolphin."

Steele laughed as well. "I keep thinking we're going to wake up and discover this is all a dream. Nothing seems real since we turned off the highway the other day."

"What are we going to do?"

"We can't just turn our backs on all of this, and act like it didn't happen," Steele said, almost as a question. "But I can't think of a way to act on the enlightenment we've received. What will our next move be if we decided to help? People are going to think we have lost our minds. I can just hear what our friends will say when we tell them we just visited my dead grandmother in another dimension."

31

The remainder of the drive home was reflective, as one or the other of them would ask a question they both knew didn't have an immediate answer. By the time they turned into their driveway neither was any closer to a plan than when they started home.

Or was this really home anymore?

"Did you leave the light on in the living room?" Celeste questioned as they stopped. Not confident of much anymore, Steele didn't say anything.

"I could use a hot bath," Celeste said. "Just relax and take my mind off everything. I don't want to think about anything right now."

No such luck. Walking to the front porch, the dogs began to growl. Then Steele saw the front door had been forced open. "Go put the dogs back in the car and call the police," he said. "Someone could still be in the house!"

Celeste pulled the dogs back to the car and called the police, while Steele quietly slid the door open to peek inside and listen for anyone who might be moving around. A large figure slammed through the door knocking Steele down as he ran to a car that screeched to a stop in front of the house. On his heels step for step was a young lady. She reached the car as the vehicle leaped forward, tires engulfed in burning rubber. Her cat-like agility was the only thing that kept her from being run over.

Steele drew a deep breath and let it out slowly, trying to regain his composure. He was getting to his feet and the young lady reached to help. She had a pleasant smile. Her eyes showed a sense of recognition you give someone when you haven't seen them for a long time. But she didn't look familiar at all. She wore her hair short and had a timeless appearance of early 20's. She was fit and agile like a dancer, or martial artist. Just short of six foot tall, she wore jeans, running shoes and a long-sleeve sweater.

"There is a patrol car in the area, that will be here soon," Celeste said. "Who are you?"

"A friend," she replied. "Louise told me you would probably need my help."

"Does this have anything to do with Jaguar being shot and our brakes being cut?" Celeste asked.

"Not sure, but I wouldn't tell the police any of that. This is just a break-in, right?" she said, turning to leave. "I have to go, but we can talk once the officers have gone."

She vanished as the police sirens broadcast their approach, shortly before the flashing lights became visible coming around the corner at the end of the street. The officers got out quickly and looked around the house. They had interrupted a burglary, is the way the police report would read. Nothing was taken and little damage, other than the broken lock on the front door. Patrol officer Dan, and his partner took little time to file the report and leave. With no more excitement than that, the neighbors all returned home to whatever they were doing.

The two wary travelers were attempting to relax and take their minds off of everything, when the doorbell rang. Figuring it was one of the neighbors, Steele answered with a ready reply that everything was fine. He was surprised by the new friend Louise sent to help. Their eyes met and he had a momentary shock of recognition looking into her clear black eyes. Stepping aside, he gestured. "Please come in."

"Thank you. My name is Akira. I have lived in your world, off-and-on, for some time now, helping those like Celeste and yourself understand this new realm of consciousness and make the transition easier."

"How do you know Louise?" Steele asked.

"Louise and I have known one another for many lifetimes," Akira replied. "Much becomes clear in this new dimension as our awareness connects us with elevated potentials of consciousness, and restores access to our memories. Louise is very talented. She is one of only a few recent graduates who has begun to move between our two worlds. I'm happy to have been able to instruct her in this art."

Akira continued. "We are all happy that you have decided to help. I can sure use your assistance." Offering a warm cup of tea, Celeste asked Akira to sit down.

She thanked Celeste and sat in Steele's favorite old recliner and proceeded. "Louise asked me to give you a message. She would be here herself, but she is still learning to move between worlds and the greater the distance the more difficult it becomes."

"There has been an occurrence in Gaia, our dimension. Something that has never happened before. Someone from your world has become stuck between worlds, and she needs your help to return."

Taken aback, Celeste asked, "What is it Louise thinks we can do, and why can't you handle it?"

"I would be happy to help, even though I have my hands full with a number of things right now, so I could use your assistance. This will be a good first collaboration for you. It should only take a phone call, but I find it is hardly ever that easy." Akira handed her a paper.

"This is the telephone number and address of Jasmine and her husband. Jasmine is the person stuck between worlds. Her husband, Ian Knecht, seems to have invented some device that is able to move people between our two worlds. The problem is that his wife is not vibrating at a high enough frequency to remain in the higher dimension and somehow she became stuck in-between. None of us are sure how long she can live this way, so she has to be moved back as soon as possible."

"Your job—if you choose to accept it-ha, I always wanted to say that, saw it in an old movie once." Akira laughed a little. "Thought it would be funnier. Anyway, contact Ian and convince him that he must rescue his wife, using his device. Tell him she is stuck between worlds above the waterfall in the photo they took on their vacation to Utah—the photo Jasmine likes to meditate in front of. He will know what you are talking about. Jaguar believes that she had a strong mental picture of that waterfall when she entered the Portal created by his invention, and that is what gave his device the destination. But because there in no Portal entrance at the waterfall, she is unable to move from our dimension back to her own. Please hurry—she might not have much time!"

"Louise also asked me to remind you to look beyond what is around you, in order to see into other realms. Thank you." With that, she was gone.

It was early evening and Akira made it sound urgent, so Steele decided to call right away. "Is this Mr. Knecht, Ian Knecht?"

With a slight hesitance came the reply, "No, this is James, his father. Can I help you?"

Not knowing what Ian's father knew about the situation, Steele didn't know how much he should say. "I would like to speak with Ian, this is important. It's about his wife Jasmine. I believe she is in need of his help."

Another pause...then, "Can you hold, I believe he just drove up, he will be with you in a minute." James put his hand over the phone and spoke to Agent Duncan, the FBI agent standing next to him. "How long will it take to trace this call?" Shaking his head, the agent told James to keep him on the phone for a moment longer.

Ian couldn't wait and took the phone from his dad. "I'll talk to him. This is Ian, you know something about my wife? Is she all right, you didn't harm her? Who are you?"

"You don't understand, I do not have your wife," Steele said, amazed that they misunderstood him so completely. "I was told by a friend where she is. Let me explain. Your wife is not hurt, but she is lost. She followed you into your machine, something about a Portal–and is stuck in another dimension."

"Stuck, are you crazy? So you have the Portable Wand and my wife then?" came Ian's response.

"No. No," Steele repeated, trying to make him perceive his intended meaning. "I don't know anything about the Portable Wand thing. I was told that Jasmine followed you into some sort of Portal opening and she is stuck between dimensions. You must rescue her before it is too late."

Ian didn't believe what he just heard. "What do you mean, 'too late,'– are you going to harm her? Who told you this?"

'He can't be serious,' Steele thought to himself. "Who told me doesn't matter. What matters is that your wife is stuck between dimensions in Utah above the waterfall in your photo, and you have to go there with your Portal thing and bring her back before it is too late."

"Before it's too late!" Ian asked again. "Is this a threat? What do you want from me?"

Steele was obviously getting nowhere, Ian was clearly too upset to listen to reason. "Just think about what I said, and I'll call back when you calm down. Please just go save your wife." Turning off his phone Steele was stunned by this conversation.

"Why would he think we had his wife and wanted to hurt her? Wow, baby, did you hear that? This is not going to be as easy as it sounded, but then Akira said it never is. I can't blame him though, I do sound crazy! 'Your wife is stuck between dimensions in Utah above a waterfall and you have to go there with your Portal Wand thing to bring her back before it is too late.' Am I going insane?"

Celeste hugged her husband and whispered in his ear. "I didn't hear his side of the call, but it certainly sounded like he didn't understand. I don't think you are going crazy, or that means we both are. What are the odds of that?"

Steele nodded his head. "I'll start a bath for you, and order a pizza once you have had time to relax. I'm going to have a drink and go read my book. Try to get my mind off all of this for awhile."

Steele loved the way his beautiful wife smiled, as she agreed without comment. After all, her smile is what first caught his attention when they met so many years ago. "Oh," she said as Steele headed for the bathroom. "Would you feed the dogs? I'll run the bath."

* * *

Ian slammed his phone down. "Do you believe the nerve of that guy! Did you get a trace, where is he?"

Agent Duncan stood very stoically, in the doorway next to the dining room table, dressed all in black–suit, shirt, and tie. Attire he always wore, awarding him the nickname 'Agent Death.' A wicked smile spread into his eyes, as he pulled the earphone from his ear and stuck two thumbs in the air. "Got him."

Standing in the other room, James quietly turned his phone on and texted: 'You bald bastard, why did U take wife - meet me B.P. 10: 2nite DO NOT B L8.'

Agent Duncan continued, "The abductor used a cell phone, but it looks like he called from a residential neighborhood and he is not on the move, so we may have gotten lucky. The phone is registered to a Steele Brandon. He lives in Durango, Colorado. We have mobilized our Durango agency, they should be there in minutes."

❯ ❯ ❯

CHAPTER 5
Unexpected

Steele sat in his friendly, dependable chair, sipping aged Scotch and reading an old Alan Watts book, finally beginning to relax. Celeste would be out of the bath soon, so the pizza place a few blocks away was on the phone. "Yes, that's all tonight, Tony." Tony owned the pizza place, 'so at least we'll have a great pie tonight,' he thought. Things were starting to look better. 'I'll call Ian again tomorrow. He will have had time to think about our conversation and go rescue Jasmine, then life can get back to normal. Whatever that is?' After reading a few pages he closed his eyes, feeling his neck muscles relax... 'better get up before I fall asleep'...

"Steele, baby, wake up. I think I hear the delivery guy pulling up." Even after twenty years, she still got him excited. His alluring wife stood next to Steele in a robe, with her wet hair pulled up in a towel.

"That bath was just what the doctor ordered, so relaxing I was beginning to feel like I was slipping between dimensions again. Everything is so clear."

Steele forced himself out of the chair, smiled and gave his wife a kiss, "Good." He started for the bedroom, to get his wallet to pay the pizza guy.

Smash! Splinters of the front door came flying through the air.

"FBI!" Four men dressed in military assault gear forced their way into their home. Steele turned, feeling a powerful silent quake of energy. Deadly flowing waves erupted from a central point where his usually passive wife stood in the nucleus.

"NO!" she screamed, as the power of lightning pulsated through every fiber of her being and exploded through the room.

Steele could see the air waves as a silent shock wave crashed outward, tearing picture frames from the walls and throwing tables, chairs, and FBI agents through the air. The windows blew out of their frames sending shards of glass into the front yard, as plaster erupted from the pulverized drywall.

Standing in the next room, away from the violent burst, Steele was hurled across the room and feeling the percussion through his skull. "HOLY SHIT! What was that?" he yelled, staggering to his feet, ears ringing. He looked around assessing the damage.

Somehow Akira stood among the wreckage, dust and smoke surrounding her. "What part of keeping a low profile did you not understand? I could feel that energy burst half way across the country. I came as soon as I felt the source. Wow!"

Celeste shook from head to toe, standing in a tiny undisturbed spot in the center of what looked like a war zone. "I don't understand what just happened."

In an instant, Akira was next to Celeste, catching her as she collapsed, both of them falling to the floor. Isis and Maya stood huddled together next to Steele, barking wildly. "We have to get out of here," shouted Akira. "Steele, grab some things and the dogs and meet us in the car."

Steele threw whatever he could think of into a suitcase, and rushed to the garage. He tossed the bag into the Xterra. Then he quickly backed out onto the street. From there he could see the damage. It looked like a bomb had gone off in their living room. Three of the agents were unconscious, or worse. One of the agents had been thrown into the yard and was struggling to his feet as they sped down their once peaceful street with neighbors gawking.

They heard sirens approach as Steele drove toward the main street, heading away from their home. They turned the corner driving past the multiple sets of flashing strobe lights, relieved to have them pass proceeding down the street.

"We have to find another vehicle—one the police will not be looking for," Akira said.

Celeste sat in the back seat in her robe, still shaking. She had lost her towel, her hair hung wet around her shoulders. Maya sat in her lap, licking her leg. And Isis pushed her body as close as possible, with the intent to protect her from any harm.

Trying to think through the confusion, it came to Steele. "We are watching a friend's house while he is in Europe on business. No one knows about his place. Let's go there, get off the street and decide what to do. I'm sure he wouldn't mind if we borrow his car." A few blocks later Steele pulled their car into their friend's garage to keep it out of view.

Celeste was beginning to regain her strength. "What just happened, Akira? How did I blow up our house?"

Akira was visibly shaken, but held her composure with a sober expression. "There are many talents you will begin to realize, now that you are moving between worlds. Physics in this new dimension 'Gaia,' are radically different from the world you are used to dealing with. Since you have access to this new world, matter around you can sometimes act differently. Nevertheless, it takes a powerful talent and very strong emotions to integrate the forces between our worlds and change the way properties of energy behave. What you just did is something very rare. Few advanced individuals have ever accomplished such a thing. For your own safety, and all of ours, please attempt to constrain your feelings."

Akira continued, telling them that Louise would like to visit now that they were somewhere safe. "Louise is able to make the transition between worlds more easily by feeling my life-force." Akira further explained that as Celeste and her husband became more accustomed to this new world, Louise would be able to visit without Akira's help.

"Hi, children," came her voice as Louise became visible. "Looks like my mentor has been doing her best to keep you out of harm's way. Easier said than done." She smiled and put an arm around Akira. "Come give me a hug, and let us have some tea. There are so many things I want to tell you." They all joined in a four-way hug.

Then Akira told them she had to go. "I'll see you soon." And she was gone.

Steele made a pot of Earl Grey tea, and they settled around a table to talk. Louise went on to explain many things. She started with 'Love'– one of her favorite subjects. "Children, the barrier between our two existences, is that our species has forgotten how to love. Most people are stuck, they need to re-learn this basic truth. As my 'guiding angels' Star and Jaguar, always told me when I was on the other side, writing my journals: 'Your title– The Art of Dying, really should be–The Art of Love.' After all, when you know one another by Love or Empathy, you will know each other again. In this way we will always be able to find one another, even between dimensions. As we have."

She went on to tell us, that from the time after we are born, our soul is testing the link between our domains, especially as young children. That is why kids sometimes have 'imaginary friends,' as we often call them.

As we grow older we experiment between our understood reality and other worlds through our dreams. People on Gaia's side refer to those visitors as 'Twinklers.' It appears that when we visit between dimensions through our dreams, we are only able to appear, or twinkle, for short times. Thus the name Twinklers.

Louise continued. "As you may remember from my journals, Star and Jaguar as my guiding angels told me: 'Dreamers never die, they learn eventually how to elude the devastating schemers and move on to other dimensions to help forward the ongoing–the ever ongoing creativities of the spirit of love.'"

Louise then looked far away, as if looking through us. "Before I passed on I once said, after glancing at the morning newspaper...'It almost looks as if God is punishing us.' The GA's had a sharp reply: 'God never punishes!' I now understand that a saving grace has been put into evolving souls, in their primitive awareness of so-called evil. First the blaming of others, any others, then the gradual awakening to Mea Culpa–'I am guilty,' then, from this new awareness of one's self, it becomes clear–the other is my brother, my kindred self."

"Star and Jaguar went on to tell me this: 'A society based on greed and lust naturally commits itself to a speedy death. But that does not mean the death of the human species. Other societies will arise from the basic potentials of this era. In the total scheme of evolution it is but a passing phase of experimentation.' Again it seems tragic to you and all your fellow idealists to watch that wonderful potential of the 'American Dream' perched on the edge of extinction, so soon. But the dream, the hope, the faith, the aspiration was the reality. The enactment was far beyond the current capacity of the entire human race, as a whole, at their current stage of development."

We could see the light in Louise's face as she spoke. "The idealists envision the way of the future. They are the gleam of Light which guides the fumbling masses toward their intermittent glimpses of a goal beyond their current understanding. It is essential, however, that you believe yourself invincible, immortal–else you would never survive to take part in humanity's real work–of slow, soul-growth, a participating process of young beings with the creativities of the cosmos."

"But wait," Louise smiled, "it sounds like I have begun to preach. How are you holding up, Celeste ?"

"Better, now that I've had time to rest, thank you for asking," she replied.

"That was some show of strength, and a wonderful understanding of the physics from this new dimension," Louise complimented. "I've never actually known anyone that was able to draw the properties of energy between worlds like that. I always thought the stories about such things were one of legend."

"Ah, but with a strength such as you have displayed, there is a fine line between expertise and wisdom. Be always true to your emotions, but attend them gently. Now get your rest, that takes a lot out of you. We will speak again soon, I love you both." With a hug, she was gone.

"I'm not sure I will ever get used to them just vanishing like that," Celeste said.

"I know what you mean," Steele replied. "We never did get that pizza. Let's see what is in the fridge." He found the makings for a tuna fish sandwich—not pizza, but it would have to do. After they ate and fed the dogs, they both were out like lights, fugitives in a borrowed bed.

* * *

Duncan appraised Ian with the strict, stone-like demeanor expected from an FBI agent. "It appears you have gotten mixed up with terrorists, Mr. Knecht. When our agents moved in to apprehend your wife's abductors, they exploded some sort of bomb that put four good men in the hospital, two of them in intensive care. However, there was no trace of Jasmine or the Portal device, so they either didn't have them at that location or have taken your wife and the Wand with them." Agent Duncan finished his assessment of the situation and looked at Ian and James suspiciously.

James took in the scene, with Agent Duncan, then thought about how long it would take him to get to the Brown Palace Hotel. He wanted to make sure he was there before 10 p.m. to meet that bald bastard, Gregory. "Ian, I have some urgent business to take care of, that may take a day or two. I'll check in with you regularly, to see if there have been any changes. Call me if you learn anything. Will you and the kids be all right? I will return to help, however I can, if you would like."

"Yes, dad, we'll be fine, and of course I would like for you to return. We could all use your support. The kids would love to have you here at a time like this."

41

"Thank you, son. I am glad we are able to put our past behind us. I know this is hard for you," James replied. "I'll take a cab to the airport and be back as soon as possible." Not trusting Agent Duncan, James was intentionally misleading him with his lie about the airport. Of course, he would take the cab to the Denver airport for appearance, then from there he would rent a car.

'Jasmine Noir Fragrance,'–an advertisement about ten feet tall, filled the brightly-lit store window at the corner where James stopped at a traffic light. He thought to himself, 'Never realized how Kirsten Dunst, in that fragrance ad, looks so much like my daughter-in-law Jasmine. Odd coincidence, the name of the perfume is the same.' A sales-girl stood a few feet away, handing out free samples. Before James started away from the light, she smiled and tossed a sample in the open window. "This is for the lady-friend you are thinking about."

James turned the corner and pulled the rental car into the downtown parking structure of Denver's Brown Palace. He was still thinking about his daughter-in-law as he pushed the Jasmine sample into his pocket. But his thoughts changed to his surroundings. 'I've always liked this old corner brick building, with its forest green awnings. It has to be well over 100 years old–so much history.'

After quickly checking in, he went up to his room and threw his bag on the carved antique bed and looked at his watch, thinking, 'Gregory won't be here for about an hour. What am I going to do about this ugly situation? I'll go down to Churchill's Bar early, order a bottle of wine and think of something.'

After cleaning up, he was on his way to the lounge. He couldn't help but to be impressed by the garish interior of the atrium gallery. Intricately designed deep green, red, black and white floral rugs led to ionic voluted Greek marble columns. Topped with an entablature stretching across the entry, where 'Spa and Salon' was carved. Arches surrounded the second floor walkway, lit with golden bezant sun patterns. Carved mahogany top rails supported by inlaid metal balusters held sconces softly lighting the interior. He gazed upwards nine-stories to where a lead-lined stained glass atrium ceiling crowned all of the opulence below.

Across the atrium was Churchill's. As he walked past the grandly carved bar, he placed an order for a bottle of 2006 Bourgogne Pinot Noir. Then slid into an oxblood red leather studded club chair, in the softly lit corner of the room. He swirled the wine around the glass and began to taste the small sample of wine the steward had just poured, when James heard a familiar voice.

"Hope you haven't been waiting long. How would you like to visit Nassau, my friend?" His associate thumped down in the matching studded chair across from James. "Pour me a glass also, bar-keep. By the way, James, I don't appreciate the text message, 'Bald Bastard'. And it took me awhile to decipher your message. 'U take wife -meet me B.P. 10: 2night DO NOT B L8.' Take who's wife? We are still working together on this. Are we not?"

James nodded approval of the wine, waited as the steward poured two glasses and walked away. James turned to scrutinize his associate with a serious stare. "Good to see you too... 'Gregory,'" pronouncing his name with a disdained emphasis. "Would you be a little discrete? Nassau, you say. Well, that depends. Why did you take my son's wife? I made it clear that no one was to be hurt in any way. Was that not clear enough for you."

With a greasy-eyed glare of disbelief, Gregory questioned. "What the hell are you going on about? I don't have her."

"Don't play me for a fool," James replied. "She followed you into the Portal and never returned, so where else would she be?"

The waiter asked that they keep their voices down, and informed them that the bar would be closing soon.

"Who is being indiscreet now?" Gregory taunted.

James decided to take the conversation to a more private place and invited his colleague upstairs. As they entered his room, James put his hand out in expectation and demanded. "You did bring the Wand with you? Let me have it."

"Of course, it's right here," he reached into his briefcase. "That son of yours is a very clever businessman. He developed this wonderful technology, offered the hardware to his investors but kept the key to make the entire process work: the DNA sequencing software. Without that, only the few people he has sequenced can make a Jump. As you know, I was sequenced during the initial testing phase when Rebel was asking Blackwater for guinea pigs. You and I are two of only a few that have been sequenced." With that Gregory grabbed James by the wrist and pulled the Wand from the briefcase. James recognized the soft inviting glow. In that instant the two of them were drifting in a mystifying white light.

* * *

Celeste and Steele laid low the following few days, trying to determine what they should do. Louise came to visit more regularly, sharing many insights into the transition between worlds.

"There are 'truths' that we can share with those ready to graduate," Louise told them during her following visit. "Earth life is an eternal struggle between the current psyche and the eternal Soul. When I was a child my mother would tell me, 'Compose yourself.' That phrase angered me then, but now intrigues me–for that is exactly what all Earth Souls are in the process of doing. Attempting to compose themselves. What masterpiece do you dream...and hope to achieve? You–a unique entity–a Soul in the making. In the eyes of eternity we are all very young, really embryonic Souls. Given the great boon, in this Earthly ordeal, of participation in our own evolution: to compose our selves."

Louise was beaming as she continued. "In my journals the GA's told me: 'Just remember...and always keep in mind...you are a Soul in the making, privileged to now take a small part in your own evolution.' So welcome! We are all a mixture of personal, cultural, and karmic needs for Soul-Growth."

"Karma is something I never quite fully understood," Celeste stated, and Steele was glad that she did for his own clarification.

Louise with a considered understanding continued. "Basically, Karma is life dramatized to suit the yearning and growing needs of the individual soul. As Star and Jaguar told me, 'Karma is simply the cosmic game for teaching its child-Souls how to play the part of the other.' For instance, if a father has cast his daughter out into the snowstorm, then it simply follows that the next game around, he will have to play a part similar to his daughters. All this is not a matter, as rigid religionists insist, of retribution, but rather the wisest way of distribution. A method of teaching and learning in this school called Planet Earth."

"It is now time we give back to our Earth. Our humanity's Karma is so inextricably involved–time and space so condensed–there is no place available for us to hide any longer. We have to deal with our own Whole World. That is why it is so important that all of us evolving Souls help one another awaken, so we can heal the wounds we have imposed on our Earth."

Louise shook her finger in warning. "Some advice to any young seeker: Never be easily satisfied with someone else's answers. The adventure is your own challenge and joy. And Star just sent me a thought: 'Remember this–It is not 'My Soul' that loves–but 'My Soul' is growing in knowing that Love is the Cosmic Power that many refer to as God, shining through.' Witness what is now happening through you and many of the graduating Souls who are responding–not to your persona–but to the Soul that is beginning to learn to be translucent… which means merely to allow the everlasting Cosmic Love to shine through."

* * *

After the Portal Jump James was becoming aware of his new surroundings. Two large men stepped to his sides and grabbed him by the arms. "I'm sorry, my old friend," came the familiar voice. "We will have to detain you until we can determine where your commitment stands. Many of us believe you are becoming soft, shifting loyalties to your family. That could be a problem with this assignment."

"Should I salute you, General?" James said sarcastically. "Since when does a previous general of the United States Marines and high ranking member of Blackwater kidnap one of their own?"

"Well, it's like this, son. I am no longer a member of Blackwater, or 'Academi' as some call it. Whatever the name, that organization is getting soft. So we have formed a new organization–UnitedOps. We do what it takes to keep the original white America strong." The General nodded to his men. "Put him someplace safe until I have a chance to interrogate him."

A bag was pulled over his head and James was led away. Damp, musky vegetation smells along with the shrill cry of a bird or maybe monkey led James to believe he was in a jungle, possibly a wildlife park somewhere. James stumbled as he was shoved in the back, forced down a dirt trail. Then his head was forced down. "Watch your head, there's a low doorframe," was a gruff command, as the hood was removed, and in the same motion James was pushed into a dark room. He stumbled to his knees and looked around.

A faint light from the full moon shining through an empty framed hole in the wall, too small to be called a window, made the stark small interior of his prison barely visible. Dust hung in the air, illuminated by the glow of the moon which created a trail of light that cast a long window-shaped glow across the floor. The floors and walls were concrete or packed dirt. It was hard to tell in the dim light. The roof appeared to be rough, heavy tree branches covered with mud. Sudden pangs of panic reached for his mind as memories of being a POW in Vietnam surfaced.

'Just relax,' he told himself, leaning back on the sole piece of furniture, an old dank smelling army cot. James quickly reconnoitered the surroundings; it was still dark so he knew he must be in the same hemisphere. No traffic sounds or city noises so this was probably not a municipal zoo. The air is damp and much warmer so he must be further south, not in Colorado anymore. 'Guess I got to visit the Bahamas after all,' James laughed to himself. Peering through the small window, James could make out another small concrete hut connected to his room by a rough path. Above the trees silhouetted against the dark gray-blue sky shown palm fronds. 'These nut cases really did take me to the Bahamas,' he muttered.

Slamming his shoulder hard against the door, James could perceive a slight give, offering hope that over time he might be able to work the latch open.

He continued through the night, trying to determine what to do, and through the next day, then the next. A small meal, if you could call it that, was served once a day on a metal plate with no utensils. They had given him a metal bucket to use as a toilet. Rains came and the roof dripped, leaving pools of muddy water on the concrete floor.

James was visited regularly by the General and one of his goons. They drugged and tortured him for information about the sequencing software. And he eventually told them what he knew—which was very little.

Time blurred from the drugs—how long had he been locked up? What day was it? Could it be Monday? Hell, did that really matter? He wasn't even sure what the General was going to do with him. It would be all to easy for him to disappear in a shallow grave, no one that cared knew he was in the Bahamas.

"Yow misstar, respek–hail up, weh yaw seh? Weh yup deh pan?

"Hello!" James desperately replied. "I do not understand you."

"Oh Aamarikien... Mister, yow whet do ay say... how r-ya a doin? Mi giv ya gud yello banana."

"Thank you, little girl." He took the banana through the small window.

"My name is James. You sound like a beautiful little lady from Jamaica. What is your name?" James reached into his pocket and retrieved the perfume sample, and placed it on the window frame for the little girl. "Here is something you might like. It smells good and has a beautiful name–'Jasmine.' That is the name of my son's wife."

"Thienk-ya Sir. Ma friends mudda, her name Jasmine. Ya call me Fa, for Fajah ie Jamaicann in ie Jamaicann settie. Ya ok in ie room. How ya stay?"

"I am okay in this room, but I need to get out. I need help. Can your father get me out of this room?"

"Mi ask im. Mie tata in bestes ever feelin in-a longa time, he geta new job we-r happie. He help, Respek." As she turned from the tiny window she exclaimed. "Oh! Caristen she frind say smile ya-r loved."

With that, the sound of her tiny little foot steps disappeared into the distance. 'What a coincidence this little girl has a friend named Caristen whose mother is Jasmine.' Like his daughter-in-law and granddaughter. That thought made James smile. At last he was beginning to have some hope of getting out.

CHAPTER 6
Dreams, Fire and Escape

"Daddy, where is mommy? My friend Fajah told me that grandpa James is with Fajah," Kristen said, rubbing her eyes from sleep, as she entered the room. "I miss mom and thought Pa was coming back to play with us."

"I miss them both, hun. Mom is okay. And don't be silly, I'm sure grandpa is not with Fajah," Ian said with a sad expression that turned angry.

He spun in outrage toward Agent Duncan. "Do you have any word about Jasmine or my father? It has been too long! I know dad hasn't been the most faithful father, but this time I really believed he would call before now." Ian looked at Duncan wondering if he ever wore anything but that black suit. It was so morbid.

Agent Duncan gave him his usual stern look. "We traced your father's car to downtown Denver. James lied to us, when he said he was going to the airport. He rented a car at the airport then drove to the Brown Palace Hotel and checked in."

Ian had to smile, though it was sarcastic. "Well, he did go to the airport."

Duncan was truly aggravated. "That is very funny, as well as beside the point. Your dad has not been seen for some time now, so the hotel manager wants you to come pick up his things, and pay them for his room. We have accessed all of the hotel's video footage and hope to learn something from that soon."

The agent pulled Ian into the next room. "Let's speak candidly, there is still no word from your wife's abductors. That is not a good sign. We should have received a ransom request before now. With the violence they showed exploding that bomb in Durango, we have to consider the worst."

* * *

'I am a bad, horrible, useless, rotten, awful kid.' Ian twisted and turned in his disturbing dream. 'It's my fault that mommy and sis are dead, and daddy doesn't love me anymore.' Ian rolled over, and over again, attempting to escape this twisted nightmare. 'But I will make everything better, like magic. Harry Potter makes things better. I will too. Mommy will come back, and so will sis. I'll make them come back, and make daddy proud of me and then daddy will want me back again.'

Ian struggled, trying to escape the bed sheets wrapped tightly around his body, then screamed out in his sleep, startling himself. Sitting up, he unwrapped the sheets holding him captive, swung his legs off the bed and stood up. Then wandered into the kitchen, rubbing his eyes. As he reached for the refrigerator, a ruckus from the dining room startled him. Turning, he ran toward the noise.

"NO! Don't hurt my family!" shouted his daddy, holding his arms up in terror. Ian looked in the dining room mirror, seeing a very young boy staring back–he was still asleep. "It's me you want!" his daddy yelled. Then that horrible little boy, 'little Ian', reached out, running as fast as he could. He was not getting any closer! Mommy and sis were just out of reach... then a loud pop, pop, pop, pop...so loud when that ugly red lamp exploded in pieces, shards of glass flying through the air mixed with little brass shell casings. So loud–so much glass and all the red, warm red flowing on his feet and mommy and sis just laying there, daddy screaming. "NO!" "NO!"

The horrible scene melted away and warped–he was now an adult again. Out of the darkness Ian heard a faint, "baby... baby..." The cry became louder, "Baby... Baby..." He strained his eyes against the darkness, and could just make out his wife. She was standing in the middle of an old rickety rope bridge, stretched across a cavernous, rocky gorge, above a waterfall. The familiar waterfall was being swallowed by a dense fog rising from beneath, when the bridge began to swing violently, with pieces hurling off in every direction. Desperately trying to get to his wife, Ian stepped precariously from one rung to another, across gaping voids, attempting to keep his balance. Finally reaching her, their fingers touched just as a loud snap threw Ian off the side. One rope holding the bridge broke, and the other began to unravel. Hanging from the side, grappling to hold onto a frayed shred of rope, he watched hopelessly as Jasmine recessed further and further away. Just before she disappeared, she looked at him and calmly said, "I need your help."

'Is that "Time of your life," by Green Day? Oh! That's my ringtone,' Ian thought to himself. 'Where is my phone?'

"Dad, dad, are you okay? You're having a nightmare." Alek stood bedside the bed shaking his father's shoulders, a scared look in his eyes. "Are you okay, dad?"

"Yeah, yeah... I'm all right. Just a bad dream, can't even remember what it was," Ian told his son, then thinking to himself. 'Humm, I really can't remember, something about my mother's old house, that horrible red lamp and Jasmine needing help. What does Jasmine have to do with that lamp?'

Alek broke his train of thought. "Dad, the phone, it's that Agent Duncan guy, he wants to talk to you. I'm going outside."

Ian heard Alek bounding down the stairs before the front door slammed. He pulled on his pants, poked his head into his daughter's room to check on her. 'Still asleep, good.' Then headed downstairs with his phone.

"Hello, Agent Duncan. Do you have some news?"

"Well, yes, we do." Duncan sounded far away, the cell phone static made it difficult to hear. "Got lucky, we have a rough photo caught by the surveillance camera from the lobby of the Brown Palace. You mentioned a large bald man when we spoke the night your wife was taken. This might be him. I emailed you the photo our team enhanced, tell me if you recognize him, he is with..."

The phone went silent. Ian ran to his office, touched a keyboard and the computers in the room jumped to life. He clicked his mail program and downloaded the image. There on the largest screen in his office was the man that took his wife and stole the Wand. Ian had only seen the man for a split second as he emerged from the Portal only to disappear with the Portal Wand. But he would never forget his face. "THAT'S MY DAD STANDING NEXT TO THE BALD MAN!" he exclaimed in disbelief. "What the hell!"

He found Agent Duncan's number in his phone's call log and returned the disconnected call. Nothing...it just rang. Finally an automated lady's voice said, "The caller you are tying to reach is out of the service area." Trying again and again he got the same response. "DAMN!" Ian thought for a minute, then decided to make some coffee. Ian hoped that Duncan would call when he got back into a hot zone. He just had to.

* * *

"Sir, here is a complementary snack. Would you like a drink?" The flight attendant went on to tell Agent Duncan, that the flight would land in Miami on time, and that he had an hour layover before his connecting flight to Nassau.

Flying into the Lynden Pindling International Airport, it appeared they would land in the turquoise surf seconds before the landing strip finally appeared. After departing and getting through customs, he took a cab to Queen Street in Nassau, just off of Marlborough Street. Duncan walked through the impressive grand lobby entrance of the British Colonial Hilton Hotel and checked in. He took his carry-on bag to the room and scanned the view from his third floor balcony. Massive cruise ships were docked just beyond the Straw Market. On the far side of the bay an isolated lighthouse stood at the rocky point of Paradise Island. Beyond the island the multicolor-turquoise Atlantic ran to the horizon where it merged with the clouds.

After drinking a bottle of water from the mini-bar, he took the elevator to the lobby and walked across the street to the U.S. Embassy. He was there to ask a consular officer to intercede with local authorities and find out if the police or customs had a passport record of James Knecht entering Nassau. If James was in the Bahamas, there should be a record. At the very least, maybe Nassau authorities had seen the bald man in the photo his team had taken from the surveillance video. If luck continued, they might even have an arrest record or his mystery man may have been detained for some reason.

After waiting for what seemed to be hours, and sifting through miles of red tape, Duncan finally spoke with Consular Odell. "Sorry to keep you waiting, Agent Duncan. Mr. Knecht has not legally entered Nassau during the past month. If you would leave the photo of the large bald man, we will review our records for him. Come back in the morning and we will share our findings with you."

Duncan bit his lip, pushed a copy of the photo across the desk along with his hotel and room number. "Please call me if you find anything. I'll be just across the street."

The following morning, Duncan pulled open the drapes, letting in the warm, fishy salt breeze that mixed with the damp musty scent of the room. He found some coffee, then got a call to meet Odell at the police station next door to the Embassy. He headed back across the street to see what the police had found.

Consular Odell walked up to Duncan soon after he entered the station. "Agent Duncan, the man in your photo may have been recognized. I believe he is the same man that was arrested about a month ago at the Foxhill Division not far from here. Come with me." A few moments later, they were headed for the Foxhill Police Department.

* * *

"We can't just sit here any longer," Steele said to Celeste as he sipped his black coffee. Louise walked into the kitchen and sat with them at the table. A bright smile seemed to make her glow.

"Good morning, make a good day," Louise greeted. "Looks like we might have some assistance to find help for Jasmine. Her young daughter Kristen and her friend are 'Twinklers' in our dimension. The girls have information that can help, we just have to find a way to contact them."

"And this can also help, Jaguar asked me to give you a lesson in observation. Try to observe everything around you in detail. Whatever is presented to you in memory, in dreams, or thought–even if things may not seem to make sense, or be what you consider 'real'. Concentrate, so that you can learn to see not only the general aspect, but eventually, even the minor details, patterns and colors, with clarity. In time the subtler meanings will become clearer."

Louise smiled, and nodded wisely. "Much of earth's communications heard, seen and felt through music, paintings, sculptures, poems and movies are attempts of the earthbound mind to receive, interpret and share flickers of wisdom, of reality. This is the path to Joy. To help observe, try this exercise. Close your eyes." She spoke in soft soothing tones. "Breathe deeply, calm your mind, body, and emotions. Stay perfectly calm and centered at all times. Meditate on a cosmic light, then illuminate your third eye by visualizing a bright golden light filling your head." Louise paused... then continued in a soft voice. "Connect this golden light of energy with your heart center and your solar plexus. See yourself as a part of Earth and feel grounded in her sea of love and light. Receive impulses of energy, see it spiral into your energy body just below your bellybutton. Let it rise up your spine, filling your entire body, then let that energy flow from you into the area around you."

The three of them sat at the table, peacefully following this meditation, visualizing the golden light. As they sent and received impulses of harmonious energy, they became aware of a ghost-like beautiful little dark-skinned girl in their presence. She spoke in a soft broken English, barely perceivable, as she flickered or twinkled in and out of focus.

"Caristen she frind.... mudda is... Jasmine... say... to tata Jiemes smile... ya-r loved... Jiemes in... ie Jamaican settie... Nassau... Foxhiell... him o-k in ie room. Tata... Jiemes nied... help." Then she was gone.

"Wow, did you see that little girl?" Celeste asked. "She looked familiar somehow."

"I saw her. But could you understand what she was trying to tell us?" Steele questioned.

"This is where you have to work on observation, listen and feel between the lines, sort of mind-speaking," Louise replied. "Jasmine obviously has a daughter 'Caristen,' or maybe Kristen. Her daughter has a friend in Nassau, Bahamas. This little girl has talked to Kristen's grandfather 'James.'"

"Yes," Steele intervened. "I spoke to James on the phone, when I called Ian."

Louise continued. "Seems that James needs our help. You might want to pack a few things, for a warm climate. I have something important to take care of first, then we can go to Nassau and see what we can accomplish. Would you do some research, see what you can find out about a 'foxhill' in Nassau? See you soon."

* * *

"You are fading, my dear," Louise said softly, staring at a rock wall, seemingly talking to herself. "Be strong, sit still, breathe deeply and picture your waterfall. I just spoke with your daughter's friend Fajah, a pretty little girl from the Bahamas. She asked us to help James, he must be your father-in-law. Hold on for your daughter, that will help you be strong. I will get Jaguar, he is a strong healer of the spirit."

Jasmine was becoming more and more diaphanous the longer she remained in Gaia. Jaguar came in a hurry, "Jasmine, can you still hear me? We're going to work with your physical connection to the planet, and keep you with us a little longer while we find your husband, so he can come get you. There is no easy way to say this. You are going through a weaning process. What you consider as dying."

Terror plastered her face and Jasmine cried. "No, not now, not this way."

Jaguar continued. "Wait, hear me out. You are moving from being nourished by Mother-Earth, to learning and preparing to adventure on toward a different stage of development, more of a cosmic connection for your nourishment, but you must be strong. Stay with us now, concentrate on your connection to the Earth."

"I'll guide you through a grounding exercise. Sit comfortably and breathe deeply through your nose, and deep into your abdomen. Relax, with each breath feel the Earth's energy flowing up your spine and spiraling into your life-center just below your navel. Hold that energy there and watch it grow, turning into a ball of warm light inside you. Yes...exhale... slowly through your mouth...continue to breathe and feel your connection with Mother Earth." After a few minutes he asked. "Do you feel it?"

"Yes." Jasmine was becoming more visible again.

"Good. Now as the connection between your world increases, visualize roots growing from that ball of light running deep into the Earth holding you here."

"No worries," Jasmine whispered uncharacteristically. "I feel my connection...and I have become aware of another here with me."

As Jasmine said that, a heavy-set, deeply-wrinkled old man with shoulder-length white hair held in place by multi-colored bandanna stepped into view. "G'day mate. I am Max Coorparoo. You are following the way of Dadirri. I will help you understand the special inner listening and quiet still awareness the Aboriginal people practice. Dadirri remembers the deep spring that is inside us all. The contemplative way of Dadirri spreads over life. It renews, brings peace and will make you feel whole again."

Max instructed Jasmine further, as the others waited nearby. "Learn to listen from your earliest times. Be still...wait, do not try to hurry things, let them follow their natural course–like nature's seasons. My people have lived for thousands of years with Nature's quietness, the great Life-Giving Spirit, the Father of us all. In time, and in the spirit of Dadirri, the way will be made clear."

"I came to you, found you here," Max explained. "We find each other in the same way as the earth, moon and the sun know each other. Much in the same way that the weight of heavenly bodies in space attract each other as they become close. As we awaken to our unique spiritual signatures, we are drawn toward one another as well...like-to-like...a truth recognized by elders and sages of past ages."

Max then turned to the group. "Good to see you again, Jaguar. How is Star? Haven't seen either of you for a very long time."

Jaguar gave Max a big hug. "Very good to see you, old friend. Star is close, you will see her soon." He gestured toward Jasmine. "Have you ever experienced anyone like our new friend here?"

Max looked expressionless. "Much the same as a dream walker, only... ah...steady, not blinking in and out. Unique. Where did you find this little sheila?"

"You do know I'm right here," Jasmine expressed in aggravation. "What am I going to do?" She put her head down in her hands and cried softly.

Max replied. "Yes, of course, dear one. We mean no disrespect. Breathe and quiet yourself."

Star came into the room and immediately ran into Max's arms. They exchanged greetings with a big hug. Jaguar asked Jasmine to excuse them so they could speak alone for a few minutes. "We will return soon with something to eat. Be still, and reinforce your grounding exercises." Star, Max and Jaguar went to find Louise.

Addressing the trio, Jaguar explained to Max what they knew of Jasmine's circumstances. "This is new to everyone that knows of Jasmine. No one has ever experienced anyone in her situation. However, I feel she is an important key to unlocking answers to Earth's condition and the problem facing all of us."

* * *

Louise returned from the Falls with a small travel bag. "Are you packed and ready for the Bahamas?"

"We don't know if we can do this, Louise," Steele said with a concerned tone. "Celeste and I have talked and we are feeling overwhelmed. We are only making things worse–I took an easy phone call and turned that into a manhunt by the FBI."

"Dear children, you cannot give up," Louise responded to Steele and Celeste's frustration and attempt to shun their destinies.

"But, Nassau–what are we going to do there?"

"We all need you more than you can understand. Everyone faces serious Earth changes–no, cosmic-changing events. It is more necessary than ever to act. As Edmund Burke from our history once said: 'All that is necessary for the triumph of evil, is that good men do nothing.'" She went on to clarify. "When we refer to Earth as our mother, or 'Father' as our friend Max does, we mean far more than just the physical planet. We speak also of her biosphere–that region on, above, and below her surface where life is possible. This eco-system is a remarkable planetary engine, or circulatory system, very similar to our own. That eco-system is the energy fueling life. Swirling wind and ocean currents spread as cold air and surface waters move toward the equator; at the same time warm air and water moves toward the poles. This is the life-blood used to equalize temperatures around the world, which comprise the entire Earth and the living organisms that inhabit her."

"Earth is a living, sentient being," Louise continued. "She receives us as we begin and live, she nourishes and sustains us to the end of our lives. Without her, our physical body would not be. You are both aware that our modern industrial society is well on its way to destroying the biosphere on this planet. Earth, the planet, will remain through any of our activities, but life as we experience it, is in real danger. In this age there are many of us that understand that we must honor the Earth. This means, more than anything else, that we are obligated to protect and defend her from the forces that would destroy her, for whatever reason. Therefore, it is time to honor the traditions of the native indigenous peoples from around the world and live our lives in dedication to the principle of sustainability. With the understanding that humanity is just one of Earth's species–not her dominator, but her loving children. We must always do our best to live in harmony with the Earth, not in opposition or rebellion against her."

"There I go again, running on with my discourse," Louise proclaimed. "Though there is one more thing I would like to share with you both, so please be patient with me for another minute. There are many political, social and economic factions that for one reason or another are fighting to dominate this world. It is through ignorance, not understanding that their shortsighted views are exterminating their own existence. War on terror, along with many word-smithed phrases, are intended to deliberately generate a culture of fear. To obscure reason and intensify fear-based emotions, which makes it easier for demagogic governments and religions to mobilize the public on behalf of the policies they want to pursue. These leaders use manufactured fear, reflected by the media, to increase their power and control over society by preying on cultural assumptions about human vulnerability and irrational fears for the future. Those of us that understand have to show that living in trust and love instead of fear is urgent."

"I understand," Steele replied. "But what can we possibly do? There are so few of us and the world is a very big place."

Louise stood with an understanding command. "Every journey starts with a single step. Being around people whose agenda is not fear-based domination, but sympathetic and supportive is imperative to spread these important truths. As Franklin D. Roosevelt said, 'Let me assert my firm belief that the only thing we have to fear is fear itself.' So long as fear, run-away materialism and greed drive our culture we are bound to be held prisoners by our beliefs. It is time mankind returns to the values of love, honoring personal individuation, growth, diversity, and creativity. Learn to flow with Earth's natural energy."

"Jaguar would like to show you two how living in harmony with the Earth helps her. If you would like to go for a little adventure." Louise told them that with her guidance and Celeste's tremendous ability to manipulate the physics between dimensions that they could travel as a group to visit Jaguar. Louise instructed them to stand in a triangle holding hands. Isis and Maya crowded together between the three. Centering themselves they began to visualize Jaguar and feel his energy.

Next thing they knew they were standing with Jaguar in an old forest in Gaia's dimension. The dogs growled softly, unsure what had just happened. He greeted them, then proceeded to show Celeste and Steele a naturally cultivated forest and explained that the forest itself used fire to prune the dead trees and eliminate crowded undergrowth.

The four stood on a ridge overlooking a majestic view. It was that perfect time of day at dusk where the soft light illuminated the valley in a magical, almost purple hue. On close inspection a series of rivers and creeks braided their way down the mountainsides that formed an organic lattice. As if a huge spider wove a series of unbound webs throughout the valley. The resplendent basin had a pure biological order that did not look the least bit unnatural.

All of a sudden a monstrous dark cumulonimbus cloud rolled over the mountaintop horizon. A blinding bolt of lightning struck a huge tree at the vertex of the adjacent ridge. A fire sprang to life, winding its way down the mountainside like a living organism. Celeste and Steele stood frozen. When Steele finally turned his gaze to Celeste, the same horrified expression that he wore was reflected in her eyes. In union, they screamed to Jaguar. "We have to do something to stop the fire."

Jaguar only shook his head, smiled and said, "Wait a minute, this is what we brought you to witness."

The fire became a rushing inferno they felt would engulf the entire basin. As they watched in amazement, the series of creeks, rivers and stone ridges directed the blazing torrent as a conductor would a work of Mozart. The ebb and flow became a harmonic orchestra where they could hear the individual musical notes in the crackling flames. The once out-of-control inferno became organized. It rushed along, dancing like tubular bells on the branches of the oldest trees, kissing the dried leaves and pine needles as a pilot fish would hygienically cleanse its host. This symbiotic boogie of completely different biological species continued from tree to tree, while tiny flame ensembles sounding like violins and flutes consumed underbrush that had threatened to choke the ancient forest. This musical concerto followed its conductor into a tight passage in the rock canyon that led over a 200-foot drop into a small lake. Most of the flames leaped over the precipice to extinguish themselves below in a billowy hiss. With the fiery orchestra's crescendo, a cloudburst spilled from the sky with a thunderous finale of the rolling percussion bass of thunder drumming and the cymbals crashing conclusion. The fire was out.

Stunned by the majesty, they stood in silence, not wanting to break the moment of reverence that nature's symphony just displayed. Louise finally broke the silence. "Come children, let us visit the Falls. I need to check on Jasmine and you can leave Isis and Maya with us to watch for awhile. I have a feeling you are going to be moving around quite a bit. Do not worry, they will be safe with us there."

* * *

"Yow misstar Jiemes mie tata here tu help yuh outa room." As his wonderful new friend Fa was talking, James heard the door lock being worked loose. A short time later a friendly, old face shyly peeked in the open door.

"Waddup? Misstar Jiemes yuh a free tugo now, hush up yuh mouth." He held his index finger across his lips. James crept out of the open door into the cover of night's darkness, and could just make out a skinny old man hurrying away, pulling Fa by her hand. She waved over her shoulder, whispering, "Walk good missatar Jiemes– respeck."

"Thank you," James mouthed, and waved in return. He saw one of the goons from the compound notice movement as they disappeared into the undergrowth. James was glad the guard didn't follow them.

Turning to avoid being seen himself, James ran down the path to what appeared to be the main building of the complex. He could hear the unforgettable snore of that bald bastard coming from the second open window he came to. His eyes had become accustomed to low light so he could make out Gregory laying on his back, mouth wide open. There on the night table next to the bed, was his handgun. Slowly crawling through the window, James reached the handgun and gently put it in Gregory's mouth. Rattling the gun against his teeth brought the snoring to an immediate stop as his eyes popped open.

"Where is the Portal Wand?" James asked. A shaky hand pointed to the safe. "Open it." The gun being pushed into his mouth became an unmistakable elicitor. Loosening only a couple of teeth, Gregory was all too happy to oblige.

With the safe open, James took the Wand and knocked Gregory out with the butt of his gun. Then he wiped off his face and attempted to cover his stench with deodorant from the bathroom. He quickly changed into Gregory's pants and shirt that hung over the nearby chair and slipped out the window. James ran like he hadn't since college track, when he had once worked to impress his wife, before they were married. Gasping for air, he slowed to a walk and found an abandoned car that had been swallowed by the vines from the nearby jungle. He forced the door open a crack and slid inside to hide for the night.

The next morning light peeked through the vines, and across the car's dashboard. James crept out of the car and stumbled out of the jungle at the edge of a town. He hurried down the street to look for a phone. James had to call his son, try to explain his situation, and get coordinates so he could use the Wand. A few blocks later, he came to an old two-story, bright turquoise building with white trim. 'Royal Bahamas Police' was painted in black lettering beside the door. Attempting to blend into the surroundings, and look like a tourist, even though an extremely dirty tourist–James walked inconspicuously past a well-dressed constable in his pressed white bush jacket sporting gold buttons, black patent leather belt and shoes, black pants with a red stripe all topped off with the familiar Commonwealth white helmet complete with a gold insignia.

"Sir, can I assist you?"

'Can I trust the police without my passport? Better not, damn, keep walking.' he thought, then changed his mind. "Yes... I am looking for Commissioner Greenslade." Luckily, James had seen Greenslade's name in the paper Fa gave him a few days ago. He would tell the Commissioner that he had been mugged and lost his passport.

"You're in luck," the constable said. "He is just through these doors on the left. Here, I'll get the door for you." Feeling trapped, James reluctantly walked through the door the constable had just opened, trying to keep his cool and not bolt down the street.

"Daddy!"

James looked toward the voice, and saw a young blond woman, about twenty-some years old. She was speaking directly at him and holding her arms out in a hugging gesture.

The young lady ran into his arms and whispered. "I'm Akira, a friend–play along."

A great relief washed over him as he saw her calm demeanor. "Hi sugar, there you are." They should have been actors, what unplanned improvisation.

"Daddy, I was so scared, I didn't know where you were," she continued. James hugged her. "Where have you been? NEVER, ever, do that to me again." They both turned to the officers and began to explain, their words rushing over one another, trying to confuse the situation as much as hide the lack of a cohesive story. Akira and James stood in the middle of the police station making a scene. Sometimes it's best to hide in plain sight.

Seeing Agent Duncan and Consular Odell walk in from the back door parking lot, James pulled Akira along as they began to shuffle toward the front doors. James was thanking every officer in sight for finding his lost daughter! Akira wrapped her arms tighter around James and whispered.

"Do not overdo it. I'm here to help you, Jasmine and Ian's family. Trust me."

She slipped the Wand from his pocket and quickly entered a set of coordinates.

Duncan spotted James. "STOP them!" Duncan shouted, grabbing for the father and daughter, as they headed for the double doors. They cleared the doors as Duncan reached them and the familiar mystifying white light engulfed them…

….something was wrong. James had only Jumped twice, but this Jump was very different. The inviting light was fading in and out, they were spinning out of control. "Duncan pulled the Wand from my hand at the threshold of the Jump." Akira's voice entered his head without words. "Hold on, this is going to be a bumpy ride. But do not worry. Trans-world conveyance is one of my talents."

After a rough ride, that could be described as what you might feel in a crashing plane, they re-appeared–landing hard on grassy turf, underneath bleacher seats that were wrapped in a green mesh cloth. James dizzily pushed himself to his feet and held onto a metal post to steady himself, then looked around. He surmised they were on a golf course, in a colder climate without any palm trees around. They were certainly not in the Bahamas any longer.

"Who are you?" he asked his dazed rescuer.

* * *

Consular Odell ran through the front door seconds behind Duncan and the father/daughter frauds, but stopped within a few steps. "Where did they go?" Odell questioned, scratching his head.

Duncan discreetly slid the Wand into his pocket and smiled. "Don't know, but they are fast, aren't they?"

Odell went straight to the district captain. "Captain, find them! You have to get your men on this right away, they couldn't have gone far. This man is important in an international case the United States is prosecuting."

After a lengthy interrogation by the Captain, Duncan excused himself, saying he was returning to his hotel, should they have any additional questions. Hailing a taxi, he stepped into the back seat, "British Colonial

Hilton, step on it." During the short ride Duncan made a call, using a prepaid Bahamas SIM card cell phone to keep from being traced. "General, meet me at the water taxi next to the Straw Market. Make it quick, we need to talk, now."

Duncan hurriedly made his way from the hotel to the water taxi. His black suit made him a target, as he pushed through the crowded market just up the street from his hotel, refusing the many local hawkers trying to sell him watches, beads, straw hats, shirts or cigars from their brightly decorated tents. When he got to the water taxi pier, he sat on the concrete wall and waited for the General. Moments later, he spotted the General crossing the street, at the corner next to 'Big Daddy.' The local street musician was playing the sax–he wore brightly colored glasses and his hair hung in long dreads.

"What do you want, Agent?" he said as he approached.

"Hello, General. You really screwed up this project. Why did you let Gregory off his leash? I had to go through the motions with the local police in order to maintain my cover. Imagine my surprise when the Consular came back to me, having recognized your mad dog from the police mug shot. You are all supposed to be avoiding attention. That means, in case you have forgotten, not being photographed, arrested or detained by the authorities."

The General clenched his fist, and gave Duncan a stare that could eat through rock, but remained silent.

"And since I'm pointing fingers, how the hell did James escape?" Duncan asked. "And with the Portal device, stolen back from Gregory, no less. Lucky for you I was able to get the Wand back. But James knows we are after him now, so he will be impossible to find. You know Bishop Daniel is going to want someone's head for this, and it's not going to be mine. I guarantee you that!"

〉〉〉

CHAPTER 7
Golf, Music and Fox Hill

Akira handed James a stack of clothes she had purchased from the pro shop. "Why don't you find the locker room, clean up and put these on, you are a real mess. Meet me at the second tee in 30 minutes."

Feeling queasy and a bit unbalanced from the rough transport, after being lock up in the jungle prison, it felt good to take a quick shower. James changed into clean slacks and a golf shirt. Then he found an attendant to get him some shoes, and take him to the second tee where Akira was standing with their clubs.

"Who are you, Akira, what is going on and how do you know Ian?"

An announcement came: "Please welcome the second pair of this foursome, father and daughter team from Denver, Colorado—James and Akira."

"I'll explain as I can," she said under her breath.

He smiled and teed up his ball. "I haven't golfed for a long time."

"Fake it till you make it!" she said kiddingly.

"Fore!" James screamed at unsuspecting golfers on the left side of the fairway. They watched as his golf ball hooked some 160 yards forward but 50 yards to the left. "Really, golfing?"

"Play along here, dad. I may need this hybrid club after that awful shot." Akira started off down the fairway, pulling a rather heavy golf bag cart. "Bring your bag, dad. After I hit, it will be your shot again. Lucky for you we're playing 'Alternate Shot.'"

They found his ball, after walking through the middle of a beautifully manicured grass fairway with its diamond-cut angles forming patterns running across the first cut, then continuing across the rough close to the out-of-bounds marker. They were just a few feet from the early blooms of white and pink colors in the ornamental trees. The earliest spring in history, thought to be caused by global warming.

"We are so lucky," she continued. "This is a lazy dog-leg to the right, you made this a long hole, but at least you avoided going out-of-bounds."

He looked around. Across the fairway, just past the green, was Peachtree

Creek, and beyond was the large white clubhouse. He grew up playing on this course, so he knew this second hole at the Bobby Jones Golf Course, in Atlanta, Georgia.

"I hope you are a better golfer than that last shot. We have 17 more holes to fake before the charity banquet being held at the clubhouse. Relax and enjoy yourself, I'll save your butt. Besides it's a beautiful day to be alive."

Akira considered the lie of the ball that James had left her with his sliced drive. Overhanging branches posed a problem. A low shot would work, to go under the obstacle. She envisioned running the ball up the front of the green... looks like about 150 yards. She pulled out a 6-iron, played the ball just off her left instep in a slightly closed stance, and laid down a creative stroke, running the ball to within four feet of the pin. "That shot should work. How is your putting?" she asked James, then got serious, noticing no one was around them. "Come on, walk with me, I know your son's situation. Ian and Agent Duncan believe his wife Jasmine has been abducted."

James was getting frustrated. "She was abducted, and I had the Wand, and everything was under control before you came along."

Akira only smiled. "Tell me then, what was your plan, to stand there and get arrested?"

"Well, miss smarty pants, where is the Wand? And what are we doing in Georgia?"

"Good shot!" came a compliment from a middle-aged woman, sporting short stylish auburn hair underneath a white visor cap. Two golfers approached the green where James and Akira sized up their putt. She introduced themselves as Morgan, and her son Doug.

"Good morning," Akira said. "I am..."

"Can't be," James interrupted. "Morgan Goodchild. I haven't seen you since we graduated from UNM. It has to have been over forty years since Albuquerque. You are looking good, how are you? And Doug, wow! I didn't know you had a son."

"Or you a daughter," Morgan said with a sly smile and a wink. "Good to see you again too, James."

"Daughter...ah.." James stuttered. "...Oh, yes. I haven't introduced you. This is my daughter, Akira."

"Nice to meet you, young lady." Morgan and Doug's ball was furthest from the hole, so they headed to the other side of the green to size up their putt.

As Morgan and Doug scrutinized their shot, Akira looked at James. "Georgia. I'm not sure exactly why we're here. Energy was asking us to be here. Besides, I do not believe in coincidence, so we are not accidentally paired with an old friend of yours some 730 miles from where we started without a reason. As my friend Louise would say, 'How much do we miss, by not paying attention to things that are obviously put in our path?' Serendipities and 'ironies' or as Louise called them the 'hearteners' and the 'challengers' are all for the basic and ultimate purpose: to help us on our evolutionary journey."

The foursome continued playing, and James and Akira spoke with their partners often, attempting to discover a reason the group had come together at this Catholic Charities golf tournament. They learned many things about Morgan and her son: neither Morgan nor Doug had any connection to Denver. They both lived in Green Bay, where she was a Realtor and Doug was a massage therapist and owned a spa and massage boutique, that specialized in Reiki healing. Morgan was thrilled that Doug was engaged to be married to Elizabeth, the daughter of the bishop of her church. Nothing they had to say seemed to have any bearing on Jasmine or the Portal Wand.

By the end of the game, James was ready to leave and head to the nearest airport to catch a flight for Denver and get back to Ian's house. Akira felt that they might still find a reason for their chance meeting and wanted to stay for the awards dinner. She told James that she would transport them to Ian's after dinner, so they would be in Denver much faster than taking a plane. James agreed.

He excused himself before the dinner to find a phone to call Ian. But what was he going to say? He stood holding the courtesy phone, staring out across the beautiful landscape not really seeing anything, caught up in thought.

"Sir, if you are not going to use the phone, I need to call my mom," a young stranger said.

James shook his head, hearing, "If you would like to make a call, please hang up and call again."

"Oh, yes...yes, I'm sorry." He handed the phone to the boy, who took it and gave James a sympathetic smile and a 'thank you sir.' Still deep in thought, he wandered through a packed room of milling strangers, all asking one another how they played. His subconscious mind found their table.

"James, I would like you to meet Bishop Daniel. I have been telling him what a surprise it was to see you again, and how proud you are of your son, Ian."

"Pleased to meet you, Bishop," James said, shaking the cleric's hand. "Morgan told me about the upcoming wedding. You must be excited." They all agreed that marriage, along with strong, loving relationships were the cornerstone of a stable society, then spent a couple of hours listening to small talk, awards and speeches about the money raised for the various charities. But James and Akira still had no more idea why the foursome was put together than they did before his first slice at the second hole.

Hugs, more pleasantries and exchanging phone numbers. 'Call, we should stay in touch'–but they all knew that would probably never happen.

As they were leaving, James turned to Akira and said, "I need to call Ian, before we just show up. Give me a minute and I will meet you in the parking lot." Finally, they would soon be on their way.

* * *

"Another turning point;
A fork stuck in the road.
Time grabs you by the wrist;
Directs you where to go.
So make the best of this test and don't ask why.
It's not a question but a lesson learned in time.
It's something unpredictable
But in the end it's right.
I hope you had the time of your life."

'I'm going to have to change that Green Day ringtone to something more upbeat. Never would have guessed how much meaning 'Time of your life' would have in my life right now.'

The cell phone had roused him. Ian yawned and rubbed his eyes, looking up from his workbench. He had been feverishly working on another Portal

Wand and hadn't slept for longer than he could recall. "Hello, this is Ian," he answered.

"Son, please don't hang up. I know you must hate me right now. I told you I would help and I just vanished. Let me explain."

"Oh, this should be good! Go ahead, explain how you know the bald man that took Jasmine and technology that can change the world. I have got to hear this. While you're at it, I would love to hear why you abandoned me after mom died. You have a hell of a lot to explain, James."

"Son, I don't want to do this on the phone. Can I come to your home so we can speak in person?"

"Dad, or James–I don't know you at all. I don't really want to see you. Where are you anyway, caller ID shows area code 770?"

"770 is Atlanta, Georgia...It's a strange story, son. Can I see you in a few minutes and explain in person?"

"Yeh, dad, you have to be four or five hours to the Denver airport, at best if you are standing at the airport terminal boarding a plane... unless you have the Wand. Do you have it?"

"Well, no, but I have something similar. You will not believe this."

"Add it to the list, James. I'm having a very hard time believing anything you have to say. Did someone copy my Portal technology? If you have something similar, why don't you just pop over. The kids are staying with friends, so you can't break their hearts again. If you show up at all."

Ian hung up and went back to work. "The nerve of that man," he mumbled to himself. Before he could get started, musical chimes filled the house, so Ian answered the door.

"Dad! You do have the Wand! Who is this girl? What have you done?"

James introduced Akira and they briefly tried to explain that she was from another dimension they call Gaia. Akira described Jasmine's situation, and told Ian how important it was that he find her at the waterfall and bring her back as soon as possible. Studying Akira with disbelief, Ian was considering if she was stark raving mad or whether his father had put her up to this wild story. Another lie in the long list.

"I know you two have a lot to talk about," Akira said. "I have to go, I have a lead on your Wand, and will see what I can do to get it back for you. Your dad can explain everything. By the way, Steele and his wife have nothing to do with taking Jasmine. They are trying to help you. That is a fabricated story, Agent Duncan is lying to you–selling you a bill of goods, as you might say. We will see each other again." And with that she faded away, leaving Ian standing there, his mouth open in mid-sentence with more questions than answers.

* * *

"Jasmine, as we explained when we first met, your vibration was not high enough to survive when you crossed to this dimension," Star explained.

"That is why you have been struggling. Not quite here nor there. But I have some good news which in a way may be bad news as well. The healing Jaguar is giving your spiritual body along with the breathing exercises and meditations, combined with your selfless love, are changing your physical vibration. This means that you are out of physical danger. Your wavelength is at a level to maintain your existence here in this world. The bad news is that by raising your vibration you are losing connection to your world. The higher your vibration, the more your consciousness shifts to align with Gaia, and the further away you get from your previous existence. Your substance... your physical matter...is changing in ways that are yet to be fully revealed to you. Your capacity and willingness of mind, heart, and spirit to raise the vibration of your physical, emotional, and mental being is adapting to resonate with this world's new energies. Put scientifically, on Earth, visible electromagnetic radiation wavelengths range between 380 nanometers to 750 nanometers. In your world this constitutes the upper and lower end points, beyond which eyes and senses do not respond to electromagnetic radiation. These wavelength ranges are beyond that which people in your dimension can see or even feel. Your energy is starting to oscillate above the visible 750 nanometers."

"What exactly does all of that mean?" Jasmine asked, afraid she already knew the answer.

"Soon you will not exist in your previous reality–at least not to anyone from that dimension."

"So I'll just disappear...I'll die," Jasmine exclaimed on the edge of panic.

"Yes, and no. It is not that cut and dried. The Earth has recently gone through a shift, moving into a Photon Belt, also called the Golden Nebula. This makes the barrier between dimensions less dense. With training, if

68

you have the talent, you will be able to travel between the two worlds. To what extent is up to your ability. One of our most gifted, Akira, is able to raise and lower her wavelength to travel between worlds at will. She can even take those with latent talents with her...it is quite remarkable. Here, like in your world, you will find different people have vastly different talents. Talents that range from trans-world conveyance, to precognition, space and time property manipulation, advanced healing and so much more."

Jasmine and Star sat up through most of the night talking about the fundamental nature of being...about the world and how love's subatomic vibration relates to energy's wavelength effecting space and time. Star even began to explain the basics of cosmology...how Earth is a sentient being, and our planet's relationship with us, along with all inhabitants, relates to the totality of all phenomena within the universe.

Finally, Jasmine stretched with a big yawn. "We should get some sleep," Star said. "These are all pretty involved topics. I am excited that you have such a fundamental grasp of the subjects. That will be a great benefit in this world."

"All of this is truly wonderful and frightening," Jasmine replied. "But my children, husband, family and friends. I can't just leave them all, they wouldn't know what happened to me."

Star's concerned expression showed in her eyes. "I'm sorry, you may not have a choice, unless your husband can soon find you with his Portal device and bring you back to your world. Wait...there might be another alternative. Work on your trans-world travel abilities with Akira, and she might be able to help you visit your dimension. In time she might even be able to teach you how to travel by yourself."

Star had one more thing to say, attempting to put Jasmine's mind at rest. "With time and training, the ability to raise and lower wavelengths to travel between worlds will not even be something that needs to be discussed. It will be deeply understood that body and consciousness are one, and that to maintain one's own spiritual and mental health, as well as the world's spiritual and mental health, lead to attunement of the entire being. There will be a time in the not-too-distant future when we understand that these restorative and enhancing energies are essential. At that time, this understanding will become more familiar to humanity's collective consciousness. Today what seems like an effort for some, impossible fantasy for others, will become a gift and an opportunity beyond our expectations."

"That doesn't do me any good right now," Jasmine said tearfully. "I'm stuck." She broke down crying again. "I'm dead."

* * *

Fox Hill Road in Nassau appeared on Google Maps. The Internet search also turned up a Fox Hill prison, police station, even a nursery garden center. Steele sat staring at the computer in their friend's borrowed house. "Looks like a good place to start might be the police station. What do you think, baby?"

"Yeh, police station. Do you think we will have time to go to a beach? I have never been to the Bahamas," Celeste replied.

Steele laughed. "What are we doing, hun? You're talking about going to the beach. Just a month ago, before our camping trip, we had a life. You were a well-respected business person running a web design and hosting company with numerous clients. I was making a pretty good living as an artist–which is a lot easier to say than do. We both worked from home, we had the ideal life. Now we are suspected terrorists on the run from the FBI. No home, no business, no way to support ourselves. Living between two worlds, trying to save some lady we never met. Oh, yeh, and we're supposed to help save the world while we're at it. Yet I have never felt so alive. Should I talk to a shrink? Maybe get some good meds?" Steele pinched Celeste with a mischievous grin. "This has to be some sort of shared dream, and we are both going to wake up in bed laughing at each other."

"Ouch. Probably so, but while we are in this dream, what do you think of this swimming suit? I picked it up down the street at the shopping center. Does it make me look fat?"

"No, you never look fat. You are as beautiful as the day we met. You did use cash, didn't you?"

"Of course I did, staying under the radar," Celeste joked.

Akira popped into view, surprising them. "I wish I looked that good in a swim suit. Louise asked if I would take you on an excursion to the Bahamas. I think we should start at the Fox Hill police station. Though you two will have to deal with the police alone. I had a bit of a run-in with them–it is a long story, remind me to tell you sometime. Let's go before the trail is completely cold, and make sure you have your passports, just in case."

Celeste changed and picked up a couple of small bags they had packed. "Ready."

Within seconds, the trio was standing on a quiet, narrow, remote dirt road, not much more than a wide path. Dense tropical vegetation surrounded them. An exotic bird squawked out a call to its neighbors, warning of the intruders.

"Yow Massi, I feel yuh a com. Yuh noa Caristen, she mi dups– a frind." Little Fajah was peeking out from behind a palm tree. Using her English/ Jamaican slang she spoke directly to Celeste as if she was a close friend. "Caristen she frind, mudda is Jasmine. Tata help Jiemes. Him nota in ie room. Mi a go ron- follow back a mi, tween see it. I-ah showa ya."

The best they could make out was that Fajah wanted them to follow her. The communication was understood more from body language than verbally. She ran down a tiny damp trail, pushing through broad-leaf plants, glancing back to make sure she was being followed. "Back a mi, back a mi a way."

They all ran down the side of a hill, sliding on the damp earth, jumping over roots and pushing the undergrowth out of their way.

Fajah stopped suddenly. She stood perfectly still, pointing to a small concrete room with a very tiny window. "Jiemes not in-a room. Jiemes giv to Fa." She held out a Jasmine perfume sample and smiled. "Saya thank Jiemes. Find Jasmine–she a sent-tee." The trio figured that Fajah wanted them to thank James and find Jasmine, the pretty smelling lady pictured on the perfume sample James had given her.

Steele turned, wearing a concerned expression. "We have to go–NOW! Someone is coming." He pulled Celeste and gave Fajah a gentle push up the trail. "Hurry."

"Hold it right there. You are trespassing, this is private property."

Startled by the strong command, the four of them turned to see three large men holding some serious weapons. From his limited understanding of guns, Steele guessed they were M-6's or possibly AK-47's. The older man, arms crossed at his chest, wore a black patch over his left eye, short shaven hair and an expression that looked like he had been chewing on glass. He was obviously the one in charge, though dressed in a dirty army green camouflage shirt and Cargo pants. "What do we have here? Three pretty young girls and yes, a pretty boy as well. This one looks like the little girl that helped James escape. Where is the old man, bonita? And what are you civilians doing on our compound with her? You know, in this country, we have the right to shoot you and ask questions later." He swung his automatic rifle, smashing it against the side of Steele's head, dropping him like a 180-pound sack of potatoes.

Celeste tensed. Akira sensed that she was pulling energy from both dimensions, about ready to release an enormous blast. She grabbed Celeste by the shoulder and whispered, "Not now. Do not let them know the power you are holding. If you let go of that energy now, it could hurt or kill all of us." Celeste shook from the tremendous effort to restrain and let the energy dissipate. Sweat beaded on her forehead from the struggle.

"What's wrong, little lady?" the grubby leader asked, rubbing his hand along the curve of her butt. "Cute ass." The three men started laughing.

"What do you want us to do with them, General?" asked the youngest of their group, a freckled-face boy with curly red hair. He ran his impure eyes over Akira.

"Throw them in the hut. I'm sure we can think of something to do with the ladies later. Don't worry, ladies, we'll be genteel. I guarantee you will never forget us." He motioned with a flip of his wrist. "Gregory, you can have the pretty boy." That got another round of laughs with a few guttural sounds and body movements thrown in for effect. "Red, find the old man that has been causing trouble with our little friend here," pointing his weapon at Fajah.

"NO!" Fajah bit the hand holding her arm and ducked into the heavy forest off the trail.

"Find her and the old man," commanded the General. "Make sure the old man doesn't bother us again, and bring the little girl back to me. I'm sure she will fetch a pretty penny–you know how they like young girls in Cambodia."

'Pigs,' Akira thought, not daring to say it aloud.

〉〉〉

CHAPTER 8
Jump About

Doug hung unconscious four stories in the air upside down, strapped by his ankles. Suspended from the eave of the bell tower, he looked lifeless.

"Wake him up!" yelled the Bishop. It had only been a short time since the charity dinner at the father and son golf tournament so Doug's memory should be fresh. Bishop Daniel was determined to find out what Doug knew about James, Akira and the Jump technology.

"Daddy, no! Don't do this. You're going to kill him." Elizabeth pleaded desperately for her fiancée.

"Wake him up!" the Bishop commanded again.

Agent Duncan stood underneath Doug with a fire hose connected outside, and braced himself as he turned on the nozzle. This action was much more to his liking, rather than the staid role of FBI investigator, that never seemed to change anything. 'That trip to Nassau was a waste of my time, if I hadn't taken the Wand–but I'm not just giving the Wand to Rebel for nothing,' he thought, before the power of the water rushing through and out of the hose almost knocked him off his feet. After regaining balance, he turned the forceful stream upward, hitting Doug, startling him into consciousness.

"What the hell!" Doug sputtered, flopping around like a fish on a hook and screaming at the top of his lungs in panic. "What do you want, you goddamn crazy man? Are you trying to kill me?"

"Do not use the Lord's name in vain, son," the Bishop shouted skyward. "No, no, you are not going to die...well...maybe not. It is up to you, so man up. If you are going to marry my daughter, you have to be man enough to take care of yourself. Stop wiggling around like that. Elizabeth would hate to see you fall." He turned, and quietly said, "Elizabeth, go wait in the car, so we can talk man-to-man here."

"No, I don't want you to hurt him any more. You stop this right now!"she demanded.

Pulling his daughter away from the bell tower, behind the trees and toward the car, the Bishop told her that he was only kidding the boy and he wanted to speak to him in private about the wedding. "We'll be with you in a few minutes. Now go ahead. He'll be fine, I promise." She left, sobbing, confused, but still the obedient child, that her father had drilled into her throughout her life.

Bishop Daniel Xavier the Fifth climbed the bell tower so he could speak without being overheard. "Now, now, Doug–let us find out what you know. Tell me how you know James Knecht and his so-called daughter Akira. Or I might have to tell Elizabeth we had a little accident."

"Why?" Doug gasped.

Bishop Daniel grabbed the strap where it was tied off from the banister and shook it violently. "Never mind that, just tell me."

"Okay, okay, just stop that...we just met," Doug said, trying to catch his breath. "They just showed up...at that father and son golf tournament. Mom and I...were paired with them. The two of them...made up our foursome. I guess... mom knew him from college." His speech was coming in short bursts of words. It was hard to speak hanging as he was, struggling to stay conscious.

"I do not believe you," the Bishop said mockingly. "You know it is a sin to lie. People like them do not just show up out of the blue." The Bishop took several deep breaths as calmness settled over him. Then with a wicked grin said, "Well, since you are going to be part of the family, I guess I will have to trust you." In stern parental tones, he went on to explain how James and Akira were dangerous people, 'non-believers', who were plotting against the Church. And that he was only concerned for his daughter's safety. After all, he had to be sure who she was marrying. "Now, get down from there. We will be in the car. Hurry up, it is time for dinner."

Doug could hear the Bishop's steps echo through the bell tower, speaking quietly to Agent Duncan as they walked away. He slowly turned his throbbing head enough to size up the situation. He spotted the leather strap with a loop, hanging close enough to reach, if he could just swing over a few feet. Contracting his stomach muscles and releasing a few times, he was able to create momentum enough to swing over and grab the strap and slide his wrist through the loop to get a firm grip. He was glad he always carried a small pocket knife, never thinking it would be critical for such a situation. He carefully pulled the knife from his front jeans pocket, being cautious not to drop it. Then he mustered all of his strength and pulled with his strapped arm so he could just reach his feet. He used his 'mighty' 2-inch blade to cut the strap. A few minutes of sawing finally sliced through the strong binding and his feet fell free, pulling agonizingly against his shoulder as they dropped. Rocking to create some momentum, he finally snagged the edge of the balcony with a foot and slid his leg over the banister rail, hooking his foot between the upright supporting rails. Then working up his confidence, he let go of the strap around his wrist as he threw himself onto the balcony, falling flat on his face. Back aching, with leather burns on his wrist and a bruised ankle, he pushed himself to his knees.

'A Bishop—that's a farce, that son of a bitch,' Doug thought, 'but he is Beth's father.' He knew the Bishop was a high ranking member of the Opus Dei–said to be a devious, antidemocratic, reactionary, semi-fascist Catholic institution. "I must be crazy to think about marrying his daughter, but it's the only way I know to get her away from that maniac," he fussed at himself, heading painfully soaked down the stairs to find the car.

* * *

Steele squinted, seeing a swirling dim light filtering through a small window. Ringing ears emphasized the splitting ache in his skull. Yet, there was a faint soothing tingle, a relieving warmth that moved slowly around the inside of his head.

"Be still," Akira said, sitting beside him on the floor with her hands gently resting on both sides of his head. He realized the warmth was coming from her, before losing consciousness again.

Akira was drawing energy from both dimensions, threading a web of vitality from this cosmic source. She wove this vibrant fabric throughout his battered head, knitting together blood veins, membrane, bone and torn tissue.

"Celeste, I have a slight ability to heal the physical body. Luckily his injuries are not beyond my abilities." Akira worked through much of the night.

Floating in his unconscious state, Steele experienced a numbing cold tingle, followed by stinging pain, ending in a welcoming warmth. Akira relaxed and slumped back against the cool wall. "That's all I can do. The rest is up to him, but he should be fine with some rest. We need to get out of here before they return. He can't take being jostled around, and I do not even want to think what those three guys have in mind for us out here in the jungle." She closed her eyes.

Celeste thought she had gone to sleep when Akira's eyes snapped open. "Room 13211. Keep holding your husband's hand, like you have all night." Akira took Steele's other hand, then wrapped her fingers around Celeste's free arm...

....the army cot where Celeste sat had now become a soft bed, and Steele was laying next to her. Akira was still kneeling, but on a plush carpeted floor. "Ah, that's better. Sure beats our previous accommodations. Shall we order room service? I'm starving–I'd like a Caesar salad. Let's get him some fish, and something with leafy greens, spinach, carrots, flaxseeds, walnuts, some fruit. Oh, and green tea with lots of honey. Avoid protein and heavy foods for your meal, since we will be traveling again soon. Jaguar and Star are putting together a gathering, and we'll want to be there. I'll get some ice for his swelling." Celeste stroked her husband's hand and shook her head in amazement. Then to avoid suspicion, she took the elevator down to the restaurant and paid cash for their dinners.

The two women quietly ate their dinner, sitting at a small table in their room at the Atlantis Resort on Paradise Island in Nassau. Both reflected on the recent scuffle with those horrible men. "How is it possible to heal someone with a touch?" Celeste asked.

Akira touched Celeste gently on the arm. "Feel the warmth. That is energy being transferred from each of us to the other. That is the basic principle. Healing can take place with a simple touch. Sometimes with only a smile or passing comment. There is a pattern resonating from the energy-body of all things–even rocks and some man-made materials. Plastic is one of only a few things that is completely dead, that has no physical energy at all. Everyone has an innate ability to perceive this phenomenon, and experience this cosmic pattern in unique and varying ways. As we understand our place in the flow of this pattern, those with the propensity for healing, can feel when something is out of alignment and realign the natural patterns within organic matter. Whether they act to understand and develop their inclination toward their gift is yet another story."

"A series that used to be on television, 'Touch' told a story about some of these individuals. Jacob and Amelia, the two children in this series, follow their predisposition toward seeing the pattern in numbers. Those around them that understood, followed their understanding of numbers and the resulting interconnection to help people. Some musicians can hear the pattern surrounding them, being played through many people and items they encounter."

"Artists are visual," Akira continued softly. "A few can actually see patterns forming. My new artist friend, your husband, describes what he sees as transparent vibrating waves of turquoise and magenta that encompass everything. He tells me these vibrating waves entwine, holding everything in this glowing pattern. He was communicating this experience with me as we were enmeshed in his healing last evening. He told me this recent phenomenon started after your visit to the Falls, and that he has been having a difficult time understanding and putting it into words."

Steele drifted in and out of consciousness, dreaming... 'so you're a sheep, and I am an elephant.' The elephant turned the painting toward his subject, the sheep. The elephant was wearing a barrette and a purple suit, the sheep wore a blue bonnet. The scene and style was fashioned after Seurat, the master of Pointillism. Many of the subjects behind and around were points of color with just enough detail to make the subject recognizable.

"Ah, yes, you are an elephant, and I, my dear, am a sheep." She smiled sheepishly. The afternoon was spent painting, moving around an abandoned amusement park, leaving masterful works on old yellowed posters or any flat surface they found. Many works were produced, as they enjoyed a beautiful day together. Then a snake slithered out from under the tilt-a-whirl ride. "I'm coming for you," it hissed.

Steele woke groggy, doing his best to force himself back to reality. "Where are we?"

Celeste ran to the bed, giving him a big hug. "Baby, I'm so happy you are back, you scared us to death. Are you hungry? We ordered you something to eat, I'll get it."

Akira smiled. "You are looking much better, you will have a slight headache for a while. Rest and have something to eat. I'll bet those pigs that hurt you have the Portal device. I'm going to take a look and see about finding the Wand. I'll be right back."

"Be careful..." She was gone before Celeste could finish.

"Wow, did I have a strange dream," Steele said, sitting up on the bed, swinging his feet to the floor. "I was an elephant artist dressed in a purple suit. You were a sheep in a blue bonnet. Odd–what do you think it means?"

Celeste thought for a minute. "Hmm, from what I know of dream interpretation, I would say you should listen carefully and take special notice of dreams containing purple. To dream that you are an elephant, suggests that you need to make your opinions and views known. You need to be strong, more vocal. Express yourself and voice your ideas. Purple resonates with strength, power, wisdom, loyalty and inspiration. As for me, being a sheep wearing blue. Interesting...the sheep sometimes represents conformity. Maybe I need to accept our new dimensional shifts. While the color blue appearing in dreams may symbolize a spirit guide, divine life path and soul mission. It also suggests clarity of mind and optimism for the future. So in the dream I am conforming to Louise and those we know from Gaia as our spirit guides. Accepting this path as our soul mission."

"Now as for your painting me as a subject, and leaving many masterful works on old posters around an abandoned amusement park... Carnivals embody out-of-control experiences. Being out of control can be ecstatic and wonderful. The fact that it is abandoned could represent the best and worst in life. The ecstatic wonderful feelings are shut off by a snake, leaving a negative aspect to the 'lack' of amusement."

"Baby!" Celeste continued. "That can only mean we are on the right path. Painting me is taking action, spreading the message of our life path. Covering shut off, negative experiences in life with our message of hope, guidance, and a bright future. Though we must be cautious of the snake trying to tilt and obstruct our path."

Celeste ran her fingers through her husband's hair and smiled. "Doesn't look like I'm going to make it to the beach this trip."

Steele smiled, picturing her standing in the sand. "I'll see you in that swim suit next time we're in the Bahamas, baby. How long was I unconscious?"

"Two days, Akira worked a full day healing you."

"Those sons-of-bitches didn't hurt you or Akira, did they?"

"No, no, we're fine. Somehow Akira found us this room–can you believe we're at the Atlantis! She moved us here from their makeshift prison before they could harm us. Thank God!"

Akira appeared in full stride, breathing hard with Fajah under one arm. She caught herself against the wall with her free hand to stop her forward momentum. "It appears that the General and the bald guy he called Gregory are gone, along with the Portal Wand. I didn't have time to try and determine where they went. The other goons had found Fajah and were giving her a hard time, and were all too eager to get their hands on me. We should be going before the hotel realizes we are not registered." She put some money on the dresser as a gratuity and to cover the night's stay. "Grab your things and we'll go see what news Jaguar has. First, I am taking Fajah to her grandfather."

Fajah broke down, crying. She turned to Celeste and told her that her grandfather was gone. The bad men shot her grandfather and told her they were going to sell her. Knowing Fajah had no one else to take care of her, Akira decided to take her with them to visit the Falls and see what Jaguar could do for her.

* * *

It seemed like decades since Akira brought James from their golf adventure in Georgia, to see his son. Ian had let James stay in the house, though they had only exchanged greetings in passing, as Ian worked feverishly, without the correct parts, to complete a Wand to rescue his wife. Alek and Kristen were staying with their friend across the street.

That evening, in an attempt to understand what was happening with his life, Ian broke down and spoke with his father. " I don't know what to believe anymore, dad, let's go talk. I'll try to keep an open mind."

Ian led the way to the kitchen table. "I could use a drink, what about you?"

"Do you have any wine, son?"

Ian found an open bottle of chardonnay in the fridge. He poured two glasses, and handed one to his father. "Dad, let me be straight with you. I have had it. I will give you one last chance to be completely honest with me. If not, I want you to leave, and I never want to see or hear from you again."

James thanked Ian for the drink, along with the chance to come clean, then took a sip of wine. "Son, I have been thinking hard about all the things I need to tell you, and apologize for. I'm not sure where to start. So please bear with me, and I'll start at the beginning."

"When you were just a baby, barely walking, a detestable thing happened

79

that changed all of our lives. This is the first and biggest regret of my life, and one I would never expect you to forgive me for. I have never spoken of this before, and cannot even find a way to forgive myself."

James went on. "I am responsible for your mother's death." His eyes became watery and tears formed as he stared absently for a long time. Ian could see his eyes darting around as if he was trying to see something fleeting. James sat frozen, lost in thought, not breathing. Finally he took a deep quick gasp, trying to catch his breath. "My God," he said in a whisper, like he didn't want to hear what he said next. "Your sisters as well. You had two older sisters, twins. I'm to blame for their deaths as well. Nooooo!" James began crying uncontrollably as he covered his face in shame. Fighting for breath he sputtered, "How did I...how could I forget the twins. Oh, Christ...Clio and Camilla, my babies."

Ian sat in stunned silence, attempting to make sense of what he just heard. "Dad, stop it. What are you talking about?"

James finally brought his emotions under control, enough to continue. "I could use something stronger to drink."

"Me, too." Ian went to the liquor cabinet and came back with two glasses of ice and a bottle of Royal Crown whiskey. "Go on, dad."

"As I said, you were just a baby. Your sisters were a year and a half older than you. We were all staying at your grandparents' house, my folks' place, while the two of them went on a vacation cruise. Your mom and sisters were sitting at the dining room table, finishing dinner. I had taken you to the bathroom." He took a long slow drink and swallowed hard. "Some armed men broke into the house after me, and to make their point shot your mother and sisters. The only reason you survived is that you were in the bathroom."

Ian gasped. "That explains the nightmares I've been having." Ian began to tear up... "go on, dad."

"I left you with my parents, and asked them not to tell you what had happened. I went away so none of you would become targets or accidentally be hurt, because of me. I started drinking to forget, drank until I lost my job at the police department. Then kept drinking until I truly did forget. My father found me living on the street, and put me into rehab. The only thing I have ever known came from the Army, and the police force, so getting a job was not easy. So I became a mercenary and spent most of the next 20-plus years in foreign countries."

"I had sisters?" Ian asked. "How could you never tell me I had sisters?"

"You were so young we thought you wouldn't remember anything from that night. I thought it would be best for you."

"That's a lot to absorb...I can't believe no one ever told me." Ian took a shot of whiskey, then shook his head side to side, not sure what to think. "Go on, why don't you jump forward– tell me about that bald fucker who broke into my home and took Jasmine and the Wand. How can you justify working with him?"

"Gregory–that's the name of that son-of-a-bitch. He didn't take her. Neither he nor I has anything to do with Jasmine disappearing. I had come to warn you that the Blackwater mercenary group attempted to hire me to steal your technology and make sure no one else had it."

"Well, that was a hell of a warning, dad"

"I'm so sorry. I sure didn't anticipate they would move that quickly," James apologized, "I was a ranking member of Blackwater, but decided to end my affiliation when they asked me to take the technology from you. That was the last straw. I wanted to warn you before quitting, so they wouldn't move on you before I had a chance to tell you what they were planning."

James went on. "The important thing now is that you find Jasmine. Akira told me she has very little time left before she will not be able to return to this dimension. Do you have another way to Jump?"

"Yes, there are two other devices," Ian said. "The first Portal built, patterned after the Portal in my office that they destroyed, is in Redmond, Washington. It was the gaming prototype. The other is in the District of Columbia at the Department of Homeland Security."

"Son, the Washington device is probably compromised. Blackwater roots are very deep. So you'll have to go to Redmond to use that Portal and find Jasmine. She is still at the waterfall in your picture."

"Hold on just a minute. Who exactly is Akira, and why should I believe her?"

"She seems to be from another world–but actually just Earth in another dimension. Gaia is the dimension your device uses briefly when someone Jumps. I met her when I was escaping from Gregory's jungle prison. Anyway, I was in the police station in the Bahamas, when Agent Duncan..."

"Stop–what? You were in a Bahamas' police station with Agent Duncan?"

"Well, yes, it's a long story. I had taken the Wand back from Gregory but I wasn't sure how to use it and just before the Nassau police and Agent Duncan arrested me, Akira appeared and whisked me away to play golf in Georgia."

"Oh, that makes everything perfectly clear." Ian took another drink then rested his head in his hands with his elbows on the table and started rubbing his temples. "You're giving me a headache. So back up–you had the Wand?"

"Yes, but just as Akira was helping, Agent Duncan grabbed it. He has it. Son, the point is that Akira saved me. She knows a lot about what is happening and she knows where Jasmine is. What more do you have to lose?"

"Other than losing my mind? I guess not much. I am glad Akira knows what is going on, because right now I don't have a clue. But I guess if we all misunderstand so often, even on our own plane of existence, how can we expect correct communications between dimensions? You're right–I have nothing to lose. Call and get us two one-way tickets on the next flight to SeaTac Airport in Seattle, and I'll throw a few things together for the trip and tell neighbors I'll be away for awhile. I'm sure the kids will enjoy staying with their friend a little longer. We seem to be the same size, so I'll get you a change of clothes. Oh, and some better shoes. Those golf shoes have to be uncomfortable. Looks like size ten? Mine should fit."

* * *

"One Micro-Program Way in Redmond, take us to the research building," Ian gave the directions to the cab driver as they climbed into the back seat early the next morning. "Take the 520 across Evergreen Bridge, I'll pay the extra toll. Please hurry."

Ian had called his contact, Mike, at the research center before they boarded the plane in Denver. "The Portal will be ready for our Jump when we get there, dad. I have the coordinates which should get us close to the waterfall, along with our sequenced algorithms on this flash drive. We will be there within the hour."

Things were finally running without a hitch, even the drive from the airport was quick with very little traffic. They arrived at the research center, signed in, took their badges and were loading the coordinates into the Portal computer 45 minutes after leaving the airport. "All right, we're

82

ready to go." Ian set the timer on his watch. "We have 20 minutes to get back to where we cross over. Follow me, dad, first we'll take a quick look around."

Ian stepped through the Portal opening, stopping immediately on the other side. He found himself teetering on the precipice of a narrow canyon overlooking the waterfall from the side. James stepped through, and ran smack into Ian before he could stop himself. Both men found themselves in mid-air as the momentum pushed the pair over the sheer cliff wall. Their screams were quickly drowned out as they fell into the cold plunge basin created by the waterfall some 40 feet below.

"Nice morning for a swim, children. Though it is a little cold for my liking. We have been expecting you." Louise sat at the edge of the water as James and his son surfaced from their unexpected tumble. "I would only give that dive a 3, maybe 4, not much for style. Here are towels, dry off. Your wife is right here, she has been so anxious to see you. You must hurry, you will not last long in Gaia, with your heavy physical vibrations."

Ian climbed out of the water and rushed to Jasmine, giving her a wet hug. "Baby, I miss you so much. Are you all right? I can barely feel you, and you're much more transparent than I expected, I can hardly see you. Jasmine, you look like a ghost. What's the matter?"

Louise interrupted their reunion. "You must hurry! Get Jasmine back to your dimension before it is too late."

Ian pulled back with concern and explained that to cross back they had to be in the same location as where his father and he entered. He looked at his watch–they had to climb the canyon wall in less than six minutes! They would never have time! "I'm going to see if I can make it before the Portal closes. I'll be back soon."

Ian was running on his way up the trail before he finished speaking. As he topped the ridge and started for the Portal opening the faint wavering mirage winked out. He missed the opening by seconds. In frustration and not wanting to climb back down the canyon, he turned and jumped back into the plunge pool. He came to the surface, swam to where his wife was standing and broke the news. "Looks like we are all lost here in Gaia's dimension together."

❯ ❯ ❯

CHAPTER 9
Fractals

Mike, Ian's contact at Micro-Programs, couldn't hold his head up. His neck strained from the weight of his head hanging limp to one side, as blood oozed from the corner of his mouth. The General stood over his flaccid body. "Tell me where Ian went, and this will all be over. I will let you go and everyone will be happy. But if you insist on keeping his whereabouts a secret, I cannot help you. Gregory will get the information from you one way or another."

They paused for an answer—when none came Gregory pulled his limp head up, gripping a hand full of Mike's hair and spit in his face. Then he pulled his head backwards, bent over and whispered. "Listen to the General. I would really hate to keep beating you." An evil smile crept across Gregory's face, and he let Mike's head drop to the side as he brought his knee up.

The sound of Gregory's knee smashing against Mike's chin, forcing his teeth to smash together made the General's skin crawl. "Enough, don't kill him yet. We need to know where Ian went."

It didn't take much more of this torture before Mike coughed up Ian's coordinates, along with a mouth full of blood. 'Mike seemed like a good guy, it was a shame it had to go this far,' the General thought to himself. Then he said, "Gregory, take Mike through the Portal and dump his body in the other dimension. No one will know what happened to him. It will seem like he just vanished."

The General entered the coordinates Mike had reluctantly given him into a map application on his phone. "I know this place—Death Hollow, how appropriate." He smiled. "Looks like we are headed back to Escalante. Gregory, after you dump Mike's body, set the timer on the C-4 to destroy the Portal door, following your Jump to Salt Lake City. Find us a room and rent a truck. We'll need a vehicle with high clearance for the back roads into Death Hollow. I'll meet you at the airport in Salt Lake as soon as I can catch the next flight. Damn, this flying is getting old, I have to get sequenced!"

* * *

The Russian shaman, Nikolay Grandstaff Noskova, stood front center stage before the crowded auditorium. He was masterfully directing a harmonic multi-sensory symphony. The tune, written by Grandstaff, had been derived from the fractal mathematics of nature. Grandstaff's contemplative bright eyes, and hoary Fu Manchu beard, led to his reputation as a man of myth and mystery. A towering Paul Bunyan-like Russian, Grandstaff gave the impression that he might consume the orchestra.

A celebrated piano virtuoso played vibrational patterns of sound, that merged with the other instruments. The melody combined with a multi-colored light show. This curious amalgam of light and sound was altering the consciousness of a handful of the audience capable of feeling the emotional truth of the moment. The harmonics of the irregular sections of the fractal composition created shifts between two and three other dimensions, uniting them through the music that rolled throughout the hall, touching many in the audience in ways they might never understand.

But for those special few, the notes took them literally to another world. Haunting harmonies touched emotions, and wove around and through their spiritual bodies. A drone over-current of the Perfect 5th explored the relationship between the notes named in Western music as 'A' and 'E' with strong undertones of G minor. This in turn resonated with the heart, dancing on the fabric that connects each individual to the universal tone. It came close to perfection.

In the reception after the performance, Jaguar found Grandstaff. "Moving concert, maestro."

"Spaseeba, rat teebya veedet. 'Thanks, nice to see you as well,'" replied Grandstaff.

This was more than attending a concert to see an old friend. Jaguar was there for a very important reason–to ask Grandstaff if he would travel with him to the Falls and use his unique talent in order to help Jasmine, Ian and James. Jaguar had devised a plan to lower the vibrations of the trapped visitors, utilizing Grandstaff's harmonic resonance in unison with his own healing abilities. He felt that by combining their skills they could reduce the trio's vibrations to a level where the three of them could slip over to their own dimension.

"I vould be gled tu help u comrrade," Grandstaff replied. "Aufter z recepsions, I hev tyme befores I hev tu ketch z plen to Arizona forr next cooncerrt. I doo hev tu keep ups appeavences u no. I ken noot joost be seen poopping ins and oout vhen I trrevel."

* * *

Maya whined and shook her entire body in an attempt to wag her tail as her older sister Isis spun a couple of circles then stood reserved with her regal demeanor. Both dogs were happy to see Celeste and Steele as they appeared following their escape in the Bahamas.

After initial greetings and catching up, Louise stood alertly with her back to the Falls. She addressed the group of friends, family and new acquaintances. Jasmine, Ian and James stood beside her. Jaguar and Star were at the center of the group with the elder Max and Grandstaff. On their left Akira stood next to Steele, who held Celeste's hand. Fajah's arms were tightly wrapped around Celeste's leg. The beautiful evening was cool, though unusually warm for the season. On the horizon an ominous, dark cumulonimbus cloud swallowed the mountains under it. Streaks of lightning lit the cloud from within, giving it a menacing air of foreboding of things yet to come.

"For those who do not know me well, I am Louise, also known as 'the teacher'–a name I proudly wear. We have all come together to help Jasmine, Ian and James find their way home. Their predicament is directly connected to other cosmic-changing events that are actually even more important to address. Universal energies have drawn all of us to this turning point in the evolution and survival of our species. We are all too aware of the ecological changes that are threatening Earth's climate and causing global warming. Earth's brain-washed, fear-based culture, that is driven by the greed of the ruling social-economic class, has led to the refusal of many to even acknowledge the problem, despite scientific proof."

"To make things more devastating, we have discovered that when unenlightened people use this new Jump technology, it causes the veil between our worlds to become more dense. This in time will greatly reduce, if not eliminate, the cosmic help provided to mankind over the last several millenniums–long before our mentor Jesus brought his early teaching through the dimensions. Every time people with heavy vibrations use the device to move between worlds, their ponderous wavelength negatively affects the veil. Those heavy vibrations affect the dimensional membrane, much like a single drop of black ink dropped into a bucket of water. A single drop will dissipate seemingly without changing the water. But drop by drop it will build until the water turns black. Or in our case, the membrane becomes solid–at which point the two worlds will be completely cut off from one another."

The group nodded in understanding, and Louise intently continued to explain. "Lacking the guiding cosmic energy of love, the human race, balanced on the edge of self-extinction, will have little hope. And with the dimensions closed, none of us will be able to assist. Even the truly enlightened, selfless ones, such as Jesus, Buddha, Confucius, and numerous others through the ages would have been unable to help. Jesus, who was able to reach through dimensions when the veil was at one of the most solid states in human history, would have been unable to cross. Humanity will be cut off entirely from cosmic, or as many people refer to it, God's Spirit. This in essence would be the true meaning of Hell on Earth."

Louise decisively concluded. "The most immediate issue will be to see what can be done to help Jasmine and her family. Then we will develop a plan to combat the Portal dilemma, with a long-reaching plan to help Earth's eco-system before much of life on Earth is extinguished. Oh, and of course, we'll continue to keep the world leaders from starting a nuclear war. As they say, a piece of cake–right?"

Jaguar thanked Louise for setting the stage with her insights, and addressed the group. He wanted to get to the task of helping Jasmine, Ian and James so that Celeste and Steele could get back to their dimension while they were still able. To do this, he needed to quickly use their strong abilities to bridge dimensions, since the trio were not yet fully transitioned themselves.

Jaguar directed Jasmine and her family to sit holding hands, forming a small circle around Max, seated at the center. Jaguar, Star, Louise, Akira, Grandstaff, Celeste and Steele stood forming a larger circle around the inner circle. Fajah quietly sat nearby, watching and wishing her friend Kristen was with her to watch her family being saved.

Then Jaguar instructed the group: "Energy cannot be created or destroyed, it is simply transformed. Every element of the universe is in a constant state of vibration, manifested to and through us as light, sound and energy. The heavier an atom, the lower the frequencies for vibrations that involve that atom. In science, the theory is known as the quantum harmonic oscillator."

"Let me quickly explain molecular vibrations this way. The Energies of all systems are related to how stretched or compressed their molecules are. The heavier the masses, or the tighter the forces are that hold the molecules together, the lower the vibrational frequency will become. Similarly, vibrational frequencies for stretching bonds in molecules are related to the looser or weaker strength of the chemical bonds and the masses of the atoms. Molecules differ in that the vibrational frequencies are quantized. That is, only certain energies for the system are allowed, and only certain energies will excite molecular vibrations. The weight and symmetry of the molecules will determine in which dimension they will exist."

"It is not important to know the exact nature of each vibration. I only point this out to give everyone a fundamental idea of what we are going to accomplish. The seven of us standing, will chant a mantra creating a state where our friends vibrate at a lower rate completely in tune with the energy and spiritual state contained within that sound. Now, let us picture and feel the cosmic source come into our circle through the crown of our heads." He paused. "Breathe deeply and feel the energy flowing counter-clockwise, passing from our left hand...through our heart chakra... and out our right hand into the person next to us. As the energy circulates and becomes stronger, concentrate on it becoming heavy...like oil...energy flowing...around...and around..."

Jaguar spoke softly, molding their thoughts. "Soon, we will use the creative projection of our minds through the form of a mantra combined with the vibrational drone pattern of Grandstaff's fractal music, played by Max on the didgeridoo, following the ancient spirit of Dadirri breathing though us. And at this point, Jasmine, Ian and James will join the outer group through a physical connection which will affect each and every cell in their bodies, lowering the rate at which they currently resonate. This should lower their wave-length enough so that they can slip back across dimensions to their world."

Dawn approached, while the inner circle sat breathing slowly...holding hands...calming their minds, preparing themselves to move back to their own reality. The larger group stood around them hand-in-hand as Jaguar began chanting a resonant mantra. Six voices soon joined his in unison. Grandstaff and Max's deep harmonic drone vibration rose from the center of the two groups, passing through the inner circle blending with the others. Time stood still. Jasmine's anxiety melted away and she could feel her partners' energy as they became aware of one another's heartbeats. Ian and James were experiencing a far deeper, soul connection than ever before.

Earth blessed the ceremony with an unusual crimson sunrise, enhancing the genesis of a united singular beat of hearts, chants and harmonics. Wild animals stopped to watch as the very air around the united groups warped, breathing in tune with the mantra that reverberated through everyone, awakening a shared spiritual life force. The chant kept repeating, their bodies slowly swaying in sync, and the unified group began to perceive the heavier weight of the lower dimension as the tones merged. When the pressure was almost too intense to continue, Star touched Jasmine. Jasmine immediately began shaking violently from the physical synthesis of energy as the two circles joined.

"Something is wrong!" came a voice rising as a shared expression of the group. Ian and James were deeply concerned for their loved one but sat untouched by her violent physical onslaught. In the midst of Jasmine's convulsion, Fajah sprang through the circles severing the connections. She pushed Jasmine away, taking her place, creating a physical connection between Ian, James and herself which grounded their energy. Coming from their world, Fajah's lower wavelength enabled the slower vibration to bond, sending the three of them back to their dimension and they vanished. Seconds later, Steele and Celeste also disappeared.

Jasmine was being torn apart–literally ripped between dimensions, unable to cross over in either direction. Every cell in her body was being disrupted. Seconds seemed to be hours, before Star was able to grab Jasmine's hand, and Louise grasped for her flailing other hand. As Louise made contact with Jasmine she became connected to the outer circle–still feeling the heavier weight of the lower energy, but beginning to vibrate with the higher Gaia dimension. When Jaguar, Max and Grandstaff realized what was happening, they quickly changed the mantra and music to resonate with the higher harmonic symmetry of Gaia. Jasmine slowly settled into her new world, and sputtered with the deep breaths of someone just saved from drowning.

Louise soothed her. "Child, if Fajah had not acted when she did, you would have had to be reborn. You have a very bright friend in the other world. I have a feeling we will be welcoming Fajah to this side very soon."

With tears forming, Jasmine looked into Louise's knowing eyes and cried. "I believe we will...but I may never see my family again."

* * *

"Sir, serious problem–Project Jump." Click.

Cryptic and short as the phone call was, Speaker of the House John Bodner knew what it meant, and he did not like it at all. Sitting back in the red-and-yellow striped office couch, Bodner stared at the ornate white fireplace and listened to the seconds tick away on the brass captain's clock sitting on the mantle. The double Windsor knot of his tie felt tighter than usual. He slowly changed his focal point to the coat rack beside the door. 'What could be the problem?' he wondered. 'This technology can change my seat of power, from being out of control to ruling the country. Hell, I could win the presidential race, bring about a new world order and put those bleeding heart liberals in their place.'

A knock on the door brought him back from his thoughts. His secretary, Bernice, informed him that the Director of Counter Terrorism from Homeland Security was here also to see him and that the Ambassador from Mexico was here for his 2 o'clock meeting.

"I'll see the Director, and get the Ambassador a drink–inform him I will be 15 minutes." She left, as he was thinking to himself, 'Damn, wish I could drop a bomb on Mexico and get rid of the immigrant and drug problems.'

"How are you, John?" his new visitor greeted.

"Enough with the pleasantry, Director Rebel. Tell me what the problem is. I should be meeting with the Ambassador from Mexico right now."

Director Aaron Rebel was 6 foot 2 inches tall, clean-cut, and looked like he was molded after the father of 'Brady Bunch,' a 1970's television series. He had a face anyone would trust, which made him all the more dangerous. Aaron frowned at the Speaker, and proceeded to tell him that the General and Gregory had gone rogue. He added that they were nowhere to be found, and that he thought the Portal Wand had been in their possession. To make things worse, Agent Duncan was now working with

Bishop Daniel.

The more Bodner heard, the tighter his tie seemed, and the angrier he became. On top of all that news, it turns out Ian and his father James had also vanished, and that they might have possibly taken the Wand from Gregory.

"So you are telling me you don't know where the hell the Wand is! Aaron–tell me that our Portal door is still in your possession. Someone didn't happen to steal that as well, did they? And you did get rid of the Door in Ian's office, correct? That leaves the only stationary Portal device, beside ours, in the research center at Micro-Programs?"

"That's correct," Agent Rebel replied, glaring at the Speaker. He always thought his boyish haircut, parted on the side, emphasized the receding hairline. His blue eyes seemed to have dulled, and turned gray, as much as his dark hair had since Bodner had taken office. However, his dumbfounded facial expressions never ceased to provide a chuckle. Rebel knew Bodner was more intelligent than he appeared. After all, they were in business together.

The Speaker continued. "We need to eliminate the Portal at Micro-Programs, then find and take the Wand back. Can you handle that, or should I find someone that will not screw things up any worse than you already have?"

"No–I've got this, MR. SPEAKER," Aaron said, with the snotty attitude of a scolded child. He turned and started to leave.

"One more thing, Director Rebel. The next time I hear from you, I want Ian in custody. I believe he is a threat to national security. Have him arrested. Make sure he doesn't speak to anyone."

* * *

Fajah, Ian and James found themselves sitting at the top of the waterfall, alone and away from Gaia. Stunned, they looked around in amazement, when Steele and Celeste suddenly appeared standing a few feet away, holding their arms out as if still in the healing circle they had just left.

"Fajah, what have you done?" Ian gasped. "I may never get another chance to bring Jasmine back!"

Fajah addressed Ian with a sad expression, blurting out a barely understandable phrase to justify her action. She stated that Jasmine would not have made it back to this world, no matter how hard everyone tried, and that she is part of that other world now. Fajah said that without her intervention, Jasmine would have died, and then she would not be in either world. She would be with Fajah's grandfather.

As tough as it was, Ian finally came to understand this new reality. Realizing how cold he had been to Fajah, he began to apologize, and then it hit him. "Fajah! Your name! You are my daughter Kristen's imaginary friend. But you are real. I am so sorry for your grandfather. And for me being such an ass, ah, I mean uncaring person."

James pulled Fajah close and hugged her, then pulled his son tight. They all shared tears and regret—not only for losing Jasmine and Grandfather, but from the deep understanding they all received from their shared meditation experience, attempting to rescue Jasmine. As unreal as recent events had been, Ian still held hope that he would see his wife again. James stood back and wiped away a tear. "We have to find a way out of here."

Ian thought for a minute. "The path that leads around the waterfall has to lead somewhere." Steele informed the group that they had been here before and that the path down would eventually lead to a road, but it was a long way. They would have to take water with them if there was any hope of walking out from where they were. Luckily, James had survival training in the military, so he directed everyone to look for something to carry water in. Gourds grew plentifully in this region. "Look for vines—this time of year the leaves and vines will be green possibly with budding yellow flowers. The light yellow gourds from the previous season will be dried. We can use those to carry water, and the seeds are edible."

They all started searching as they descended the tight trail, looking in every open space along the sheer rock walls and creek bank. Something had to turn up before the water disappeared underground and the high desert took over.

Before they had gone far, Akira showed up with their dogs Isis and Maya. She informed them that she would have been there earlier, but they were making sure Jasmine was all right and secured in her new environment. She explained that Jasmine was unable to lower her vibration to shift back with her family. She had become acclimated to the other reality.

"Your wife is healthy," Akira told them, "but it may be some time before you are able to see her again. Jasmine is now living in Gaia. In time, and with our help, she may learn to travel between dimensions. Whether or not she will ever have the ability for a sustained visit to your dimension all depends. She will need the talent and will have to learn how to raise and lower her molecular wavelength at will. If she is capable, then visits to your world can last days, or possibly a week at a time."

Akira went on to explain that she was unable to take them back to Gaia, or transport them out of the back country. The ceremony had lowered their wavelengths sufficiently to ground them solidly in this dimension. "I have alerted someone in this world to meet you at the bottom of the trail. Celeste and Steele–you know Vicky, Louise told me that she helped you once before. She drives a tow truck and will take you to Cedar City, the nearest town that has rental cars. You can arrange transportation home from there. Please take care of Fajah for now. We believe she will be able to shift over with a little training. All of you be very careful. As you know, Ian, there are some very dangerous people who want your technology and will stop at nothing to obtain it."

Akira handed Ian a hand-carved gourd with a leather strap. "Here is some water." She bent and pet Isis behind her ears, rubbed the top of Maya's head, and addressed the dogs. "You two take care of your family, they'll need your help. It will be best if you make camp here tonight and walk out in the morning. See all of you soon. Goodbye."

"I would sure like to be able to just pop in and out whenever I wanted," James said, and gave Ian a wink. "I think you are really on to something with this Portal technology stuff, son."

* * *

Stories about the ghost people of Death Hollow have circulated around Escalante for well over a century, with legends going back a millennia or more. The Navajo Dineh believe they are sustained as a nation because of their strong spirituality, and enduring faith in the Great Spirits that live in this area. These tribal people believe in a spiritual resonance that lives after the life cycle is over. They describe this as a spirit, rather than a ghost. Spirits that reside in certain rock formations were once living, breathing beings. There are spirits in living trees which live on in the grain of the wood, or the smoke when burning dead wood. Though in appearance a tree may appear non-sentient, yet they believe it a living spirit. In fact, Vicky's late grandfather used to tell her that the medicine man of the

Dineh, claimed the Ancient Ones–the Anasazi–had legends about the spirit people. The Anasazi had to pass through four different worlds before emerging into the fifth world or spirit world. It was thought that when one was ready, they could enter the spirit world somewhere around the slot canyons of Death Hollow.

Escalante had grown slowly through the years, and was still growing. The township of 818 was soon to be 819–the bartender Jake was about to become a granddad. His daughter Tracy and her husband Ed, were soon to become new parents.

Still Escalante had a small town feel. The city still had not agreed to put in their first stop light, but there were rumors. On the outskirts of town you drive past the cemetery, gas station and high school. Nearer town, there are random farms and the gray weathered wood of what's still standing of the old prospector's cabin. Next is the mayor's house with the white picket fence. There's another gas station, two restaurants and a single room post office complete with posts where the residents still tie their horses. Escalante is proud to have a modern bank next to the outfitters. Those are the main businesses in town. But of course there is the Prospector's Inn as you leave town.

Many people came to explore the massive wilderness areas, and tackle sandstone climbs, as well as take photos of the mysterious Hoodoos, Fairy Chimneys, Slot Canyons and other rock formations. Vicky could remember sitting wide-eyed next to her grandfather, when he told wild stories from the old bar stool, at the local watering hole. That was back when there were only 700 people up and down the valley that called this town home. Her granddad would tell old stories about the ghost people, to any traveler that would buy him a beer, or even listen to his tall tales.

But she couldn't remember any travelers in these parts that scared her, the way those did who came through around several weeks ago. The bald guy and his friend, he called the General, gave her chills–the kind that ran up your spine leaving a creepy, sick feeling. They had been asking around town about the legend of the ghost people.

Now Jake, the old-timer who had been behind the bar since she could remember, had a story of his own. After he told Vicky about his daughter Tracy expecting a baby girl, and how his grandson Little Jake was turning five, he went on to tell her, that the bald guy and the General who were in town some time back, were in Escalante again. And that they gave him a sawbuck, to tell them the story that her late granddad used to tell. The tall-tale about the ghost people–and he also gave them directions to Death Hollow. That's the biggest tip he ever got, and all they wanted was a glass of water. What greenhorns.

That got Vicky to thinking. Akira told her that about the time the General and his friend first showed up –that a friend of hers had been shot up around the Hollow, where Jake had sent those fellas. She wondered if they had anything to do with that? Strange, this was now the second time that Akira had asked her to meet friends of hers up there. That nice couple, their grandmother and their dogs, with that strange brake line problem. Now that couple was back again, along with a little girl and two men. This time without any vehicle, and were needing assistance again...guess they just magically appeared out there...like the ghost people. She smiled to herself. And oddly, now at the same time the General and friend were back in town. She had better be careful, that canyon was strange enough, with the Hoodoos, and legends of ghost people. "Better hit the road, and 'get the haul on', like dad always said." Akira had asked Vicky to be at the trail-head to the Hollows Slot Canyon by late afternoon.

* * *

Maya ran ahead of the group, while the larger dog Isis strolled along just behind. Fajah and the rest of the five reluctant hikers emerged from the steep trail and saw the tow truck waiting their arrival. "What a welcome sight," James said.

Ian nodded in agreement. "It will be great to sit down and relax on the drive out of this forsaken land."

Isis reached the truck with a deep growl, her sister whined and started to run back to the group. As Maya reach Steele, he bent down and picked up her front paw. It was crusted in damp red mud, with a brighter red in her fur above the mud-soaked paw. He pinched the red fur and rubbed it between his thumb and finger, then smelled the red smear on his thumb. Celeste saw her husband's concerned face and screamed. "That's blood!"

"Everyone take cover!" Steele yelled. Something was wrong, where was Vicky? Between the tight canyon walls, there was little room to take cover. Steele ducked behind a large boulder, following the others, and came face to gun barrel, behind which stood a large man with a patch over his left eye. The remainder of his group stood in back of the man, face against the cliff wall, with another man pointing a weapon at their backs. Steele saw the fur on Isis' back standing straight. He didn't want her to be shot so he told Isis to lay down.

The man guarding the group jabbed James in the back with his AK 47. "Why don't you introduce us to your friends?"

"Dad, who are these men?"

"Let me introduce you, son. The ugly character sticking his weapon in my back is Gregory." That comment received a strong jab to the ribs. "Uh," James moaned... then taking a deep breath, he continued. "The cute guy with the patch we call the General. I'm ashamed to say, these men are part of my past, when I was with the Blackwater group."

"Oh, don't be so harsh–no hard feelings, James," the General smiled. "Hello, little Fajah, good to see you again, I believe we have some unfinished business." He walked to the canyon wall and turned Ian's face away from the sandstone. "So this is your son-genius," then patted Celeste on the butt, "and his sexy–voluptuous wife. But what's with the dogs? They don't seem to care for me."

"My name is Celeste, and I'm not Ian's wife–that is my husband," Celeste pointed to Steele–"those are our dogs, and I'm sure they don't like you."

"Well, well, now that we have all been formally introduced, let's be on our way. Move!" The General roughly shoved Steele ahead of himself. When he did, Isis jumped at the General, only to be knocked to the ground with the butt of his weapon.

Celeste ran to Isis and knelt to care for her. Isis rubbed her paw over her snout, whined then shakily got to her feet and growled. "You bastard!" Celeste cursed her captor.

"Keep that mutt under control–or the next bullet will be for it. Which is really against my better nature." He laughed and straightened his eye patch. "That little puppy of yours spoiled our surprise. I'm afraid your friend Vicky was on the wrong side of an argument with Gregory's knife. Looks like she will be permanently visiting your ghost friends."

"But enough small talk," he said, pulling Celeste to her feet. "Leash that mutt, and let's get down to business. James, what have you done with the Wand?" He glanced toward Ian. "I'm getting very tired of having to fly everywhere. It takes so long. It is long past time that you sequence me for your device. I get pissed every time I see Gregory blink out and know he will arrive ahead of me. Now get moving."

The General had a look of anticipation as they approached the truck. But instead of seeing Vicky's blank dead eyes staring infinitely into the distance, his gaze was greeted by only a dark red mixture of blood and sandy dirt next to the truck.

"Where is she?" he yelled, then turned with a grim smile. "No matter, she will not get far losing blood like that."

Maya and Isis bolted off through the sagebrush—either chasing a rabbit or maybe looking for Vicky. The General ignored the dogs, and proceeded to zip-tie everyone's wrists, then searched for the Wand through the few things they carried. "You don't have the God-damn Wand!"

He shoved James to the ground, grinding his foot on the back of his head, and pushed his face into the blood-stained dirt. "You had better cough-up the Wand or your friends are going to regret it." Then he swung his large arm and struck Steele, knocking him back a few steps. "We can finish this later, I've been out here in the desert too long."

"Gregory, throw our new friends Celeste and Steele in our truck, along with the traitor James here." "I'll take Ian and my little girlfriend Fajah in the tow truck. Let's get the hell out of here. Oh, Ian, if you get any funny ideas about escaping, I will let Gregory loose on your dad, with his extraordinary negotiating powers. I'm confident he will convince you and your father to give us the Wand and the software."

Gregory twisted his face with a wicked smile, and held up his knife. "My negotiator here can hardly wait."

The General laughed. "You can't kill them—we'll just tease them, until we get the Wand, and Ian gives us the sequencing software."

❯ ❯ ❯

CHAPTER 10
New Life

Vicky lay in the sandy arroyo as far from her truck as she could stumble before collapsing. She struggled to take a breath as the last drops of life slowly left her body. Maya lay next to her making a sympathetic whine, as Isis gently licked her hand. Focused and unaware of the drama being played out at the tow truck, Jaguar and Star knelt on both sides of Vicky, working desperately to heal her bleeding body, but they had arrived too late to heal her.

Star wiped away a tear. "Hold on, love." Her heart ached from empathy. "We will know each other again. Through our love we will always be able to find one another, even between dimensions." Star remembered that finding one another again through love was something she had shared with Louise, for her notebooks, before she crossed over. The world goes round and round.

Vicky smiled, recognizing Star's true essence. "Star, you are so beautiful this time...in this life. How did I not recognize you before now? I'm afraid to die, tell me everything will be all right."

Star nodded through her tears, realizing she was about to share another truth she had given Louise so many years ago. "You will be fine, Vicky–dying is the process of learning to be more aware of the new dimensions which will eventually be your next home. When we die, then again we are born...growth, learning, growth and learning...it is a long process, the learning always linked to–and limited by–the rate at which we learn. But at various stages of the soul's gradual awakening, the process may be, however imperceptible to the receiver, speeded up. I will see you again, Love."

Vicky took her final deep breath and whispered, "Goodbye, love." Her soul withdrew, leaving the lifeless body she had used for this time's earth adventure.

Star gasped. "Jaguar–even though I'm sure she and I will find one another again, this empty feeling is still here in my chest. It hurts so bad."

"I know, dear heart," Jaguar murmured. "It never gets any easier when a loved one leaves us. But knowing how the cycle works does make the pain dissolve more quickly. You two will find each other again soon. She did finally remember you, before she passed on. I am sure she will not go far this time, she was so close to making it across the barrier to join us. I am sure she will join us during her next life—boy or girl? Which do you think she will choose this time?"

Star looked away from Vicky's vacant body, with a twinkle in her eye. "I think she will return as a boy. Funny how it works out. In our first encounter she was my father, we have been brother and sister, we were married in a previous live together. I faintly remember our life in ancient Rome. This life she and I were acquaintances living in different dimensions. Wonder what our next encounter has in store for us?"

* * *

It takes concentration, moving through Earth's energy field without a body. Vicky floated free of her corpse, feeling misplaced, in a dream-like state, out of control. Everything was in a fog, soft and out of focus. More than that, in this reality, nothing was solid. Everything was constantly shifting—like multiple realities imposed on layers of gentle ripples, layered over and through one another. Here time and space have not congealed.

After an indefinite period of time, Vicky's primordial instinct realized that she could control this bodiless space in time. She decided to look around to experience this new weightless environment. Directing her consciousness, she discovered that her thoughts would take her in any direction through time and space. As she moved along, less animated areas became apparent—seeming more mirror-like, with a vague sparkle. These areas were very faint, until she directed her awareness to one specifically. Then they seemed alive with an electromagnetic field.

Vicky fixed her attention to one of these spaces, and an apparition appeared in her mind. Yet in this new space, she had no physical mind. This vision appeared to be part of her. The longer she fixed her attention to this space, the more real it became, gaining the substance of life. In time, the life became vivid. Vicky felt a blink, then instead of watching the life unfold, the life became her. She was being led across a footbridge over a little stream toward a pleasant lawn or meadow where a small group of people were enjoying the view, and conversing with one another in a social gathering. In the background was a large Victorian-style house–but her being there was detached. A strong thought came to mind–'You choose your own parents'–and a feeling–'Oh! This is what I am doing. This is a pre-view of a possible new life for me.'

Vicky pulled her attention back–'Wow, that was enlightening,' she thought. She had recognized the landscape, and the little girl in the family seemed to be...Louise! That life appeared to be back east...possibly around Philadelphia? It even appeared to be in the past, maybe the late 1800's. Her essence conjured what felt like a smile–that warmed her entire being. Could that have been Louise's childhood?

Moving on, she discovered another of the electromagnetic fields. No– that one didn't feel right. Inquiries continued, many areas she sensed were not for her. Others were possible, so she probed them more deeply.

Additional possible lives followed. There was the nighttime bonfire in an old quarry that appeared to be Ireland, or possibly Scotland? A very pregnant mother was arm-in-arm with her husband, as they watched their son and daughter with pride. The kids struggled to collect the most wood for this annual event. The children from the neighboring farm always came up trumps though, dragging larger branches with their tractor, making an impressively high wood pile. Darkness fell, and the huge heaps of wood were doused with petrol and set alight. That seemed like a happy family– but it wasn't for her, that life would be halfway around the world from Star.

Vicky saw flashes of many lifetimes. Some were tempting, others frightening. She found that the longer the vision held her attention, the more difficult it was to withdraw. The longer she stayed with a scene, the more she became enmeshed in that reality.

Another exceptionally alluring lifetime appeared. Here was a five-year-old preschool boy holding his mother's hand. He was being led to a boat on dry land. The little boy was holding his crotch and squirming around, obviously having to go to the bathroom. The boy was in awe as his mother helped him up the stairs–of a boat on dry land! The boat was a restaurant, and mom had asked to use their facilities. Her caring husband she had called Ed was also helping the young boy–Ed! So this lady is Tracy from her home town. 'That's right,' Vicky thought, 'she was with child last time I saw her. I have always liked her as a friend.' If Vicky picked that new baby's life, she would live in Escalante, close to Star.

She considered this as a possible life–but wait. Tracy was about five month's pregnant. Vicky couldn't wait four months. But she continued to be drawn to this life, wondering if it was even possible to enter the baby's consciousness this far before birth? She listened intently as Ed spoke quietly to his wife.

"I am thrilled to see Little Jake so happy before his operation, but we must get to the hospital. It's time we check in for his procedure."

Tracy had told Vicky a few weeks ago that Little Jake was very sick, and they would be going to California for his heart operation. He had been named after Jake, his granddad, so they always added the 'Little' when they were talking about the boy.

Vicky had become immersed with this family, so she followed them to the hospital. Little Jake was taken directly into pre-op for preparation, while Tracy and Ed were directed to a waiting area. As Little Jake was put to sleep with the anesthesia, Vicky was immediately drawn to his side.

"Hello…I'm Jake, who are you?" Little Jake was talking to her!

"You can see me?" Vicky asked in surprise. "I'm Vicky...well, I was Vicky before I died…but I guess that was really only a name."

"So you are a ghost, and I can see you. Does that mean I am dead? What are you doing here? Is this heaven? Maybe you are an angel!" Little Jake fired so many questions Vicky didn't know where to start answering.

"Hold on. I don't have all the answers either, but I will tell you what I can. First, I guess I could be a ghost or angel or maybe a spirit. Whatever I am, I do not have a body. And it turns out I am here shopping for a new life. I was thinking about becoming the baby your mother is going to have in a few months."

"You can do that?" Jake asked inquisitively.

"It appears you can, though this is the first time I can remember doing it. I guess we forget once we choose," Vicky replied, also confused. "I don't know if everyone can make a choice, or if life just happens to most people."

Then Vicky steered Little Jake's attention to the operating table. "That is your body on the operating table. It appears you have a bad heart that the doctors are attempting to fix–and it looks like you are breathing, so you are still alive."

"So it is. My body looks funny from here, doesn't it?" Jake floated down and took a close look at himself then asked, "If you can choose a life, could you take my body and let me go choose another?"

While they were visiting, the doctors completed the operation. "Great success, doctor. Congratulations," one of the nurses complimented. "This little man should go on to live a long natural life."

Vicky twirled around in excitement. "Jake, you are going to be okay! You should go back now."

Jake looked confused and frightened, instead of excited. "I don't want to. I feel like there are other things I have to do…and I have to go now. You take my body. Tell my folks I really love them." And with that last statement, Little Jake was gone.

"Doctor, something is wrong! Little Jake is not responding…we are losing him!"

"Code blue!" the doctor immediately responded. "Keep the blood pumping and supply oxygen to his brain, while I revive him, stat."

Vicky was stunned. What was she going to do–she couldn't let that precious little boy just die! Then it struck her–she wasn't here to take the baby's consciousness–she was here to become Little Jake. She thought quickly–Tracy and Ed seemed to really be in love. They would make good parents for her and for the new baby, and the old bartender Jake would be her granddad. 'This is it! This will be my new life.' She directed her energy toward the unconsciousness boy laying on the table, then coughed and sputtered for breath. Then she took a long deep breath.

"Well done, team," the doctor told everyone. "That was a close one, let's close him up and get Little Jake into post-op. He needs to get back to living life."

The doctor had just given the family the good news about the success of the operation when grandpa Jake took a necklace from around his neck. A beautiful crystal dangled from the chain. "Tracy, Ed–this isn't much, but I want Little Jake to have this. Tracy, your mother made it for me from a crystal I found up around Box Hollow. That was a special place for us. We loved hiking up to the waterfall to have lunch beneath the old pine tree, and swim in the cool water at the base of the falls"... Old Jake's thoughts drifted to another place and time... "found this crystal in that very pond. Your mother would have been proud to give this to Little Jake herself. I'm sure she is looking down from heaven smiling as big a smile as mine. Bless her soul."

Tracy began to cry softly. "Thank you, daddy." She gave her dad a big hug. "I am going to hang this in his bedroom window so he can watch the beautiful sparkles of light from this wondrous crystal."

* * *

Smash! Murderous sounds from the impact echoed through the canyon walls, in the middle of nowhere, on Highway 12 in Utah. Twisted metal cut into Gregory's side with all the violent intensity of two vehicles attempting to become one at 50 miles an hour. Truck tires screeched as Gregory's vehicle spun sideways from the impact, rolled on its side and skidded across gravel to a stop. Then all turned deathly silent.

Seconds later, two unmarked vehicles pulled beside the Humvee that was barely scratched from ramming into Gregory's truck. Director Rebel jumped from the gray BMW and started shouting directions. "Let's bug out, gentlemen. Grab Ian, and the others. Move it, move it!"

"Sir–Ian is not in this vehicle. Do you still want the others? They are pretty banged up."

"Stand down, let me see who they are." Rebel walked to the truck, stood on the undercarriage and looked through the broken window. "Okay, take the old man, he's Ian's father James. Don't know the others, leave them."

Agent Duncan stepped from the other unmarked vehicle, a dark SUV.

"Duncan–you were a combat medic. Patch-up James, and take him back to DC," Rebel ordered. "I'll see you in a few days. You two in the Humvee get after that tow truck, Ian must be in it with the General. Bring them to me."

* * *

Looking at the carnage in his rear view mirror, the General decided not to stop. In fact he didn't even slow down. He had what he'd come for, and there was nothing he could do for Gregory who would have to fend for himself. He looked over at Ian and Fajah and thought to himself, 'This is one hell of a pay-day. This little one will get a good price after I have my fun with her, and Ian will enable UnitedOps to finally become a world power. With his Jump technology, I will call the shots. Governments will have to negotiate with me. Hell, I might start my own country–the country

103

our forefathers intended–a white race where the black man is our slave, not the goddamn president."

He pulled off the highway, and headed down a dirt road toward what the sign promoted as 'The Double JJ Ranch' and switched off the engine. "They won't see us here." The General checked the ties on his captive's wrists, and legs, then adjusted the gag on Ian. "Don't worry, little one." He patted Fajah on top of her head. "Everything will be just fine. Now you two be quiet, we'll wait here awhile, and they will get tired of looking for us, then I'll find us another vehicle."

The General pulled the phone from his pocket. "Call Red, Ops 1," he said. His phone dialed, and a few seconds later was answered.

"This is Ops 1."

"Red, all is going as planned. Move on Ian's house."

* * *

"No sign of the tow-truck, Mr. Director."

"You are telling me a tow truck just vanished into thin air? I want you to take every side road between here and the border if need be–FIND them! Let's go, gentlemen, before the police get here." Rebel pulled out his phone. "Call Switchback."

Moments later as they drove away from the accident, he directed a team to move on Ian's home.

* * *

Dazed and confused, Steele stared blankly, attempting to focus his eyes, in the dim blurry flashing lights. He shook his head, trying to clear his mind. All that did was hurt his neck. Red and blue police lights played off the broken windshield, creating a spiderweb from the shards of glass. The refracted light inside the dark truck gave the appearance of a gory kaleidoscope.

Hanging sideways from his seatbelt, Steele looked through the changing patterns of lights and shapes to the front seat. There he saw the bloodied Gregory, dangling lifeless. Blood gushed from him, falling in slow motion, pooling on Celeste's still body laying beneath him. 'Was she still alive?' he worried. 'How much of that gore was coming from her?' The seatbelt cut into his side, making it hard to breath. The ringing in his ears overcame him and blackness ensued.

* * *

An elite counter-terrorist team, code name 'Switchback', battered in the front door of a beautiful home on the quiet Black Widow Drive, in the outskirts of Denver. Alek, Kristen and their friend Grace watched from the neighbor's house across the street as men and women removed boxes of computer hardware, monitors and files. The children both knew their father was no terrorist, something wasn't right. Kristen began to cry, then hugged Logan, her friend's mother, and asked when her daddy was coming home.

"I'm sure he will be home soon, hun." With the same question running through her mind, Logan pulled Alek aside. "Alek, take the girls to the park. I will make some calls and find out what the federal agents are doing in your house."

The three kids hesitantly started up the street toward the park at the top of the hill. About a block from the park, Alek ran ahead. "Come on, you babies," he taunted from three houses away. As he turned to tease them again, a car swung around the corner. A big man jumped from the back seat and pulled Kristen into the car, knocking Grace to the ground.

"NO!" Alek yelled, running as hard as he could. Black smoke burnt from the tires and a sickening rubber smell filled his sinus, and blurred his vision, burning his eyes. He watched helplessly as his sister disappeared down the street in the back of a stranger's car. Alek pulled Grace to her feet, then ran for his life, pulling her behind him. "Hurry, we have to tell your mother, and tell those men in my house!"

The agents from Homeland Security were finished with their investigation and climbing into their vehicles. Alek was completely out of breath, when he ran up to one of the agents, and started pulling his arm. "They have my sister!" He stopped only long enough to catch a breath. "Sir...hurry...they have my sister. You have to go after them...this way. Hurry!"

"Settle down, son," the man said. "Sit down here in the car, and we will go after them." He turned speaking into the phone, "Sir, Ian's son just came to me with a story about someone taking his sister. Do you want us to bring him in?"

Hearing that, Alek turned to get out of the back seat when another man shut the door. "Relax, son, you are in good hands. We will take care of you, and find your father and sister."

Struggling against the back door, Alek realized there was no handle, and the door was locked. Then he saw the heavy metal grate between him and the front seat. "Am I under arrest?"

CHAPTER 11
Hell and Healing

Gregory's disembodied soul bobbed like a discarded piece of trash, floating out of control across ocean waves. His consciousness misplaced, in a nightmare-like state, where nothing was solid. Time and space were no more substantial than he was. His barbarous habits and emotions of lust, hate, anger and destruction, began to fabricate his environment. Everything around him was constantly shifting, like multiple realities imposed layer on layer of violent waves, crashing over one another.

His thoughts and twisted passions created raging torrents comprised of undulating, discarnate beings, locked in lust-filled savage battles–beings like himself, in a mixture of their personal, cultural, and karmic hells. "So this is what death is–I could get used to this."

Gregory smiled and stroked what he believed to be his manhood, as he watched naked bodies twisted around one another. Not realizing his physical body existed only in his consciousness. Everywhere he looked, he sensed unimaginable deviant intercourse, derived from his perverted subconscious. A sea of bodies, tied, twisted, tortured and broken. This orgy of bodies in bondage, more of a contorted battle than sex.

His thought told him he was breathing heavily. Degenerate sex and violence, now that was something Gregory understood. Something he was good at. He dove into the swirling battle of bodies, penetrating what he could, slashing anybody unwilling with his trusty knife. Oblivious that the knife was only a figment of his twisted psyche. He turned and twisted in an impotent frenzy of lust. Licking, biting, thrusting, gouging, punching and laughing with cacophonous joy.

Flinching from violent pain in his side, he suddenly realized he was being gnawed on. Consumed–bite-by-bite–he was being taken apart and eaten alive.

Gregory's lust-filled violent passions during life, were being rewarded through malignant, karmic consequences of pain, suffering and agony. But he was dead–how could things hurt the way they did? In sudden horror it dawned on him. He had no escape. He could not die—could not sleep in death. He had created his own hell!

* * *

Bishop Daniel handed the ambulance team the agreed-upon sum for delivering Steele and Celeste to his private plane. He assured them, that his private doctor on-board would care for them. It was early morning around 2:00 am. His son-in-law Doug realized how agitated the Bishop was, as he was shaken awake and told to heal this young lady and her husband. Daniel told him that they had been in an accident and couldn't go to a hospital, that he would explain more about their situation after they were stable. The Bishop kissed his daughter on the forehead and thanked her and Doug for accompanying him on this business trip. Then he directed the pilot to get in the air as quickly as possible.

After they were at a cruising altitude, Doug did what he could medically for Steele, who wasn't hurt severely—mostly bruises, some strained muscles, and one laceration deep enough to require a few quick stitches. Then he was ready to work with Celeste's injuries. She had more serious internal injuries, and he was not a doctor.

Doug decided to use his knowledge of Reiki to work with Celeste's energy body, and try to stabilize her until they could reach a hospital. He placed his hands on her shoulders and gently pushed then released, pushed and released, intermingling their energies. Mirroring his breath with hers, in...out...in...out, feeling the energy exchange between them. Relaxing, moving her energy body very gently forward, then letting her slide back. Again and again, like a wave's rhythm flowing against the shore. Replicating her body's natural rhythm, a tempo in tune with Earth's meter, that all living beings possess. He was opening her energy-body to remember this cadence from when she was a baby, rocking her again and again. Allowing her body's energy to slosh back to her accustomed equilibrium, opening up blockages in each appendage and throughout her torso. Treating energy as if it was liquid, helping it flow, simple and basic.

Repeating a healing mantra to keep his mind focused, Doug held a meditative state. That is when Jaguar slipped into his receptive psyche—gently pushing Doug's being to the back of his mind, and taking control of his body. Doug's wrists curled. One hand over the other. Somehow

Doug understood that he was cradling an energy that was pulling together the physical properties of matter. Connecting positive and negative ions from the basic building blocks of life. Using the fundamental principles of charge interactions to manipulate protons and electrons. Creating a positively charged weave of water, air, earth and fire.

Doug's muscles were being driven by a foreign pilot. Jaguar felt as if he was wearing a new suit of clothes, with two psyches steering the same vehicle. Working in harmony with Doug, they manipulated this ball of energy, like kneading a ball of etheric clay. Doug watched from a cognitive state of mind. The energy was so strong that he could see it: a rotating ball of transparent fluorescent air danced between his palms, shifting color and shape. It was alive with pure energy. During hundreds of healing Reiki sessions, even through his third year of the undergraduate program of his medical degree, Doug had never experienced anything like this. His essence sat in the back of his mind and watched as his senses–mind, body and spirit–moved with an undetermined grace. Controlled by an unknown driver, Doug's Reiki and medical background made him a perfect channel.

Together Doug and Jaguar sent this ball of energy into Celeste with a complete emotional intent to heal. Jaguar's essence moved through Doug, directing this cosmic universal influence to a cellular level in Celeste's body. Flowing with a natural tempo, he could feel a restorative light from the element of fire move between them, entering the dead matter from the trauma in her body. This white fire-driven light simply burned off the expired tissue and unwanted putrid blood from her wounds, allowing a clean slate for living tissue to grow. With Jaguar as his pilot, Doug instinctively knew how to work with this perfect restorative weave of essential elements. Together they wrapped her torn tissues in spirit, interlacing the fabrics of bone, blood vessels and muscle, guiding them back to their natural state of being. Extreme energy pulsated through every fiber of Doug.

Hours of this intimate healing connection passed before Doug collapsed from exhaustion. He fell into a deep sleep from the fatigue of being this vessel for healing energy. Jaguar slipped from his psyche, leaving Doug again in complete control of his senses.

* * *

Returning to the Falls, Jaguar knew that Celeste would be fine. 'I haven't done any remote healing for a long time,' he thought, smiling. 'And healing at 45,000 feet going 600 miles an hour added a new wrinkle.' Then he told Star, "I am glad Doug has such a receptive spirit, he made that much easier than it could have been. I need some rest."

Jaguar excused himself as Star held Louise's hand. "I am sorry we didn't realize their imminent danger before the accident. We were so distracted by Vicky's passing and Jasmine's situation. But I am thrilled Jaguar was able to heal them."

Louise smiled. "Thank you, my dear. I'm relieved and pleased Jaguar was able to restore my family."

* * *

Celeste slowly regained consciousness. The faint drone of what sounded like a jet engine became louder. Quiet voices intermingled with the engine's drone. As her head cleared, she was barely able to make out a conversation.

"What are we going to do with them, Bishop?" a strangers voice asked.

"Give them something to eat and make them feel at home. Let me know as soon as they are awake. I have to know what their connection is to Ian and this blasphemous technology. Then we'll think of something. But right now, I have a speech to write for the Bishop's Appeal. You know—our annual fund-raising campaign that supports the ministries, services this plane and pays your salary," the Bishop said with disdain.

He stepped into his private room, closed the door, took off his jacket and loosened his starched collar. He glanced at the bedroom where his daughter Elizabeth and her husband Doug were fast asleep. Then sat at his desk and turned on his laptop. Duncan appeared on the screen.

"Your Excellency, a quick update: First, let me tell you that I have James, the General has Ian, and his men are holding his daughter Kristen. I believe Ian's son Alek is being held by Director Rebel's men. One of Rebel's counter-terrorist teams took boxes of files and all of Ian's computer equipment."

The Bishop frowned. "Damn, I was hoping to beat them to Ian's work. Well, well, we will have to round up all of our lost little sheep and bring them home to the flock. Bring me the Wand after the fund raiser and we'll finish our transaction. You are about to be a very rich man."

In the outer cabin, Celeste sat up on the plush tan leather couch and wrapped her arms around her husband. "Where are we?"

"We are in Bishop Daniel's private plane," Steele whispered and hugged her tenderly. "I'm so happy you are awake, baby I thought I had lost you in the wreck."

She woozily looked around the plane's cabin. Near her was a table with matching leather recliner chairs at either side. An inviting plate of crisp vegetables and a creamy looking dip sat on the table along with a pitcher of iced tea. Leaning back in one of the recliners was a frail little man, clean-cut and shaven, with a thin black tie and a button-down white pressed shirt. At the back of the cabin was a door leading to what must have been the Bishop's private quarters.

Steele helped her sit up on the couch. "Good afternoon, baby. Glad to see you awake, I have been so worried." She shook her head gently and looked at her husband with a question in her eyes. Steele squeezed her hand tenderly. "I'll tell you what is going on. We are in a private jet heading to a Catholic diocese somewhere in Wisconsin. This is Reverend Paul, Bishop Daniel's right arm. He was just telling me how they rescued us from a serious auto accident. Gregory died in the crash and the vehicle that smashed into us left the scene."

"What happened to James, Ian and Fajah?" Celeste asked.

"Nice to make your acquaintance, young lady. I'm afraid there was no sign of any other cars or people at the site," Paul answered. "Who is this Ian you speak of? Oh, never mind. You two are lucky to be alive, being left alone after such a bad accident. It is fortunate we were there to find you. No telling how long you would have been there, undiscovered in such a remote place."

Reverend Paul got up from his chair, slid the plate of vegetables across the table, and poured two glasses of tea. "Here, have something to eat, you need your strength after your ordeal."

"Nice to meet you as well, Reverend," Celeste reciprocated. Then she picked up a few carrot slices, broccoli, and some cherry tomatoes and put them on her plate with a dab of dressing. A sad look came across her face. "Where do you think our girls are, babe? I miss Isis and Maya so much."

Steele had an uneasy feeling about Isis, but not being sure what this sense meant, he decided to keep it to himself. "I'm sure they are all right. I'll bet Louise has them. They have been spending a lot of time at the Falls, they seem to like it there."

"Ah, yes. Is that where you two were coming from–out there in the middle of nowhere? "Bishop Daniel said as he entered the room. "So glad to see you up and about, you gave us quite a scare."

Steele frowned. "Speaking of the middle of nowhere, why were you and the Reverend out there? Seems like a long way from Wisconsin."

"Yes, it is a long way from home. We are considering a retreat in the region, and were looking at property. Funny how providence works, is it not? God is truly looking out for you two. I am convinced he has a mission for you."

Reverend Paul pushed a glass of tea to Steele. "I think this mission of yours might have something to do with Ian. This Ian you are so concerned about isn't perhaps the same gentleman we hear about who invented the Portal technology, is he? There are rumors that he is spending time in the Utah area. Do you realize that this technology is blasphemous, and it should be stopped?"

"Oh, so the truth comes out. This is no mere coincidence, or providence. You and the Bishop were really out there looking for Ian," Steele countered.

"Son, are you accusing us of something? Do you believe that the Reverend, and I–a Bishop for the Catholic Church–are lying to you two? We are looking for property. We just so happen to also be looking around to see if these rumors might be true. We believe this technology is a serious problem, that it is in a league with the devil. Lucifer has enough of a hold on this world without this device giving him a helping hand."

Then Celeste spoke her mind. "My husband and I also believe that it could be hurting the environment. We too agree that this technology should be investigated."

"Maybe we should work together to come up with a plan then," the Bishop suggested, smiling at everyone. "Yes, that is why God put us all together. Now get some rest, and we can talk about our plans later. I have some work to do. We should be landing soon."

"Bishop, are you saying our meeting is destiny?" Celeste asked.

"I'm saying it is God's will–that God has given men and women the capacity to choose good or evil in their lives–and with that free will, we all must have chosen to be here." With that he turned and entered his private quarters, pulling the door shut behind him.

A few minutes later, the pilot's voice came across a speaker. "We will be making our final approach into Outagamie County Regional Airport. Please make preparations for landing."

CHAPTER 12
New Beginnings

"Welcome to the Diocese," Bishop Daniel greeted Celeste and Steele. "Doug will take you to your apartment. After you get settled, he can show you around the complex. I have the Bishops' Appeal fundraiser tomorrow, so I will excuse myself to prepare. If you and your wife need anything, ask Doug or find Reverend Paul–they can help you. It's past dinner, but if you would like, we will see if the kitchen can send something up to your room. And if you are up to it, please join my table at the fundraiser tomorrow evening around 6:00 in the Bishop's Hall."

Doug motioned them to follow him. They walked silently to the Retreat Hall, past the depressing entry gardens, where semi-circular walls of roses stood with the empty branches, patiently waiting to display their promised beauty and to rejoice in the new life of spring.

Their apartment was up a flight of stairs, and down a long hall. Doug opened the apartment door, and handed keys to both Steele and Celeste. "Don't say much to anyone. We'll talk later, I have some important information for you. Get some rest, you need to heal." Doug turned suspiciously, glancing around, then hurried down the hall.

Celeste and Steele thought his reactions and cryptic warning pretty odd, but figured they would eventually learn what it was about. So they turned their attention to their new accommodations. The apartment was in a large two-story brick building called the Retreat Hall. It was tucked between massive trees overlooking a meandering creek. The apartment was small, with all the hotel style furnishings necessary to make it comfortable–although hospital-like sterile. Celeste was happy to see the closet was well stocked with warm clothing. She quickly slipped on a sweater and handed a jacket to her husband. There was a decent-sized bedroom with 3/4 bath, a galley-style kitchen and a small dining table between the kitchen and living area. A balcony, large enough for two comfortable-looking chairs, overlooked a natural setting without a building to be seen. Below, a light snow covered the manicured lawn, that slanted gently about thirty yards to the slow water, that wandered lazily between thin patches of ice. The stark contrast of the birch trees' beautiful white bark, was scattered among the evergreen foliage of hemlock and spruce along both creek banks. The trees artfully surrounded a large pond formed long ago by industrious beavers.

Steele picked up two glasses and a welcoming bottle of wine from the dining table and urged Celeste out to the porch. He poured their wine, then turned and stroked her hand tenderly, tears forming in his eyes. "I was afraid I had lost you back in the crash." She gave him a reassuring smile and a long hug, then they both sank into an over-sized chair, clinked glasses and enjoyed being alive. He pulled a warm blanket over them and put his arm around her. She snuggled close to keep warm in the crisp evening air. The slow water rippling gently over the old beaver dam created a relaxing resonance that quickly lulled them into a calm sleep.

Celeste stretched, awakened by the sun's early greeting. It peered over the trees, casting the creek in soft morning shadows. The smell of coffee wafted out from the quiet kitchen. Waking more fully, she glanced from the porch and spotted her husband wearing a warm parka, sitting on a rock by the morning's golden pond. Steam rose from the coffee cup that sat next to him. Celeste freshened up, poured herself a cup of coffee, put on her warm clothes then strolled quietly across the white grass toward her husband. She stepped quietly, reaching to place her feet into the footprints he'd left in the light snow on his way to the creek.

Steele sat preoccupied by his thoughts, watching the reflections sparkle from a spot of light that found its way through the trees to play on the ripples, before the water formed bubbles as it flowed under the delicate ice and into the still, deep pond created by the master builder's handiwork.

"Penny for your thoughts," she said softly.

He shook an impression of Isis and Maya from his mind, smiled up at her and asked, "What do you think? Should we work with the Bishop? Do you think our meeting is destiny, or something more?"

"Wow, I got my penny's worth. Well, Louise once told me that we are intelligent and free creatures and have to journey toward our ultimate destinies by free choice. So I guess it is really up to us if this is the path we want to take."

"You should be a politician, the way you talked your way around that one," Steele said with a sly grin, then continued. "Even though neither of us is Catholic, I'm thinking that we should work with Bishop Daniel and see where this takes us. Besides, we have nowhere else to go and we need to keep our heads down for awhile."

Celeste agreed, but wanted to talk to Louise to see what was happening before they told the Bishop.

"I have the crystal pendant Louise gave us to help communicate with her. Let's contact her and catch up with everyone first."

Steele nodded, so she took the pendant from around her neck. They held it between their hands, closed their eyes, took a few deep breaths to relax their minds and thought of Louise. As they thought of Louise, a strong impression of Star developed.

When they opened their eyes, Star stepped out from behind a large tree. "I'm happy to see you are both well, what a beautiful place to recuperate. Louise sends her love and regrets that she is unable to come right now. This has been a tempestuous few days, and there is an issue with Akira that she is handling."

"I know you have many questions, so I'll fill you in on what I know to be true." Star sat on a large rock next to them and proceeded with an update: "The serious car crash you were in killed Gregory. We believe the crash was staged and that someone took James from the crash scene and left Gregory and you two behind."

"So the General still has Fajah, and Ian, we have to help them," Celeste asserted.

"We suspect the General has them, along with Ian's daughter, Kristen. No one is sure where they took James. Louise, Jaguar and Grandstaff have gone to save the girls. After the accident Akira went to rescue Kristen and Fajah when Akira just vanished, so we believe she is with Kristen and her friend."

Steele shook his head, trying to take it all in, and hit on the last part. "Well, Akira vanishing is not unusual. You are all vanishing and reappearing a lot," he pointed out.

"No, this is different—I mean she really vanished. None of us can sense her anymore." Star went on to explain. "With the heightened senses that occur when moving into Gaia's dimension, when someone is as close as Akira is to all of us, we can feel her essence anywhere she travels. In this case, she just blinked out."

Concern spread through Celeste's energy. "Does that mean she is dead?"

Star reassured them that Jaguar and Louise were also pretty sure that she did not pass on. "You see, even when someone close passes over, their energy does not just go out. In our dimension, we can continue to sense them–their soul or spirit just feels different. So we are not sure what happened to Akira."

"Let me explain this way," Star went on. "Just before you were hurt in the car crash, our friend Vicky, your tow truck driver, passed away."

Steele and Celeste both let out loud gasps, then Celeste consoled, "We are so sorry. When the General captured us, and couldn't find Vicky, we had hoped that she escaped and might have found help."

"Jaguar and I found her, but we were too late to save her." Star wiped away a tear. "I'm sure I will see her again. Anyway, the point I was making, is that I can still feel Vicky's energy. She was born again in your world. We have shared many lives together and are very close. Even though we live in different dimensions, I can still perceive her essence."

"There is one more thing I must tell you. There is no easy way to tell you, and this will be hard for you to hear. Just know that, as I have just explained, death is not what it appears to be in your world." Steele and Celeste both had an air of trepidation hanging around them, but Star had to continue. "I am so sorry, your Isis is no longer in your world. She is with us in Gaia now."

Celeste looked at Star with confusion and doubt, and Steele's eyes began to tear. They both felt like they had been kicked in the chest, making it difficult to breathe. When they could finally catch their breaths, their emotions overtook them, and together they broke down and cried.

"NO! Not our baby!" Celeste sobbed.

Steele hugged his wife, attempting to offer comfort. "I...ah.." Working to steady his emotions, he took a deep breath, wiped away tears and started over. "I... I had a bad feeling something was wrong back in the plane yesterday, but couldn't place what it meant, so I didn't say anything. The General hurt her badly when he hit her with his rifle."

"Is Isis okay, now that she is in Gaia with you? Is she out of pain?"

A smile crossed Star's sad features. "Yes, yes, she is just fine, restored to health and the vigor of her youth. And Maya can still be with her, as can you when you visit Gaia."

Celeste stared past Star and Steele. Steele noticed a calm joy emerge from her tears, so he turned his head to see what held her attention. A few feet away, in the morning light, Isis spun in a circle of pure joy at seeing them again, and playfully sprang through the light snow, knocking Steele and Celeste sprawling.

The three of them rolled in the dry morning snow, Isis licking and spreading her unconditional love. 'I love you guys,' came a wordless sense that was unmistakably Isis. Her thoughts entered their minds more surely than if she had screamed the words out loud.

Together Celeste and Steele told Isis how much they loved her. "We are so happy to see you, girl," they declared in one voice. "We love you so much!" Isis love and happiness filled them as she rubbed her sides against them.

'Do not worry about me, I feel magical. I will watch over Maya. But as much as I want to, I cannot stay here with you...I love you...see you soon...' Isis looked at them with the smile she always had and slowly faded.

Star smiled at Steele and Celeste. "I'm sorry Isis is no longer with you in this world. Though I feel you will be joining us in Gaia before long. In the meantime, stay in touch. I have to get back to the Falls. I will see you soon."

* * *

That evening, Celeste and Steele joined Bishop Daniel at his table for the fundraiser. They looked festive in their new wardrobes provided by the Bishop, and had decided it would be a good way to take their minds off of the morning news. Besides, following the Portal technology leads would probably be the quickest way back to the Falls to see Isis and Maya again. Just thinking about Isis was punishing, as they both wiped tears away before entering the Hall.

The company was cordial, the evening full of all the pomp and circumstance they had expected. Bishop Daniel was quite flamboyant and over the top. Too much fire and brimstone talk for them, though it seemed to work well for his rich influential gathering, that were donating handsome amounts to his charities. During the charity check presentations, they quietly excused themselves to return to the apartment.

The night was dark, showing a sliver of a waxing crescent moon sneaking between high clouds. The chilled night air made for a brisk walk across the considerable distance to the Retreat Hall. As they approached a small group of pine trees, near the rose garden, a dark figure stepped out, startling them .

"Do not be alarmed, it's Doug. Can we speak for just a minute?"

Steele and Celeste nodded, and he continued in a whisper. "I have to warn you, before you get in too deep. Don't trust the Bishop, or the Reverend. Are you familiar with the Opus Dei? I believe the Opus Dei is a devious, anti-democratic, reactionary, semi-fascist Catholic institution, hungry for absolute power. The Bishop is a high ranking member."

Doug cocked his head, listening, then went on. "The Bishop will stop at nothing to get his hands on the Portal device. I heard him mention it again at dinner. He recently threatened my life, asking about James Knecht and a girl named Akira." That got Steele and Celeste's attention. Doug continued, "After some research, I found that Mr. Knecht is Ian's father. 'Ian!' You know—the man that invented the Jump technology. I'm certain the Bishop and Reverend were in Utah looking for Ian and some connection to a legend about ghost people, when they found you."

A sudden noise spooked Doug, and he anxiously looked around. "I have to go, you never heard any of this from me—got it?" He turned and melted into the deep shadows among the blue spruce.

* * *

After entering the door-lock code, a blast of cold air met Director Rebel as he entered the IT room of the Homeland Security building. One of hundreds of server cabinets sat open, displaying a maze of colorful wires. Sporting a bright red insulated vest, with his back to the door and parts neatly scattered across the work table was the man Director Rebel had come to see. His disheveled long gray hair hung in a loose ponytail down the middle of his back.

Rebel was looking for good news. "Walter, have you finished the Wand? You sounded excited when you called."

"No, well, not exactly."

"What do you mean—not exactly? Why did you call me down here?"

"As you know, I have been working night and day, reverse engineering Ian's technology since you confiscated his computers. I have discovered some very ingenious hardware and software Ian has developed." Walter continued, "Did you know that Ian has invented a chip that somehow

119

changes the frequency of anything that comes in contact with it? It reverses the poles almost like a battery. I believe that..."

"Cut to the chase, Walter. Why did you ask me down here?"

"Well, take a look at this." Walter slid a dull metal ring-shaped object out from in front of him. He had been working on this doughnut-shaped object. It looked like a piece had been taken out of it, leaving an open space about the size of a man's neck. Rebel stepped up for a closer look, and Walter picked up the object and snapped it closed around Rebel's neck.

"What are you doing? Get this off of me. What on earth is this? Great, so you have invented a heavy necklace – good work," the Director said, tugging at the metal doughnut.

Walter smiled with the excited look of a 12-year old boy. "It works! Look at this display." He jumped up and down with excitement. "All right! This has changed your electromagnetic energy. Do you feel anything, like maybe... do you feel heavier?"

"NO! Walter, get this confounded thing off of me."

"Try to get it off, I have built in a seamless lock that requires a light key to remove."

Rebel was getting angry, so he reached up and yanked on the tight Collar, he pulled, pushed, even took one of Walter's tools and banged on the side, but that only hurt his neck. The Collar didn't budge, didn't even feel like it was loosening. "WALTER!"

"Hold on, boss, don't blow a fuse." Walter waved a small laser light across the side of the Collar. Rebel could see in the reflection of a server door a sequence of blue lights swirling around the torus Collar, turning color with each complete rotation. A moment later, the lights all formed a solid band of green light encircling the Collar and it snapped open.

"That was pretty, Walter," Rebel mocked, rubbing his neck in relief. "Is this some kind of new rave necklace? You going to take it out to the clubs?"

"Don't be silly, Director. This is the answer to the problem you have been having with people popping in and out of space. If someone uses a Wand, or the other Portal door, you just snap this around their neck and they are frozen in place."

"What do you mean? I could still move. I was not frozen."

"In a way, you were frozen. If you had tried to enter the Portal door, or use the Wand, nothing would happen. This literally makes your frequency so heavy that you cannot move through dimensions. You or anyone else that has this Collar on is stuck. Watch this."

Walter picked up the Collar and snapped it shut. The object seemed to shrink. Then he took the solid disk and hit the side of it against his own neck. As he did, the Collar opened and snapped back shut around his neck, locked as tight as it was on Rebel. "It is easy to carry, and even easier to lock on your subject. Here, you take these two, I'll begin production of more. That is, if I have funding."

Rebel smiled, thinking of how he could use the Collar. "Make them." He started to walk away, and then turned. "Good job, Walter. Send me a request form for what you need to cover the project. When can I have more of these, and how many?"

"I can only make four more. This device only works with this." Walter held up a wafer-thin, semi-transparent hexagon crystal, the circumference of a dime. "These were confiscated when your team raided Ian's home. I have no idea how he made these–yet."

* * *

Director Rebel greeted Agent Duncan with a strong handshake attempting to stress his authority. Rebel ushered him into his private office, and they settled into comfortable chairs for the Director's briefing. "As you know, Agent, one of the functions of the Counter Intelligence Strategic Partnership between the FBI and The Department of Homeland Security works to determine and safeguard new technologies which, if compromised, would result in catastrophic damage to national security. Through our agencies' relationship, we are able to identify and effectively protect projects of great importance to the U.S. government. This provides the first line of defense inside facilities where research and development occurs, and where intelligence services are focused. It is because of this alliance that I'm able to share this important security device we have just developed."

The Director continued, "That, and of course, to discuss our approach to the millions we stand to receive from the many special interest groups. They will be standing in line to throw billions at this technological achievement when we let them in on this. You and I are two of a privileged few who are aware of the Jump technology and its implications regarding our national security–and our off-shore bank accounts. If we work together, we will be very wealthy men." There was a knock on the door.

"Enter," the Director sanctioned. "I believe you know Walter from our IT department." They shook hands, then Walter handed him another Collar. "Hot off the press," Walter said kiddingly. Rebel continued, "he has developed a device that will level the playing field–maybe even tilt it in our favor. Look at this." Director Rebel held up the Collar Walter had just handed him, then deftly slapped it on Duncan's neck.

"What the hell are you doing? Get this damn thing off of me. What is this?" Duncan's angry words reflected Rebel's reaction when Walter first locked the Collar on him–only with a few more expletives.

Rebel turned Duncan toward an ornate wall mirror to watch, and quickly waved the laser light across the Collar. They watched the sequence of lights swirl around the Collar until the Collar snapped open, then Rebel removed it and held it in the air. "This is our answer! An answer that will stop anyone from misusing the Portal devices. If someone abuses a Portal, just snap this around their neck and they are frozen. They cannot Jump again while wearing the Collar. It's like a portable prison. Here, these two are for you."

He handed Duncan the Collars and light key, then showed him how to use it. "These are two of only three Collars currently made, though Walter will have others completed soon. Keep them with you at all times, no telling when someone might pay you a visit. By the way, the General has been a lot of trouble recently. You are still in contact with him, correct?"

"Yes, I know where he is."

"Good. I have reason to believe he might know where Ian is. Talk to him and find out what you can. While you are catching up with the General, I'll see what is going on in Utah. There has been a lot of activity around Escalante. Meet me there after you speak with the General."

"One other thing, I understand that James wasn't hurt badly in the crash, and that you have reunited him with his grandson Alek."

"Yes, sir," Duncan answered. "They are in a well-guarded safe-house, secure, and comfortable. We can use them as bait to find Ian, whenever you are ready."

* * *

Turning off of International Drive in Washington, DC, the General stopped his truck near the hydraulic retractable bollards in front of the black metal gate. He pulled the camouflage hat with the American flag lower, covering most of his face in order to disguise his appearance, as he had noticed at least three closed circuit cameras capturing his every move. Behind the foreboding gate, an angular concrete fortress rose from the circular cement drive that entered the Embassy of the People's Republic of China. As he waited, a face appeared on the video intercom at the entrance and questioned his business at the Embassy.

"I am here to see Minister Cui Chao Qian from the Ministry of National Defense. Tell him the General is here with something of interest."

Within seconds, two armed guards emerged from their fortified outpost and inspected the under-carriage of his vehicle with mirrors, then checked his identification. "Tong chàng."

From his limited understanding of Mandarin, he took the guard's comment to mean 'clear', which must be the case, since the shiny steel bollards began to retract as the gate slid open. He pulled 200 feet across the drive toward the concrete building with huge angular walls, and parked beside a glass dome positioned squarely beneath a perfect isosceles triangular window. Inside, the sole window in the front of the icosahedron-shaped, concrete building, filtered a strong light across the gray floor, casting a warm light on the otherwise cold, stark lobby desk.

Two guards escorted him from his car, and left him at the double glass doors beneath the dome that covered the front entrance. The General entered the sharply defined, angular lobby and within a few steps, was following his long shadow. The shadow cast from the elongated V-shaped light, coming from the triangular window above the entrance behind him. When he reached the immaculately clean reception desk, a young Chinese lady asked him to sign and date the ledger, then handed him a badge, and directed him have a seat to wait for Cui Chao Qian.

Impatience grew as the General sat and waited. He had re-crossed his legs for a third time attempting to find a comfortable position, when Cui Chao Qian finally came walking down the hall. He was a graying man in his late 60's, a stiff demeanor, with a sober appearance. He wore a permanent frown that appeared to be etched in stone.

Qian was talking to a heavy-set Asian man who had a knowing gentle smile with a long beard, streaked with gray. Qian addressed the man as

Yaozu Lei, the infamous Chinese artist.

As they came close, he heard Qian say, "We cannot help you with your project at this time."

When the two men passed the General, Yaozu bent away from Qian and whispered, just loud enough for the General to hear. "Don't do it, you are on the wrong path. I will see you again."

"Don't bother our guests," Qian said to Yaozu's back.

Yaozu turned and bowed as he left. "Thank you for your time, Minister Qian."

Qian then faced the General, "Sorry if he bothered you, General, please come with me." He pivoted with a military demeanor and led the way past the reception desk, out of the filtered light, and down one of the halls to the elevators.

"I have something you will be very interested in..."

"Not here," Qian interrupted. "We can speak soon." Moments later, he opened a door and motioned his guest to enter a room on his left. "This is a secure space," Qian said, after closing the door to his office. Then he directed the General to a chair across from his desk. "Sit down."

The General sat with an arrogant, ostentatious stature flaunting his previous military rank. He slid a key on top of a closed envelope across the desk and addressed his partner in crime. "Inside is a password-protected Internet link to a video feed where you can see Ian. You will also find offshore bank routing numbers. I expect the finder's fee will be transferred without delay. When my account has been credited, I will email you Ian's location."

"You will receive confirmation by 1800 hours, General. I'll escort you out, and don't think about crossing me."

"Wouldn't think about it," the General said, thinking to himself, 'this little chink won't know what hit him.' He smiled and gave Qian a halfhearted bow, really not more than a nod of his head.

* * *

Crossing underneath the railroad viaduct in the rundown Northeast side of Washington, DC, the General parked on the street beside a railroad siding with a rusted-out boxcar that wore a few remaining chips of red paint along with colorful spray-paint tags from local gangs. He entered the warehouse behind the boxcar, through a metal security door. Red was kicked back on the cheap furnished apartment's couch. His feet were propped up on the cluttered coffee table next to a half-empty pizza box and ashtray full of unfiltered cigarette butts, drink in hand. Red swirled the ice around, through the dark liquid in his water-stained glass and asked, "How did your meeting go, sir? Tell me you don't really plan on giving our Ian to the Reds."

"Don't get your panties in a bundle, you know better than that. Qian thinks I am working with him, so I'm going to take advantage of the situation and take his money. Then we'll head back to the island compound with Ian. He will never think to look for us there. We can sell Fajah and use Kristen to get information from her father. You see, we hold all the cards. Where are our little angels?"

"I nailed the window shut and locked the two of them in the bedroom. They know better than to make any noise, I told them what you would do to them. Anyway, no one could hear them if they screamed bloody murder, with that damn train that runs by all the time."

"Red, show Kristen how to play poker or something to keep her busy. I'm going to introduce Fajah to her new lifestyle in the international sex-trade." He pulled Kristen out of the bedroom, and shut the door behind him. Fajah realized what he had in mind as the General approached her with a sick grin and nauseating hunger in his eyes. He reached for her, and she backed into a corner and began a silent scream.

Then everything became quiet–an aura of calm enveloped her and every fiber in her body and mind became focused. She had a clear picture of pushing the General away. The air around her became thick, almost visibly creating a cushion of air that surrounded Fajah. The General came for her, entering her protective shield, and found himself struggling against the thick airwaves of energy being created by Fajah. He fought as if swimming upstream against a strong current. Forcing himself harder against the unseen pressure, a perplexed look came across his face. The harder he struggled, the more solid the invisible obstruction became. His face turned darker and darker shades of red in anger as he fought.

"What the hell are you doing, you little..." Before he could finish his verbal attack, the air was wrenched from his lungs and he froze in place, unable to even blink. An isolated anguish wrapped him in this transparent cocoon, slowly absorbing his anger and pain, filling every molecule in his body with a fire. A fire of love that began to burn away emotional scars, starting with his most recent self-inflicted memories, searing away the damaging sexual thoughts that filled his mind just moments ago. Replacing the voids left by those vacated intentions with tender intimate introspection.

At the precise instant he was fully bound by his most intimate soul-searching introspection, Fajah filled her silent scream with a thunderous vibration that suffused the room with a violent wave of sound that nearly split his skull. As she did, the solid air snapped back into its natural state. He shrunk to his knees, tears cascading from his eyes. His body collapsed as though his spine had been pulled from his skeleton.

Red smashed in the door and ran into the room, finding the General laying in a fetal position on the floor, whimpering uncontrollably.

* * *

When Duncan entered the warehouse apartment, he found the General laying on a stained couch with a pillow propped under his head and a glazed look on his face. Red was returning from the kitchen with a wet washcloth, and placed it on the General's forehead. "That should help with the headache." Then he realized someone was standing in the doorway. "Oh, Duncan, I'm surprised to see you here."

Duncan gave Red a crooked grin, then looked through a cracked opening in the smashed door leading to the bedroom. A filthy spotted window filtered enough light to barely illuminate the room, just enough to chase the shadows into the corners. Scarcely visible, two young girls sat back-to-back under the window on the floor. They were tied to a rusted old hot water radiator heater next to a mattress in the tenebrous corner of the room. The chipped paint on the walls and baseboard leading to the bedroom exposed layers of long-forgotten paint colors the room had once modeled. The cracked laminate floor with missing tiles finished the room's bleak decor.

"What a piss-hole apartment, General. I feel like I'm going to catch a disease in here. What are you doing with those young girls in the other room? Never mind, I really don't want to know. The reason I am here is to find Ian. I understand you have him."

The General squinted, as if trying to focus his eyes. "What gave you that

126

idea, Duncan? Oh, you recognized Kristen? Yes, I have Ian's daughter, and her little friend. I figured we can use them to barter with her father when we find him. But I was under the impression that you, or rather Rebel, has Ian."

Duncan ignored him, and nodded to the back room. "Well–DO NOT harm the girls, they will prove to be an important part of our Jump master plan. This technology will secure our country as the world's super power for the next millennium. We cannot allow another country to get their hands on Ian or his toys. Anyone found interfering with this will be considered a terrorist and tried accordingly–if you catch my meaning. I will send a team over to secure the girls. We will hold them in a more appropriate location where they will be cared for properly. If anyone should ask, you do not know where they are."

Duncan turned as he was leaving the apartment. "Do not go anywhere. I'll be back with a team to pick up the girls within the hour..." Before he finished that statement, Duncan saw a slight glimmer come from the bedroom. He recognized this, as not really a light, more of a disturbance in the air. In an instant, he was halfway to the bedroom, pulling the Collar from his pocket.

127

CHAPTER 13
Collared

Jasmine, the most recent addition to their Gaian family, walked with Louise and Akira along a naturally flowing spring, surrounded by wildflowers. Louise was telling her about living in Gaia, after having introduced her to some of the many families living along the canyon, that called the Falls home.

Then Akira instructed Jasmine about the different reality she would find in this new dimension. Jasmine was having trouble with her first lesson–creating objects. Being new to Gaia, she attempted to create a simple cup in order to take a drink from the natural spring water. Midway during her creation the vessel's shape changed, then fell apart. The cup actually warped before her eyes and returned to its natural state. She didn't know whether to laugh or cry.

Akira patiently continued her instruction. "In order to understand why your cup changed, you must first understand physical creation in Gaia. Physics work very differently in this world. On Earth, let's say you were going to build a room. In order to manifest this room–first, you would have to decide what that room would look like. Make a blueprint, get the materials you would build it from, decide where you would build it, etc. Have those materials delivered to the site. And then finally, physically construct those materials according to Earth's physical laws."

Louise inserted a note into their lesson. "Remember, dear, in Gaia things are built of Spirit. Spirit is not a force, like gravity or electromagnetism. Consciousness is derived of Spirit. The universe is alive, and we are a part of it. All matter originates and exists by the virtue of an omnipresent force that we all know as Spirit."

"Thank you, Louise, I could not have said it better." Akira continued, "Things in Gaia manifest much more quickly than on Earth. Thoughts create on Gaia. They build from the image you hold in your heart, combining Spirit and the available physical materials from Mother Earth. These natural elements manifest according to the strength of your desire.

In other words, Love Creates."

"You do not have to understand the physical compounds necessary to create glass, though those compounds would need to be available in the area you are influencing. You create that glass by firmly holding an unmistakable vision of the size, shape and place you want the glass to materialize. Glass will behave as glass does anywhere, even in Gaia. There are physical laws for the thickness that can be created without it failing, just as on Earth. For instance, too thin a glass in a size that is too large will shatter from its own weight. When building in Gaia, we cannot build unnatural, unsustainable elements. That is an understood physical law, different than on Earth. We work in harmony with our physical world. Unnatural compounds such as plastic will not manifest here—because they are not built entirely from natural elements."

At exactly the same instant a disturbing feeling struck the three of them. "Something is horribly wrong," Jasmine screamed. "Kristen...my baby... we have to help her!"

Louise tightly held Jasmine in her arms. "Take a deep breath, dear. There is a strong feeling of love being emitted from Fajah, that surrounds the fear-filled energy you feel from your daughter. I am sure that she is all right for now, but we should do something quickly. I haven't felt such a burst of pure energy since Celeste blew apart her home."

Jasmine's eyes popped wide open. "Blew what up? Where?"

"Do not worry, this is somehow different. I sense no physical destruction, just a scorching light of truth burning away an intensely dark persona. Fajah is helping Kristen, though they are both very frightened." Akira asked Louise to watch after Jasmine. "I'll help Kristen—be right back." And Akira was gone.

* * *

Standing in the dark corner of a dingy room, Akira's eyes took a few seconds to acclimate before she could make out Fajah and Kristen, tied to a decrepit cast-iron radiator. She could feel their fear hanging in the air. Their terror merged with the shadows and seemed to fight the murky light filtering through the grimy window above their heads. Akira bent down to free the captives when she sensed someone rushing into the room.

Duncan charged into the room and saw a young lady kneeling beside the girls, working feverishly to untie them. He dove at Akira and swung the Collar at her neck. 'Click.'

Stunned into silence, Akira sat heavily, unable to pull energy for defense or escape. She felt helpless and alone, cut off from her very existence. Powerless! Akira had never felt so forsaken. She knew there were others in the room, and around her throughout the block. She had felt them just seconds before. Now there was nothing, she couldn't even feel her own heart beating. This void was overwhelming, the silence so profound it hurt.

* * *

Two thousand miles away, Louise lost her breath. "Akira is gone!"

It was hard to explain to Jasmine, the connection she and Akira shared. She could perceive her energy from thousands of miles away. Her presence was a tiny pressure that rested in her mind's eye just behind her right ear inside her skull. Almost imperceptible until it was gone. Where that presence once lived, there was now an empty hole. Where was Akira? What has happened to her? She just blinked out, like a light switch was flipped off.

Louise and Jasmine sank to the ground overcome by a shared vision. Sitting on smooth sandstone overlooking the Falls, their familiar surroundings became immersed in a celestial battle. Many hundreds, possibly thousands, set siege against a group of seven. Faces were unclear, but they could sense a goodness pulling this group of seven together as a single strength, standing against this torrent of terror.

Their valley became engulfed by darkness as the battle raged through the rocky canyon filling it with crying children, fear and chaos. "Our valley has become a vale of tears," Jasmine whispered and began to cry silently. They cringed as the evil, heavy gloom overwhelmed their glorious home with a horrific struggle, like neither of them had ever witnessed. All was lost in blackness. An eerie silence extended seemingly forever.

* * *

That was a new sound. For countless hours, not sure how many, Ian had been sitting in the dark, with a mask over his eyes. The coarse rope cut into his wrists that were tightly bound behind his back. He had heard, recognized and categorized numerous sounds. The sound of traffic from a nearby highway formed an almost soothing flow, like the waves in the ocean, as the daily commerce moved, slowed then moved again. He estimated the train rail was five, possibly six blocks further away than the highway noise. He felt akin to the distant haunting sound of the train whistle–as it moved away in the night, it sounded as isolated as he felt. The old building creaked once in a while, and the sound of mice scratched behind the walls–he hoped it wasn't rats. There was a broken or open window somewhere, pigeons roosted in the rafters a couple of stories overhead. The dusty old smell of machine oil suggested the warehouse he was in had been abandoned for a long time.

In the distance, church bells chimed regularly, so he knew it was 12:00 midnight. Time for the late shift whistle at the metal recycling plant down the street, and the train was due along the tracks about now. Church bells sparked an anamnesis of Jasmine. He missed his beautiful wife so much. For all extents, she was dead. But not really? How was he going to tell Alek and Kristen about their mother? Were they all right, staying with their friend Grace, and what was Grace's mother Logan going to think– that he abandoned his children? His life of a few weeks ago had been turned on its head. That existence seemed like another lifetime.

What was that–footsteps? This new sound pulled on his mind, forcing him back from his thoughts. Something or someone was in the building. That made his skin crawl. "Hello, who are you? What do you want? Don't hurt me, I have children."

A few seconds passed before he had a reply with a heavy Asian accent. "No, I will not harm you. I come in peace. That is what they say in your American movies. I came to get you out of here."

The mask was pulled off, but there was only enough illumination to make out the vague features of a man standing behind the glare of a flashlight. Ian rubbed his eyes and questioned, "Who are you?"

"You do not know me. My name is Yaozu Lei, I am an artist. But right now that matters little. Akira is a mutual friend. She told me you were in Washington, DC and in trouble. She asked me to find you. And lucky I found you when I did. I have been trying to get some dirt, as you might say, on Qian. The other day I was able to plant a bug in Cui Chao Qian's office, before the General and he spoke."

"Hold it, what are you saying? The General, the same nut case that kidnapped me? And who is Qian?"

"Qian is the chairman of the Ministry of National Defense at the Embassy of the People's Republic of China. He is attempting to buy you from the General."

"This is getting more insane all the time. Let me get this straight. A world famous artist from China–I know your work–is saving me from a crazy person who calls himself 'The General,' that is selling me to the Chinese Embassy?"

"Yes, that is about it. Let's get out of here, they will be here soon. I looped their video to show the same five minutes over again but they will figure it out soon and come to check on you." Yaozu told Ian to hold onto his hand and he might be able to Jump them to another location using a similar principle as his technology. "Akira told me it is the same as when she brought your father to see you after your unique golf outing." Yaozu swung his arms holding an imaginary club in jest, then took Ian's hand.

Nothing happened.

"Stop right there!"

Pigeons scattered from the strength of the insistent command as it reverberated through the warehouse. Startled, Ian looked up toward the fluttering sound of the bird's wings. Particles of dust floated in the moonlight filtering through a broken window, where the birds escaped. Rushing, heavy footsteps came their direction echoing in the darkness.

Yaozu pulled Ian along. "Hurry, we have to get out of here now!" They ducked around a nearby corner and took off running . Hurrying down a short hall past the broken windows of old offices, the pair turned again, entering another large open room. Ian saw a faint light squeezing through a cracked door opening about 20 yards ahead. He started for the door, with the promise of escape and being able to see again.

Yaozu grabbed his arm. "Over here." He headed for a dark corner of the warehouse without any means of escape.

Ian pulled back. Yaozu continued. "Trust me, I can see a dimensional energy shift that will allow us to Jump." He pointed to a corner. "Over there–the veil between our worlds is attenuated there, much thinner." Yaozu pulled Ian forward. "Now!"

Without time to think, Ian sprang ahead, stumbling as his next step brought him head-long toward a turn-of-the-century old brick castle, bathed in the bright daylight of early afternoon. Startled and half blind, he squinted from the burning light making it difficult to see. Ian could just make out pine trees bordering a pristine grass lawn. The lawn was growing on a steep hill, surrounded by rock walls leading to a large building.

As Ian's eyes cleared, he realized that it was not actually a castle, though it was built in a similar style. Four tiers of steps led up to a grand medieval-style Scottish baronial three-story brick building. The entrance with a corbeled arch spanned four framed doors with eight panels of stained-glass lancet windows above the doors. He saw four dormers protruding from the roof, each with two windows. The uneven roof had two towers adorned by small turrets and an ornamental chimney with four round clay stacks. Ian felt like he had been transported back in time.

"Welcome to Montsalvat artist studios in Victoria, Australia, outside of Melbourne," Yaozu said. "The Montsalvat patron was kind enough to offer me studio space after the Chinese government tore down my studio. You can stay with me to keep a low profile while you figure out your next move. Let me take you to my studio where you can shower and change clothes, and I'll give you a quick tour on the way there."

Yaozu showed Ian a varied mix of buildings making up Australia's oldest artists' colony. He explained that with the bug in Qian's office he had discovered that the General had his daughter Kristen along with Fajah.

"That monster has Kristen! Why didn't you tell me that first? I have to go get her."

"That is exactly why I did not tell you before now. You cannot charge in to save Kristen, like some super-hero without a plan. Ah, we are here, this is my studio. Come inside, get cleaned up, then we will all develop a plan, and have a much better chance of saving Kristen and Fajah."

Ian's demeanor was obviously anxious, but he agreed with Yaozu. "We'll come up with a plan after I wash up. A shower sounds really good. But have you heard anything about my son or father? Gregory had my dad, Steele and Celeste last I know of. Are all of them all right?"

"I am sorry, I know nothing about any of them. I will check with everyone at the Falls and see if they can tell us anything."

* * *

"Director Rebel, good...glad to see you. I have it! Look–look–right here."

Rebel had never seen Walter so excited, and that was saying a lot, since they had worked together for over fifteen years, and Walter could get quite animated at times.

Walter was on the verge of exploding with excitement. "Here–look–Ian's notes on sequencing the human DNA are so totally innovative!" He pointed to a white-board full of scribbled formulas. "Pyrosequencing is it. The method of DNA sequencing he is using. Brilliant! This determines the order of nucleotides in DNA, based on the 'sequencing by synthesis' principle. You may not know that it relies on the detection of pyrophosphate release on nucleotide incorporation, rather than chain termination with dideoxynucleotides. This is very exciting, very exciting indeed, from the standpoint of high energy phosphate accounting. The hydrolysis of ATP to AMP and PPi requires two high-energy phosphates, as to reconstitute AMP into ATP using two phosphorylation reactions. Look at this formula–it is so simple...it's...it's dazzling." He was pounding on the board with a green dry erase marker, pointing along the scribbled formula–(AMP + ATP $\rightarrow$ 2 ADP = 2 ADP + 2 Pi $\rightarrow$ 2 ATP). "Can you believe that!"

"Walter, slow down. I know you are trying to tell me something, and it appears to be very exciting. But I have no earthly idea what you are talking about."

Walter had obviously been working for many hours. He had two open cans of RockStar energy drink on his desk, along with half a dried-out pizza. Strands of his long gray hair had pulled free from his ponytail and were sticking out every direction. His eyes were wide with excitement. "Oh, yes... I'm sorry. Guess I get ahead of myself sometimes." He looked around his office and IT area quickly as if getting his coordinates and making sure they were alone.

"Take a breath, Walter, and see if you can explain to me what it is that has you all stirred up."

"Oh, Rebel, that's simple. I recreated the sequencing formula that enables us to Jump!" Walter leaped into the air as he finished the word 'jump.' "I sent you an email as soon as I returned."

"Returned from where, Walter."

"That doesn't matter. What matters is that I went, and I returned!"

"Walter, you are talking nonsense."

"Not at all, no, sir, I sequenced my DNA and took a Jump over there, and here I am right back here again—so it works!"

* * *

Commander Victor Gholam addressed his platoon the following Friday in a secure briefing room. "Gentlemen. As Navy Seals, we demand discipline. We expect innovation. The lives of your teammates and the success of our mission depend on you—on your technical skill, tactical proficiency and attention to detail. As you know, your training is never complete. We train for war—to fight, to win. Stand ready to bring the full spectrum of combat power to bear in order to achieve the mission and the goals established by our country."

He continued. "The execution of our duties will be swift and violent, when required, yet guided by the very principles that we serve to defend. Your brothers are brave men who have fought and many died building the proud tradition and feared reputation that you are all bound to uphold. In the worst of conditions, the legacy of your teammates' steady resolve will silently guide our every deed. You will not fail."

Director Rebel and Walter stood beside 'Free Jump' Commander Gholam as he spoke to his men. "Your ASVAB scores are top notch, proving your mental sharpness and ability to learn. The sixteen of you have been divided into eight man squads, each with two 4-man Fire Teams. You men are the best of the best, brought together for operation Free Jump. You are here for training in secret technology, known to exist by only a select few in the entire world. The missions, following your training, will be dangerous. You will not speak of this to anyone. This information will go to the grave with you. Do you understand me?"

"YES, SIR!" the sixteen shouted in unison.

"Today you will have your DNA sequenced." Commander Gholam directed the men's attention to Walter. "Men, this is Walter from Homeland Security. He will take samples of your blood for sequencing. Jump training begins in the morning. This training will allow you to move freely around the world. This training will enable us to deploy you anywhere in the world within seconds. Report Wednesday at 0400. Now, line up single file for Walter's needle. Dismissed."

Saturday morning, pre-dawn in the Homeland Security IT department, found Walter standing at the Portal door, grinning ear to ear as the last man vanished through the opening.

The platoon re-grouped quickly in a dark field wearing their full combat gear, firearms drawn, many miles from where they stood just seconds before. They recognized the deserted airstrip from previous trainings.

Commander Gholam yelled with authority. "Not bad. You sixteen men have just traveled one hundred miles in ten seconds. I want to see it done in half that time. Go back and be ready to do it again on my mark." This was already the sixth Jump that morning, and the sun had not yet decided to join the Free Jump platoon.

* * *

After their shared vision Louise and Jasmine hurriedly found Jaguar. He was talking to Max, Grandstaff and Star. "Kristen is in trouble, and Akira is gone!" Louise interrupted. "She went to help Kristen and just vanished." Jaguar's concern was visible against his normally calm demeanor.

He looked around the hastily assembled group. "Where is Yaozu Lei?"

Max looked at Jaguar. "Yaozu went to DC to rescue Ian. I'll fill him in on what we decided to do when I see him again."

"All right, then I'll continue. Akira, Fajah and Kristen are not our only concern." Star walked to Jaguar's side as he continued. "There have been many disturbances in the energy between our worlds. It is evident that the United States government has learned to travel using Ian's technology. Star and I followed the resulting energy corruption to a computer science building in Washington, DC, where an entire military platoon has made numerous Jumps over the last few days."

"Since they do not resonate with Gaia's dimension, the heavy energy from this large group of people is quickly damaging the veil between our worlds. If this increased pace of Jumps continues, our ability to help our brothers and sisters in Earth's dimension will cease. We will be unable to reach across the barrier in any fashion. Dreams, premonitions, and intuitions will all be gone. Even the strongest of us won't be able to give someone that gut feeling–NO contact! Those on Earth who do reach a higher energy level will be unable to graduate to this world. Mankind will be stuck again in a dark age similar to the time following the collapse of the Roman Empire."

Then Star addressed the group. "We are not sure at this point if Akira's disappearance has anything to do with these increased Jumps. All I could feel is..." She paused and swallowed back tears. "I could feel her spirit in the DC area, then instantly she was gone. I'm not sure what that means. With the connection Akira and I share, I would feel her essence, even if she were to pass from this world."

Louise forced a weak smile. "So she has not passed on?"

"No, we do not believe she has. I am confident you could feel her passing, as I do, Louise–though you have not had that experience yet. This is different. Not like anything I, or even Jaguar, has ever experienced in his thousand years in Gaia."

"I'm going after her," Star insisted. "I know where she was less than an hour ago, when she vanished. Who is coming with me?"

Grandstaff took a step toward Star and placed a large hand on her shoulder. "Letz goo, I aum vith you."

"Hold on just one minute," Jaguar insisted. "We have to put together a plan. Quickly gather around." Jaguar waved his hand over a nearby table, and a faint map appeared to draw itself out of thin air. "This is where I last sensed Akira." The area he indicated was about a four square miles area around the Potomac River and Washington Channel in Washington, DC.

"Close–she was right here." Louise moved his finger about six miles north and east just above a knotted interchange where the John Hanson Highway and Baltimore Washington Parkway entangled. Louise enlarged the detailed aerial map, showing an area of rundown old warehouses and gently re-positioned his finger on one particular building. "I could feel the location when she went to rescue Kristen and Fajah. She was there not long ago, so we must be quick if we are going to find her."

"Let us go then," Jaguar said. "Max, would you find Yaozu, and see if he and Ian are together? Louise, Star, Grandstaff and I will go to DC and find Akira. Let us all meet back here by this time tomorrow."

"That is a good plan, Jaguar, thank you. But you three can find Akira without me," Star said. "So I am going to check on Celeste and her husband. They were hurt badly in the accident, and I have to tell them about Isis. I know you healed them, Jaguar, but they are new at dealing with the dual dimensions and must have concerns right now."

Louise took Star's hand. "I feel energy from Celeste and Steele now, they are using the crystal. Feel my connection, and go to them. Please tell them I am sorry I could not come to them right now, and that I will see them soon." Star could tell exactly where they were by Louise's connection to them through the crystal, and began to organize her thoughts.

"We have to find Akira, and discover a way to stop the disintegration of the veil between our worlds before it is too late," Jaguar said. "Be very careful everyone. We have no idea what they used to erase Akira, or if they can do it again to any one of us. See you all tomorrow, have a safe journey."

CHAPTER 14
Rescue

From the looks of it, the overhead street light had obviously been broken for some time. That masked this part of the block in an inky darkness—even more gloomy than the rain and almost moonless night already made this industrial district. A van slowly approached as Louise, Jaguar and Grandstaff huddled next to an old rusted red boxcar covered in gang-marked graffiti. The group retreated behind the boxcar and watched the headlights reflect from the rain-soaked street as the van passed. Jaguar's black onyx eyes stared trance-like, extending his consciousness around them.

"Kristen and Fajah are up there, and Akira must be with them." He pointed to a small window in the back corner of the old brick warehouse, near the boxcar where the three of them stood.

"Can you sense Akira?" Louise asked.

"Not sure, but there is tremendous residue from an ethereal energy burst emanating from that room. Akira is one of only a few that can generate that kind of spirit. Grandstaff, would you keep watch while Louise and I see if we can rescue our friends?" The shaman stroked his graying Fu Manchu mustache and bowed his head in agreement.

Jaguar and Louise disappeared, materializing seconds later in a dingy, dark room. Louise knelt next to Akira with a finger across her lip, miming silence, and whispered, "Dear, are you all right?" Light from a cracked open door formed an angular shaped glow, that filtered across the tiny room. Akira's form was suffused by the faint light that barely reached her limp body. She was laying on the dirty floor, handcuffed to an old cast-iron radiator, with an odd Collar around her neck.

Faint voices drifted in from the adjacent room. "Hit me, and it better be a good card. Kristen, fetch me a beer from the back of the fridge, make sure it's cold."

Jaguar surveyed the other room. He could sense the two men along with Kristen and Fajah. He turned and whispered to Louise, "Akira doesn't look well! That thing around her neck is affecting her energy, dropping her resonance to a dangerous level. We have to get her out of here. Can you Jump to the street with her?"

Concern radiated from Louise. "No! That Collar is holding her energy too low, I cannot travel with her."

"See what you can do for her, I'll be right back." Jaguar scrutinized the two captors playing cards. He recognized the General from the impressions Akira had given him, after she met the General in the Bahamas. But Jaguar had no idea who the red-headed kid was. He was certain there were only four people in the room—the two men at the table and two young girls in the kitchen.

Compacting the air around the table, Jaguar silently held the General and his friend captive. Sudden looks of confusion and terror crossed their faces when they realized neither of them could move. Jaguar stepped into the room to rescue the girls.

"Click." Duncan snapped the Collar in place.

Surprise struck Jaguar, like a hundred pounds thrown around his neck. Why didn't he sense another person in the room? Jaguar was unable to withstand the heavy energy keeping him captive. He felt helpless and alone, cut off from everything. Powerless! He pulled on the Collar around his neck. Freed from Jaguar's force field, the two men leaped from the table. The General grabbed the 9mm from beside him.

"Don't move." A wicked smile contorted the General's face. "Well, well, whom do we have here? I see you like the Collar our mad scientist Walter created. That was some display of power, holding us in place as you did. I must learn that trick. You have to be one of those from the other side—one of Akira's friends. I believe little Fajah called you Jaguar. She threatened, saying you would come after me. But you don't look so tough, now that you are Collared. Jaguar, you are on the losing team. Homeland Security has Ian's father and son, James and Alek. While I have Ian, Kristen, Fajah, Akira...and, oh, yes you—the mighty Jaguar."

"Red, look in the other room, and see who came with our friend here." Kristen and Fajah cowered in the corner, hugging one another, as Red walked past them into the bedroom. With help from Louise, Akira had pulled herself to a sitting position against the wall. One arm propped on her knee, with her head resting on the open palm. Louise had Jumped seconds before Red entered the room. "No one here but that bitch."

"All right," agreed the General. "Keep an eye on her. Duncan, I told you to stick around and someone would come for Akira. I'm really beginning to like those Collars. Tell you what. You give me these Collars along with the bodies they're attached to and I'll give you Fajah. Does that sound fair, two Collars for the little girl? That's cheap at twice the price."

Duncan considered the options, he knew what the General would do with her, and he hoped Jaguar and Akira could find a way to take care of themselves. Damn, he hated having a conscience–maybe he would keep the Collars? His better side won his inner conflict and chose to save Fajah. He reluctantly agreed, handing the light keys for the two occupied Collars to the General. "I want Kristen also," he bargained.

"Not for your life, Duncan, you greedy son of a bitch," the General yelled. "Get out of here before I change my mind."

Reluctantly leaving Akira, Louise had popped onto the shadowy street next to Grandstaff, expressing to him her grave concerns. "Akira has a Collar around her neck. It is draining her energy. I believe it is killing her! If we do not save her, she will be pulled back to the other dimension and have to be reborn. And somehow, they were able to put one of those godforsaken Collars on Jaguar. The Collar shields the person holding it, by some means, so Jaguar did not realize another person was in the room until it was too late. What are we going to do, Grandstaff?" Louise was beside herself. How could everything have gone so wrong?

As the two considered their options, they saw Duncan come out of the building, mumbling to Fajah as he pulled her to a sedan parked across the street. "I'll get you to safety then I'll come back after Kristen." Fajah pulled, and dragged her feet, screaming. She was glad to be away from the General, but was afraid for Kristen and didn't know what Duncan wanted with her. Glancing around the dark, scary street, she thought about running. But where would she go?

Duncan opened the car door, and pushed her inside. "Don't move, if you know what is good for you." Slamming the door, he walked to the driver's side, climbed in and started the car.

Grandstaff gritted his teeth, "I hav haad enouff." He vanished, appearing in the back seat of Duncan's car, and immediately wrapped his massive arms around Duncan, pinning him against the front seat. Louise was suddenly standing by the vehicle and tried to wrap their antagonist in air as Jaguar had been teaching her, but the attempt failed.

Duncan bit Grandstaff's wrist, pulled free and pushed a handgun against Fajah, and commanded–"Either of you try anything else and she gets a bullet." Duncan motioned to Grandstaff, "Now get out before I shoot all of you."

As the big shaman stepped out of the back seat, Duncan hit the gas, knocking Grandstaff to the ground. Seconds later, Duncan's car turned out of sight around the corner.

Louise was helping him to his feet when the van that passed earlier rounded the corner. Louise and Grandstaff scurried to the boxcar's shadow. The van quickly stopped in front of the building. One man immediately jumped from the sliding cargo door, ran to the warehouse and quietly opened the door. He was followed into the building by four other men, all dressed in black loose-fitting clothes with their entire heads masked.

Louise gave Grandstaff a puzzled look. "They look like something out of the movies. Are there really ninjas anymore and do they dress like that?"

He shook his head. "Noo, I believe zey Chineze mielitery spesiel fourrcez grooup. Loouise, juomp oover to z tops of zat buildink acrrooz z streetz, yoou vill be saef. Ond keep ah eye oon thinkz. I aom gooink insides end sees voot I con doo. Doon't vorry, I vill kep my distense, I hav noo intentions of beink Coollared."

Louise Jumped, and watched from a hidden spot on the roof across the street. Focusing her complete attention on Grandstaff, she could feel his anxious energy. The faint hum from the van's idling engine was the only sound escaping the gloom of the starless night.

Pop! A single muffled gunshot from inside the building cracked the silence, causing her heart to skip a beat. Then nothing.

A few minutes later, Louise saw the men in black push four people out of the warehouse. The captives' wrists were bound, with bags pulled over their heads. The night's ebony darkness made it difficult to see, but Louise was sure two of the four were Akira and Jaguar. The others must be the General and his accomplice. That would account for everyone except Grandstaff and Kristen.

Was Grandstaff okay? With his energy so scattered it was hard to determine. Louise worried, but waited.

The van slowly pulled away. As it turned out of sight, Louise popped over to the apartment. Grandstaff was standing in the kitchen consoling the crying Kristen. Louise spread her welcoming arms. "It will be all right, Kristen, we have you now." She ran into Louise's outstretched arms, receiving a big hug.

"The bad men have Fajah!" Kristen whimpered, trying to catch her breath.

"Do not worry, we will get her back," Louise said, then asked Grandstaff what had happened "I heard a gunshot. Who were those people?"

"Noo oone vas shout. Thes General hardlys hed time too greb heis guns, oon did noot hit anyvone. As for vho they vere? They ver orgoonezed lekea mielitery groops. Spooke z Chinezea, boot seda verry little. I herrd von ofs zem sayz somthings aubootz Qian."

Unexpectedly, Louise and Grandstaff felt Max attempting to communicate from Australia. They tuned into his energy , and within a few moments they had exchanged recent occurrences with one another. Louise thought back to the first time she communicated this way. It was so much more concise than a phone call or even video conference. With thought transference, they all exchanged emotions, ideas, even visual impressions along with their thoughts. They created a complete picture of recent developments, like you were inside the other's skin, experiencing what they felt.

"Let us all get out of here." Grandstaff nodded his head to Louise.

"Yoou tekes Kristen too sefetyz at z Faulls und meetz vith the oothers. I aom foulloinks Akira and Jagvuar, befoore I looz z energizes froom thoose in z van." Grandstaff wavered, merged with the air and vanished. Louise hugged Kristen, they took a deep breath together, and flash...

...they appeared at the Falls. "That was fun!" Kristen exclaimed. Then shouted, ecstatic at seeing who was there waiting. MOM! Kristen sprang into Jasmine's waiting arms.

* * *

Max was translucent, so Ian hardly noticed him when they entered Yaozu's studio at Montsalvat in Melbourne, after their escape from the DC warehouse. Max stood in a hypnotic state, staring blankly at the door. He didn't seem to notice that Ian and Yaozu were in the room.

"Hello." Ian looked at Yaozu questioningly, then hesitantly waved his hand in front of Max's face.

"Ah... g'day, mates." Max became more solid as he spoke. "I was just visiting with Grandstaff and Louise." Yaozu introduced Ian and Max and they shook hands. "Good to meet you, Ian. You will be happy as Larry, to hear that Louise has Kristen."

"They have my daughter! Oh, thank God–she is all right. That monster didn't touch her, did he? Where are Alek, Fajah and my dad, wait–who is Larry?"

"Ha, so many questions. Yes, Kristen is right as rain, with her mother. And Louise tells me that Alek and James are safe for now–Homeland Security has them. And Larry? Oh, that's just an expression down under–it means very happy."

Max went on. "Seems that a Chinese military special forces group just liberated your daughter, and captured the General, his friend Red, and our friends Akira and Jaguar. Duncan took Fajah from the General. The bloke Duncan, and the General have some sort of Collar that anchors the person wearing it in a limbo between our two worlds. Akira and Jaguar are being forced to wear this new jewelry and they cannot remove it or escape."

"Chinese special forces? Collars? Kidnaping my kids, and the Department of Homeland Security is after me, not to mention, transparent people, different worlds in new dimensions?" Ian sunk heavily onto the couch, holding his head in bewilderment. "I feel like I'm caught in the twilight zone. What has happened to my life? Jump technology really opened Pandora's box. What was I thinking?"

Yaozu calmly walked to the refrigerator and pulled out a six-pack of beer, handed a can to Max, took one himself and gave the other four to Ian. "Relax and try to take your mind off of things, Alek and Kristen are safe for now. Once you have had some rest, Max and I will help you get Alek back."

Yaozu nodded reassuringly. "Feel free to take a shower, you are ripe. Then you can crash on the couch. There is plenty of food in the fridge, if you're hungry–make yourself at home. No harm will come to you here."

Ian looked up, Max and Yaozu had moved to the doorway. "We have a meeting at the Falls, but we'll be back in a few hours."

As they shut the front door, Max turned to Yaozu. "I do not know how you maintain your body for extended visits in the lower Earth energies. I have a difficult time there–my body feels so heavy."

Yaozu nodded. "That is why I excused us when I did. I could tell you were having a hard time holding the lower dimension. We can explain this to Ian later, he has enough to grasp right now. Let's go, it is about the time Jaguar asked us to all meet back at the Falls. We have to figure a way to straighten out this mess." Yaozu and Max both vanished into Gaia.

"Ian, wake up, dear, you have been sleeping for 12 hours." Louise sat next to Ian on the couch, gently urging him out of a deep sleep. She had both a smile and strong cup of black coffee waiting. "I hate to wake you, but we need to talk and then we'll find James, Alek and Fajah." Ian slowly sat up and took a sip of coffee, rubbed his eyes and looked around the studio.

Yaozu was rustling through some sketches next to an easel and Max sat at the table eating an apple. Louise continued. "We have just returned from the Falls, where Yaozu, Max and I met with the others to determine the best way to free your family and little Fajah. Kristen is safe at the Falls with her mother, and from what I overheard, your father, Alek and Fajah are being held by Homeland Security."

"We developed a plan to save them, and if it works, will also alleviate the negative influences from the Jumps that are destroying the veil between Earth and Gaia. As you remember from our previous gathering at the Falls, when people who are not enlightened use your Jump technology, it causes the veil between our worlds to become more dense. This reduces the resonance of the mantle between worlds. We will not be able to move between Earth and Gaia, if these Jumps are not stopped—or at the very least used only by those with a higher spiritual awareness."

Ian was feeling guilty about creating the technology. "I am so sorry, I never intended any of these consequences. I didn't even realize the Gaia dimension existed. The dimensional shift was figured into my equations, but the fact that people actually lived in this dimension never occurred to me."

"We know that, dear, do not feel guilty," Louise reassured. "That is not my intention for telling you about the ramification of this technology. My reason is to help you understand and to ask for your help. You understand from an intellectual level that increasing the vibrational energy of a person actually helps them reach a higher state of awareness. And that this state of being is necessary to move between our worlds. That must be an important part of your equations that enabled you to create this technology. We believe this understanding will help you make others recognize the necessary transition between intellect and understanding. Pure understanding. That is, understanding in your being, in your soul–an understanding that will ultimately transform your energy to a higher dimension, without the use of technology."

Ian smiled. "Louise, I would be more than happy to help any way I can. I understand from my yoga trainer, that killing my ego is a first step to this state of higher understanding."

With the knowing grin of a true teacher, Louise replied. "Well, yes and no. Many spiritual teachers instruct their pupils to eliminate the ego, which in itself is not the only initial path. There is not one path to enlightenment. An old Yogi instructor of mine, Yogi Ramacharaka, believed people must first use their ego to understand their place in the world. To personalize that, Ian, you must use your ego, not let it use you."

Ian nodded an understanding so Louise continued. "Earth is one of many worlds that are schools for the development of our cosmic self. Earth compacts spirit, forcing it to require a physical body. This body is necessary to survive, until which time the spirit awakens enough to function independently. Gaia is a step between the need for your body and the spiritual freedom to function fully without your Earth suit. I believe the ego is necessary to help the uninitiated to understand that they are the center of their universe–to understand the absolute spark they carry within themselves. We will go into all of this more deeply at another time."

"But right now, our plan to alleviate the problem is to ask the government agency using this technology to create a training program. This program could recruit and train Jumpers to understand these truths and increase their frequency to a point that does not harm the mantle between our worlds. This would take some time, but it would solve a very serious problem."

"That all sounds good," Ian said, "but how is this going to save my family and little Fajah?"

"This government program is Homeland Security, their interest in your technology and your family are all related," Yaozu interjected. "We are confident that we can discover more about Alek and James while we are speaking with them. And convince the government to release them into your custody."

Ian thought for a minute. "That sounds like it could work. However, I don't believe they will understand, or for that matter, even listen to any of this."

Max threw the apple core in the trash and wiped his mouth. "Well, son, that's where a bloke like you comes in. Mean no disrespect, calling you 'son.' Seems everyone is younger than I am, so I call everyone 'son.' Tell me if it ruffles your feathers. Anyway, with instruction, we believe you can increase your frequency to a point that will not harm the mantle. Then we need to find a sympathetic person from the government, preferably a scientist, whom we can instruct to run tests proving our argument."

Ian shook his head. "There is another big issue here. First you need to convince them that the Gaia dimension actually exists."

Louise took Ian's hand in hers. "We never said it would be easy, but what would be the fun in that? Nonetheless, we have to try. The alternative is to destroy the technology, and somehow erase the knowledge from everyone who understands how it works."

A sad expression moved through Ian's body, causing his shoulders to slump. "That might be best. This technology will ultimately be used for war, and in the wrong hands can cause catastrophic consequences. I was planning to destroy everything just before they attacked me in my home and took the Wand, and my life away. I don't trust anyone with this."

Louise smiled. "Destroying it all will be a last resort. There is value in what you have created. But first-things-first. Let us outline our plan to rescue Alek, your father and Fajah."

CHAPTER 15
Opulence

Bishop Daniel smiled to himself as he walked through the empty foyer in Bishop's Hall. The fundraiser, a few days ago, had been a great success. The money raised would help so many families. From his church's donations through Daniel's charities, of course. Not to mention paying off his private Gulfstream G5 jet. He made a mental note to order the upgrades for his jet when he paid it off next week.

As he approached his office, he noticed the door was slightly ajar. Daniel slowly pushed the heavy, carved mahogany door open, listening for an intruder.

His Tiffany desk lamp suddenly switched on, adding a warm green glow to the dark furniture in the room. Duncan sat back in Daniel's 19th century green leather desk chair with his arms propped behind his head. On the Bishop's antique French walnut Louis XV writing desk was an empty crystal candy dish, next to a partially filled brandy snifter and an open bottle of his best Louis XIII Cognac.

The Cognac and snifter should be sitting on the marble top of the French hand-painted side table, next to his rare antique three-piece rosewood Victorian parlor set. Bishop Daniel really hated to see his things out of order–everything has its place.

"If it isn't the Most Revered Bishop Daniel Xavier the Fifth. Come in, Your Holiness. I haven't seen you since our little escapade, hanging your future son-in-law by his ankles. How is your daughter dealing with her new marriage?"

The Bishop gave Duncan an irritated smile as he leaned against the silent alarm button hidden next to the door. "My daughter is fine, thank you. I see you have made yourself at home. Is there anything else I can get for you?"

Duncan winked with a nod of his head. "Well, as a matter of fact, yes you can. I believe you have a briefcase full of cash for me. In exchange, I will be happy to give you this."

Duncan held up the Portal Wand and turned it on. Alternating white and florescent blue lights started flashing in rotation. The lights grew and spiraled outward, filling the area around Duncan and he disappeared. Seconds later, Duncan put his hand on the Bishop's shoulder from behind him.

Daniel jumped from surprise. "I wish you would not do that, son."

"Just wanted to demonstrate what you are purchasing. And don't call me 'son'–Father."

"Good, looks like the Wand works. Do you also have the sequencing program?"

Duncan did his best to hide his aggravation. "Well, no, I will have that for you soon."

Daniel walked to his safe, put his thumb on a pad and entered the code. The safe popped open and he removed a briefcase. Setting the case on a table, he spun the lock code on the briefcase, opened the top and proceeded to remove half the bundles, stacked them neatly in the safe and closed the door. "Give me the Wand and take this. You can have the remainder when you give me the sequencing code."

Reflected in the beveled-door mirror of the French Victorian wardrobe, the Bishop saw Duncan reach for a concealed gun. "Gentlemen!" Daniel said firmly.

Two large bodyguards stepped into the room, the lasers on their weapons sited on Duncan's chest. Daniel spoke as he turned his back to Duncan, "Let's not do anything rash, that could be detrimental to your health, son."

"I'm hurt, Your Eminence, that you don't trust me. I'll call you when I have the program. Oh, by the way, I have a very interesting piece of jewelry, actually a Collar, that I will show you when I come back." As Duncan was leaving he bent close to the Bishop and whispered, "This Collar restricts anyone that wears it from Jumping. In fact, we have captured two people using it." Duncan turned as he got to the door. "Daniel, I have another bidder for the jewelry, so I'll let you know what the going offer is. See you soon, Father."

* * *

Speaker of the House John Bodner sat behind his over-sized desk, looking very patriotic with the American flag hanging behind him on the wall. The Director of Counter Terrorism for Homeland Security Aaron Rebel was escorted into his office. Bodner stood to shake hands, "Thank you, Bernice. Please hold my calls until we are finished." His secretary left the room, closing the door behind her.

"I understand that Walter saved your butt again..." Bodner said, motioning for Aaron to sit down, "...by discovering how to sequence DNA, which will allow us to create others able to Jump."

"Yes, he did—at my instruction. And I have additional news that will interest you. Also under my authority, Walter has designed a Collar that when locked on a person will keep them from Jumping. And in addition to his ongoing work to complete the Wand, he is now working on a laser rod that will also keep a person from Jumping when touched by a whip-like laser. We will be able to neutralize anyone using the Jump technology."

Bodner smiled broadly as he sat down at his desk, and gave a rare commendation. "Excellent work, Director. This will give us complete control. We have to discuss our approach to the many special interest groups vying for this technology. I will direct funds from these groups to JBR, our new technology subsidiary of Hellibenson. Then any additional monies that Congress grants, to this project through its legal authority and internal budgeting process will be gravy. Of course our favorite weapons manufacturer, along with a few lobbying groups, including an unnamed set of brothers, will receive a healthy sum to act as our umbrella should any fallout come our way, and of course to lobby for this technology." Rebel nodded in agreement.

"You will develop the budgets," Bodner continued. "It goes without saying that you should find creative ways to enhance the expenses. As new and unknown as this technology is, we should be able to hide a billion or two within development and manufacturing. And these funds will reimburse you and me for our extraordinary efforts to secure this technology—for the security of our great nation." Bodner leaned forward thoughtfully, and Rebel just waited patiently for what he had to say.

"In the next few years, before my term ends, I'll introduce additional legislation for contracts which will be awarded to JBR for production. JBR will produce the hardware and software for the Portals, Collars and Laser Whips to equip all branches of the United States military. Between our salaries, bonuses and stock options in JBR, this will be a very good run for us. We will go down in history, known for saving our country from terrorism. And our grandchildrens' grandchildren will be set for life."

Bodner sat back in his chair and crossed his arms over his chest. "Enough about that for now. Aaron, I trust the Jump Platoon's training is on track. I have a mission for them."

"They are ready, John. This elite team of Navy Seals is ready to deploy anywhere in the world in minutes."

"Good. Our first target is in Syria. As you know, the Islamic State has beheaded a journalist along with an aid worker. What you don't know is the President has ordered airstrikes against their home base Raqqa in northern Syria to take place soon. There was no alternative but to target their headquarters, along with other locations where the terrorist group has built up a considerable infrastructure. The Islamic State is currently holding five American captives, and have threatened the same torture and beheading in the coming days. I want the Platoon ready for briefing in two hours and able to Jump in four. We have the exact coordinates of the compound where the hostages are being held."

Aaron was concerned. After all, this mission was invading another country. "Do these orders come from the President, sir?"

Bodner gave Aaron an angry sneer. "Just don't you be worried about that– I wield the Speaker's gavel. Besides, no one else needs to know, until our men are home safely. Do you understand?"

Bodner walked around the desk, put his hands on Aaron's shoulders, and gave him a solid shake. "You be sure to let me know where Ian is, and what has happened with the only working Jump Wand as soon as you know anything. You have Ian's father and son in a private room under 24-hour surveillance. Ian will be happy to know we are taking good care of them. When the Platoon returns from Syria, Ian and the Wand will be the next targets for our Seal team. I will see you and the team for briefing in an hour and a half."

The Speaker pressed a button on his phone: "Bernice, Director Rebel is leaving. Would you get the commander in charge of the reconnaissance team for the Syria mission on the phone. What is his name again, Galum?"

Bernice entered the room. "Yes, sir, his name is Gholam, Commander Victor Gholam."

* * *

No mistaking it. The sickeningly-sweet smell of restaurants, produce stalls with fruit and vegetables, mixed with live seafood and the smell of stale grease. Those were only some of the clues. There was also the distant lady's voice screaming at someone in what sounds like Mandarin–she was not at all happy with her husband. Put all that together with someone beating on a pot and the Asian music resonating from the street below. This was either Chinatown or a market somewhere in Asia.

These thoughts became less a dream and more reality as Akira returned to her senses. She reached to her neck. The Collar had been removed! She immediately tried to travel. No use, her energy was much too heavy. Her physical buoyancy felt like the weight of the stale grease she smelled coming from the street.

Akira pushed herself to her knees and looked around the small, empty, windowless room. She had been laying on a mattress in a corner on the floor. There was a single, bare light bulb hanging from a short wire protruding from the center of the ceiling. Quietly trying the doorknob confirmed that the door was locked. Her Collar had been removed and she had not been restrained, though without being able to travel she was trapped.

She returned to the mattress and plopped down, trying to remember. She felt so heavy, so ponderous. Flashes from her past lifetime–this is what it was like to live on Earth, before she became enlightened. Was it part of a dream or did she remember Louise attempting to help her. And there was a gunshot! Did someone shoot Louise?

How long had she been captive? Akira's head was throbbing, she began to feel faint–couldn't hold her head up. Her chin dropped, and she saw needle marks in the veins of her arm. The room became blurry as her body melted into the bed. What kind... of drugs had they... injected into.. her? Everything went black.

Conscious again? Unable to move, Akira stared at the dangling light. Slowly she became aware of a hazy face staring back.

"She is still alive."

"Good. Keep her sedated for now until we decide what to do with her." Another needle...she drifted away into a dream...

...she ran through the beautiful valley at the Falls. Darkness spread behind, chasing her as she ran for her life. Bam! Bam! 'Were those gun shots?' Murky black shadows were coming toward her from every direction. She knew that if the shadows caught her, she would die a horrible death.

The shadows almost had her! There was nowhere to run. Darkness was overtaking her–when a bright door appeared. Bam–Bam! There it was again. With her last effort, Akira dove through the door.

She rolled, then came up to her feet in a crowded oriental kitchen. Bam! Turning, she watched as the famous chef Emeril Lagasse, came toward her. "Bam!" he exclaimed with his familiar flair, throwing spices at her. A Chinese chef came threateningly toward Akira from the other direction, a huge cleaver in one hand and holding a fish in his other hand. "Bam!" Spice flew into the air. She was surrounded by chefs, fish, dish washers and waiters–a multitude, pushing against her. Panic was holding her tight– it was becoming difficult to breathe. The world around her filled with the shadows creeping in from beneath the door and everything began to spin.

"Quiet your mind, little one."

Akira knew that voice! "Jaguar, help me!" she screamed.

"Remember your training–gain control." Jaguar's voice was clear through all the turmoil. "In the world of dreams, much like on Gaia, what you construct in your mind becomes your surroundings."

Akira squeezed her eyes tight. Breathing deeply, she built a picture in her mind.

When she opened her eyes, she sat in a bright, grass-covered meadow with Jaguar sitting next to her. He smiled, and explained. "As ethereal as Gaia appears, we continue to have a physical body. Our bodies are lucent, almost intangible in Gaia. But when we lower our vibration and move to Earth's realm, we become palpable and subject to Earth's more substantial physical laws. That does not mean our essence has to be completely tied to the physical plane."

"Now concentrate on raising your energy, we do not want to lose you. Physically, I am also captive in another room next to yours. Meet me in the dream state each evening after they feed us, and we will work on plans to escape. We..." Jaguar vibrated, then vanished.

Jaguar opened his eyes to see a young man with curly red hair shaking him by the shoulders. "Wake up." A strong backhand snapped his head back, a trickle of blood ran down his chin. "What have you done with Ian? We know you, or your pals, have taken him from the warehouse."

Jaguar wiped the corner of his mouth on his shoulder. "Who is Ian?"

That met with a closed fist, sending a spray of blood from his nose. "Don't be a smart guy. We know you had something to do with Ian's escape." Red pulled back to send another fist into Jaguar's unprotected face.

"Stop it." An older Asian man grabbed Red's arm before he could deliver another blow. The man wiped Jaguar's face with a cold wet cloth. Jaguar felt a brief moment of relief, before the man grabbed a handful of Jaguar's hair. He pulled his head back, and looked into his eyes. "These men promised to deliver Ian to me. They are crudely attempting to retrieve him, so they may honor this agreement. I propose that you help me, to help you. So you do not have to endure any more pain. Think about that for a minute. Come with me, Red."

The General confronted them as they entered the next room. "Minister Qian, let Red finish his interrogation, so we can complete our business here."

Before they closed the door, Jaguar heard Qian's rage. "General, I do not have time for this. Return my investment. And for my wasted time, give me the Collars your two captives were wearing, and we will call our agreement complete." Then through the door, an angry, muffled argument ensued.

CHAPTER 16
Animal Totem

She dropped 100...200 feet...plummeting toward earth, the rocky ground rushing to meet her free fall, promising certain death hitting at this speed. Seconds before smashing into the ground she spread powerful wings, caught the air and soured up into the sky. She turned, caught an eddy of air and banked sharply, zipping between outstretched branches of huge, beautiful pine trees. The trees disappeared behind her as she shot out across a jagged cliff. There she found an updraft, flapped those magnificent wings a couple of times and soured into the clouds above.

This was freedom. At this altitude everything was so quiet. She breathed the chill of the cool air into strong lungs. White clouds drifted by, dampening her plume with condensation. Wind from this speed rushed through feathers that tickled as they fluttered in the breeze. Her vision was so sharp. Below, a sparkling clear lake lay huddled between mountain ridges, fed by a creek falling step by step from a natural spring above. As she jetted free from within a cumulus cloud, movement caught her eye a thousand feet below—there at the bank of that majestic lake.

She dove. One hundred feet above the prey it became clearly defined. A small cottontail sat munching grass, ears alert, yet unaware of the silent, deadly talons a moment away. An instant before the kill, Akira pulled up sharply.

'What am I doing?' Akira thought. 'I'm hungry, but there is no way I'm eating that little rabbit.' She had nearly lost herself in the rapture of souring freedom which she found in her totem.

Akira pulled her mind back to the tiny room where her body lay—but she didn't return to her body. What was going on? Why wasn't she in her body? Her thoughts were unnerved.

"Welcome back, Little Hawk," Jaguar said, sitting beside her on the bed.

Before she could say anything, Minister Qian stepped into the room, startling Akira. "Get out!" She screamed a warning to Jaguar.

He only smiled. "Qian cannot see us. As far as he can tell, he is the only conscious person in the room. Our consciousness is in a dream state right now, not fully in Gaia or Earth."

Qian picked up Akira's arm, his fingers across her wrist.

That was odd. Akira saw her arm being lifted, but it seemed like she was feeling someone else's arm—not her own.

"How much Special K did you give her?" Qian hollered. "I can hardly feel a pulse."

Aggravation in the General's voice came from the other room, where he was with Jaguar's body. "Enough. Relax, damn it. She should be conscious soon. As we agreed, I gave your money back, along with one Collar and the girl. So Red and I will be on our way with him." Jaguar sensed a sharp poke in the ribs from his body in the adjacent room.

Qian rushed into the other room, signaled his men, and they stepped in front of the door. "Not so fast, General. You are not leaving me with a dead girl. When she wakes up you can go. So you relax."

Akira's concern was growing. "Jaguar, why can't I re-enter my body?"

"Be patient, Little Hawk. The problem must be with the drugs they gave you, combined with the residual effects of the Collar."

"Okay, Big Cat," Akira teased. They both laughed. As she giggled, the corner of her physical mouth formed a slight smile. "I can almost feel my body, but it doesn't FEEL like me!"

Hours passed. It was difficult being patient. Akira's body began to stir. "Look, I'm moving, I am awake. Finally!"

Hurriedly, she tried to push her spirit back into the body that lay in bed. "Nothing!" She jumped on her body, took a running dive, stretched out on top of herself and willed her return. The harder she tried, the more upset she became. "That's not me anymore, Jaguar." Akira's physical form swung her legs off the bed, and sat up. Her spiritual essence stood next to herself.

"Sure it is, Akira. Your consciousness has been separated from your physical body—that's all. You are traveling in a discorporal form between the physical and spiritual worlds. Somehow you have lost contact with sensory input from the body."

"The General has reached an agreement with Qian, and is leaving with me. But I'll keep trying to help you make sense of your corporeal situation. Stay close to your body and try to reconnect with your physical senses. Pinch and slap yourself. You have to...feel again..." Jaguar blinked on and off...

As he disappeared, his faint thought appeared in Akira's mind. "I'll contact you...soon as... I'm able. Be strong, Little Hawk."

* * *

"Grandpa, I'm scared." Tears ran down Alek's cheeks as he hugged James for dear life. "Where are my mom and dad and sis? Why do these bad men have us? Why do they think dad is a terrorist?" Alek stood back and pounded his fists against his granddad's chest. "I hate you. I hate you! You never, ever came to see us! My dad always gets so mad when sis or I talk about you and grandma." Alek covered his face and ran into the corner, throwing his shoulder against the wall.

James didn't know what to do. He wasn't good at being a grandparent. Hell, he wasn't even any good at being a parent. He was beginning to question whether he was any good at being a man. Slowly crossing the room, he hesitantly rested a hand on his grandson's shoulder. "Now, now, son, we'll figure something out. Don't cry, we have to be strong. Courage isn't about not being afraid, it's that we make something else more important than our fear. Now it is more important that we work together and find a way out of here, so you and I can help our family."

Alek sniffed and rubbed his eyes. James took his grandson's hands and gently pulled him over to the couch. "Sit down, son. I feel horrible, not being around to see you and Kristen grow up. I have not been a good father, or grandfather. But that is going to change. Over time, I had convinced myself that you would all be better off without me in your lives. I couldn't even speak of this, before your father and I had a heart-to-heart discussion, after the golf tournament I told you about with Akira. Never expected your father would forgive me."

"It is past time I ask for your forgiveness, please understand," James continued slowly. "When your dad was a little boy, a detestable thing happened. Something I've regretted all of my life, and been unable to forgive myself for. I believe that you are old enough to hear this now. Your grandmother's death was my fault. More than that, your father would have had twin sisters, if not for me."

Tears came to his eyes as James continued. "Your father wasn't much

157

more than a baby, his sisters were a year and a half older. We were all staying at my parent's house–your grandmother, father, the twins and me, were watching my folk's house, while the two of them went on a vacation. My wife and daughters were sitting at the dining room table finishing dinner, while I took your father to the bathroom." James took a long slow breath, swallowed hard, and squeezed his grandson's hand compassionately. "Some armed men broke into the house after me, and to make their point shot my wife and daughters. The only reason your dad and I survived, is that we were in the other room." James took another deep breath, and sat staring at memories through the tears in his eyes. "Remember, son. You can never hide from your problems. Don't make the mistake I did. Face your problems and mistakes."

"Grandpa, I don't really hate you, I didn't mean it. I'm sorry." Alek hugged his granddad, crying loudly.

"I know, son, I know. I'm sorry too. What do you say we man up, and go rescue your father and sister? Let's find a way out of here."

A heavy feeling cleared as Alek shook his head, stretched, took a deep breath and stopped crying. He felt twenty pounds lighter, as if a huge weight had been lifted from his shoulders. A huge emotional blockage had been stripped from him, allowing his true essence to be freed. It was like crawling out of a cocoon after a long sleep.

Alek sensed a tactile difference in his being. 'What?' Alek thought. Two seconds ago, he did not know the meaning of 'tactile'. And he had never given thought to the essence of his cosmic being. A strange voice spoke to him from the back of his mind–'Now we remember–we are one again.' Was that his subconscious? Was he going mad?

James studied his grandson's demeanor. "You look like you're feeling better, son."

Alek was standing taller, with a strength and composure unlike anything he had ever felt before. Everything was brighter and clearer, like viewing things through a magnifying lens. Alek looked at his outstretched arms, turned his arms over and raised them in the air. "I have never felt better!" Alek jumped up and down a couple of times. He was obviously himself, but he was different somehow–more alive. "Granddad, I love you," he said, taking him by the hands. With the clearest thoughts of his lifetime, he formed a precise image of his mother. "I want to see mom and dad now," he stated knowingly.

The air in the room wavered–seeming for a second to become liquefied and glowed a white hot–yet their surroundings were cool. Before closing his eyes, James actually saw his breath as he exhaled. "What the h..."

Nine thousand, eight hundred miles away, in Australia, the air in the room around Ian wavered, liquefied then flashed a bright cold white. Ian vanished before he had time to question the strangeness around him.

* * *

The creek always relaxed Jasmine. She listened to Star intently as they strolled along the water's edge. Star had given Jasmine an exercise to help her learn about travel between worlds.

"I think I understand," Jasmine stated. She picked up a pebble and tossed it into the still water pooled above some rapids and watched the circular ripples spread. Jasmine concentrated on the motion of the water and attempted the exercise. Straining with the lesson, the tension in her body began to show through quick breathing and anxious movements.

"I can't do it!" Jasmine threw a stone at the water in frustration and spun away. Turning her attention to her daughter, she started up the hill to be with her.

Kristen played on the river bank above the creek, in a sunlit area between tall trees. Maya and Isis frolicked between the trees, Isis fetching a stick Kristen threw. Star followed Jasmine as she walked over the nearby embankment toward the dogs and her daughter. "Be patient, Jasmine." Star called from a few steps behind. "Traveling is not an easy accomplishment. It takes time. Do not try so hard, you must let it happen naturally."

Jasmine opened her mouth to reply...

An instantaneous split in the air emerged with a bright white flash. Jasmine's mouth hung open in amazement with unformed words hanging from her lips. The hair on the backs of Isis and Maya stood up as they gave protective growls. Where the flash just occurred, Alek, Ian and James stood next to Kristen.

"Yeah!" Alek screamed, and jumped high with excitement. He had done it. He brought his family together. Alek dropped to his knees, overwhelmed from the sudden rush of energy that just coursed through every cell of his body. Looking up from his hands and knees at mom, dad, sis and his granddad, he broke into tears of euphoria. He had never been so happy!

Ian helped Alek stand, supporting him with a strong hug, grinning from ear to ear. "Are you all right, son?"

As he regained some strength and composure, Alek smiled. "I feel great, dad–like a whole new person. Let's all go home."

Louise, Max and Yaozu materialized a few yards away from the happy family's reunion. "What was that disturbance?" the three asked. Star stood nearby, shaking her head in disbelief at the event. Louise walked over to Alek, sensing a residual energy still circulating around him. "Did you transport Ian, James and yourself here, young man?"

Alek looked at the ground, his chin down, as if he had done something wrong, and hesitantly nodded his head. "Yes, ma'am. I just had to. Please don't be mad."

Louise smiled. "Oh, quite the contrary, young Alek. Your mother has told me much about you–though she neglected to tell me how powerful you are."

Max marched over with a suspicious look. "Elders among our Aboriginal culture have shared many stories since before the written word. But through history, never has such a thing been spoken. Remote transport of others separated from each other has never been done from more than a few feet. Who are you, mate?"

"I can answer that," Jaguar said, suddenly appearing next to Max. He approached Alek, dropped to one knee and bowed his head in respect. "Greetings, Manco Cápac, son of Inti. Welcome. You have not visited us for over a millennium. What brings you here, now, mi maestro–my teacher?"

Alek, startled by Jaguar's translucent physique and odd greeting, gave a bewildered reply. "Ya... a.. ah... 'Pull yourself together' came the voice in his head. Alek cleared his throat, "Hello, sir. I'm Alek, Alek Knecht, not Manco, whoever." Alek stared in amazement, wondering if this guy was a ghost or something.

Yet, distant memories from Cápac started to surface again in the back of his mind. Alek frowned, closed his eyes and rubbed his temples with both hands. "This Cápac guy you're mistaking me for does seems familiar, somehow. I must have read about him in school. Or maybe he is a character in my video games." Alek was so confused. Impressions, memories buried in the recesses of his being, all but forgotten, bubbled up in his conscious mind. Advanced information, knowledge, understanding and wisdom accumulated from thousands of years of experience.

Jasmine, seeing his confusion and discomfort, put her arms around her son protectively. "Well, we will sort all of this out in time. First I have some catching up to do with my family."

"That is a grand idea," Louise said, taking Jaguar by the arm. "We need to speak as well." She asked Star, Max and Yaozu to join them. "We will take our leave and let you all visit. Excuse us."

Louise hurried her group away, past a small stand of pine trees and stopped next to the creek. With concern, she addressed Jaguar. "You are not well. Your physical substance is wrong. You should not be diaphanous here in Gaia." Star, Max and Yaozu expressed their concerns as well, even as Jaguar permeated the entire area with a radiance of peace.

"Relax, my friends. I am more than fine." Jaguar's transparent body was now more the shape of his body embossed in the air. His image wavered with the slight breeze. The group felt an overwhelming sense of pure joy as Jaguar continued. "I have graduated, shifted to a new state of being, to an eternal consciousness. I am now more firmly bonded to the absolute creative and sustaining source of everything. As we all know, this state of being is known by many names: Buddhists experience Bodhi, Christians heavenly body, Jewish d'veikut, Zen kensho, Hindu moksha, or Sufi nafsil mutma`inna. I have come to see you from this dimension, where a physical manifestation is unnecessary. The materialized form you see I created in order to make our speaking with one another more comfortable. My actual physical form is trapped on Earth. I chose not to remain tethered to that body any longer. So it will pass on soon. As I had earlier shared with you, my treasured friends, I have put off this dimensional transition for many decades. And now the time is right. With all of your continued help, my assistance to Gaia and Earth will be much stronger from this other dimension."

"Now is the time of prophecy," Jaguar continued. "Prophecy, long told through time, speaks of Manco Cápac, son of Inti–the great Sapa Inca ruler of Cusco from the Quechua people, will come home again. It is told that Cápac reappears during a heavy time–a time of few words and no world voyages. He will stand before the world killers, and heal the splitting of worlds. It is now becoming as foretold."

* * *

Akira's mind reeled. She had tried everything to re-enter her body. Nothing worked. It was strangely sadistic. She'd slapped and pinched herself frequently, sometimes violently, out of desperation. It must have hurt. Nevertheless, she was feeling less, growing more distant. Attempting to travel was of no use. She couldn't even communicate with anyone.

Qian and a couple of his men entered the room. Akira didn't bother to move. She knew they couldn't really see her spirit self, though she was only feet away watching in horror. "See for yourself, xiānsheng. Oh, sorry, sir–always speak English. Anyway, she is useless. Watch." The man moved like a cat over to Akira. He slid his hand inside her shirt, groping her breast. A smile crossed his face as he pinched her nipple and twisted. "See, she is worthless, no one will pay to lay with this one. Not unless they get off on dead people. You know–I think Americans call it necrophilia. That even disgusts me."

Qian moved closer and stroked her hair, gently pushing strands behind her ear. He slapped her cheek, placed his hand between her legs, as he bent close and whispered. "It is a shame, little one, we could have had fun." Qian stood abruptly, smelled his finger, then winked at her and gave her a disgusting grin.

"I'll get the General for this–dumping a brain-dead girl on me. Leave her. We'll make an anonymous call to the police in a day or two. No one can trace us to this building. Gather everything, leave nothing behind."

A few minutes later, the light was turned off. She heard the men leave, closing the door behind them. It was so dark. She was truly alone. And afraid! What was she going to do? Her physical body had been awake sitting on the edge of the bed with a glazed, far away look in her eyes– seemingly unaware of the abuse that had just been forced upon her. Akira sat next to herself, putting an arm around the familiar stranger and cried.

Hours passed, sitting alone in the dark, rocking gently. Eventually she felt an odd comfort–having her spirit self sitting closely beside her physical self. Somehow she was less lonely. 'I must be losing my mind. I'm keeping myself company,' she thought. Akira stood up and screamed at herself. "GET UP, STUPID! We have to get out of here. Stop feeling sorry for ourselves." Attempting to move, her emotions turned from anger to frustration and exasperation followed by annoyance, to finally circle back around to depression. Akira's desperate spirit slipped into her totem animal to escape.

Floating through the clouds relieved her anxiety, watching the ground below shift and change as she soared above. Her unresponsive physical body was slowly pushed into the recesses of her mind as she flew. It would be so easy to forget her body. Forget her troubles and frolic in the breeze forever–how wonderful. She lifted a wing and banked. Rolled, looped and played, forgetting.

Then she knew she was home, landing on her nest perched high in the tallest tree close to the lake. A strangely aggressive male hawk landed on a tree branch next to her, seemingly flirting with her. She ignored him watching every movement around her nest. Sparrows darted around the grass below after bugs. A dragonfly sat on a flower near the creek. Fish, mmm...

...that trout just broke the surface of the lake. Instinctively, Akira lifted off, circled, then pulled both wings tight against her sides and dove into the lake. Pulling up, dinner clutched tightly, water falling from feathers as she skimmed across the water's surface. Lost in the moment–in the primal kill and urge to devour her prey. Wings spread wide, she caught the air, lifted quickly, then slowed her flight and came to a soft landing on the edge of the nest. All right, dinner...

"Akira?...Little Hawk..."

'What was that?' She turned her feathered head to listen. Turned her head again, and again, side to side, listening. Her eyes and ears catching everything. But where was that sound coming from, it sounded human...

"A-ki-ra."

'Who was calling?'–she knew that name, though she wasn't sure how she knew it?

"Akira! Little Hawk! Come back, you have entered into your totem too strongly!"

She shook her head, the hawk looking past the fish and nest to the foot of her tree. At the base, sitting on an exposed root was a large spotted cat. "A Big Cat...Oh...Jaguar!"

"Focus, Little Hawk. We cannot lose you. Your life going back will not be easy, but be strong. You have an important role to play before this is over. We will never leave you alone again. Grandstaff is with you now. Concentrate on being you–Akira."

* * *

Jasmine guided Ian along a winding path through tall pines, their children having been left to play with new friends. Rounding a large rock, they came to a beautiful quiet pond in the creek. "This is one of my favorite places," she said, spreading a blanket on the grass and matted needles, under a pine tree near the water.

Ian sat next to his wife. "You are becoming acquainted with your new life in Gaia, and able to hold the dimension around us so we can be together. I love you, baby."

"I love you, too," Jasmine replied, kissing Ian passionately.

Ian laid back on the blanket, staring up through the tree branches circling the tall Ponderosa pine. He watched as drops of rain began to make their way through the few empty spaces between clusters of bright green needles. A drop fell on Jasmine's face as she rolled on top of him, the raindrop hanging from the end of her nose. "We're going to get wet," he whispered, gently kissing the drop away.

Jasmine gave Ian a seductive smile that found its way into her eyes, as she raised her brows. "I have a solution." She pulled his shirt off and slid it under the blanket. Then began to unsnap his jeans.

"Wait a minute," he protested mildly.

"Since when have you become shy?" she replied, sitting back, pulling her shirt off.

Ian smiled. How he loved her round firm breasts, nipples erect from the cool mountain shower.

Jasmine stood up, flirt-fully removed her shorts, then slowly slid off her panties and ran into the pond. He pulled off his pants, almost stumbling as he ran after her.

Together they swam, played and explored one another in the strangely warm water with a steady gentle rain falling around them. Countless drops fell, caressing their head and shoulders. Drops penetrated the calm waters' surface nearby, pushing droplets squirting upwards, defying gravity. Other drops pulled a thin mantle of water percolating over a pocket of air creating bubbles–flimsy transparent pearls that sparkled and reflected their naked surroundings briefly, before relinquishing a delicate gasp of satisfaction, merging once again into the water's surface–never to be the same again.

Nature rejoiced as they aroused one another, re-acquainting themselves with every inch of the other's body. The afternoon dissolved in their passionate dance, with a climax to the day as the sun set. Then they retreated under the tree, rolled up in the blanket, and laid cuddled arm in arm, both drained from the emotional and physical release.

Darkness began to overtake the sunset. Ian sat up. "We'd better get back. There is something I have to tell you and the kids." They playfully dressed one another, then slowly strolled along the path, back to the Falls, neither of them wanting to let this day go and face reality.

* * *

"No! Alek has only just brought us all back together," Jasmine complained, but knowing in her soul that Ian was right. Shoulders slumped, her chin dropped and bottom lip pouted, she sighed. "I can't live without my family."

Ian's somber expression gave away his despondent feelings. She looked like a dejected child when she pouted like that.

Kristen held tightly onto her mom's leg, matching Jasmine's expression. James stood silently as an observer to the family discussion, having very mixed feelings as to his own future. "I know, baby, but we can 't stay with you in this dimension. The kids and I are not prepared to transition to this existence yet. You must understand."

"I understand, you know I do, hun." She stroked her daughter's fine hair. "But it doesn't make losing all of you any easier. And Alek, he moved heaven and earth bringing you here from Australia. That must mean he is ready to join me."

"That was magnificent, though no one is sure how he did that." Ian gave Alek a proud punch in the shoulder, followed by a high five. "Yet despite that fact, and that Jaguar claims he is the reincarnation of Manco Cápac, the Incan elder, Star does not feel his vibration is consistently high enough to transcend."

Ian embraced his beautiful wife, as if holding her close would keep her with them. "I love you. How did I ever get so lucky to fall in love with such a wonderful person, and have such great kids?"

"Dumb luck, I suppose," she kidded, trying to lighten the mood.

He stood back, holding her at arm's length and grinned. Then he leaned close and whispered, "Smart ass." It worked–she had softened the anxiety a little for both of them. He pulled her back against his chest and held her tight, not wanting to let go. Not saying a word, feeling their hearts beating in combined rhythm. Ian kissed her ear and spoke softly, "Coming back to visit will be easy, once I get a new Wand built. We'll be back before you know it." He struggled emotionally, to pull himself away from their embrace, then said, "Spend the next day or two smothering the kids. I am going with Max and Louise to convince a government scientist to help make the Portals safe to use."

A horrified expression crossed Jasmine's face. "You can't go. The government is after you, in case you have forgotten."

"No, daddy," Kristen ran into his arms. He gave her a big bear-hug, growled and shook her gently. She loved that, giving a growl in return.

"Jasmine, I have to help alleviate the problem that I've created. It's the least I can do."

"Be careful, then," she said sternly.

"You know I will. And since Jaguar's passage, he is able to move between worlds without being seen. He checked out Walter, the scientist we're going to visit. Jaguar believes he is the correct person to contact for our cause. Walter is becoming emotionally torn about his role in reverse engineering my technology. We believe this might be a way of helping him come to terms with himself." He gave Jasmine a hug, a deep look between souls, then a tender kiss. "Love ya...see you soon." Then he shook hands with his dad, and pulled him into a hug, telling him to look after the family. He held Alek and Kristen tight and long, then left on his urgent mission.

CHAPTER 17
Realization

Black smoke rose from what was left of an old building next to a Syrian Mosque. The destruction could be seen from the second story window of the complex in Syria, where the American prisoners were being held by the radical Islamic State. Minutes earlier, Major Mariam Mansouri, the United Arab Emirates' first female fighter pilot, had led a strike by the country's fighter jets against Islamic State targets in Syria. The bombing had started ahead of schedule, but it was obvious the intelligence gathered was correct or this building would also be a pile of rubble.

The U.S. Navy Seal team charged in with full combat gear, firearms drawn ready for any aggression. The Jump team had materialized in the complex eight seconds after the Jump started. They were surprised to find the room was empty, with the exception of the five hostages, who were dumbfounded by the sudden appearance of the team.

Outside, Syrian streets were unusually frenetic. Terrorist soldiers rummaged through what was left of buildings looking for survivors. Minutes later, the five U.S. hostages were safe inside Homeland Security's computer room in Washington, DC.

"Outstanding success, men," exclaimed Director Rebel. "Better than could have been expected. Not one shot fired. They will never know how their hostages escaped."

He turned to Walter and pulled him aside for some privacy. "Be ready. Bodner will push this project into full gear after such a success. He will want every branch of the military equipped with this technology. Figure out how to put this into full production."

* * *

Walter's room had returned to the quiet hum of the servers' cooling fans. The earlier tumult had gone with the Jump team and hostages when they left. He liked the cold and quiet of the room. "What have I done?"

he said to himself. Then he lost himself in a labyrinth of thoughts. 'I have been so focused and excited about this new technology. It has such promise. Yet, now... "Full production...every branch in the military?" All those uneducated hands on this technology would be dangerous.'

Walter considered the difficulties. 'Adequate tests have not been done. What long-term effect would this technology have on the men using it? What effect might it have on the environment? I'll speak with Aaron about my concerns. NO. That wouldn't help. Aaron only cares about his position and the money he's going to make.'

Walter sighed and went back to work. A resolution would come to him—always did when he kept his mind busy on something else. He did some of his best thinking, when he wasn't thinking. Walter worked through the night. He did his most productive non-thinking at night, when everyone left him alone.

Yawning, nothing significant had come to him. He thought about blowing everything up. But he was no terrorist, and besides, someone else would just continue his work. Walter turned off his desk lamp and was gathering things to leave—when a familiar flash and the corresponding warp in the air pulled his attention. But he was sure he'd turned off the Portal door.

As he turned to check on the Portal, three people were now visible—shadows standing between server rows in the eerie dancing glow of blue LED lights. "Who are you?" Walter questioned. "I'm going to call security."

"No need for that, Walter," came a woman's soft voice. "We are friends. Sorry, didn't mean to startle you. We are concerned with what the Jump technology is doing to the environment. Can we talk? Privately?"

"I still don't know who you are, or what you know about this technology."

Ian stepped closer, into an overhead security light so Walter could see him, but he avoided the camera's detection. "I'm Ian Knecht. Inventor of the technology you are using. You might say we know a thing or two about it. Can we talk without being interrupted?" Ian signaled at the camera with raised eyes and an upward nod of his head.

"Oh, of course," Walter whispered under his breath. "I have an A/V loop recording I play when I want to be alone." He positioned himself at his desk, picked up a book as if reading, then reached down and flipped a switch under his desk.

Walter's eyes opened almost as wide as his mouth gasped, then he ran to Ian, shaking his hand. "Of course we can talk! You are Brilliant! The order of nucleotides in DNA, on which you based the 'sequencing by synthesis.' Brilliant! Simply brilliant. And the detection of pyrophosphate release on nucleotide incorporation, rather than chain termination with dideoxynucleotides. That is very exciting! How on earth did you come up with such a unique approach to hydrolysis of ATP to AMP and PPi? That is gifted, I mean, you are gifted." Words were flying off his tongue faster then anyone but Ian could make sense of.

"Walter, slow down, you are exhausting me."

"Oh—oh yes, I do that sometimes. It's just that this is earth-changing stuff, Ian, I have so much to ask you."

"We'll get to that, Walter. But first, we are here, asking for your help. Something just as earth-changing, that we pray you can help us with."

"All righty then, let's hear it. You and your friends come sit down. Can I get you a Rock Star?" Walter saw the confused looks. "Energy drink, coffee or something?"

"Thanks heaps, mate, but we can't stay long." Max pulled out a chair for Louise. "I am Max, and this is Louise. Would take an apple though."

"Pear, I have a pear in the fridge." Walter started toward the refrigerator. "Or grapes, yes, I have grapes."

"Just a minute, you two fruitcakes," Louise said, kiddingly. "We have something more important to talk about than fruit. Let me get to the point, Walter, for this will be hard to believe."

"Try me. I have a good imagination."

"Take a close look at Max," Louise said.

Walter was confused, but he did as asked.

Max grinned. He pulled up the sleeves of his shirt. "Nothing up my sleeves." There was a warp in the air and he vanished.

"Impressive," Walter commented. "Ian, you have reduced the size of your Portal Wand. Show me—how small can you make it?"

"That's not what Max did," Ian replied. "Walter, you understand the equation that enables this technology to work. It increases the vibrational weight of a person's energy in order to move between dimensions."

"Yes, yes, of course. Brilliant." Walter shut his eyes, brought his fists in front of his face then exploded his fingers outward and popped his eyes open, animating the point.

Ian continued with a smile. "It turns out the other dimension used by this technology is inhabited."

"I knew it." Walter jumped to his feet. "What did you find? Amoebas, insects possibly?"

"Not exactly, Walter." Ian rolled his chair next to Louise and put his arm around her. Max reappeared standing behind them. "These friends of mine live there. Max and Louise, along with many other people who consider that dimension their home. They call their dimension, Gaia, and it's inhabited by many people who have increased their vibrational energy to a point where they have shifted their physical essence to Gaia."

"Wow!" Walter sat down, almost missing his chair, a thoughtful look in his eyes. "Hmm, well, I, ah... You're not playing with me now? No bull?"

"No bull, Walter. If you are willing, we can use the Portal door to visit their dimension for a short time. You have been sequenced."

"Sequenced, yes, yes. This will be better than my medical marijuana. You understand." Walter winked at Ian. "Let's go."

Louise smiled with relief, this was easier than expected. "Max and I will see you in a few minutes. Ian, meet us on Star's patio, there is plenty of room at her table to talk. Give us a few minutes so I can warn her. After all, it is very early."

* * *

Star gazed through tears from her patio, across the Falls, watching the moon. Though it was a couple of hours before sunrise, sleep eluded her. Jaguar's voice mixed with the sound of the creek cascading over the falls. His words resonated with so many meanings. "Star, I am with you, anytime you want. No matter the distance between us, I am less than a thought away. I love you. Always will. There is no separating that from us, whether my body is here or not."

The embossed appearance of Jaguar's body refracted the moon's pale light, producing a watery ghost-like impression of him sitting beside her on the ledge overlooking the Falls. Star blinked, causing a tear to blur her sight. "Our love for one another is without question. Though the physical form is quite cumbersome, heavy and awkward at times. I want to hold you, feel your body against mine. I miss you so much!"

Amazingly, as she completed her thought, the unmistakable warm feeling of Jaguar pressed against her. Star closed her eyes and felt his familiar strong arms hug her. His gentle fingers tenderly caressed her face. A soft kiss brushed her lips. In her mind, Jaguar was there, holding her, dissolving away her anxiety of being alone.

"We can always be together, love," he whispered. She smiled, so did he.

Star opened her eyes, surprised at not finding Jaguar in her arms. Their embrace had been so real. Then her attention shifted. 'Louise and Max are back from their meeting with Walter,' she noted, nodding to Jaguar's apparition.

A moment later, Louise walked onto the patio followed by Max. "Thank you for meeting with us at this hour. You know the importance of not delaying this get-together. Ian and Walter will be along shortly."

Max put cn a big smile and clowned about. "That Walter is a dag, he could be fun at the pub. He is an intelligent bloke though. Be good to have on our side. If anyone can convince those pommy bastards to stop Jumpin' about, Walter will."

* * *

Ian and Walter hung around in the server room, talking technology to kill time while Star was informed of their visit. "You know, Walter, I feel like we know each other—like we have met before."

"I catch your drift. If you weren't so young, I'd bet it was at Woodstock."

"Well, maybe not," Ian laughed, "I can't quite see myself at a big rock music festival—too many people for my taste. Jumping is enough of a head trip for me. We'd better go. Do you mind if I use your rig?" He indicated Walter's computer.

"Not at all," Walter said, pushing the keyboard to him. Ian programed the coordinates, then said seriously, "Walter, promise me you will delete these coordinates when you return. Can't chance the wrong people getting these."

"Will do—race you to the Portal door." Walter sprang to his feet and took off running.

"Walter, be careful!" Ian yelled.

"Come on, slow poke—you going to let this old man school you?" He stopped before the Portal door. Then hopped across the threshold, Jumping right through Jaguar's projection on the other side.

"Well, that was an odd experience," Walter jested. "I just Jumped through someone." He stopped and thought. Then with a horrified expression, he pleaded. "Please tell me I didn't hurt anyone."

"Walter!" Ian stepped into view. "You don't know the meaning of be careful, do you? I was concerned the Portal opening was too close to the Falls. Had a horrible thought of you running off the edge of the drop."

"Everyone is all right, no harm. The person you walked through is my partner, Jaguar." Star extended her hand in greeting. "Everyone calls me Star. Nice to meet you, Walter."

He took her hand, bent at the waist, and kissed close to her wrist. "The pleasure is truly mine, Star. And Jaguar, I'm happy to make your acquaintance." He bowed again. "Can't say I've ever met anyone in quite that fashion before. I apologize for the intrusion."

Max looked at him oddly. "Since when did you become a gentleman?"

"There is more to this old dog than you might guess." He looked around in all directions, just shaking his head. "Wonderful place you have here, Jaguar and Star."

"Thank you, Walter. We love our home here at the Falls," Star replied. "Sit down, please. Louise just brewed some sage tea. Would you care for a cup?"

The group sat around the table and sipped hot tea while they discussed the unexpected trouble caused by the massive number of Jumps. They outlined the plan to alleviate the problem with the technology. Then asked Walter to convince Homeland Security to create a training program. A program that would recruit and train Jumpers to increase their personal energy frequency to a point that would not negatively impact the mantle between worlds.

Ian looked at the glow threatening to peek over the horizon. "Walter, we need to get you back. We've left the Portal open long enough. Don't want someone wandering through and discovering the Falls inadvertently. I have one more request of you. I would like to Jump back with you and bring my father, son and daughter, then use the Portal to return to our home. We cannot stay in this dimension any longer."

"Gather your family," Walter said without hesitation. He looked at his watch. "Let's get a move on, I'm expecting people in about an hour." Walter turned to Star, Louise and the wavering representation of Jaguar. "It has been an unusual pleasure to meet you all. Thank you for your hospitality." Then he swirled his hand with a theatrical bow to Max. "You and I need to visit Australia together some time. I've always wanted to visit your part of the world, and I cannot think of a better guide." Addressing the rest of the group, he added, "I'll see what I can do to help with the Jump situation. It may take some time to find a sympathetic ear. How can I contact you?"

"We will stay in touch," Louise said, handing him a paper. "This is where you can reach my grandson Steele, and his wife Celeste, if you need to reach us before we contact you. They live in your world, but have a unique ability to communicate with us. You can trust them. I believe the three of you would make a good team."

Ian walked in with James, Jasmine, Alek and Kristen. Jasmine hugged her children, and even James, who had brought such turmoil into their lives. "I love you all," she expressed with a soft voice, wiping tears from her eyes, then kissed Ian. "I have been thinking that your old partner Rico would be a good person to contact for help. You are going to need a place to stay out of sight while you finish another Wand."

"Love you, mommy," Kristen said tearfully, followed by Alek's attempt to appear strong, "Yeh, mom, me too." Then punched his sister gently in the shoulder. "Don't be such a baby, we'll see mom again soon."

"Rico–that's a good idea, baby," Ian said. "See you later, my friends. Take care of my special lady." Ian looked at his wedding ring, turning it in contemplation, then kissed his wife one last time. "See you soon, baby." Then he took the hand of each of his kids and nodded to James. "Let's go, dad."

They all vanished through the Portal door. Walter waved. "See you later, alligator." Then he hopped through gingerly, followed by a quick flash.

* * *

Emerging from the Portal, Walter was relieved to see everything was quiet and just the way he'd left things. Ian asked Walter for access to the keyboard in order to delete the coordinates for the Falls, and program the location for his family's Jump home. "Make yourself at home," Walter replied, putting his arms out referring to the large room.

Walter picked something up from his desk."Before you leave, Ian, I would like to ask how you made this." Walter held up a small wafer. It was paper-thin semi-transparent hexagon crystal the circumference of a dime. It gave off a faint glow. Walter held the disk under a desk lamp, about a foot above his white desk. It projected the image of a ghostly circuit board onto the desktop.

"Yes, I call that the Ancient Horologe."

"Amazing," Walter exclaimed. "Didn't take you for a Whovian. The Ancient Horologe was a time travel device from the tenth Doctor, of the Doctor Who series. If memory servers me correctly."

"Your memory is very sharp, the name is from the tenth Doctor," Ian smiled. "I always liked the word Horologe. Seemed to fit, though my technology is not time travel. It is futuristic. My Horologe is created using energy transmitted from a focused mind, by holding a mental picture of the microchip design. I'm using a crystalline form of magnetite and single strands of viral DNA, in a mixture of different short synthetic oligonucleotide strands. The chip self-assembles around mental patterns projected into the mixture."

"But the mind must be extremely focused," Ian noted. "When the mind enters a high vibrational frequency, it creates 'sticky patches' within the viral DNA mixture, enabling the DNA strings to align. The end result is the Horologe chip, a high-speed optical data connections capable of transmitting elaborate optically-encoded information. It takes only 1-trillionth of a second–thousands of time faster than current transistors–to flip the on-off switch. This speed is necessary to transmit optically-encoded data fast enough to power the Portal technology. I'll show you how that's made when we have more time. Make sure to remind me." Ian extended his hand to shake.

Walter grabbed his hand and pulled Ian into a hug. "I'll take you up on that offer. Now all of you get out of here."

Ian put an arm around Alek and Kristen and they stepped through the Portal. James nodded to Walter, "See you again..."

* * *

...they appeared in Ian's shadowy home office a second later. The room was a mess. All the computers and monitors were gone. The file cabinet drawers were strewn across the floor, along with the few papers the Department of Homeland Security didn't think were important. Desk drawers lay piled on one another. A ragged hole in the wall where the Portal door once stood. Not much left after it was bombed.

Ian flipped the light switch. Power had obviously been turned off.

"Daddy, no!" Kristen cried, at the orderly office in shambles, and ran out the door. She headed upstairs to check her room. "Alek, take care of your sister, would you? Oh, and you two get some clothes together quickly. There are suitcases in the guest closet. We can't stay here long," Ian stressed.

He started sifting through what was left of his office. James looked around the room. "Looks like they didn't miss much."

Upstairs, the arguing, banging and rummaging noises stopped. Kristen came running down the stairs. "Daddy, I'm going across the street to see Grace. Be right back."

The door slammed behind her before Ian could say anything. "Dad, please see to Kristen's safety, and bring her home soon to pack. Alek," he yelled, "get your things together! Don't straggle, we have to leave soon."

Alone, Ian picked a paperweight up from the littered floor and stared into the crystal. Encased inside was the first crystallized hexagon Horologe he had attempted to make. Jasmine had surprised him with it the day he took his first successful Jump. Seemed like a lifetime ago.

'If I had only...' he thought to himself, then cursed. "Yeh, should-a, could-a, would-a, and if only frogs had wings...damn!"

He threw the paperweight against the brick wall, shattering the crystal. The Horologe bounced off the tile floor, then spun around like an off-balanced top. Ian watched mesmerized by the motion. As it settled, Ian remembered his safe. Maybe they hadn't found his safe. It held a working Horologe and most of the parts necessary to build a new Wand!

Ian rushed to the laundry room. Good. The dryer had not been moved. He pulled the dryer away from the wall and pried up the loose tile. He looked around to be sure he was still alone, then entered the hour Kristen was born, the date when Alek lost his first tooth, and the degrees of latitude and longitude of the location he kissed Jasmine for the first time. When he placed his thumb on the scanner, the door on the safe popped open. Taking a deep breath, he looked inside. The cell phone with the secure line was there, along with the flash drive with the sequencing software and pieces of an incomplete Wand, that Jasmine must have snuck into the safe.

Ian was ecstatic! He quickly entered a number on his cell phone.

"Hello, is this Rico Gori? Rico, this is Ian. How are you, my friend?" Ian had not talked to his former partner in about six months.

"Good, I'm very good, Ian–I mean Mr. Peabody." Rico always called Ian by his nickname Mr. Peabody. That came from the 1960's television animated cartoon series 'Rocky and Friends,' which they watched together as kids. "How is the family? And what is this I read about you being a terrorist? Hate to say it, but always thought the technology we were working on would lead to trouble. You know that is why I broke off our partnership."

"Yes, I know that, Rico, I should have listened, you usually were right about things. Buddy, my life has turned into a horrible nightmare. Jasmine passed on, she is no longer with us," Ian said, his eyes starting to tear. "The kids are safe with me. But as you apparently know, the government is looking for me and we have no place to stay. You still live at Arcosanti, in the Arizona's desert? Would it be possible for us to join you there for a few days, until I figure out what to do?"

"I am so sorry to hear about Jasmine," Rico said. "You, Kristen and Alek are welcome to stay with me for as long as it takes."

"I hate to impose, but my father is with us now, so we would need a place for the four of us."

"Your father?" Rico almost dropped his phone. "Did I hear you right? Your father is really with you? I didn't think he was still alive–I have to hear this story, you must come stay. Arcosanti has a volunteer program where you can stay a few months or longer if you would like. As a department manager, I can sponsor you to work with me."

"You will like it here," Rico continued. "Arcosanti seeks to embody what they call a 'Lean Alternative' to hyper-consumption through a smartly efficient and elegant city design. Leanness is inherent to the sustainable health of any living system. The city works to be such a system. It's all the things we talked about in college."

"I truly appreciate the offer, my friend. Would it be possible to work on my own project while we are there? I need to finish an incomplete Wand, so we can see Jasmine again."

"What!" Rico was floored, and beginning to worry about his friend. "You said Jasmine passed away."

"She did, pass on," Ian confirmed. "You will not believe this..."

Kristen ran into the room. "Daddy, Grace's mom Logan wants to talk to you."

"Rico, we'll talk in two days. We will head your direction later today, after I tie up some loose ends. Thanks again, my friend. I'll tell you all about my father, Jasmine and the craziness in my life when we get there. I have to go."

Walking across the street, Ian was concerned that the recent developments were going to hurt their eight-year relationship with the neighbors. As he spoke with Logan, he quickly realized how distraught she was–feeling responsible for Kristen and Alek being taken. She told Ian that an agent with the FBI assured her that the children would be fine. And she emphasized how sorry she was that Jasmine had passed away and asked if there was anything her husband Phil and she could do.

Ian thanked her for their concern. He felt bad making up a story, telling Logan that Jasmine's services had quietly been held in her hometown–but figured the truth would be hard to understand, plus he didn't have time to try and explain. He assured her that he was no terrorist and that he was working to clear his name. Then Ian told her that he, his father, and the kids were going to stay with a friend until the misunderstanding was put right.

Ian turned at the doorway as he was leaving. "I'll call once we are settled. A management company will take care of the house while we are gone, no need for you to water. Give my best to Phil, when he gets home from work, and tell him we'll have a beer when I get back."

It was wonderful having good neighbors, they made this part of his life easier. Ian contacted the management company to take care of his property. He made sure all the utilities and mortgage were on direct deposit. Then he threw some clothes together for his dad and himself and they were on the road. 'Thank God Homeland Security hadn't taken the family vehicle. Next stop–Arizona,' he thought with a weak smile.

* * *

Duncan hated giving the Collars to the General. But he could not have lived with himself had he left Fajah with that madman. He shuddered to think what the General would have done with her. But now that he had her, what was he going to do with her?

"Fajah, hun, do you have family back home that are missing you?"

Her eyes began to tear again. "Na, dat bad man, he kill mi Tata. Tata he onley famley."

"Now, now, don't be afraid, I will not let that bad man hurt you ever again." Then he remembered hearing something about gifted children. Yes, the Sentient6 Corporation was studying children with psychic sensitivities, to help them understand and work with their unusual abilities. They were looking for special kids with unique skills. Fajah would be perfect for that live-in program, and it would get her out of his hair. Plus Sentient6 was offering $600 a week for the clinical studies. That would go a long way toward paying off his bookie.

As an FBI agent, Duncan could easily get documents proving he was Fajah's legal guardian. This would work for a few months, while he figured a permanent place for her. He knew that having let the old probate court judge slide on that illegal sentencing, a few years back, would come in handy one day. After a visit to remind Judge Reinheart of that earlier injudiciousness, Duncan walked out of the court with guardianship over Fajah.

* * *

The Sentient6 Corporation seemed overly secured for a simple research facility. The massive twelve-foot walls, and the guard at the gate made it look more like a prison. Duncan convinced himself that she would be better off here, than in the foster-care program.

"We are here to see Elanor Maddie," Duncan said to the front gate guard.

Fajah was scared and concerned, but was quickly developing a cocky, obstreperous attitude. "It's all right, hun," Duncan consoled her, patting Fajah on the shoulder. "These are good people that want to help you, don't be afraid."

She pulled her shoulder away, angrily giving Duncan a rebellious look. "Mi nota fraid."

The guard was not dressed in a uniform, though he did have a military air. "All right, you may proceed. Go past the lawn, turn left at the fountain and proceed about half a klick and park. The reception desk is inside the double doors."

Elanor Maddie had a pleasant enough smile. Though it was forced, the smile nearly lightened her stern expression. Short, curled, naturally dark hair was streaked with gray, framing her face. Slight wrinkles around steel gray-blue eyes that looked right through you, was a sign of her 50-plus years. Her only adornment was a porcelain, coat-of-arms lapel pin, in the gray vest of her suit.

"You must be our little Fajah," she said in an austere voice.

"Ya ayem," Fajah stated, hands on her hips with a glare of defiance.

"It appears that you and I will be having some fun together, little missy," Elanor Maddie said sarcastically. "Duncan, we will contact you in a few days. Come, Fajah, let me introduce you to some of the other children."

She clutched Fajah's shirt collar, turned her away and ushered her down the hospital-like hallway. Duncan wondered briefly if he had made a mistake, but then, they wouldn't let her starve here—better than being on the streets. As he was leaving, he heard Fajah denouncing Elanor asking, 'What is wrong with you?' in her native slang. "Fiyah bun, a wa do yu?" He smiled as he walked away, hoping for Fajah's sake, that Elanor was not familiar with Jamaican Patwa.

* * *

"Concentrate, Little Hawk, come back to us...come back..."

"I'm trying, Jaguar, but I can't return. I do not feel the way." Akira was lost, cold, so cold. Space around her was more than black. It was devoid of color, of substance, of existence. She ached to return to her free, floating hawk, where everything was so bright, so clear. 'That is not real," she thought, 'or is it?' The hawk was more tangible than this nothingness.

"Follow me," came Jaguar's crackling voice. A spark flashed in the blackness, out in front of her, vanishing in darkness. Flash.. there ahead. Yards away? Miles away? Discernible distance did not exist in this blackness. Another... and again...then again. This time the golden spark arced a short distance—an electrical charge, twisting, turning. Lightning-sparked legs struck like bolts from a slender cat-like form, springing forward through the darkness. Akira followed the luminous electrical discharge as Jaguar lashed through the void.

"Good! Stay with me, Little Hawk." Jaguar bounded ahead—lightning striking with a purpose, a direction of being, a destination. He sprang ahead with the grace of a cat, combined with the blind fury of an electrical storm.

Akira did her best to keep up. The current was leaping far ahead with every spark. Far off came Jaguar's voice, rattling like distant thunder: "Feel where the lightning is going to strike, not where it has been."

Reaching into the distance Akira felt an electrostatic charge in the atmosphere. Excitement coursed through her being, as she realized the colorless non-existence had turned to this magnificent electrical torrent. She threw all of her essence into a leap of faith aimed at the building electrical field.

FLASH! She ripped a connecting charge of her own into the ionized air far ahead creating a conductive channel. This channel was a void, bridging the ionized air between the negative charges in this space and the positive surface charges ahead. Like a balloon of energy popping, a massive electrical discharge followed.

She appeared in a blinding corona discharge, far from where she had been nano seconds before. As her vision cleared, she was standing in the presence of Grandstaff, Jaguar's ghostlike projection, and her own body.

Grandstaff was sitting next to her on the bed in the dingy room where Qian had abandoned her. He was holding her hand. "Spaseeba, Rat teebya veedet." His Russian came to her fully understood: "Good to see you, my friends." He smiled at Akira's spirit and nodded to Jaguar.

"You, too, my friend," she said, very pleased to hear her own voice, and to not be alone in that dark room any longer. Akira's body was fully awake and semi-conscious of her surroundings, glancing back and forth between the three of them with a confused look. They heard footsteps in the hall outside the apartment. Grandstaff walked into the other room and listened. "Whoever it was is gone, but we must get out of here before Minister Qian or his men return."

Akira sat next to herself and put an arm around her shoulder. "Hi, kiddo, do not worry, we are in this together. I won't leave you again, promise. Funny–this gives new meaning to talking to yourself." The Akiras smiled in unison.

Jaguar's voice appeared in their mind. "I'll check to see if we are clear to leave." A moment later he was back. "Let's go. Akira, there is a café in the Smithsonian Art Museum, not far from here. They will not look for you there. Grandstaff can get you something to eat. You are functioning well enough to have some nourishment, while he rents a car down the street. No one can see me, so I will watch for any trouble. After we are mobile, we can decide where to go from there. How does that sound?" Akira and Grandstaff expressed their agreement.

The physical Akira stood up, as her spirit attempted to test her legs. After a few staggered passes across the room she was becoming somewhat familiar moving her body remotely from outside herself.

An hour later, after bumping into a few tables, at the café, and dribbling water like a baby, they were on highway 270 headed north out of DC. Steele and Celeste were a two day's drive away, in Wisconsin. Akira had decided she would like to hang with them if Bishop Daniel would let her stay for awhile.

CHAPTER 18
Jaguar's New Look

Startled, Celeste stood staring through his projection. Jaguar's body refracted just enough light from the room to give him the appearance of being embossed in the air. Steele sat at the dining table behind him, with the same stunned expression as his wife. "It is all fine, my friends. Do not be alarmed. I had no intention of unsettling you so. Please forgive me. I did project communication announcing my arrival. You must not have been listening."

Steele smiled. "Good to almost see you again, Jaguar. You are always welcome. This is a new look for you."

"Yes, it is," Jaguar said matter-of-factly. His voice appeared in their minds, more than being heard. "I have graduated. Shifted to a new state of being, to an eternal consciousness. I created my materialized form, which you see, in order to make our speaking with one another easier."

Celeste walked over to Steele at the table, putting Jaguar between them and the open patio door, that framed him in the dwindling evening light. They both watched in amazement as layers of faint luminous colors wavered around Jaguar. An almost imperceptible, mirage-like aura, alternating through a spectrum of semi-transparent colors. It was beautiful.

"Pardon my abruptness, but I have to get back. I must ask a favor from you. Akira needs your help. She was captured using a device that has effected her physical vibration. She is caught between our two worlds. Her physical body is stranded on Earth, while her spiritual body is stuck between Gaia and the dream world."

A concerned expression passed between Celeste and her husband. "What can we do to help her?" Celeste asked.

"She needs a quiet place to stay, to heal. If it is all right with you, could you speak with Bishop Daniel? Ask if your friend Akira can stay in an apartment next to yours. Akira is learning to function physically. She can walk and maintain normal day to day functions without full time assistance. Though she has not said a word physically, she does understand, and communicates telepathically. Akira needs help dealing with the outside world here on Earth. Her spiritual presence usually stays close to her physical body. You may be able to hear her spirit, if you quiet and focus your minds and listen carefully."

"Akira means a lot to us. We are more than happy to help," Steele said. "We'll speak with Daniel this evening. I am certain he will allow her to stay."

"Thank you. This is a great relief." Jaguar's aura shifted from a concerned cadence to a soothing modulation. "One of us from Gaia will check on you regularly while we are still able." The ambient wave around him shifted again to one of concern and tension. "Children, we may not be able to shift between our worlds for much longer though. There have been numerous Portal Jumps recently. These Jumps are destroying the veil between Earth and Gaia faster than anticipated. In recent years, transition between worlds was smooth. But since the increased use of the Portal technology, moving between dimensions is more like breaking through to the other side. I am not sure how much longer I will be able to make this transition or even communicate. This barrier is becoming quite substantial."

"Let me quickly explain the communication process between our worlds. This might make the process easier for all of us." Jaguar's aura transformed again, swirling between colors, showing signs of his thought process. "Let me put it this way. In current communication, if two parties want to communicate, something needs to be sent, and something is allowing for its passage. Physical sound waves, converted to electronic signals transmitted as radio waves over long distances. Spiritual communication uses a counter-factual language of quantum communication. Thoughts are sent using remote entanglement between atoms. Many on Earth consider such communication psychic, or telepathic, even magic. Those are terms for what is not yet currently understood. Remote entanglement of two or more beings separated by a large distance is a fascinating phenomenon. Yet it is a universal constant that science will eventually understand. What is sent and received is a mental image. So your thoughts must be clear and focused. The crystal pendant from Louise will help focus your mental picture. When Akira arrives, use this method to communicate with her. You might want to contact your grandmother Louise, while you are able. I'm sure she would like to talk to the three of you."

Jaguar continued. "Grandstaff and Akira are headed your direction as we speak. Earlier today, I assisted in her escape from Cui Chao Qian, the Minister of National Defense for the People's Republic of China. She was being held by Qian in an abandoned China Town building in Washington, DC." He proceeded to tell them as much as he knew about her abduction and rescue. "Grandstaff rented a car and started this way a few hours ago. The drive will take two days. Here is his cell phone number." He projected the number to Celeste. "I will communicate your number to him so he can call when he gets close. Again, thank you. We'll see you again soon."

The room seemed to lose luminance once he was gone. Not really darker, just more like the room was less alive. Celeste shut her eyes and stilled her thoughts. In the back of her mind she felt Jaguar's smile with the thought– "Thank you for listening, good job."

* * *

Bishop Daniel agreed to let Akira stay in an apartment next to Celeste and Steele. Daniel explained that he had met Akira and her father James at a charity golf tournament, and expressed concern about her physical condition. The Bishop had one stipulation–that they introduce him to Akira's brother Ian when they had a chance. The Bishop's belief that Ian and Akira were siblings surprised them, but they played along agreeing to his request.

Akira and Grandstaff arrived the following evening. Grandstaff helped Akira to the room, his strong arms supporting her as they walked up the steps to the second floor. Steele kicked himself for not thinking about the stairs being a problem. She moved painfully slowly, having to concentrate on every movement. Manipulating her body from outside of herself was like making a robot move. Walking, picking up something, drinking, even eating was very difficult. But she was happy to have her own place next to friends. She gave everyone a big smile. That was the easiest movement she could accomplish. When her spiritual body smiled from the heart, her physical body copied the movement.

Once Akira got settled, they all got together in Steele and Celeste's room for dinner. As they ate, Grandstaff would grow quiet sometimes as he communicated with Akira. Afterwards he would speak for Akira and she would nod, smile or frown depending on the sentiment of the conversation. It was odd hearing a feminine expression, with a heavy Russian accent, coming from a Paul Bunyan-like man, with a Fu Manchu mustache, who looked like he might consume you along with dinner.

After they ate, Steele looked at Akira and said, "We would like to attempt to communicate with you directly. Jaguar told us that using the crystal Louise gave us will help. Would you try to speak with Celeste and me?"

Akira nodded her head and smiled. Steele and Celeste held the crystal between their palms and took a deep, calming breath. After a few minutes Steele got frustrated, and gently pulled his hand away, leaving the crystal with Celeste.

The second he pulled away, Celeste received a thought from Akira. "He cannot hear me. I feel your thoughts and understand you clearly. Can you understand me?"

Celeste smiled and gave Akira a big hug. "Yes, I can," she said excitedly. "Yes, I understand you." Celeste concentrated on sending her thoughts. "I'm communicating with you, this is wonderful. Oh, I'm sorry, it is not wonderful what you communicated—being locked out of your body...that you feel, think, and understand, but have a difficult time moving and cannot speak. That your body is a prisoner."

A wave of concern washed across Celeste. "That must be horrible, being locked out of your body. I am so sorry. But your thoughts are so much clearer than just talking. I not only understand what you are thinking, I receive your emotions plus I get a visual picture of what you are seeing in your mind. It is almost like I'm thinking it...your last thoughts of being a prisoner really hurt me."

"Let me try again. Hand me the crystal, baby." Steele took a breath and looked at Akira. She smiled and looked deep into his eyes. A foreign thought drifted through his mind just out of reach. Like a dream you try to remember when waking. As if there was something you can almost remember, but it is just beyond assimilation. "Damn. I almost understood. It feels like there is a screen between us keeping me from remembering what I saw."

"It takesa prractiz soometiemez," Grandstaff said. "Do noot voorry. Yoou vill geet it."

"I believe with practice, I mean 'prractiz', I 'vill' walk easier, maybe even learn to talk again." Akira sent in jest. Celeste and Grandstaff laughed.

Steele looked at everyone questioningly, with signs of annoyance and aggravation. "What?"

"Oh, Akira was kidding Grandstaff about his accent," Celeste replied. "She said, 'with prractiz,' she 'vill' learn to talk again."

Akira continued, sending her thoughts. "I have seen and read stories in the news about mind control devices, such as computers, prosthetic limbs and wheel chairs. Even played around with a friend's brain wave sensor game. I never thought I would have to think of my body as a device—though that is how I have to visualize myself in order to move. My body connection is remote, alien. Like I am moving someone else. Moving works best if I visualize playing the piano with either hand to move my arms and hands, or see myself jogging, in order to move forward. But after a few weeks of practice, my accuracy should increase and hopefully my movement will become more effortless."

"That is wonderful," Celeste said, then explained to her husband what Akira had just told her.

"Voondurfull, I vill teel Jakvaar."

"That will not be necessary." Jaguar's voice projected from the corner of the room, as his embossed image materialized. "That is wonderful news. Akira, you will have to show Grandstaff your technique and teach him how to talk."

"Veerrie fooney," Grandstaff chuckled. Everyone had a good-natured laugh together.

Louise flickered into view. "That was funny. Good to see a lighter mood than I was expecting."

"Vell, auls ookaa, so I moust goo. I haava cooncerrt in Arizona. Sea yaoo saoon."

Grandstaff's body blinked in and out a few times—with a static-like interference, then he was gone. Louise watched as he vanished. "It appears he is having trouble traveling also. I am having the same problem. Was not sure I would make it here, the veil is getting very thick."

"We may have to begin traveling in groups so we can boost one another's energy." Jaguar's image blinked in and out. "This is disconcerting. We may have to destroy the Portal technology if Walter is not successful in convincing Homeland Security to stop the Jumps, until they can train the Jumpers properly. Louise, join me and we will go figure what to do."

Louise hugged Steele, Celeste and Akira. "See you again soon. I will try to stay longer next time, so we can visit." She smiled, turned to Jaguar, and they vanished without any interference.

Steele nodded to where they had been, "Looks like the group-traveling thing worked for them, it's time I turn in. Good night, Akira, nice to have you here with us."

Akira smiled and nodded.

"I'll walk with Akira to her place. Be right back, hun."

Next door, Celeste shared a quiet good night thought and gave Akira a hug. Then she started back down the hall.

As Celeste walked back to their apartment, Louise sent her another thought. The thought took only seconds to communicate with precise meaning. Celeste entered their room, hugged her husband, and attempted to give justice to what Louise had communicated.

"Baby, your grandmother sent a final big thought to me as I walked back to our apartment. I'll try to tell you exactly what she communicated." But then Celeste's verbal communication was taking her so much longer to translate. She was frustrated at the lack of clarity as she attempted to verbalize what Louise had shared, so she focused her thoughts very precisely. "Baby, this is a quote from Louise:

'You will find what I am about to tell you in my journals. Before I passed on to this dimension, Star and Jaguar, whom at the time I considered my Guiding Angels, told me: Images on your current gadgets, 3-D, TV, Internet and electronics devices are beginning to open up new possibilities for better communication. But until the human mind and soul, so steeped in its own superiority, can recognize the possibilities of intelligences beyond itself, then communications from other worlds and dimensions, will continue to be rather rare and suspect to your world. But you must keep trying.'"

Celeste spoke haltingly, quoting the guidance of Louise's Angels, as Steele listened intently to every word, trying to absorb it all: 'At mankind's sundry stages of growth, misinterpretations are rampant. If you all misunderstand each other so often even on your own plane, how can you expect correct communications between dimensions? However, even with all the difficulties, it is not impossible for there to be glimmers and flashes sent out and received. There are subtle awarenesses of communications going on all the time beneath and above your current focus. They influence your responses and your reactions in ways— in waves–that is not quite understood, usually translated into lucky, jinxed, good or evil.'

'Yet even when misinterpreted, the single most important fact remains– The potential, the embryonic, the yet-to-be developed systems of communications between what you now term other worlds... that 'other' being merely the yet-to-be explored, vast part of the Cosmos...' Celeste stopped to stress the importance of one last thought Louise had sent. '... that we must learn not only to give, but to receive with Grace. Remember, Love is the basic and ultimate communication in the universe.'

Celeste's voice diminished to a whisper as she quoted the poetry of an enlightened soul:

'Souls flicker,
even through dying:
Ray withdrawn to Light.'"

〉 〉 〉

CHAPTER 19
Unforeseen

Walter had been working diligently with the leading neuroscientist at the National Institute for Neurological Disorders. Electrodes ran from points scattered across the EEG swimming cap he wore, attached to a state-of-the-art, inference-based biofeedback system. He looked like some crazy cyborg. They were using electroencephalography to measure the mental functions of the experimental neuro-enhancing drugs in combination with Walter's special meditation.

Walter was optimistic about the meditation. It started with 126.22 Hz, the platonic energies of the Sun, a regularity signal that produces energies that resonate between Earth and the Cosmos. The chakra carrier wave graduates up to 320 Hz frequency providing information about creation, and communicates intelligence about different dimensions. Tones then evolved through A=432Hz to C=256Hz, which harmonizes with the speed of light, the human light body and Earth's rotation. Ending with the sacred Solfeggio tones at 528 Hz, the healing tones used in ancient Gregorian chants. His hypothesis was that the frequencies produced by these chants and their special tones would help him enter the high vibrational frequency necessary to create Ian's Horologe.

After numerous attempts, Walter was making great progress. The doctor checked the biofeedback equipment and gave him the green light. "Dim the lights and start my meditation tape," Walter instructed. "This time it's going to work."

Resonant harmonic tones filled the office where Walter sat, wired to the equipment, meditating. He held a mental picture of the Horologe microchip design as his consciousness entered a heightened alpha state. Blue light from the glass case he stared into bathed Walter's face in an eerie glow. In the glass case was a viral mixture of DNA strings aligning in the crystalline structure of magnetite to his mental projection. Millions of intricate paths were forming before his eyes, connecting microscopic switches, thus creating the Horologe.

"Finally!" Walter leaped out of the chair, only to be yanked back by the wires still attached to his cap. "This one is going to work! Help me. Help me get this contraption off my head. We have to get this chip into the oven to cure."

As the chip cured, Walter had a battle raging within. He was torn between conflicting realities. The scientist in him could hardly believe what he had just accomplished. This method of chip manufacturing would change the world.

But the humanitarian in him wanted to destroy the chip before anyone saw it. If what Jaguar and those from the other dimension told him was true, this WOULD change the world–it would doom the world to the dark ages, cutting off Earth's spiritual sustenance. Unless he could convince the Director to start a recruitment and training program for the Jump teams. He had to try.

Walter met with Director Rebel later that evening in the computer lab. "You may have a hard time believing me, Director. Just please keep an open mind."

"Walter, after all the amazing accomplishments you have come up with since I've known you, especially since you've been working with this new technology, I'm not sure what I won't believe. You have really been pushing the boundaries of my imagination."

'This might be easier to explain than I had hoped,' Walter thought. He stopped to think of the best way to approach this. "Good, I'm happy to hear that you have an open mind...I'm not sure how to say this..."

"Spit it out, Walter." Rebel was obviously getting irritated. "I have a hundred things to do. What is it?"

"Well, remember the unfortunate accident on Highway 12 in Utah. The reason Ian and his father James were in Utah, was to meet with a group of people that live in the mountains."

"WALTER! What does that have to do with the price of tea in China?" Rebel said acrimoniously.

Walter ignored his friend's anger and continued. "These people are different. They live in another dimension–in the dimension our Jump technology uses to travel."

Rebel frowned. "So you are telling me there are aliens living in the Utah Mountains. Please tell me this isn't about the crackpots and Area 51."

Walter shook his head. "No, nothing like that. These people are real. Only they live in another dimension. It appears that as mankind–you and I learn about the world and how life works–how spiritual life works, we can graduate to this other dimension. This is the next step in human evolution."

"That make me feel better," Rebel jested. "So instead of going to heaven–or hell–I can move my things to Utah and live in the mountains." He paused. "I think you are working too hard, Walter. Go home for a few days–get some rest." He got up to leave.

"Director Aaron Rebel!" Walter said in exasperation. "You and I have known each other for years. I was there when you were married. When your daughter was born and graduated from high school. Do NOT write me off, without hearing me out first. This is important, and you are going to hear this. So sit down!" Rebel was surprised at the outburst, but did as he was told.

Walter went on to explain about the dimensions, the technology and how the Jump Platoon was destroying the veil between dimensions. Walter asked Rebel to talk with Commander Gholam and develop a recruitment and training program to eliminate the destruction being caused.

Rebel listened, but wasn't sure if he should be getting his old friend medical or psychological help. Or...if he could possibly be correct? "Shit, Walter, you have either lost your mind or this is going to change the world."

"Aaron, you know you can't tell everyone about this," Walter said with concern. "People will begin to think you are as crazy as I am–that I'm rubbing off on you. We have to be discrete about this, about who we trust, who we confide in."

Rebel rested his chin between his thumb and index-finger of his hand and thought. Then he rubbed the side of his face and temple. "I did not say I believe you."

Walter smiled. "But neither did you say that you didn't believe me either. I'll set up a meeting with someone from the other dimension. They can prove to you what I am saying." He unfolded the paper Louise had given him at the Falls and made a call to Steele.

* * *

Walter and Director Rebel appeared standing in the moonlight, 124 floors above the ground. "This is neutral ground, just as you asked," Walter said. "An out of the way place where we could meet and talk that is not in Washington or in Utah. Someplace secure. At 2 a.m., I figured this is one of the most secure places we could find. No one will be up here at this hour. The elevators shut down to the upper floors after midnight."

"Walter, tell me where we are. No more suspense," Rebel demanded, gingerly stepping away from the chrome and glass rail surrounding the observation deck, where they had both Jumped a minute earlier.

Walter smiled. "Hope you are not afraid of heights. I have always wanted to see the view from here. We are on the observation deck of the Burj Khalifa tower in Dubai, United Arab Emirates. This is the tallest man-made structure in the world. Really some view, isn't it?" Walter stuck his arms out like a kid playing airplane and spun in a circle. He stopped and pointed off toward the horizon. "Look, there are the lights from Palm Jumeira Island."

"You could have killed us, Walter! If your calculations were off by a foot when we stepped through the Portal, we could have found ourselves standing in mid-air 124 stories above the ground."

"Aaron, I thought you knew me better. I used NASA's Global Positioning System to measure the latitude and longitude values and the WGS 84 geodetic systems of datums to calculate our exact position. Of course, I cross-referenced the calculations using the seven-parameter transformation method of three-dimensional space in association with geodesy formulas. You are standing within 2cm of my calculations. And look at this view!"

"How could I have doubted you, Walter?" Aaron said.

"Quite a view, Walter," came Star's voice from behind them.

"Yes, very interesting choice for our meeting," Louise agreed, standing next to Star and Grandstaff.

"Voud yoo look at zet. Goud too zee yoo, Valltuer."

"Nice to see you all again," Walter replied. "Star, Louise and Grandstaff—this is Director Aaron Rebel. Aaron, these are my friends from the other dimension."

With a rigid air of suspicion, Rebel acknowledged the semi-transparent, ghost-like group. "Interesting, good to meet all of you," he said with trepidation. Then took a step back, straightened his shoulders and stood more confidently. "Walter has apprised me of our meeting's agenda. Let me get right to the point. First, why should I believe you are from another dimension? Second, why should I care if you travel between dimensions or not?"

Star explained the situation. "Walter understands the equations that enable the Jump technology to work. It increases the vibrational weight of a person's energy, changing their molecular wave-length in order to move between dimensions."

"Yes, yes, of course. I understand," Rebel said indignantly.

Star continued, patiently. "This other dimension used by your technology is inhabited."

Walter walked over to Louise and put his arm around her. Grandstaff vanished, and reappeared standing behind Walter, Louise and Star. "These friends of mine live in the other dimension," Walter said. "Louise, Star and Grandstaff, along with many other people, consider that dimension home. They call that dimension, 'Gaia.' It's inhabited by numerous people from Earth, who have increased their vibrational energy to a point where they have shifted their essence to that world. Gaia is mankind's next stage of human development."

"We came to speak with you and ask for your help," Louise said. "The technology you call Jump, is destroying the ability to move between dimensions. Before long, mankind will not be able to advance to their natural stage of spiritual growth."

Rebel looked at the group speciously. "Why are more people not aware of this dimension?"

Louise stepped next to Rebel and took his hand. Rebel started to pull away, but found she had a comforting way about her that melted his apprehension. "There are many in your world that attempt to share this understanding. Very few listen to these people. They are considered new-age crack-pots, among other labels."

"Let me explain further, young man," Louise said. "Due to recent celestial alignments, Earth is in a quantum shift which aligns our planet with its destined position in the cosmos. This shift has attuned Earth in a perfected state as a planet, to make a shift into an evolved cycle of life. This means the veil between dimensions is thin enough right now, to allow enlightened people from your plane of existence, to move to our world more easily. In highly advanced situations, even physically transforming their bodies to this evolutionary existence."

Louise continued. "As people from your dimension leave behind greed and selfishness and learn to dance in the energies of unconditional love and unceasing light, access opens to the mind's energies. This process enables those to consciously transcend time and space, so one's conscious awareness is able to visit, then ultimately move to the higher dimensional levels of existence in the universe. This activates multi-dimensional understanding and an awareness that vibrates at the same resonance as Gaia. From this place of being, they will be able to communicate, then even see into our dimension. We will first appear very ghost-like, though as they become mindful of their surroundings we will become more opaque, more solid in appearance."

Director Rebel was not sold. "This all sounds like a science fiction story. I do not believe–I have not risen to 'your Vibration'– yet you stand before me. Ghost-like, but here all the same. This is only a trick of the Jump technology. What is your game?"

"Zhis is noo games." Grandstaff took a threatening step toward Rebel.

Star softly placed her hand on Grandstaff's arm. "Let me speak to Aaron. May I call you Aaron? We are only attempting to help. Throughout history, glimmers of hope, wisdom and knowledge have filtered through many dimensions to help all of us understand–to grow toward our higher self. Many religions speak of this and teach their version of this awareness. If you are a religious man look to your God, to your bible, Torah or whatever teaching you follow, and you will find the same truths. We will speak again, glad to make your acquaintance."

Star dipped her head in a light bow to acknowledge his spirit and show respect. She then took Louise and Grandstaff by the hand. The air around them wavered then they blinked away, leaving Walter and Rebel standing in darkness.

* * *

Late that night, Rebel found Walter sitting at his desk, long hair disheveled, Rockstar in his hand. "Did you get any sleep, Walter?"

He looked up from the gadget he was working on. "Yes–I believe so. What day is this?"

"Sunday Walter. We met with your friends early this morning, standing on top of the world– remember?"

"Of course I remember. In fact, you were rather rude to them–as I remember."

Rebel put on his best guise of genuine sincerity. "That's why I'm here,

Walter. I would like a chance to apologize. And tell them we will begin recruiting and training for new Jump platoons. I did a lot of soul searching this evening, and decided that working with them wouldn't hurt anything. If they have correctly ascertained the situation it may even help."

Walter leaped to his feet, with a look of shock. "Aaron!"

"What is it?" Rebel blurted out in surprise.

"My god, you have a soul. I never realized."

"Very funny, Walter. You have always been such a wisecracker. Talk to your friends, and arrange another meeting." Rebel turned and started to walk away, then stopped and looked over his shoulder. "Oh, I do NOT like heights–no skyscrapers. I would like to see their dimension, this Gaia, if they are willing. Let's meet there."

* * *

At home that evening, Walter sat back in his favorite recliner, Scotch in hand, reading an article in 'Science Journal.' It referred to classified CIA documents that had been released in 1995. The documents revealed that in the 1970s, the CIA had sponsored a program at Stanford Research Institute in Menlo Park, California, to determine whether such phenomena as remote viewing might have any utility for intelligence collection. The intelligence community had been involved for more than two decades, investigating so-called parapsychology or psi phenomena. That program presumably ended in 1985, though new information had come to light. In that same year a corporation by the name of Sentient6 was formed to continue the research.

In the past few years, the Sentient6 Corporation had been working with children that displayed strong psychic talents.

Walter sat up in his chair, eyes wide. 'That's it!' Walter said to himself. He sometimes talked to himself when working out problems. After all, he usually came up with the best answers to his questions. 'If Sentient6 is government-supported, they might have the clearance to help me manufacture the Horologe chip. I'll teach some of these kids how to apply their talents to a useful project. They can help me build the chips.'

* * *

Ian pulled into a hotel with his tired family, after hours on the road. The drive from Denver had been filled with tears and questions about mom, loads of complaints about leaving friends and moving to the middle of nowhere along with a few friendly-ish fights between brother and sister. They were all exhausted by the time they reached Albuquerque, so the overnight stay was relaxing and uneventful. It was a welcome change after all the intense heartache, and full spectrum of emotions they were all feeling.

The next day nothing much was said on the drive from New Mexico into Arizona. Alek, Kristen, James and Ian were mostly consumed by their own thoughts. After another long drive, Ian turned the car off Highway 17 at Cordes Lakes. They stretched, filled up at one of the only two gas stations, then turned on Stagecoach Trail toward Arcosanti.

"Kids, I know neither of you are happy about this, but we all need a place to stay out of sight until we figure out what to do. This will only be temporary, so make the best of it," Ian urged. James added that they would find a way to have fun together.

Approaching Arcosanti, they found a community that looked otherworldly, a mix of the future with organic curves and shapes from the past. Rico was standing at the Visitor's Center when Ian and his family entered. "There you are, my friend." Rico gave Ian a big hug. "It is so good to see you, Mr. Peabody."

Alek and Kristen gave each other a look somewhere between confusion and skepticism. "Who's Mr. Peabody?" Kristen whispered to her brother.

Alek shrugged his shoulders and shook his head. "Hell if I know."

Kristen covered her ears. "Omm–I'm going to tell dad and grandpa."

Alek pinched her and showed his fist. "You better not."

"Ouch! Daddy!"

"Behave, you two. Rico, this is my son Alek, daughter Kristen and my father James."

"Welcome everyone," Rico said. "Kristen, I can't believe you are so big. Alek, you play basketball yet? Where did you get that height? And nice to meet you, sir," Rico shook James's hand.

Then he stepped back and spread his arms. "We are all standing in the Visitor's Center of the Crafts III building which provides housing on the first level, a cafe on the second level, a bakery on the third floor mezzanine, and a gallery on the fourth level. If you don't mind, I will tell you about

Arcosanti's design principles on the way to your apartment."

They left the building and walked slowly, Rico guiding the way. "In nature, as an organism evolves, it increases in complexity and it also becomes a more compact or miniaturized system. Similarly, a city should function as a living system. This is called Arcology, architecture and ecology as one integral process. Arcology is capable of producing positive results to the many problems of urban civilization–population, pollution, energy and natural resource depletion, food scarcity and quality of life. Arcology recognizes the necessity of the radical reorganization of the sprawling urban landscape into dense, integrated, three-dimensional cities in order to support the complex activities that sustain human cultures. The city is the necessary instrument for the evolution of humankind."

Rico spoke ardently to Ian and James, with the children lagging behind exploring. "Arcosanti seeks to embody a 'Lean Alternative' to hyper consumption through a smartly efficient and elegant city design. Leanness is inherent to the sustainable health of any living system. That is the general idea behind this city. I can tell you more sometime if you're interested." Alek looked at his sister, crossed his eyes, made a goofy face and whispered, "Yeh, tell us more," and they both giggled.

"Here we are, the East Crescent complex." Ian could see how much Arcosanti meant to Rico, as he continued. "You will be staying in the Sky Suite, while your apartments are prepared. You'll enjoy the large two-bedroom unit. It is usually rented to overnight guests, but I pulled some strings for you."

As they entered the apartment, Rico flourished his arms in the air again. "Look at the extensive use of glass in the living area, it takes advantage of the fabulous views from the third floor. This room overlooks the Sky Theater of the Colly Soleri Music Center. And through that window is the Agua Fria River valley. Beautiful, isn't it? There's a small kitchen and eating area, one bedroom has a double bed, another bedroom has a single and sleeping pads are in the living area. So there is enough space for the four of you for a day or two."

"Follow me now," he said excitedly. "The suite opens onto a roof terrace with a great view of the landscape to the south and access to the top of the South Vault for a 360-degree view. It's also a great place for star-gazing. You all have full access to all the amenities, cafe, library, swimming pool, classes, and the amphitheater."

Rico was long-winded, but they all listened patiently. "We have a wonderful guest artist scheduled to play next week. Nikolay Grandstaff."

Ian raised an eyebrow and looked at his father. "Did you say Grandstaff will be here next week?"

"Yes. Have you heard him play?"

Ian pulled Rico away from the kids. "We met not too long ago. Can you come by this evening so we can talk privately?"

"Sure, I'll meet you on your terrace around nine tonight."

Then they joined Alek and Kristen in the middle of an argument about who was going to get the bedroom. "I am sure you are all sick of hearing me ramble on. Make yourself at home. I stocked the refrigerator, if you are hungry. Let me know if you need anything at all."

After Rico left, James gave Ian a vexed look and blew out a heavy breath. "Whew, I never thought he would stop talking." The family laughed quietly.

* * *

That night, Ian sat on the moon-drenched terrace, staring out across the high desert landscape. The surrounding architecture blended with the valley, lending the panorama a mystical aura. He could almost see the Native American medicine man from the prehistoric Hohokam tribe, conjuring the spirit of grandfather and animal totems to guide his healing. Arcosanti seemed to honor the ancient culture's way of living with the land.

His thoughts drifted across the valley...when he became aware of a hand waving in front of his face. "Hello, earth to Ian, come in, Mr. Peabody."

Shaking his head brought him back to reality. "Oh–Rico, how long have you been standing there?"

"Long enough to catch you in a daydream, or trance or something. Are you all right?"

"I'm not really sure any more, my friend."

Rico had brought a bottle of wine, he poured a couple of glasses, and handed one to Ian. "I don't mean to add to your uncertainty, but I have something to tell you."

"Rico, I'm not sure I can handle anything more. Please tell me you have good news. Or that you have some answers to life's great mysteries."

Rico smiled reassuringly. "There are more things in heaven and earth, Mr. Peabody, than are dreamt of in your technology."

"If you say so, Mr. Shakespeare," Ian said. "That's from Hamlet, I believe –and I am beginning to see that's true. I smell foul play, Sherman."

"So you're quoting scholars also," Rico replied. They both laughed, remembering Mr. Peabody and Sherman's cartoon from their childhood. "You remember what the cartoon announcer usually said?" Rico took on an air of the radio announcer. "Well, you're just in time for what might be a very unhappy ending."

Ian tried to smile as a tear ran down his cheek. "I could use a happy ending instead. Or at the very least some happy thoughts." Ian took several gulps of wine.

Rico took a sip of his drink and sighed. "I do not know how to say this, so I'm just going to say it. I am from Gaia–from the dimension where Jasmine now lives."

Ian choked on his drink, coughing, as Rico continued. "Are you all right, buddy?" Ian nodded, clearing his throat. "Anyway, a number of people living here are from Gaia's dimension, the same as Montsalvat and similar to the Falls. However, the Falls is a different place, because it has no Earthly component. Those living there live strictly in Gaia."

Ian cleared his throat again. "What did you say?–Are you kidding me? This world is turning inside out. Two years ago, I thought I had most everything figured out. The first Jump was successful, and I was on top of the world. Now, I feel like the world has swallowed me and I'm churning in Earth's acidic stomach."

"I'm telling you the truth, buddy. I spoke with Jasmine, Louise and Star just this evening. Jasmine asked me to tell you that you are full of 'dumb luck' and she loves you for that."

Ian remembered her telling him that dumb luck is how she and the kids ended up with him. And that it was Jasmine who suggested he contact Rico for help. He took a deep breath. "You ARE telling me the truth. Is Jasmine all right? Why didn't I ever know this about you before? How long ago did you cross over to Gaia?"

"Ian, slow down, have a sip of wine–here, let me pour you another glass. Jasmine is fine. In fact, she is in the other dimension, standing next to you as we speak. However, she is unable to cross over to Earth's dimension because she has not learned to lower her vibration sufficiently. She is so high-spirited!" They both laughed. "Plus the veil between dimensions is becoming so corrupt, making it difficult except for the most talented from Gaia to move between worlds. I'm not sure how much longer I will be able to cross over. I may be leaving soon."

Ian drained his glass. "Can Jasmine hear me? Tell her I'm sorry. I know the dimensional cataclysm is my fault."

"Yes, she is able to hear, and even feel a subtle energy from you. She is asking me to tell you that she loves you and the kids very much, and misses you tremendously. She also thinks you should relax, that your energy is feeling very tense."

Ian's emotions caught in his chest, so that he couldn't swallow, and was having trouble taking a breath. After a minute, he whispered. "Baby, I love you so much. I want to hold you, feel you nibble on my ear again."

Rico turned his head, listening. "She said to take care of yourself and the kids. She just kissed you, said good night. She needs to be alone, it hurts too much to see you and the kids right now. She asked you to meditate, to calm yourself, so that you might learn to hear her yourself. Be still and listen when you first wake. That is a good time to communicate, before you are fully awake, and she will try to reach you then. She plans to stay here in Gaia's Arcosanti, and to work with me to help your family hasten your abilities to communicate between dimensions. As you may or may not know, Arcosanti is much like Montsalvat artist studios in Victoria, Australia, along with many other locations around the world, that share an Earthly and Gaia world in the same location. Now get some sleep, buddy. You look bone-tired."

Rico looked past him, obviously listening to someone unseen. "Louise would like to share insights from the Journals she wrote, about passing over, before she joined us in this world. She asks if that would be all right with you?" Ian nodded his head in agreement.

"I will tell you, word for word what she is saying: 'Jasmine has not left you. It is only your perception that is not strong enough. Insights from others will help you on your path, until you can find your own way. And know that borders are no barriers to souls in love. Good night.'"

With that, Rico put his hand on Ian's shoulder, gave him a reassuring squeeze and walked away into the night.

> > >

CHAPTER 20
Meany Maddie

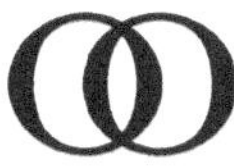

Fajah stood at the window, doing her best not to cry. She wouldn't give Meany Maddie the satisfaction. A friendly-looking man with long gray hair got out of a car in the parking lot below her window. He had a kind smile, it reminded her of Tata. She really missed her granddad...and the little house they had lived in...and her room with the flowered wallpaper. She wanted to go home and play in the trees, by the creek, where she had found that wallpaper. People used to throw things away, down by the creek. The wallpaper was the prettiest thing she ever found there.

Ms. Elanor Maddie poked her mean headmistress head into the room. "Fajah, find the other children–all of you meet me in the class room in five minutes."

Mean Maddie always ruined her dreaming. Fajah opened her mouth wide and huffed warm breath on the window glass, then in the fog she drew a frown with dots for eyes. "Okay, Mea... Ms. Maddie," she yelled, running out the door and down the hall.

Fajah found the other eight kids in the game room. The few times they didn't have chores or classes, most everyone played there. She didn't like it there, the games were lame, not fun like memory games and stuff like that. All the other snotty kids thought they were so smart, kidding her about the way she talked.

Fajah saw her one friend, Linda. "Ya com wid me Lienda, the kids, not no nothin. Ya tell em Meany Maddie wantus ina class."

Linda told the kids, then she and Fajah took off running down the hall toward the classroom. Fajah and Linda sat in the back of the class, watching the others find their desks. "What did you do?" everyone was asking one another. Who was going to be scolded? By the time Ms. Maddie arrived, the kids had narrowed the culprits to five of them, and everyone looked guilty.

They were all happy to see Ms. Maddie walk in with a stranger. He didn't look threatening. Fajah smiled, it was the nice man from the parking lot! "Class, this is Mr. Walter Walter." Walter stepped forward with a grand bow. Fajah stood and bowed, copying his grandeur as best she could. Everyone laughed.

Ms. Maddie frowned at Walter's theatrics, gave the kids a sour look and clapped her hands. The room got quiet. "Glad to meet all of you. Please call me Walter, not Walter–Walter. My father stuttered when he named me."

He got a couple of giggles which quickly died under Mean Maddie's glare. "Children, Mr. Walter has a fun game. He would like to test everyone and find one of you to help him make a special computer chip."

The kids all drug out long moans. "A tesssst...."

Ms. Maddie looked across the class. "Who would like to go first?"

Fajah's hand shot up. "Mea, me."

"All right." Walter smiled at her.

"Not her, she is a little trouble-maker. Benjamin here is a good boy." She pulled Benjamin out of his seat at the front of the room.

"If you say so, Ms. Maddie," Walter said. "Then the little girl in the back can go next. What is your name, hun?" he asked her.

"Fajah, mi namea, it Fajah."

Another boy in the front stood. "It Fajah," he mocked. The kids laughed.

Ms. Maddie threatened an hour of extra homework and the room got deathly still. "Come." She pulled Benjamin by the collar.

"That's not necessary, Elanor," Walter said as the classroom door shut. He patted Benjamin on the shoulder.

"Ms. Maddie," she snapped. "You may call me Ms. Maddie." She turned abruptly and marched away, ordering, "Follow me." At the end of the long hall, she opened a door to a dark room, and flipped on the light.

Walter shielded his eyes from the bright white light, as it illuminated the sterile room. From what he had seen, this Sentient6 facility would make a better hospital than school. Except even in hospitals there is an occasional plant or picture on the wall.

"You can use this room. Let me know when you are ready for another child."

"Have a seat and relax, young Benjamin," Walter invited. "Would it be all right if I call you Ben?"

"Okay. Is this test going to be hard, sir?" Ben looked nervous.

"Just chill, young Ben," Walter said casually, opening his briefcase.

"Would you like a Tootsie Pop?" Walter unwrapped a grape sucker and popped it into his mouth, then held out an assortment to Ben.

"Thank you, sir." Ben took an orange pop. Walter smiled, then took an orange and green pop and held one in each hand behind his back. "Choose the hand with an orange pop and you get another."

Ben picked the wrong hand. Walter switched the pops and brought out the orange and gave it to him. "Good choice, son. That is as hard as the tests get."

He ran a few more tests. Some had six cards with different symbols–wavy lines, an x, circle, square and such. He tested child after child with mixed results. Some of the children seemed promising. Others must have been too nervous. He was yet to see little Fajah, as he had requested. Mean Maddie had ostracized Fajah, leaving her for very last, then pulled her into the room by the collar. "You behave, young lady."

"You know, Elanor...you can catch more flies with honey than with vinegar," Walter admonished, receiving a glare from Ms. Maddie as she reminded him sternly of her formal name. Then she huffed and stormed out of the room. Walter stuck out his tongue, put a thumb in each ear and waved his fingers as the door closed behind her.

Fajah giggled and copied him. "Thata bea fulljoy," she said with a smile.

"Yeh, it really was fun, wasn't it? Is she always so mean?"

Fajah mocked Mean Maddie. She stomped her foot, pinched her lips tight, squinted her eyes, dropped eyebrows and looked mean. Then she placed her hands on her hips, shifting her weight back and forth. "She be allaways mean ta mi anda Lienda."

Fajah had fun with Walter's tests. When they finished, she gave him a big hug and growled. "Thisa how mi friend growl ta her tata," then she lowered her voice–"Mi no wanta ya ta go."

Walter growled back, and said, "I have a feeling I will be seeing you again soon." She had far surpassed the other children's tests scores. "In fact, how would you like to take a trip to Washington, DC, and see my office sometime?"

Fajah started to jump up and down in excitement. Then she stopped with a pout. "Lienda, she coma tu?"

"I'll see what I can do," he said, already thinking to himself. 'These two must have become friends because they can relate to one another, they had the two highest scores from the group.'

"I will contact Ms. Maddie as soon as arrangements can be made for you and Linda to visit me. See you soon."

After Meany Maddie excused them, Fajah ran as fast as she could, throwing the door to her room open as she sprinted to the window. Walter was just getting to his car. She banged on the window to get his attention, then blew her hot breath on the cool window, drew a happy face and waved.

This little one made Walter happy. He waved, then took his first two fingers, pointed to his eyes then pointed to her with the same fingers and mouthed, 'See you soon.'

* * *

"Congratulations on a job well done, Commander Gholam," Director Rebel saluted, then turned to address Bodner. "Mr. Speaker, as you know, the Syrian mission was an outstanding success. The prisoners were rescued without a shot being fired. The Islamic State will have no idea how their captives disappeared. I would love to have been a fly on the wall, when they discovered them missing."

The three men were meeting in a secure bunker deep underground, that was built for privacy. Jaguar had attempted to follow and listen to their conversation, but the electromagnetism encompassing the room was more than he could penetrate.

"Yes, well done, Commander," replied Speaker Bodner. "The President will be honoring you surreptitiously with the National Defense Service Medal in the next few weeks. Right now, however, we need to focus on an immediate situation. Ian Knecht is still at large. And now his father and son have also escaped our surveillance. Good news, though. They were all seen at Ian's home in Colorado."

"Ian sold his vehicle attempting to cover his trail, which worked for awhile. But we have the license number for the gray SUV he is now driving. We have also placed Ian on the FBI's most wanted list, so it is only a matter of time before he is spotted. Commander, your team is on 24-hour alert. Split the platoon into shifts so a team is ready to move within minutes of Ian being located. Understood?" Bodner then dismissed him with a nod to the door.

"Mr. Speaker, I need to speak with you about another subject," Rebel urged, rather hesitantly, once they were alone. "Walter and I recently met with a group of people, that know more about this technology than they should. The three people we met with are–odd, to say the least. Louise, is a young lady, yet has a mannerism much older than her impression. There's a tall, attractive young lady they call Star, who has a dark complexion, long black hair and strange obsidian eyes. And a threatening Russian, they referred to as Grandstaff, who had a look like he might take a bite out of me."

Bodner stood impatiently waiting to hear some significance to this information. Rebel hurried to explain: "They claim to be part of a much larger group. These people have a Jump device with which I am not familiar. But here is where their story gets really strange. They claim to live in another dimension–the same dimension that Jump technology uses to move from place to place. I believe they are a grave threat to national security and to our business endeavors."

Bodner crossed his arms and took a defensive stance. "Well, we can't have them upsetting our business plans, now can we? What are we going to do about it, Aaron?"

Rebel smiled, and felt invited to a first-name basis. "John, they claim to need our help. We can use this to our advantage." Aaron went on to explain about how the Jump technology is supposedly damaging the dimensions. He broached the idea of spiritual awakening and mankind's next stage of human development.

Bodner shook his head in disbelief. "Sounds like a crock of shit, Aaron. What is their game, and how can we use this against them?"

A wicked smirk spread across Rebel's face, glad to be treated as a confidant. "Star asked me to seek guidance from my God, from my bible. And to meet with them again. Can you believe that? I don't remember any scripture about crazy people living in another dimension. But they actually believe we might help them. I can arrange an ambush. I'll set another meeting. Our Jump platoon armed with these new Collars and Laser Whips will just happen to be waiting. We can capture them and move them to Guantanamo Bay detention camp for questioning. That will enable us to interrogate them with any means necessary to find the rest of their terrorist group."

> > >

CHAPTER 21
Elec-Toads

Fajah stood at her bedroom window watching for Walter Walter. That was a fun name, she said it over and over, waiting to see his wonderful smile again. Whenever she had any free time she would stand at the window and watch for Walter Walter. She smiled thinking of his name again.

Meany Maddie had called the kids together again. This time Ms. Maddie looked like her favorite cat had just been hit by a car. Everyone was anxious, and afraid of what she was going to tell them. "Children." Meany always started that way. "Remember Mr. Walter, the gentleman who visited us recently to run some tests?"

It wasn't much fun when SHE said his name, Fajah thought. In fact, she made his name sound dirty, bad somehow. Must be the way she twisted her face and sounded like she was scolding him. Fajah just wasn't going to listen if Meany was going to be nasty to Walter. "Bla, bla... bla-bla-bla-bla..."

"Fajah...FAJAH!"

Linda jabbed her with an elbow, bringing her attention back to the room. "Ouch," she exclaimed. "Yow weh yuh a seh?"

Meany scowled at Fajah. "Come to the front of the room right this instant."

'Aht-oh. Waa mi doo?' Fajah wondered. She looked at her feet, and shuffled her way to the front of the room. "Yesa ma'am."

"I do NOT for the life of me, see why. Nevertheless, Mr. Walter would like to take you to Washington, DC, and work with you to develop his computer chip."

Fajah screeched with excitement, before covering her mouth. "Aum sarry ma'am, mi forget mi mannars." Fajah tucked her chin to her chest, and looked up with her best big-eyed puppy-dog look.

"Do not give me that look. It–will–not–work." Meany pronounced each word separately. "Notwithstanding, Mr. Walter will be here tomorrow to pick you up, so pack some things. Oh I almost forgot. He would also like your little friend Linda to make the trip. Linda, get your bag packed as well. It will be nice and quiet around here while you two are gone."

* * *

"Hes a herea now Lienda!" Fajah said, turning from the window. "Walter Walter hea fanally herea, get u bags–harrys up." Fajah grabbed her backpack off the nightstand and bolted down the hall. "Com a naow Lienda."

"Hello, Mr. Walter," Maddie said, meeting Walter at the reception desk. "As you know, we have run a thorough investigation into your background. This is procedure for anyone working with our children. It is nothing personal, but we must make sure our young ladies are taken care of while away from us. You appear to be quite a colorful person, though there were no red-flags that would make you suspect for any wrong-doing. I also made arrangements for the girls to stay with a foster family, close to the National Institute for Neurological Disorders. Someone from Sentient6 will check on the girls regularly."

Then she pulled him aside. "There is a matter of that payment we discussed. After all, we cannot allow the girls to work as interns for free. Then I will find Fajah and Linda and bring them right out."

Walter handed her a sealed envelope.

"Very good then. This is the address of the foster home, they are expecting you. Wait here in the lobby, I will only be a minute." Ms. Maddie started to march away when Fajah came sliding around the corner. Linda skidded into Fajah as they came to a stop in the hall, face-to-face with Meany Maddie. "YOUNG LADIES–Manners!" The girls stood up taller, brushed their skirts down and straightened their shirt collars.

"Sorry, Ms. Maddie," they said in unison.

"You both behave, and mind your manners while you are with Mr. Walter. Do you have all your things, girls?"

"Yes, ma'am." Fajah and Linda walked very properly past the front desk and curtsied to Walter. "Good to see you, Mr. Walter," the girls said together.

Walter flourished them with a deep formal bow. "Nice to see you two again." He winked to Fajah, receiving a beautiful, natural smile in return.

"I will have the girls back before you know it," Walter said as he picked up their small bags and they all walked to the door.

Once outside, Walter smiled at the girls. "We're free! Last one to the car is a rotten egg." He took off running toward the parking lot. They both giggled, looked over their shoulders at Meany Maddie, and ran as fast as they could.

The next day Walter met the girls at the private residence, where he had delivered them the night before. This was going to be their new home for now. The Haywards were nice foster parents. The girls took to their daughter April immediately. April was a couple of years older and made Fajah and Linda feel right at home. The Hayward's home looked like it was out of a fairy tale, with two big brick fireplaces, many pointy roofs and a basketball hoop in the driveway. It had a large nicely landscaped yard, with manicured shrubs surrounding the house.

Across the street was a forest with big trees and a path. "Wonda whar da patha run?" Fajah said as she and Linda got into Walter's car. They were going to the research lab where he was going to show them how to build a Horologe. "Da ta fulljoy name," Fajah smiled. "Walter Walter an da Horologe chip, solika a spy film," she giggled and whispered to Linda.

Linda smiled and whispered back, "Maybe Walter Walter is a cook and the Horologe is a potato chip he cooks." They laughed together, happy to be in a new place, and away from Meany Maddie.

On the way to the National Institute for Neurological Disorders, the girls were wide-eyed, making up stories about the tall buildings, all the people and cars. Then Fajah thought how very important Walter Walter must be, when she saw that the 'Neuro-Disordered' building was so very big–maybe ten floors high with at least a million windows.

A large fish tank in the lobby, with all the pretty fish, held the girls' attention while Walter talked to the receptionist. When Walter was finished at the front desk, he walked over and made a funny face from the other side of the fish, then came around the tank and clipped badges on Linda and Fajah. "Come on, girls."

Upstairs, Walter showed them some strange equipment. He told them how the equipment attached to the electrodes on the swimming cap, and would read their minds and make the chip from their thoughts.

"Wow, obe maagick," Fajah said.

Then he gave them drawings of the microchip and wanted them to study it–to memorize all the details.

After some time, Walter asked, "Who wants to go first?"

The girls looked at each other. "Will it hurt?" they asked.

"I would never hurt you girls, promise."

"Mi go, dat elec-toads no gona hurt?" Fajah asked.

Linda snickered at Fajah. "It's not electric toads." They all laughed.

"You look funny, like a robot-monster, with wires coming from your head," Linda noted, after the cap was on Fajah.

After the kidding around, they settled into working. Fajah had a hard time concentrating. All she could think of was toads hopping on top of her head, attached to the swim cap with wires.

* * *

Time slipped away and Walter was beginning to think the experiment was a bust. He was about to end the research, when…one afternoon the three of them were working after lunch. Fajah was attached to the electrodes, concentrating hard when Linda walked over and held her hand. "You look like you are going to explode. Relax, let's play the game we play when Meany Maddie sends us to our room. You know, when we look at each other's thoughts."

The girls sat together, holding hands and closed their eyes. Walter watched the monitor and noticed Fajah's brainwave frequencies begin to calm. The two girls worked so well together. With astonishment Walter observed Linda's brainwaves appeared on Fajah's chart, though she was not being monitored. Their EEG, Alpha, Beta and even Theta graphs were almost identical, it was like they were one person. Their breaths came together in chorus, and when they reached an identical deep Delta state, Walter saw the mixture of DNA strings start to align to their combined mental projection. He waited and watched, with amazement.

"That's it, girls, you did it!" Their combined energy was the missing ingredient.

The following days the girls made eleven chips. As they got more familiar with the process, the chips became easier to create, and the last one only took 25 minutes to generate.

As the girls worked, Walter sat at the desk blocking their view and made a quiet phone call. "Set up the surprise, the girls will be so excited!" Then poking his head out from behind the computer, Walter announced,

"Help me clean up, we are leaving early today. We must go to my office, I have a secret for you."

"What is it?" the girls questioned in unison.

"You'll have to wait, I told you it's a secret."

A few blocks away in his office, Walter went to his computer and entered some numbers, then he grinned at the girls. "You are doing a marvelous job, my little ladies. Let us celebrate." Walter produced three pointy party hats decorated in colored polka dots, with rubber bands for under their chins. He put one on and gave the others to the girls. "Come on!" he said excitedly. "I sequenced you both the other day for just such an occasion."

Walter started to skip toward the Portal. At the door, he stopped, took both girls by the hands, and together they leaped through the Portal, reappearing behind an old silver-colored trailer.

"Mon dat isa arr sa priz?" Fajah frowned in disappointment.

"YES! Come on, come with me." Walter led the girls around to the front of the trailer.

They could not believe the difference. This side looked like pure fun. The front of the trailer was shiny and had neon lights, bright yellow awnings, and pretty plastic flowers around a white-fenced patio. One table on the patio had a big rainbow umbrella decorated with balloons dancing on strings, and the banner over the door read 'CONGRATULATIONS!'

"Let's explore!" Walter suggested. So they all walked inside. The floors had black-and-white checkered tiles, and at the front counter were tall metal stools with round red leather seats. There was even the front of an old car inside the diner. It looked like it had driven right through the end of the trailer.

A pretty waitress greeted them on roller skates. Walter ordered three banana splits, with extra cherries on top of the whipped cream.

"Let's sit on the patio," Linda said.

"Mi wana raad baaloon," Faja screamed, racing through the front doors.

Fajah couldn't remember ever having so much fun. Walter even put whipped cream on all of their noses and they pretended to be clowns.

When they finished playing games, Walter said they had to get back to the office, but first he had something to tell them. "I have to go on a trip, I'll be away for a short time. While I'm gone you can work with the nice lady at the Neuro-Center and create more chips. How does that sound?"

They were both disappointed, but eventually Fajah took Walter's hand. "Oanly lettel tyme, ok."

"Yes, yes, my darlings, I will be back before you miss me." Walter paid the waitress and thanked her. Then when the three were alone, he took out a Wand, and FLASH–they were back in his office.

* * *

Alek was moody. It seemed like a lifetime since the Knecht family had driven to Arcosanti. Kristen and he had recently learned to speak with their mom, using Rico's meditations. Talking was great, but he and his sister wished they could hug her again. Their dad was so upset, because he was the only one of them unable to speak with her. Alek didn't have the heart to tell him he was beginning to actually see his mom. He wondered why his dad had such trouble?

The sun had been up for about an hour, as Alek walked along the Agua Fria river with his thoughts keeping him company. He loved it down here under the huge cottonwood trees. When he had time after studying and working in the bell chime foundry, he liked to skip rocks in the pools of cool water. It was quiet here, plus the birds and animals were fun to watch.

He was deep in contemplation about their new lives, when Alek stared across the river, slowly becoming aware of a great stone city that was beginning to manifest in the hills above the riverbank. He knew he was awake, but clearly in a dream–a dream that was part of him, somehow. He instinctively knew the city was high in the mountains. As he watched, the surroundings along the river dissolved and the high mountains became real.

He looked at his arm and became aware that he wore a grand gold bracelet embossed with a sun symbol and he was gripping a golden staff. He held the 'tapac-yauri' staff high in the air and watched the morning light glimmer off the pure gold. How did he know the staff was a 'tapac-yauri?' He now stood at the top of stone stairs, next to an altar. Rings of native people on their knees, at the base of the stairs, bowing to him wavered into view. These were not people from Arizona–they appeared to be from South America. Then a clear memory welled up from his subconscious, or was it coming from the mad-man in his mind? They were in ancient

211

Peru, and a sudden realization struck him– he was witnessing a previous lifetime.

From a great distance came the voice. Was it a voice, or a memory? Whatever it was, a declaration from Manco Cápac came from deep inside his mind.

"Splitting of the worlds has begun, we must be ready!"

"Alek, hello, Alek..."

Was that his sister? How was his sister here, high in the mountains...?

"Hey, stupid. Dad said you're late for your lessons."

That brought Alek back, standing at the river bank. He looked around– it was gone–the city had been so real.

"Come on, hurry," Kristen said. "You know if we miss our home school lessons, we'll have to start school in town–that's Cray-Cray."

"You're Cray-Cray talking all street like that," Alek said, poking her gently in the forehead with his finger. "Race you. Give you a 20-step head start. 1, 2, 3..."

* * *

On the outside, Agent Duncan seemed to be a good Christian. He was a pious, church-going Catholic, a loving father, husband, and a dedicated FBI Agent. No one ever guessed his dark secret life within.

In a similar way– Bishop Daniel was pious, but seemed dedicated, because he repeatedly put on a public exhibition of his devotion to living an ordinary, respectable God-fearing life. Yet on closer examination, the reality was that he lived in a self-created dualistic system that disconnected his manipulative and deceptive actual practices, from the lofty ideals of his diocesan peers and parishioners. In the Bishop's mind, he justified his selfish actions and ways of thinking, that would otherwise be clearly wrong if taken out of the context of his 'higher' goals.

That's why, deep inside, Duncan respected Bishop Daniel. He was a kindred spirit and great adversary. Duncan decided he would strategize with the Bishop, in order to draw potential members closer to the church, by manipulating behind the scenes to make their humanly-orchestrated plan look like a spontaneous vision from God. In turn, that would help Duncan create his illusion of what the world should be like. This, of course, would be for the flock's higher good. There were so many sinners that needed saving, whether they knew it or not. And he was going to help them by allowing the Bishop the ability to appear more than human. The Jump technology would surely convince even the most skeptical of his followers, that the Bishop was a heavenly disciple in direct touch with God.

Duncan knocked on the door to the Penthouse Royal Suite at the Waldorf Astoria on Park Avenue in New York City.

Reverend Paul, the Bishop's assistant, opened the door. "Come in, Agent, the Bishop is expecting you."

Bishop Daniel sat on a luxurious antique couch, upholstered in silk cloth with gold brocade. The large room was furnished with period furniture. An intricately-carved coffee table with matching end tables and two fine chairs completed the sitting area. A baby grand piano in the corner was dwarfed by the size of the room. Elaborate swags and fringed valances hung in the tall windows, the white frames topped with ornate gold crown moldings.

Duncan glanced through the windows, down at busy Park Avenue and the stately St. Patrick's Cathedral. He also noted the dining room where the formal table settings would easily accommodate twelve. "A little extravagant, Your Eminence? It appears your upcoming Leadership Convocation must be another lucrative fundraiser."

The Bishop smiled. "Always unabashed–are you not? But let us get down to the business at hand. I believe you have the sequencing software for me."

"Better than that, Your Grace. This is a sequencing kit, just invented by Rebel's man Walter at Homeland Security." Duncan sat in a chair across from the Bishop and laid the kit on the coffee table. He unzipped a soft shell case that held a small monitoring device. It looked like a blood glucose meter, used for diabetes. "You see, Bishop, this is the finger poker. You just prick yourself with it, and squeeze your finger until a big drop of blood appears. And this is the monitor."

Duncan handed the meter to the Bishop. "It has a test strip inserted into it, waiting for your blood sample. Touch the test strip to your finger and the blood is drawn up. The meter then runs the program, and your sequence number will show on this digital readout. Enter the number into the Wand, along with the location coordinates from GPS and you are ready to Jump." He smiled with anticipation.

"Now if you please, I'll take the remainder of my fee. Oh, and one other thing..." Duncan walked around the table and sat next to the Bishop. "I have been a parishioner with your Diocese for over a decade. For my continued support, and silence, I will be given an important, high-ranking position with your church administration. We can work together to orchestrate your plan to appear as a messenger direct from God. I will work behind the scenes to promote Your Eminence to a position within the church, placing you above the Pope himself. People will see you as an incarnate God on Earth, the second coming of Christ. What we can achieve together is of biblical proportions."

Duncan's phone rang. "Agent Duncan here." He listened intently, then answered, "Yes, sir, right away, sir," and hung up. "Bishop, I'll take that fee now, but I'll have to return so we can discuss my new position with the church–right now I have been ordered back to DC."

* * *

When the kids ran in breathless from Alek's vision at the river, and the family was together in their Arcosanti apartment, Ian announced, "We are all getting stir crazy. What do you say we visit the Grand Canyon today, instead of studying your lessons? If the government knew where we are, they would have come for us by now, so a short trip should be safe enough, if we keep our eyes open."

"Sick, dad, beats school work."

"Yeh, no lessons, let's go!" Alek and Kristen agreed.

"I would enjoy seeing the canyon, son. Good idea."

"I'm glad you all think so. Rico made reservations, under alias names for us at the El Tovar Hotel on the South Rim for three nights. There are many hiking trails, we can rent bikes, and take the Grand Canyon Railroad tour."

They packed, and arrived a few hours later. With apprehension, Ian waited in line at the National Park Service pay station. He paid for a week's pass in cash, and was relieved when the station attendant didn't pay undo attention to him or the vehicle.

At the Mather Point Visitor Center he picked up some maps. They took a quick look around, and all agreed the canyon was the most breathtaking site ever. The 100-year-old El Tovar Hotel was pulled from an old-west

214

movie. The massive three-story log cabin with a brick base was perched on the edge of the canyon. Elk were grazing in the green winter grass lawn at the entrance when they arrived. Ian and his dad went inside to check in.

Alek and his sister raced to the rail fence at the rim. There were no words to describe the immenseness in front of them. "Wow, that's big," Kristen said.

"Yah. You think–dummy," Alek teased. "Let's go find dad, and pa." They had started to call James pa, which pleased him more than they could know.

Everyone decided to go for a hike before dinner, so they took their bags to the room to change. Ian stopped a hotel employee to ask directions for their hike, as they headed through the enormous, rustic grand room. That's when he noticed a man at the front desk, watching him, or was he? 'I must be imagining things,' he thought to himself. 'I'm beginning to jump from shadows.'

Alek and Kristen bolted through the door facing the canyon. Another race was on. "You two stay away from the guard rails!" Ian shouted after them, as he got to the door. He looked around and the man at the front desk was gone. 'I really am afraid of shadows,' he said to himself.

Heading east on the Rim Trail, every other word was an exclamation– "look, wow, that's amazing, it's so big, beautiful!" The trail wound along the canyon's rim, too close for Ian and James' comfort, as Alek and Kristen raced and played along the path. Mesquite, piñon, pine, juniper and sagebrush trees were intermixed with yucca, agave cactus and a few sprinklings of wild flowers.

"Look!" Ian pointed out. "A golden eagle." The magnificent bird effortlessly soured in an updraft along the rim a hundred feet ahead. James wiped away a tear, he could not remember being so happy. There was a time he never thought he would see his family again. Smiling, he ran and picked up Kristen and tossed her in the air. She returned a surprised giggle.

* * *

Twenty minutes before Ian spotted the eagle, and 2,000 miles away, the large Homeland Security computer room was a beehive of activity. "Time to mobilize, men," Commander Gholam ordered. "A license plate just showed up at the Grand Canyon's South Rim, matching the vehicle

Ian was last seen driving. I will take point and scout ahead, so be ready to move in five minutes, on my return."

The Commander had changed from the usual Navy fatigues, to casual outdoor clothing. He looked like a fish out of water, but would blend in at the Grand Canyon.

"I'll return as soon as I have found the target," then he turned and stepped through the Portal.

Seconds later, Gholam walked out from behind a group of piñon and juniper pines growing next to the Canyon. He entered El Tovar, going directly to the front desk, discretely showing the clerk his military credentials. "Do you have an Ian, or James Knecht registered today?" As the clerk looked, Gholam turned to scan the large room.

Ian and family were headed for the doors. Gholam overheard him ask directions for Yavapai Point, then look his direction, so the commander turned away to not look conspicuous. Thanking the clerk, he slipped through the back door, stepped behind the same trees–and vanished.

* * *

Not far from where they spotted the eagle, there was a little side trail that took them closer to the canyon for a better view. Kristen ran to a point next to the rim. "Dad, take my picture."

"Be careful, hun –don't get any closer. Alek, stand next to your sister and watch her. I'll get you both in the picture." Ian took a few steps back to get a better photographic angle .

The air behind him liquefied then wavered gelatin-like and four men appeared. They grabbed James and Ian, disappearing as fast as they had arrived.

Alek yelled, "Dad!" He ran toward the group as they vanished.

Startled, Kristen flinched, and caught the heel of her shoe on a loose rock. She teetered for a split second, attempting to catch her balance. Turning toward her scream, Alek watched horrified as she plummeted from the sheer canyon wall. Instinctively he pictured his favorite deep pool in the creek at Arcosanti, and reached for his sister with his mind. The air around her screaming body quivered, then she splashed into the water, after falling only a few feet.

Alek appeared seconds later, and jumped from the bank of the Agua

Fria and pulled her to the shore. Kristen crawled through the sand at the creek's edge, coughing and sputtering for breath.

He pushed her up to sit on the sandy beach. Raising her arms she looked at her body in total disbelief. "I'm not dead! What did you do?" Then her whirling emotions shifted. "Stupid–why didn't you make me fall into my bed? The water is freezing."

Their laugh was cut short.... "Dad and pa," Kristen suddenly remembered. "Those army men got them."

"We'll get them back," Alek vowed, putting his arm around her shoulder and pulling her close. Huddled together they sat under a mighty oak at the creek's edge, shivering but alive.

CHAPTER 22
Power Struggles

Kristen and Alek sat in the mud, wet and shivering, under the massive old oak, on the bank of the Aqua Fria. They were happy to be alive, after Kristen's fall over the rim into the Grand Canyon. They were feeling very alone and were at a loss as to handling the kidnapping of their father and grandfather.

The sun was setting, leaving them sitting in the cold, deep shadows of the valley. Slowly a warmth began to surround them. A feeling of recognition engulfed the warmth, wrapped lovingly around them. In the weaning light, a translucent shape formed, backlit by the last rays of sun peeking over the canyon walls.

"Mom!" Alek screamed.

Kristen's bottom lip quivered. "Where! I don't see her." She began to cry... "mo.. mo.. mommy, the bad men have daddy and pa!"

Jasmine's calm voice permeated everything around her children, with a peaceful tranquility. "Do not be afraid, everything will be all right, my babies."

Alek gritted his teeth. "Why don't they leave us alone? The government, and the corporations–or whoever they are, have taken everything from us. They killed you, mom! Blew up dad's Portal, stole all his work. Even took my computer. I hate them, I really hate them!"

"Alekander James Knecht." When his mom used his full name like that, he knew she wasn't happy. "You know better. We have always taught you that love will always be the answer to any problem. Hate only destroys things, and makes things worse."

"Mom–it can't get worse!" Alek exclaimed. "Kristen and I are wet and cold, sitting in the mud. You're dead, dad's gone, our home destroyed. We have nothing!"

"Nonsense, you have each other, I will always be with you both and we will find your dad. Now reach inside and find your inner-self. Feel your warrior spirit from lifetimes ago, Manco Cápac, then fight through this with the loving hearts I know you both have. Now listen–I am having trouble speaking to anyone on your side, so this may be the last time we talk for awhile."

Kristen started to protest, but Jasmine interrupted. "Listen carefully, for I cannot stay with you long. Rico will help you. Trust him, he is a good friend of your father, and his heart is wide open. He will do whatever it takes to find your dad. Also contact Celeste and Steele at the Diocese in Wisconsin where Bishop Daniel is the head of the church, but do not trust the Bishop. Celeste and her husband live there and will know how to reach Walter, who is another person you can trust. Celeste, Steele and Walter are good people who are on your side. I love you both so much, and I will be thinking about you every minute, so be strong. I will see you both again as soon as I'm able." Jasmine wrapped the loving warmth tighter, giving her children an ethereal hug.

Suddenly the warmth was gone and the cold returned. "Come on, Kristen! Race you to our room before we freeze."

* * *

Seven of the world's leading theologians stood behind their chairs around the large dining table in the Penthouse Royal Suite at the Waldorf Astoria Hotel. They were in New York City making plans for the upcoming Leadership Convocation, and tonight they were special guests of Bishop Daniel. Dinner was being prepared by celebrity chef English and would be served after the blessing was said.

With Duncan's help, the two conspirators had decided this would make an intimate stage for the premier of the Bishop's direct mystical communion with God. This would be a perfect precursor to the international debut at the Conclave, displaying his special association and communication with the Lord.

Bishop Daniel looked around the extravagant table. The ornate room and dinner setting was overshadowed only by the flamboyant apparel of the assembled group. For a brief moment, the Bishop studied the details of the ceremonial attire they had all chosen. After all, he soon would be selecting a wide variety of formal wear for his world-wide tour of acclaim by the faithful. The traditional white simplicity of the Pope's robes left a lot to be desired.

This elite hierarchy of Roman Catholicism had come at his bidding. Their formal ankle-length black or gray cassocks were complemented with ornate piping along with capes and vestments of rich amaranth shades, bright scarlets, and deep purples. The elders displayed a museum-worthy assortment of chains with gold and silver crosses, their designs and crafting dating back through the centuries.

Bishop Daniel stood at the head of the table, carefully holding the pre-programmed Portal Wand inside his opulent white and gold robe. He tapped his water glass with his spoon for silence, then bowed his head preparing to say the blessing. But as he spoke the first words, he stopped, and silently stared trance-like, then whispered... "Do you see them?... Are they angels?... Look...Look...My God..."

He pressed the button on the Wand as he spoke. The fellowship of clerics around the table observed a heavenly transparent blue-white light surround him, the air nearby liquefied, wavered, and he vanished. For all to witness. A miracle!

Seconds later, he reappeared through the same heavenly illumination. He dropped to his knees. "I have had a revelation from God!"

The assemblage was in awe. Those closest to Bishop Daniel stepped away, not knowing what to expect from the next occurrence. Cardinal Dove dropped to his knees, while Cardinal Biestone crossed himself. Piarro clasped his hands in prayer. Bishop Matthew looked upwards to the heavens, arms raised, like the roof might open and a host of angels appear. The others were all postured in states of worship, disbelief and wonder.

Bishop Daniel waited for the impact of his transformation to settle on the unsettled minds around the table. None had dared approach him, or even speak to one another. He prolonged the sacred moment for full lasting impact.

"My brethren," he finally said in his most theatrical, heavenly voice. "The Lord spoke to me, using David's last words from the Bible in Second Samuel, chapter 23, and I quote–'The Spirit of the LORD spoke through me; his word was on my tongue. The God of Israel spoke, the Rock of Israel said to me: When one rules over men in righteousness, when he rules in the fear of God, he is like the light of morning at sunrise on a cloudless morning, like the brightness after rain that brings the grass from the earth. But evil men are all to be cast aside like thorns, which are not gathered with the hand. Whoever touches thorns uses a tool of iron or the shaft of a spear; they are burned up where they lie.' Bishop Daniel paused, and took a deep breath. "This is the Word of the Lord," he declared.

"Thanks be to God," the clerics responded with reverence.

Bishop Daniel continued, strongly interjecting his own message, as if given direct from God's throne: "We must be strong and rule over men through the fear of the Lord. The end times are near, and we must follow the Lord's wishes. We must cast aside evil men as we would cut away thorns. It is time to gather God-fearing men, and create the Lord's will on Earth. We cannot stand for homosexuals, or for women's rights to abort and kill their babies, along with the multitude of horrors perpetuated by evil. We will be firm. Speak to your congregations about what transpired here today. And of the Lord's will for man to fear his wrath. I have been directed to speak of this at the Leadership Convocation."

"And now, my brethren, let us eat the food we are about to receive in silence, and give thanks to the Lord for speaking through me and choosing us as the righteous eight to spread his newly revealed word. In the name of the Father, and of the Son, and of the Holy Ghost. Amen." They all solemnly made the sign of the cross, and sat down.

He felt all eyes on him. An evil smirk sat in Bishop Daniel's mind, with the only outward display being a dull twinkle in his eyes and the small upturned corner of his mouth. He hoped his face showed only as a shining countenance, radiating the happy holiness of an obedient servant chosen by the Lord.

* * *

Director Aaron Rebel was furious with Walter. He stood four feet away from a 100-foot drop at the edge of a waterfall. "Walter, no heights. I told you I do NOT like heights."

Walter smiled inside, showing a stern outer persona. "Aaron, you told me no skyscrapers. This is all natural."

Rebel quickly walked away from the edge and looked around. He was standing on a patio of sorts. The rock around him appeared to have weathered in such a way as to create a natural balcony. Complete with a retaining wall guarding the edge, overlooking a deep pool of water, which paused quietly before diving over the precipice, cascading noisily to the rock-enclosed tarn below.

It also seemed that Nature's weathering had etched from the sandstone patio a table with a stone bench-style seating that could easily seat sixteen people. High above, an outcrop of stone covered most of the balcony. Delicate stone arches created three doorways leading into the mountain. The entire scene seemed out of a dream. If Rebel looked directly at any element on the cliff other than his immediate surroundings, it would vanish into the landscape as if not actually there. He couldn't hold the image in his mind long enough for it to become real. Any more than he could force a dream to be reality after waking.

"Good to see you both again, Aaron and Walter." Star's voice was a soft whisper, gentle, but easily heard over the sound of the waterfall. Star, Louise, Max and Grandstaff appeared ghost-like, as they first walked onto the balcony from one of the arches in the mountain. As they approached, their appearance as well as the area around them became solid. Aaron watched mystified as their presence seemed to pull the perceived dreamscape into reality.

Rebel shook his head to clear his senses. "I'm glad to see all of you as well," he replied. "Where are we?"

Star's soft voice took on a melodic tone as she answered. "You are standing on the balcony of our home at the Falls in Gaia's dimension. That is the reason the surroundings seemed out of focus when you arrived. While you are influenced by your Portal technology, you will scarcely be able to perceive this dimension. Everything from this world will appear ghost-like, shifting in and out of focus. As you step away from the Portal's influence upon you, everything from our world will vanish. This dimension is not perceivable from your Earth's dimension without the assistance of your technology. The four of us have lowered the energy of the surrounding area, allowing you to see us and the immediate surrounding space."

"Nice trick," Rebel said.

Max stepped toward him. "That's no trick, Walley–just simple science." He took Rebel's hand in a strong grip and shook it firmly. "Glad to make your acquaintance, mate. I'm Max. But enough earbashin. My friends tell me you were undecided at the previous meeting in Dubai. Have you come to help us?"

"Beautiful place you have here. I meant no disrespect when I called this a trick," Rebel said. He was killing time, giving the Jump platoon time to pinpoint his coordinates for the ambush. Rebel walked further away from the waterfall and toward the others, so his team would not materialize too close to the edge, or even in mid-air over the falls. He strolled over to Louise to talk. "I was short with you and the others when we last met. I would like to apologize. And to ask what we can do to eliminate the problem this technology is causing."

Walter stood next to Star, giving Rebel a questioning look, wondering why he was acting so strangely. When Walter opened his mouth to ask Rebel what was going on, a familiar flash split the air, and a squad of armed men burst onto the patio.

Before anyone could react, the first two intruders slapped Collars on Max and Grandstaff. They immediately disappeared. Another smaller man grabbed for Louise, but she sprang away from him and ran toward Star and Walter. The man swung a strange blue-light Whip in an arc that wrapped around Louise's arm.

Walter watched in dismay as he realized the Laser Whip was one of his inventions. It was never meant to harm anyone. He had designed it to help protect the Jump technology from others, who might attempt to steal Ian's discovery. The Whip reduced the frequency of anyone touched by it, keeping them from Jumping. Or unfortunately in this case, reduced the target's energy, removing them from the higher dimension of Gaia.

The Whip immediately dropped Louise's energy, and she started to slip from their dimension. Star took hold of Louise's free arm to pull her back. But the powerful reduction leaped through Louise and pulled Star with her. The air split around them, and the three of them vanished. Another henchman took Rebel's hand, and they disappeared with the final flash of light.

It had all taken less than a minute. Walter stood alone on the cliffs at the top of the waterfall, shaking in shock, trepidation and anger. The patio, his friends and that lying bastard Rebel had all vanished. And without his etheric friends' energy, he had returned to his own dimension in the natural environment, at the creek above the waterfall. All signs of their wondrous home had vanished.

* * *

Swirling between worlds, Star pulled Louise with all the physical and mental strength she could muster. It hurt! Searing pain entered Star through the grip she had on Louise. The agony coursing through Louise was unbearable. Star was not sure how much longer she could withstand the ache pulsating through her energy field.

'Poor Louise,' she thought, then, 'Oh my god! Poor Max, Grandstaff, Akira, and Jaguar!' Had they all felt this horrible suffering from those Collars? It felt like her soul was being torn from her body. It had only been seconds that Louise and she had been swirling in this white light. Was it physical light, or a brightness scorching their minds from the excruciating pain?

From this nauseating spiral, Star saw a split in the air in front of them, and instinctively pulled away. Then she combined every last ounce of her energy along with everything Louise had left to give. Together they screamed into the pain and pulled away. Star threw as strong an energy pulse as Louise and she could gather at the Portal door, that was splitting dimensions.

SNAP. Seconds before they exited the dimensional split, the energy pulse created a massive electrical surge that blew in on itself. The gateway collapsed–throwing them away from the door.

Star fell backward through space, landing hard on her patio at home. Louise, being pulled through, fell on top of her in tears. "My God!" Louise screamed. "That was horrible!" Tremors shook both women unmercifully. Then slowly, their bodies seemed to calm at the feeling of solid unmoving cool stone of home beneath them.

Louise was the first to sit up, and hazily look around. Walter was gone. They were alone.

"We have to help them," was her first lucid thought, putting others first, as usual. "Max and Grandstaff must be feeling that same torment, but what can we do?"

Star lay exhausted on the balcony beside Louise. "Send for Jaguar, he'll know what to do," she was able to weakly reply.

Louise looked through her tears, and another horrifying scream rushed from her lips. "What is that?!"

Laying at Star's feet, still holding the Laser Whip was a hand, severed at the wrist.

"NO. What have I done?" Star whimpered in disgrace, squirming away from the appendage. "I have disrupted life's natural balance. Gone against Gaia's principal doctrine, not to harm or kill from anger or hate. This is the opposite of love. How could I?"

Louise crawled over and hugged the gasping Star. "This was not intentional."

"Of course it was not," Star mewled meekly. "But that does not negate the ripples this action has set in motion. Who knows what consequences this has created? And that poor boy, without a hand. I have changed his life forever."

Louise released their hug and held Star by the shoulders at arm's length. "Hear me–from another perspective you may have just saved many lives. It may be possible to take that Whip apart and see how it works. Find a vulnerability we can exploit in order to stop this destructive technology. Find out what makes it tick."

* * *

Walter looked around, he was alone in the natural mountain landscape, where moments before the Falls patio stood. He had to decide what to do. The road, at best guess, must be twenty miles away or more. He would never make that hike before dark.

There was a sudden bright flash, accompanied by a snap, the air splintered as he watched Louise and Star fall through a space in time. That's the only way he could describe it. They fell in and right back out of the dimension he occupied. As if they had fallen through an invisible doorway that was slammed shut. Then all was quiet again.

He hoped that meant they were safe back in their world. Walter sat on a boulder next to the creek to think. What was he going to do? He could find shelter in the caves across the creek, and build a fire for the night. Walking out in the morning would be a challenge. But then what?

Could he honestly go back to work, with Director Rebel, after all of this? Knowing that the very work he did might be destroying their worlds? What would the repercussions be in breaking his contract with the government? So many questions.

"Hell, it will all work out," he said aloud, just to hear a voice and test his sanity. He was just glad for his late lunch, before this fiasco. It might be a long couple of days before he ate again. Walter set to work finding a place to stay the night and gathering firewood.

* * *

The massive electrical surge short-circuited the Portal door slamming the opening shut, throwing the last men through the door across the room. Edward, the man who had been holding the Laser Whip pulling Louise behind him, lay on the ground a few feet from the dazed Rebel. His hand was missing below the wrist. There was no blood, the wound had cauterized from the heat of the electrical explosion, mixed with the dimension slamming shut on his arm.

"Get this man to the hospital," Rebel yelled above the confusion, rubbing his temples between his palms attempting to clear his mind. "Commander, take the detainees down to the bunker. I do not want Max and Grandstaff escaping. But take the Collars off of them once firmly secured. Those Collars are deadly if left on too long. We have already lost two people that appeared to have been from this alien Gaia group. I cannot believe that a Navy Seal could not hold onto a small lady like Louise... we will discuss that during debriefing. Where the hell is Walter?" Rebel screamed at no one in particular. "Why didn't he Jump back with us? They must have him captive."

The Commander gave orders to four of the platoon: "Once you secure Max and Grandstaff, return with those Collars." He turned back to Rebel. "My men can use Wands to go back and recon the situation at the waterfall, and retrieve Walter. Can we use deadly force on the insurgents if necessary, sir?"

"Of course. If the situation calls for force, use whatever is necessary," Rebel replied. "This is obviously a very dangerous terrorist group. And Commander, I want you to personally lead your men. Make sure you have Collars and the Laser Whips. Use those to subdue Louise and Star first. Remember only two or three people can Jump at a time using a Wand."

For several persons using a Wand to Jump simultaneously, they had to be in close physical contact so their movement through dimensions had to be coordinated. Commander Gholam held a Wand and gripped Chief Petty Officer Arland's hand, and they stepped in tandem as the Portal opening engulfed them.

They stood on the empty ghost-like balcony at the Falls. Petty Officers Kent and Landell followed, holding hands as well. Neither group of men was comfortable holding one another's hand– it was following an

226

order they would not talk about. After they emerged from the Portal, they immediately dropped hands and let the window close. As it shut, the balcony on which they stood vanished. The four men stood back-to-back in the dim light of dusk at the bank of a small creek, looking around nervously in the unfamiliar territory.

Commander Gholam memorized the Jump code for the return home, then erased it from the Wand. Holding the button down to produce a localized Portal effect he looked around. The familiar ghost-like balcony appeared around him, visible for some ten feet.

"Do you men see anything unnatural?"

"No, Sir." came a unanimous response.

"Interesting," he said, letting go of the button. His surroundings returned to the natural landscape. "Hmm, very interesting. Officer Arland, come touch my arm and tell me what you see."

Gholam pressed the button again. "Yes, sir, I see a faint patio around us, sir." As Gholam let go of the button, he thought he saw movement entering the perimeter of their localized illusion.

"Watch your backs, men," Gholam commanded. They carefully put away the Collars and Laser Whips, and armed their automatic weapons. "We'll stay together and head up this stream. Keep your eyes peeled for signs of Walter. Let's find him and get out of here. This place gives me the willies."

* * *

Star and Louise Jumped into the cave that Walter was using for his night's shelter, near the creek. Even though the cave physically was in Gaia, Walter's consciousness was not able to see them until they joined him in Earth's dimension. He sat next to a small fire at the mouth of the grotto, jumping to his feet when they appeared.

"I was hoping you would find me," Walter exclaimed, "I'm so sorry for the attack. I had no idea what they were planning. Rebel had assured me that he was coming here to learn how to fix the problem the Jumps are causing." Walter looked at his feet, kicked a small rock and said, "Rebel and I have been friends for many years–I feel so betrayed."

"Do not feel badly on our account, Walter," Star responded. "We trust you, but I must ask you something quickly before they reach here. There are four men a few minutes from here, their energy is quite angry and dark. Can you help us get our friends back? Those Collars are deadly to those of us from Gaia. Please help us."

Walter smiled. "Of course I will help."

"Thank you, Walter," Louise exclaimed, giving him a hug. "When you learn of Max and Grandstaff's whereabouts, meditate with us in mind. We will come for them. Steele and Celeste are with Akira at the Diocese in Wisconsin. Contact them if you need assistance reaching us."

A spot in the sandstone next to Star's head shattered, microseconds before the sound of a shot echoed through the valley. Shards of stone pierced Star's skin above her eyebrow, forming spots of blood.

Walter shoved both women to the ground and fell over them for protection. "Are you all right?" he looked at them and whispered.

Star wiped a hand across her face, producing a small smear of blood. "I'll be fine."

"Then go!" Walter ordered.

Star took Louise by the hand, and just before they vanished Louise told him they would send their friend Yaozu to help.

Minutes passed while Walter peeked out of the cave watching four heavily armed men snake their way across the creek toward the cave. 'Guess this Yaozu's not going to make it,' he said to himself. Then let out a heavy breath, put his arms over his head to surrender, and began to sing a favorite Stones' song, "I said, baby, baby, baby, you're out of time–Well, baby, baby, baby, you're out of time..."

Out of the blue an Asian man with a gentle smile and a long gray streaked beard materialized, bending low. Yaozu quickly introduced himself and in the same breath asked Walter to follow him. Yaozu ran toward the back of the cave encouraging Walter with urgent whispers. "Hurry, they will be here soon." Walter gladly complied.

When he reached the back wall of the cave, a doorway simply appeared. Walter turned as he stepped through, and saw the door dematerialize, just as Gholam and his men rushed the mouth of the cave in attack formation. He would have loved to see their faces, when discovering no one in the cave.

Walter looked around, realizing he had been so caught up in the events at the cave that he had not noticed his new surroundings. "Where are we?"

"Not sure," Yaozu replied. "As we were free-falling between dimensions, I envisioned the room where Max and Grandstaff are being held prisoner.

I was able to tune into the general vicinity of their transference. So that is where we ended up. The image of the room they are being held in kept changing. Must be that Grandstaff was unable to form a clear picture in his mind of the room's physical attributes. Grandstaff was doing his best to create a mental picture of the room, but he must be sick, possibly weak from that damn Collar. He is unable to hold a clear image of the room or its location in his mind. So here we are, as close as I could get to their location."

They stood on a dark street, underneath a highway overpass. Obviously in a good-sized city. There was no sign of life under the bustling thoroughfare, buzzing with traffic above. It was not a place that either of them would care to be under normal circumstances. 'But what was normal anymore?' Walter thought, then said, "Let's get out of here before we get mugged."

Yaozu and Walter found a 24-hour diner a few blocks away. It was an old converted trailer with a small patio built in front. Walter ordered a piece of cherry pie a-la-mode, and they both had coffee. Walter took a bite of pie, then held up a fork-full. "Hmm, this is good. Take a bite, Yaozu. Oh, and thank you for saving my life."

"Good news, Yaozu!" Walter then exclaimed suddenly. "I know where we are. This diner is a few blocks from where my computer lab is. We're in Washington, DC. There is an underground bunker about six stories under the overpass where we first appeared. I would bet Max and Grandstaff are being held down there, it's like a prison." Yaozu took the bite of pie Walter had offered and still waved around on the fork in the excitement of the moment.

"Mmm, that is very good. Miss, I would like a piece of pie also," he ordered with a smile. Then he leaned forward and told Walter that he could still feel a weak presence from Grandstaff, and that he thought it would be sunrise soon. They could look around when it was light.

"After we discover their location, Louise told me we should find Akira, Steele and Celeste–that they could help. "But first I need to go to my apartment to pick up a change of clothes and a couple of things. They won't be looking for me back here yet," Walter told Yaozu. "I saved a Wand for myself, in case I might need it one day. I believe this is just such a day."

❯ ❯ ❯

CHAPTER 23
The Hawk, The Jaguar and The Speaker

Walter and Yaozu materialized behind a stand of spruce trees on the Diocesan grounds in Wisconsin. A red balloon floated in front of them as they made their way through the festive gathering. Walter stopped to watch as the red orb, caressed by a gentle breeze floated carelessly into the sky. The balloon seemed to have a mind of its own, as it danced around the tree branches that reached to stop it from reaching the lofty heights to which it aspired. He stood trance-like and watched it grow smaller until it vanished into the light clouds above. Childhood memories frolicked through his mind, tickling a spot that made him smile.

"They are here." Walter's thoughts tickled Celeste's mind, as she received mental images conveyed from Akira's connection to Walter. Funny how Walter's childhood memory could carry such strong, happy delight, when translated through Akira.

Those simple words, 'They are here', triggered Akira's jovial excitement at sensing Walter's memories. Though they had never met, Akira knew Walter and his friend were there to see the three of them. They have news, something troubling Walter deeply. Yet he had the joy of a child in his soul. She already liked him.

"Steele–Steele Brandon?" Walter reached out and shook hands, then smiled. "This must be your beautiful wife Celeste, and friend Akira. This is my friend, Yaozu." Yaozu nodded his head, as he shook hands, saying nice to meet everyone. Walter bowed in his cheery old-fashioned way, and lightly kissed the back of Celeste's hand.

She scrunched her brow suspiciously. If not for Akira's earlier thoughts, she would have been concerned about his intentions. "Oh, sorry, I have not introduced myself–I'm Walter, a friend of your grandmother, Louise. I met Louise awhile back at the Falls. What a lovely woman. Very interesting place, the Falls."

"Yes, Walter," Celeste smiled. "Louise said you might be contacting us. Good to finally meet you. Louise is quite taken by your charm. Let's go back to our apartment where we can talk more privately."

Steele put his arms out, indicating the festive gathering around them. "All of this is a celebration of Bishop Daniel's recent meeting with angels. He had a religious experience while preparing for the conclave."

Akira took Walter's hand and smiled. Celeste translated her thoughts. "Akira likes you, Walter, and would like to hear the latest news about Louise and Gaia. Come, our apartment is not far."

Soon they were all sipping tea on the apartment's balcony. Walter proceeded to apologize to them for the ambush he unwittingly brought to the Falls. About how he was betrayed, while attempting to help solve the problems which the Jump technology was causing. And he told them how Max and Grandstaff had been captured.

Yaozu then explained how they had found Max and Grandstaff. That Walter had talked to an old friend from the agency and discovered that they were prisoners deep in a shielded, underground bunker. And they were scheduled to be moved to Guantanamo Prison next week.

"I'm surprised Louise has not told us about all of this," Celeste questioned. "In fact, we haven't heard anything from her for some time now. That is a concern we were discussing earlier today. We have not been able to communicate with Louise or anyone in Gaia."

"That is a concern," Walter agreed. "We've been attempting to tell those at the Falls where Max and Grandstaff are, and to inform them of our plan to free them, but Yaozu has been unable to communicate. We have to get them out before they are moved. It will be impossible to spring them from Guantanamo."

Unable to participate in the conversation, Akira drifted into her totem dreamworld, as the other four sat on the patio making plans for the rescue.

* * *

Crouching in the tall grass, close to the grizzled, lone pine tree next to the lake, he waited patiently–watching every movement around him. He was prepared to remain motionless for hours, hiding from his prey. The tall grass bunched beneath him tickled his stomach, but he would not budge. The slightest movement would give away his location.

His prey has about the best eyesight in the animal kingdom, so he dared to breathe only lightly. Blending into his surroundings was a trait not entirely unique to his species, yet amidst the feline kingdom, he took pride as being one of the best. Nothing escaped his razor-sharp awareness. Not the small bug crawling between blades of the tall dry pasture grass, nor the squirrel hanging from the tree branch above. 'That squirrel would make a tasty bite. NO, that is not the reason for this hunt.'

She would come eventually. He'd seen her hunt during the day along the shore of this lake before. Now the hunter had become the hunted. When she wasn't searching for prey, the updraft coming off the lake shooting up the tall rock cliffs made for a perfect place to play. She would be here soon. His long day's repose would not end in vain.

Was that her? The small speck soured into view, high in the air above him. As the hawk moved closer, she became clear. That was the little hawk for which he had so patiently awaited. Circling on the current above, she gradually came lower. The squirrel caught her keen attention. The unsuspecting rodent now sat beneath the tree, munching on a fallen nut. She began her dive from above. Talons out, death from above.

It was only a matter of time before she was his. Patience... timing had to be perfect. That's it. Just before Akira took her prey, she became his. Tortile muscles uncoiled instantly, pushing his powerful legs, shooting him into the air a split-second before the squirrel was to meet its end.

The large cat caught the hawk, pulling it to the ground, rolling from the momentum, then held her down between powerful paws. The prey was his.

Panic surged through the hawk. She looked death in the face, then...

"Shit, Jaguar, is that you? You scared me to death! Why did you do that?"

The communication flowed naturally between them without an actual word being said. "Instinct, I guess—wanted to see if I still had it. It has been a long time, Little Hawk, good to see you." Jaguar continued. "Actually, this is the only way I was able to get your attention—at least without you flying away. I have attempted many times, but here, in your dream, you have truly become master of your domain. When I approached you as another hawk, you didn't recognize me—did not want anything to do with me. And as a Jaguar, you avoided me the instant you saw me."

Akira smiled. "Funny, that other hawk—I always thought he was horny, making advances. That hawk was too aggressive. I'm not ready to set up a nest and raise any little feathered bundles. Not ready to stay in this reality yet. I have things to do back in Gaia. Would you let go of me now? You're getting heavy."

"Good," Jaguar said, lifting his powerful paw from her pinned body.

Akira flew to a nearby branch and ruffled her feathers, shaking loose dry blades of grass. "Good? You almost hurt me."

"Oh, I'm sorry. I did not mean 'good,' for me having you pushed against the ground." Jaguar would have blushed if a jaguar was capable. "I meant– 'good,' you have things to do in Gaia. Because we need your special talents on Earth right now."

"Jaguar, I have no talents in that world. I can hardly move, and communicating with Earth-bounds is impossible."

Jaguar turned his paw over, licking dry grass from it, then shook to eliminate the grass and pine needles from his fur. They tickled. "Your communication with those bound to earth is not weakening from your lack of talent, Akira. Communication between worlds has all but been cut off entirely. From the plane of existence where I now live, it is arduous to even interact with Gaia. Earth is impossible, though I feel a connection to your energy. I believe you may be a conduit between worlds. Your unique situation–being caught outside of your body–has opened a channel between worlds. That may allow those from Gaia, and maybe even my new world, to not only communicate but travel between dimensions again." His smile, with the large canine teeth, would have been frightening if Akira hadn't known him.

"Are you up for an experiment?" Jaguar asked her. She nodded her feathered head in agreement. "Return to Earth and feel my essence in your heart. I will come visit if I am able."

Akira vanished, leaving a thought with Jaguar. 'Come on, what are you waiting for?'

Time is a funny thing. What had been hours on Earth passed in moments in the dreamworld where Jaguar sat. He directed his spirit toward Akira and found himself hovering in the kitchen of a small apartment.

* * *

"There you are, finally," Akira stood next to herself. The eyes of Akira's physical body had a faraway look. "I wasn't sure you were going to make it. It has been hours."

"Yes. Yes! Akira, you are truly a unique gift to us all–to our worlds! So good to be with you again. Is that Celeste and Steele on the patio?" Jaguar asked.

Sensing Jaguar's presence, Celeste turned her head away from the conversation on the patio. "Jaguar! That is you. I thought I could feel your charisma. I'm so happy to see you, and relieved to make contact with one of our friends outside of Earth."

"How...what?" Jaguar interrupted, sending greetings and mental hugs to Celeste and Steele. "I sense someone else there with you. How are you, Walter." Walter poked his head around the patio door. "Glad to almost see you again, Jaguar." It was going to take time before Walter could get used to Jaguar's appearance being no more than a wavering light. "I haven't seen you since walking through you at the Falls–that was an experience I'll never forget."

Jaguar smiled. "That is a certainty. Walter, join us. And hello, my friend," he said to Yaozu, as he walked into the room. "It is good to have all of you in this fine partnership. I'm here attempting to find a way to communicate with Gaia. All of you know, this new technology has created a tear between dimensions, cutting off communication and travel between our worlds. Earth-bound souls are an odd breed. Just as they are beginning to discover new dimensions, referring to them as Multiverses, they cut themselves off from those same worlds. I'll never understand the third dimensional intellect."

"But I am regressing, let me continue. Akira and I were about to communicate with Gaia. She seems to have a very unique ability to bridge the 'multiverses' and communicate, even hopefully travel between our worlds. Akira, are you up for another test? You may be the key to saving mankind from themselves."

* * *

Speaker of the House Bodner greeted Director Rebel, Agent Duncan and Bishop Daniel from the couch in his office on Capitol Hill. He didn't bother himself to remove his feet from the coffee table when they entered. "Good morning, Your Grace, Director Rebel, Agent Duncan."

Bodner then got up, having reaffirmed his authority, put his arms around the shoulders of Rebel and Duncan and walked them across the room. "You two have managed to make a mess of things from your lofty position as Director of Counter Terrorism and Senior FBI agent. I'm just not feeling very secure these days."

Bodner dropped his arms, turned to Agent Duncan, and looked him hard in the eyes. "God damn it–excuse my language, Bishop–you can't seem to keep anyone from the Falls in custody. Please tell me that the terrorists Max and Grandstaff are both still secure in your safekeeping."

Bodner didn't wait for a reply. He walked over and stared out the window, then he turned to face the three of them. "Let me tell you a story: Puppeteers control our world," he began quietly. "They pull the strings that make all their good little puppets jump, twist and turn. They manipulate these strings to control the public. They tell the public-puppets when to wake up, what to eat, and drink, which vehicle they drive, even control the electrical grid everyone is plugged into. They even scare the public into voting in their favor."

"Remember the movie 'Matrix?' Earth's society is much like those people. Like Nemo before he awakens from the pod–where he was being fed, and maintained in his perfect dream. Look around you. Most people are wandering Earth in a self-imposed dream. They wake up to the alarm, that tells them it is time to go to work. They have their coffee, Jolt, Monster or whatever other energy drink the commercials convince them is required to get started. They dream of driving their idea of what the perfect car will be, when lucky enough to finally 'Make It.' They use the gas or electricity bought from the grid's regulated surcharges. They go to work for a menial salary–just enough of a salary to keep them plugged into and hoping for that perfect life. And all the while the Puppeteers suck as much life-force as possible from their little puppets."

"Are you still with me?" Bodner asked his silent audience, and they nodded strong agreement. He continued with added fervor. "In order to keep this mechanism working, the puppets have to feel somewhat safe and believe there is a way to escape from the life they have so masterfully built around themselves. So to keep them focused on something other than their mundane lives, the masses are entertained with hundreds of television channels, more movies, sports, day-time dramas, reality shows, and even so-called news."

"We, the privileged, feed the masses a mind-numbing mix of prescription drugs, alcohol, fatty and sugary foods. Funny they even think legalizing marijuana was their idea. All of this keeps the pawns sedated enough to not think for themselves. Our media tells them what to think. The Puppeteers keep the minions functioning at just enough of a level to produce and keep the wheels greased and running."

"When the doldrums set in, we promise the masses something. The lottery, win a dream vacation. Give them a menial raise or promotion. Game shows. New car. Win a house. Make them believe."

"Enough of your personal diatribe," Bishop Daniel interrupted. "I believe we all agree with most of what you are saying–but does any of this have a point?"

"Yes, you are paying attention, Bishop–Religion is a wonderful tool. That is where you pull the strings. You get your parishioners to go to their knees, bow and pray, promise them an afterlife–give them hope. Faith does the trick for many. Anything to keep hope floating."

"Let me make a final point and my sermon will get to you, Agent Duncan, and Director Rebel. A select few have sucked so much wealth from others they don't know what to do with it. Sitting above the world's stage, pulling the strings from the top. They have become so jaded, their only reason for living is to feel the control they have over others. Because these puppet masters' emotions are buried so deeply under piles of greed, they must feed from the emotions of others in order to feel alive."

"This select two percent pull the puppet strings from the apex of society. In succession, the top brown-nosers pull their strings. Leading to the yes-men and women to dance and pull strings. Creating their trusted sycophants to work. It leads on and on. The parasites are all too content to wiggle the controller holding the threaded restraints attached to the arms, legs and heads animating their groups of marionettes."

"Some politicians call this trickle-down economics. But politicians are bound by their own threads, eventually leading to the well-connected filthy-rich Puppeteers orchestrating this hidden hideous cacophony from their thrones toward the top of the pyramid. The web of strings is so tangled that any one puppet will never trace their threads to the top. Every puppet's strings are eventually lost in an intricately-tangled maze."

"This brings us to you, Director Rebel and Agent Duncan," Bodner continued. "When I pull your strings, and you men are not able to pacify the masses–to make them believe they are safe–then that makes me look bad–and the strings begin to unravel. More and more good little puppets are realizing that life does not depend on government. Yes, society's grid makes things convenient. Who wants to think and survive on their own? So much easier to be a taker and suckle on the government for nourishment."

"Because of the mess you two have created, people are becoming aware. They will start cutting strings, unplugging from the grid. Lessening their dependence on our great society. They will return to their roots, grow food, use solar and wind energy. Worst of all, society will think for themselves. Which to the horror of the discarded Puppeteers, will lead to enlightenment and the total lack of dependence."

"In short, your lack of performing your jobs is causing anarchy. But the greedy two percent do not go down easily. So disconnected and afraid of the natural order of life–they are willing to do anything to maintain their power. This elite group, through the chain of command, has instructed me to use the Portal technology and our newly developed weapons to eliminate the threat from the terrorist group at the Falls."

"This is where you come into play, Bishop. It is no secret that you recently 'saw angels'–had a divine revelation where 'God' spoke to you of David's last words from the Bible. If I may paraphrase: 'Evil men are all to be cast aside like thorns, which are not gathered with the hand. Whoever touches thorns uses a tool of iron or the shaft of a spear; they are burned up where they lie.' I believe you went on to say 'the Lord's will is for man to fear his wrath.'"

"Well, Your Eminence," Bodner said in arrogance, "those sentiments are of mutual interest. So let's cut the shit and speak honestly. We both know you somehow got your hands on a Wand. Either that or God will be striking me down by the end of our conversation."

"You have no right to speak to me in such a condescending tone, Mr. Bodner," Daniel raged. "I do not have to listen to your blasphemies any longer." The Bishop turned to leave.

"Sit down and listen, Bishop," Bodner hissed. "Or I might have to expose a certain pedophile case. Which is now sealed under the 'secretum pontificium'–your faith's code of confidentiality in accordance with the Roman Catholic Church. This sex abuse coming to light would entail grave ecclesiastical penalties, with the possibility of spending time in jail. Turns out inmates take special care of pedophiles."

Bishop Daniel turned red from either embarrassment, rage, maybe both, bit his lip and sat quietly on the couch.

Bodner continued. "You obviously have a Wand and have been sequenced. And you are familiar with the religious sect in Utah. They are using the Jump technology to give the appearance of living in an alternate dimension, in the canyons outside of the town of Escalante. They call their encampment the 'Falls.' Your 'miraculous' Jump makes you a natural choice to contact this group on our behalf."

"With my authorization, Director Rebel recently brought together a nonpareil group of combat experts to attack the terrorist group at the Falls. I will share details with you, Bishop, since you now have a need to know, but you are not to pass this on. Commander Gholam and his elite group of Navy Seals accomplished a successful first strike. Moving with an uncanny stealth, striking with frightening accuracy. Two of the Falls' group known as Max and Grandstaff were successfully captured. We are planning to interrogate them for information necessary to rid ourselves of this terrorist threat. You will be our lead operative, Bishop. The terrorists at the Falls will not expect you, garbed in your robes of famous holiness, so you will head Project Annihilation. We need you ready before the end of the week."

* * *

The following morning, Duncan entered Daniel's hotel in DC, his hand out in greeting. "So good to see you again, Bishop."

"Yes, you as well," Daniel said, turning away without shaking Duncan's hand, suspicious of his agenda. There was no love lost between these antagonists. As adversaries, they had agreed to disagree on most subjects. Though between them remained a mutual understanding of needing one another, for each of their twisted agendas.

Duncan put on his best salesman's smile. "Your Eminence, I'm here to outline your role as lead of our mission to attack the Falls. Your involvement will also be in the best interest of your Church. After our initial interrogation of Max and Grandstaff, it appears that the culture at the Falls stresses the idea of a new paradigm for living. They are taking an active role, wanting to change culture and bring about a new spiritual awareness."

"Their philosophy is to be in tune with nature, with the cosmos. But they are blurring the distinction between good and evil and creating the mindset where there is no need for condemnation, so that nobody needs forgiveness. They call this spiritual attitude 'Gaia,' claiming it to be in harmony with the profound knowledge of God. But you and I know that this blasphemy will result in distorting God's word, lead to anarchy, a state of disorder and nonrecognition of the Catholic authority."

The Bishop's suspicions turned to contemplation. "You might just have a notion there. When are we moving forward with this mission, and what exactly is my part?"

CHAPTER 24
Gathering

"This plan will work," Walter said, addressing the group standing in Celeste's kitchen. "That is, if they haven't canceled my security clearance yet."

The look of uncertainty was obvious in Steele and Celeste's demeanor. Akira and Yaozu looked to Jaguar for reassurance.

"A wanted government employee strolls in the front door of a secure government building, and walks two fugitives out. It is just crazy enough to work," Jaguar mused in an attempt to alleviate everyone's concerns.

"We'll need four of us to get Max and Grandstaff out of the bunker," Walter continued.

"The trick will be getting away afterwards," Steele observed.

Walter ran his hands through his hair, leaving it disheveled with a few strands of hairs pulled free from his long gray ponytail. Opening his eyes wide and tucking his lips under, leaving a flat, lip-less smile, and exclaimed, "Never said it would be easy. Guess that means you have volunteered."

Then with a big smile, Walter pulled a Wand from his backpack. "I hope everyone is sequenced."

The group figured that Yaozu's energy level was high enough that he could Jump without being sequenced, as long as he was touching whomever was using the Wand. However, Steele and Celeste's energy was questionable—they had visited Gaia without the Portal before, so with a little luck they could Jump with the Wand's assistance. "Once we get Max and Grandstaff away from the Collars, and the bunkers, their vibrational energy should rise so they can also travel with the aid of the Wand."

"So it is settled," Jaguar confirmed. "Steele, Celeste, Yaozu and Walter will Jump to DC and rescue Max and Grandstaff. Akira and I will test her ability and travel to the Falls. And we will all meet there the night of the moon's eclipse, in two days"

"Works for me," Walter said.

"Yes, it will be great to have all of us together and to see Louise and

Star again," Celeste noted. "Good luck. Everyone be careful, we will see you soon."

* * *

"I am reporting this truck stolen to the DC police, later this afternoon," Walter's buddy said. "It has been fun knowing you, my friend. Please don't go and get yourself shot."

"Not planning on it, see you around," Walter replied with a wink. "Thanks, give my best to Mary and the kids."

Steele and Celeste were able to change their body's energy just enough to make the DC Jump, though it was a little rough on the first attempt. That afternoon, the rescue group was on their way. Steele, Celeste and Yaozu in the truck they had borrowed from the Department of Transportation. Walter followed in a rental car. The truck made a perfect cover for their plan. Bright reflective orange vests and hard hats finished the deception. Steele stopped the truck under the overpass. Then Celeste placed orange and white-striped barricades behind the truck and a couple around the curved sheet-metal air duct, that Walter had indicated next to the adjacent building's wall. Walter passed the would-be street workers and continued up the street, pulling into the parking structure beside the Homeland Security building.

Yaozu started the compressor in the back of the truck, connected the canister of gas Walter provided and pushed most of the hundred-foot hose deep into the air duct. Then flipped open the valve and odorless gas rushed through the tube, into the vent. Within minutes, everyone in the hall outside the bunker cells should be asleep. There were four separate air ducts feeding the bunker complex. Steele hoped Walter had the correct one or this would be a very short rescue attempt.

Up the street, Walter stepped through the metal detector just inside the lobby of U.S. Immigration and Custom Enforcement in one of the Homeland Security buildings. 'Whew, so-good-so-far,' he thought. The fact that only a select few knew about the bunker, hidden deep beneath them, would work to his advantage. Security was minimal in order to keep the facility undisclosed. Generally only a guard or two from the Army and no video surveillance.

'If I'm lucky, this will simply be the end of my career with the government. Better that, than being arrested or shot,' Walter thought stepping into the elevator. Three glass strips ran around the inside of the elevator, an interesting design element. He swiped his security card through the reader, scanned his palm on the center glass strip, just right of the elevator button pad, then entered an eight-digit code. The elevator plummeted six floors, giving him just enough time to wipe the glass free of fingerprints. This was all part of the protocol keeping the bunker secure.

Before the elevator doors opened, another thought crossed his mind. 'Hope the vent I picked was correct.' Walter pulled a mask from his briefcase and slipped it on. His descent stopped and the doors slowly slid open. Outside he was greeted by an armed guard with an M4 Carbine pointed at Walter's chest. "Shit," came Walter's muffled voice from beneath the mask. "Must have been the wrong vent."

A confused look crossed the guard's face. He pushed the Carbine into Walter's chest with a command. "Don't move!"

Suddenly the guard's knees buckled and he collapsed to the floor. Walter pulled the keys from the comatose body and started unlocking cell doors. Behind the third door was Max. He was unconscious, but he had a pulse. The next room held Grandstaff, sitting tilted woozily on the bed.

Walter figured the building's exhaust system had cleared the gas, so he pulled off his mask. "It's me, Grandstaff–can you walk?" Grandstaff shook his head affirmatively. "Good. We have to get out of here. Help me with Max, he isn't looking too well." Grandstaff's large girth made it easier to support Max as they lurched down the hall. Max was waking up and slowly getting his legs to work. As they exited the elevator on the main floor, Walter pulled the fire alarm to create a diversion. Then they slipped out the side door, where the remainder of their partners in crime waited in the rental car they had retrieved from the parking garage.

Driving away, the team all breathed a sigh of relief. "Can't believe your plan actually worked," Yaozu said.

Walter punched him in the shoulder. "Thanks for the vote of confidence." They all laughed.

"One more stop we have to make before we Jump to the Falls. Fajah and her friend Linda have been making computer chips. These chips are key to the operation of the Portal technology. We must get them away from the project. That will keep Bodner and his team from manufacturing any more devices. The girls should be at the National Institute for Neurological

Disorders by nine tomorrow morning. I need to go into the lab, save the girls, wipe the computer program and destroy the DNA magnetite mixture."

"Ve doo noot all hav to go ofter z gurls," Grandstaff pointed out.

"That's right," Yaozu agreed. "I can Jump to the Falls with Grandstaff, Max, Celeste and her husband. Then come back for Walter and the girls at ten in the morning, after he has destroyed the DNA stuff."

"Hold on just one minute," Celeste exclaimed. "Have you all lost your minds? That is putting Fajah and Linda in too much danger. Walter can pick-up the girls at their foster home in the morning, as he usually would going to the lab. Yaozu can take them to safety, then return for Walter, after he has taken care of things at the lab."

They all agreed that Celeste's plan made more sense.

Max and Grandstaff needed some rest and nourishment, to regain their strength before the Jump. Using cash, they checked into a small hotel off Wisconsin Avenue, about ten minutes from the Institute for Neurological Disorders.

They were all exhausted. Max and Grandstaff collapsed when they got to the room they shared with Walter. Waking only long enough to eat something before falling into a deep sleep. Even Walter's snoring didn't keep them awake. Celeste and her husband had an adjoining room and needed no encouragement to sleep either.

Early the next morning, the day of eclipse, Walter put together a makeshift breakfast of juice, coffee and rolls from the convenience store around the corner, and woke everyone.

After coffee and a quick review of their plan, Yaozu and Max made the first Jump to the Falls with the assistance of Walter's Wand. Grandstaff Jumped next. "Be careful, Walter," Celeste warned.

"Always am, I will see you soon," Walter said with a reassuring wink, then when Yaozu returned, Celeste and Steele vanished with him.

* * *

"Hydrochloric acid, that's it, that will destroy the DNA magnetite mixture," Walter said, looking up from the bottom shelf holding various swimming pool supplies. Walter's ranting, as he wandered through the DC hardware store aisles talking to himself, had drawn attention. A store clerk stood next to a few shoppers at the end of the aisle, watching suspiciously and keeping their distance. 'I had better pay for this and go pick up the girls,' he thought. 'I'm beginning to gather a crowd.'

Walter looked over at the gawking shoppers, then ran his fingers through his disheveled hair in an attempt to comb it into place. "Go on with your shopping, I have found my elusive pool product. Carry on." He smiled at the clerk he passed on the way to the checkout counter. "Oh, one more thing, sir. I will require a small glass jar—where can I find that?"

After his early morning rant through the local hardware store, Walter was on his way to pick up Fajah and Linda.

Screams could probably be heard by the neighborhood, when the girls saw Walter and ran into his arms. "We missed you!" came their united voices. Fajah smiled and giggled. "Walter Walter, u bea so happi—we make many of Horologes. We gettin ok width da frogs on a heads, we makin chips fass te fass. Mr. Reabel he bea happi he taka many many to yuh builders. He tell wi ya gata team of smadi, buildin spacial Collar an a Magic Wands wid um."

Linda interrupted— "Yeh, Fajah and I think those must be really, really magic, and the prettiest Collars in the world! Can we see them?"

"I am so happy to see you girls," Walter exclaimed, frowning slightly at the loss of the chips. Then he forced a smile and patted them both on the head gently as they hugged him. "Of course you can see the Collars and I will show you how magic the Wands are. But first, go and get a favorite toy and a sweater from your room to bring with you today. It's a special day."

On the way to the lab, Walter pulled the car off the highway and turned into the hotel parking lot, where he had agreed to meet Yaozu. "Girls, we are not going to the lab today. I have a big surprise for you both," Walter said, throwing his hands in the air. "We are going on a short vacation. You won't even need a change of clothes or bring a toothbrush. A friend will show you one of the magic Wands, and use it to take you to see our friends at the Falls. Fajah, you've probably told Linda about your adventures with them." The girls exchanged excited looks. "Now hold hands, and concentrate like you do when you make the Horologe chip. That will bring your energy up so you can Jump to see Star, Louise and the dogs. Oh, this is going to be so much fun! Girls, here comes my friend, he will travel with you, while I take care of some business."

As they were speaking, Yaozu walked up to the car and climbed into the backseat with the girls. Fajah squeezed Linda's hand harder and looked to Walter for reassurance. "Yaozu is my friend and a very good person," he assured them. "You two will be just fine. And I promise I will see you very soon. And you know I keep my promises. Now go have fun, and pet Isis and Maya for me."

Fajah and Linda looked at the magic Wand, smiled, then took Yaozu's hand and the three vanished.

Ten minutes later, Walter walked into the Institute for Neurological Disorders.

"Good morning, Walter," greeted the receptionist as he approached the desk. "We haven't seen you around for a while, good to have you back. Will those two precious girls be joining you today?"

"They will not be in today, good to see you as well," Walter smiled, and gave her a wink. "Please hold my calls, I have some catching up to do."

As the elevator doors closed, the receptionist picked up the phone and made a call. "Walter is back, sir, I am sure he will be happy to see you." She paused listening. "Okay, I won't tell him you're coming, he will be so surprised. Good day to you as well, sir," she said, then hung up the receiver.

Walter entered the lab, and locked the door behind him. He unlocked the refrigerated cabinet where the Horologe chips were stored. 'The girls have been busy,' he thought to himself, taking the container of the remaining chips. Then he rushed to the glass case holding the viral DNA magnetite mixture and unlocked it. He sighed heavily in disappointment, and hesitated. Then firm in his decision, he dumped the chips into the mixture, and pulled the small jar of hydrochloric acid from his jacket pocket and poured half the bottle into the mixture. The mixture started to bubble and turn white, releasing a gas. Walter quickly closed the top of the case to keep the fumes inside. Next he inserted a flash drive into the computer and started to download the programs and experimental data.

Bang, Bang, Bang! The lab door rattled from the force of the knocks. "Walter, we know you are in there. Let me in so we can talk. You have created quite a mess for yourself. We have been friends for a long time, so let me help you," Director Rebel said loudly with false sincerity.

"You have played me for enough of a fool, my old friend," Walter said through the door in dismay. "I'm afraid our friendship cannot withstand your bamboozling nature, Rebel."

"Sorry, buddy, I truly wanted to help you out of this situation," the Director responded. Then he screamed the order, "Break down the door!"

Walter ran to the computer and checked the screen. The download was not complete, but he could wait no longer. He pulled out the drive, opened the side of the CPU and poured the remainder of the acid into the hard drive. He was happy he had insisted from the beginning of the experiment, that the computer not be connected to the network. He hoped it had not been hacked by his so-called friends.

'It's after 10, where is Yaozu?–He's late!' Walter thought as the door came off its hinges. Armed men rushed through the door, so Walter closed his eyes and held his arms over his head in surrender.

"Hold tight, Walter!" Yaozu shouted, appearing suddenly. Walter opened his eyes wide, he was never so happy to see the light surround them. Just as they began to shift into the other dimension Walter saw the flash from the muzzle of a weapon.

* * *

It had been a frustrating time for Little Jake. So much had happened in Star and her friends' lives that he was unaware of. The reincarnated Vicky as 5-year-old Little Jake had been too busy recovering from heart surgery to think about much else. His parents Tracy and Ed could not understand why their son was suddenly so fixated on his imaginary friend Star. In fact, his very first words after the operation were about finding Star.

Little Jake wondered why his parents insisted that Star was a fictitious, make-believe friend. He had tried to explain that his real friend's name was really Star, so why didn't they just believe him?

Following Vicky's passion from her previous life, Little Jake started reading about auto mechanics on the home computer, instead of playing games and learning his ABC's like other kids his age would. Then one morning Ed found Little Jake in the garage reprogramming the computer in the family car, insisting it would improve the gas mileage. His mom and dad were sure surprised when it actually worked.

Now they were calling him gifted, and had him standing in some child psychologist's office pointing at barnyard animals on a silly IQ chart. "Show me the cow," said the doctor.

'Oh yeh,' Jake thought. Maybe he should tell them why the methane gas from cow's poop was causing global greenhouse gas emissions that were destroying the Earth's ozone layer. He was sure that would interest them.

None of that really mattered though. He had to figure out how to contact Star. That had consumed him since his rebirth. There were times he wished he hadn't remembered any of his past life, about Star. Being concerned about little boy things would have been so much easier. That evening, after his bath, Little Jake made a mental note to wake up to see the moon's eclipse. Then he drifted off to sleep, thinking about Star and looking at the crystal that grandpa had given him after the operation. 'I love that crystal' he thought drifting into a dream...

....'Star, she's in trouble!' Startled awake, little Jake sat straight up in bed. Star needed his help. Looking around, he saw that an odd light filled the room–light from bright moonlight refracting through the crystal hanging in the window. 'Is this still a dream?' he wondered. 'Could I still be sleeping?'

Jake rubbed the sleep from his eyes, got up on his bed and looked out the window. The earth's shadow was starting its trail across the moon. The light danced through the tree's leaves outside the window, sending multi-colored radiance across the walls of his room. The colors began to darken, the light turning orange... it was so...sooo.. hypnotizing...

....the lights... Jake shifted into a transcendent state where he could feel Star's presence. Suddenly he sensed another presence–it was Akira! And instantly the room changed. The air around him was somehow dimensional. It became liquid-like and glowed. Appearing as if in a mirage, he could see Star, standing overlooking a beautiful valley, shrouded in darkness.

At the Falls, Star immediately felt his presence–the little boy–and at the same time her old friend Vicky. Her mind instantly joined with Little Jake's essence. A spark of recognition flashed between them, reuniting their many loves throughout time. Lifetimes of the love they shared, which had proliferated through centuries. Life upon lifetimes of their unique loves, layered one upon another, growing ever stronger with each layer. Innumerable feelings from so many different relationships. Love shared between mother and child, father and son, siblings, platonic loves, physical lovers, all building their understanding of what true love is.

Suddenly Little Jake was standing looking up at Star, their combined auric field pulsated and glowed with a brilliance that flooded their surroundings with great power. A power that drew the energy fields of loved ones like a magnet draws iron shavings.

Louise appeared. "What is all of this? I was literally pulled here, from an enormous energy that holds Vicky, Star, and Akira's combined signature," she said breathlessly, then looked more closely. "And who is this wondrous child here with you, Star? And where is Akira? I can feel her, yet she is not here. What in all the worlds is going on?"

* * *

Standing by the creek down the hill from her apartment at the Diocese, Akira watched the blood moon of the eclipse. She listened to the murmur of the gentle breeze rustling the leaves of the trees. The babbling brook and distant croak of frogs merged with nature's chorus.

Jaguar's soothing voice resonated with the sounds as if it came from Earth herself. "Center your life-force, Little Hawk. Listen to the rippling water flow over pebbles and around the stones. Feel the earth beneath your feet...now feel the air moving around you... relax…"

"Now, concentrate on Star...and Louise...and the Falls..." Jaguar gently took Akira's hand in his. "...see them in your mind's eye..." Jaguar smiled, "...let us go there together when you are ready."

The air around Akira appeared to liquefy and glow with a modulating iridescence. Spreading slowly, it engulfed Jaguar. Akira was somehow bending space, in a gravitational, space-time singularity. Through a quantum drift, she copied the super symmetry in both Earth's and Gaia's dimensions and with a spark of love–merged the two worlds. Jaguar and Akira were suddenly with Louise, Star and Jake, all bathed in a loving radiance.

* * *

Across the country, Alek stood on the patio in the Arcosanti night, gazing at the Aqua Fria. He could barely see the old oak tree on the river's bank where he and Kristen had spoken with their mother a few days earlier. He kicked the guardrail in frustration. He was unsure how he should find Steele, Celeste and Walter, as his mother had instructed. How were any of them going to help his sister and him anyway?

Standing there with more questions than answers, he glanced up at the moon. What was happening? 'Oh, that's right,' he thought. 'The lunar eclipse is tonight. The news lady the other day said tonight would be the blood moon. Perfect, as if my mood wasn't bad enough.'

Kristen walked out of the apartment rubbing her eyes. "What are you doing up?"

"Couldn't sleep," Alek replied. "Besides, I wanted to see the moon eclipse."

"Oh, yeh," she said, looking up. "Wish mom could be here to see it with us." Tears swelled in Kristen's eyes. She began to cry.

Alek hugged his sister. "Me, too. I miss mom so much. But we will find a way to be with her again–promise." Holding his sister, under the blood moon, their united love and desire to be with their mother was palpable. Never had Alek wanted anything so much in his life.

Then, amazingly–a dimensional energy shift occurred. Alek felt as if the universe opened. He sensed everyone–Akira, Jaguar, Louise, Star and a little boy he didn't recognize. MOM! There was mom! In that instant, he stood with his sister next to their mother and the rest of the group.

Isis and Maya bounded across the balcony toward the group, followed by Celeste, Steele, Max, Yaozu, and Grandstaff.

"Vhoots oul z rookuz?" Grandstaff asked in his broken Russian-English dialect.

"Let us figure that wonderful mystery out," Louise said. "Did you do that, Alek?"

He stood tall, chin up. "No, ma'm. That wasn't me this time."

"Most likely, Akira pulled us together," Jaguar stated. "I believe she is a conduit between worlds. Her condition, being stuck outside her physical body, has somehow created her unique talent. Akira has brought us together for a reason. There is no such thing as coincidence."

* * *

"Gentlemen!" the host threw out a salutation across the room. "So good to finally meet you, Ian. Good to have you back, James, how is that fine grandson of yours? Please have a seat."

Three FBI agents escorted Ian and his father to the couch. "Excuse me for not shaking your hands, but I'm weary of fugitives these days. Nothing personal."

"I understand, Mr. Speaker, or can I call you just plain John?" Ian said, sitting next to his father on the uncomfortable ornate office furniture. "Nor would I shake the hand of a criminal–masquerading as a government official, anyway. Nothing personal, of course."

Bodner smiled. "Your obstinate tone will change soon." He nodded to the FBI agents and asked them to wait outside the door, in case his guests became uncooperative.

Then continued. "I asked you two to join me to witness the end of your terrorist organization. I believe you refer to the group as 'The Falls.' Yes, you see, I have my sources, Ian. I know your wife Jasmine is living in the canyons with them, outside of Escalante, and my bet is that your children may be there with her. Oh, and how exciting–you will be here first hand, as an eyewitness to see how your very own technology will take down these ridiculous radicals. For that, your country owes you a debt of gratitude. And I personally do as well. It's just a shame that this is the only commendation for service which you will ever receive in your remaining short life."

"Our very capable Commander Victor Gholam will use the Portal Door in the computer lab, along with your very own Wand–one of many we have recently manufactured–to bring us first-hand reports on the campaign against the Falls. You see, Walter has been busy sequencing hundreds of men. While the Commander's team has worked around the clock to train these special forces platoons, to use this new technology of yours. And you will be with me to experience the attack and witness everything as it unravels." Bodner's laugh was not good-humored.

CHAPTER 25
Oblivion

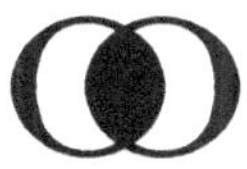

Bishop Daniel appeared on the patio at the Falls, Wand in hand. His other hand was extended, holding an olive branch.

Jaguar, Louise, and Star nodded suspiciously to him at his arrival. The three of them were here at this uncertain scene as a last effort for a peaceful resolution to the conflict. Director Rebel had told Walter that he had made a detestable mistake in conducting the earlier assault on Gaia, and was sincerely penitent. He wanted to send a high representative from the Catholic Church to make amends, and set up a conciliation meeting to find a way to live in peace. Walter finally relented, and made these arrangements, but the group was far from trusting.

The Bishop was taken back at seeing Jaguar's diaphanous appearance, no more than a wavering light. 'Spirit-like.' His impression was angelic, or was it demonic. "Th... tha...thank you all for meeting me on such short notice." Daniel cleared his throat attempting to regain his composure, and straightened his white robe. "I understand you were assailed by Agent Duncan's men, and that they took friends of yours prisoner. Then a short time later that you also were assaulted by Director Rebel, and prisoners again were taken. Those two officials asked that I, as a neutral third party meet with you, apologize for those ill-conceived and unnecessary offensive actions, and to ask if your group would meet with an arbitrator to alleviate tensions between our organizations. Of course, this meeting would be held on neutral ground."

Bishop Daniel was doing his best to keep those from Gaia occupied. The plan was to divert their attention away from Commander Gholam and the platoons, amassing down the valley from the Falls. And to not run from this aberration they referred to as Jaguar. He silently prayed to himself, waiting for their response. 'Yea, though I walk through the valley of the shadow of death, I will fear no evil, for thou art with me. Thy rod and thy staff they comfort me.'

The group remained silent, so Daniel changed the subject and continued.

"The belief and teachings you give your followers here at the Falls are false hopes. You must understand the truth. In Heaven we will remain human, therefore finite, therefore our knowledge will remain finite. Only God's shoulders are strong enough to carry the burden of infinite knowledge."

Jaguar finally addressed the Bishop. "First, we are not an organization, we are a family, sir. The ideologies you and many religions propose are rigid doctrines and utterly hopeless to approach by rational argument. Many of these beliefs are fabricated on prejudices, and arrogance, perpetuating ignorance, and used as a means of control. Only when you awake to the wisdom and joy of the infinite dimensions of Spirit can enlightenment begin to come. We are going to have to agree to disagree, with no hard feelings, only love."

"No hard feelings," Daniel agreed verbally, hiding his indignation. "Though I am frightened for your souls, son. As God-fearing human beings–we must suffer gladly the blow and shock to our pride. That is Heaven's gift of eternal childhood, thus eternal hope and progress. So what you offer as successes or self-actualization–that is what Heaven denies us all. That is what Purgatory and Hell offers us. In your version of heaven, we will find despair instead of hope, ennui instead of creative work, and the emptying of all our joy and hopes. You must heed Jesus' teaching, 'Unless you turn and become like children, you will never enter the kingdom of Heaven.' Heaven is not something to be outgrown."

"Heaven cannot be outgrown," Star interjected. "As we have taught through numerous lifetimes and a wisdom we imparted to Louise many years ago–Nobody puts you through 'Heaven', 'Purgatory' or 'Hell' but your own self. It is simply a rite of passage from one phase of existence to another...whether on Earth or between dimensions. I must reiterate: only when you awake to the wisdom and joy of the infinite dimensions of Spirit can enlightenment begin to come. Then humanity can realize that Heaven, Purgatory and Hell are simply a state of being. Not a physical location. They are tailored to each single Soul's basic need for evolution."

"Stop your intentional delusion, Bishop," Jaguar interrupted, then turned his head, listening to frequencies beyond the others' ability to hear. "These theologies can and have been argued throughout time. But we do not have time for that, now do we? Why are you really here, Bishop? You are attempting to distract us for some reason. I feel the universe developing a defense to stand against an approaching darkness, though I am not certain of what this defense consists. Or against exactly what?"

Jaguar stood back, taking hold of Star and Louise's hands. The three of them concentrated, feeling the energy from the darkness and the light being drawn to a single point there at the Falls.

"What have you done, Daniel?" the three said in concert.

Louise moved forward, one slow step at a time. "Bishop, think about the people you are aligning yourself with. You are siding with a group using science to sever mankind's connection to your professed God. They have caused the veil between Earth and the higher dimension of Gaia and beyond to degenerate to a point where communication between spiritual dimensions is being cut off entirely. Without what you consider spiritual guidance, the evil being perpetuated by a growing number of governments, corporations, religions and misguided people on Earth will spiral out of control. The deluge of greed and lack of empathy may ultimately cause mankind's destruction. Possibly cause irreparable harm to Earth's ecosystem."

They were now toe to toe, as she spoke her condemnation. "Your misguided decisions could make the planet inhospitable for eons to come. Or worse, could destroy the atmosphere, killing the planet and every living organism that relies on her for existence."

Louise began to tremble. Jaguar stepped beside her, resting a hand on her shoulder for support, as she continued. "Earth, aligned with Gaia's wisdom, is drawing an energy together right here at the Falls, to stand against this growing darkness. You—you Bogus Bishop—are being used as a Trojan Horse, a puppet, whose ultimate goal is to tear apart the very spiritual nature you pretend to pray to for guidance." Louise turned her face away, and in a very unladylike manner, spat on the ground in disgust.

Jaguar's attention was tugged away from the conversation as he focused intently on the forces of the negative energy that were coming ever nearer. He could sense the numerous Jump platoons that were gathering in the valley below the Falls. Their heavy energy along with the weapons they carried was affecting the dimension around them. And they were advancing on the Falls rapidly and would be here soon.

Just then Rico Gori materialized. "What is happening around here...?" His words stopped short as he felt a shiver run down his spine. "That's nasty," he exclaimed. "Where is all of this cynicism coming from?" The

Bishop was startled by this new display of understanding, knowing that he himself was the answer.

In response to Rico's question, Jaguar sent everyone in the group a clear impression of what he was seeing–a vision of the razor-edge of darkness, being led by Commander Gholam. This arrogant group was bent on attacking their own source of survival. How could they not see that? None of those at the Falls could fathom the depths being dredged by these people to justify attacking the true nature of one's self.

So Jaguar made the underlying cause for their dysfunctional behavior clear by giving them a quick summary of recent decades, and how mankind's technological advancement had greatly surpassed their spiritual growth. It became obvious that man's understanding of his soul, in relation to the universal soul, was truly lacking. Even with his limited connection, the Bishop shuddered at this truth.

* * *

Commander Gholam considered the most optimal maneuvers in order to take advantage of the limited available Wands. He had insisted they wait until the Horologe chips the girls had made were developed into weapons, but orders were orders, and he had to make use of the resources available. He gave orders to Chief Petty Officer Arland, along with Petty Officer Kent, to each take a Wand, and Jump two squads of four men to the head of the canyon and flank the terrorists from behind. Even with the limited resources and rushed training, the commander was proud of his men. Project Annihilation was coming together without a hitch. They moved out quietly.

Gaia's defense against the advancing forces was not obvious to those standing on the patio. Powerful individuals for the light were being drawn to the Falls. How they fit together to combat the darkness was yet unclear. For Daniel's own protection, and the group's security, Max and Grandstaff appeared and escorted the Bishop to a room off of the patio, then secured that entrance with an energy shield composed of a weave of earth and air.

"It is no coincidence we are all here simultaneously," Star noted with a tone of urgency as the entire group assembled. "Akira, your timing could not have been better–bringing us together at this specific moment, in response to the extreme negative energy surrounding the Falls. You are obviously in tune with Gaia's life force."

Louise acknowledged Star, "Very true indeed." Then she addressed the rest of the gathering. "And Akira is far more than the key to move between worlds. She is also our connection to one another–she alone is able to open a doorway of integration. Through her unparalleled worldly and spiritual bond, she is able to reintegrate the individual spark of cosmic consciousness, held locked within each of us. This enables the wholeness from where we came to be restored–in turn allowing higher states of consciousness and our assimilation into oneness." Their thoughts were flowing in rapid uniformity from one being to the other, without the need for slow words being spoken. Much remained to be done.

"Profound insight, Louise," Jaguar stated. Then he held Alek by the shoulders, looked into his strong eyes, and addressed the group. "This young man is the genesis around which our group is uniting." He gently shook Alek with pride. "That is why you returned at this time, Manco Cápac, my teacher. You have always been the one to bring people together around a cause."

At the urging of Jaguar's touch, Alek searched deep within himself, and listened to Cápac's inner voice. He understood what Jaguar said to be true. He felt this great burden, like a stack of bricks on his shoulders. Yet at the same time he found humor in the dichotomy that a 12-year-old had knowledge from thousands of years. He and Cápac had the strength of youth and the wisdom of age, which relieved some of the pressure.

However, Alek's youth and lack of confidence showed in his slumped shoulders as he stepped to the edge of Star's patio, and looked out over the Falls. Jasmine could see his insecurity, so she picked up Kristen and walked to her son. He put an arm around his mother and poked his sister in the forehead with his finger. "Hey, sis, what about all of this– you little dork?"

She punched him. "I think you can do this. Just don't get a big head– stupid." They stood by his side, as the others joined them at the retaining wall and watched the troops–now numbering hundreds–spreading through the valley.

The heavy gloom was thick from the fear, anger and hate coming off of the battle-hardened militia below. Their emotions were so incredibly stagnant, that their very existence in Gaia consumed energy from the living matter around them, shriveling the plants. Jasmine kissed her son's cheek and whispered in his ear, "Your father and I are proud of you, son. Be strong, all of us are with you..." She turned with her free arm out indicating the makeshift family gathered around them.

"Yeh, dork, get them for us...I wish daddy was here." Kristen jumped from her mom's arms and ran off to prevent her brother from seeing her cry.

* * *

It was up to him—and from deep inside came an idea. As a means to stand against the growing darkness, Alek concentrated on the feeling of his parent's pride and the glimmer of hope from each of those standing with him. Cápac whispered from the back of his mind, 'We have all been drawn here by the fabric of the universe for this purpose—dork—whatever that is.'

Alek smiled at Cápac's attempt at humor. He shook his head and thought, 'I must be going mad, listening to the voice of an old fossil in my head.' Then he rotated his head to better hear Louise instruct the group about the process used to pass into Alek, by means of Akira's integration. She stressed the importance of this action in order to generate a combined power and stamina capable of standing against the growing forces. 'Am I up to that?' he wondered, almost aloud. But he readied his strongest self for the task, and whispered to himself, "Let's get them, Cápac."

Akira was the first to blend herself with Alek. She took both of his hands in her own, closed her eyes and took a deep breath. A familiar light and quiet space enveloped them, exposing an intimate understanding and expanded knowledge of one another as their spirits became one. Alek-Akira now shared a united psyche. They took a moment to adjust to this brand new way of being. It was strange...and huge...very wonderfully incredibly powerful.

"I love you, be careful," Steele said, hugging Celeste, not wanting to let go. She kissed him tenderly and nodded, then bent to pet Isis and Maya. Her intuition felt that Alek still lacked the confidence in his young strength. So she kissed Isis on the nose, turned and stepped forward extending her arms. Taking her place across from Alek-Akira, she mustered a confident smile, then her inner-being reached for the Akira bridge, finding an open path to their unified mind—and melted into their reality. As she let go of herself and their energies combined, Alek's confidence grew from her positive assurance. Celeste was astounded by the unity and expanded understanding that flooded her awareness.

After Celeste's energy settled into their merged unity, Alek focused the combined power of the threesome and pushed a weave of air and earth at the front troops of the advancing army. But the pressure from such a negative force was too strong–the darkness continued to advance up the valley, sucking life-force from Gaia's dimension. The long years of fear, control, ego and greed from the amassed troops was too much for the three to combat alone.

Gaia embodied the essence of goodness emanating from every soul who resided in her peaceful borders. And as a sentient being, Gaia sensed the desecration being perpetuated against her residents. So in response she changed the surrounding environment in defense, reshaping the weather to reflect the overwhelming feelings that consumed the approaching forces back at them. Black clouds boiled and thunder growled, voicing Gaia's reflection of the overbearing emotions of descent. More troops poured through the Portals. In response, lightning flashed and the ground rumbled. Earth, the very emblem of solidity, moved beneath everyone. Fissures formed, ripping apart the ground beneath the advancing hordes, swallowing whomever was near.

Star and Jake knew that their deep understanding of love was needed in the mix, so they stepped into the circle of friends, reached into Akira's essence and merged with the group. They swirled into Alek-Akira-Celeste becoming one with them–uniting with their encompassing essence, to form a strength of five-as-one. Each unique being a part of the other, becoming an amalgamation of Alek-Akira-Celeste-Star-Jake. Yet each of them was still themselves within this unity. This was a volatile mix. So much energy, so much love. Yet the equilibrium of their four energies surrounding Alek, who had moved to the center of their group, was unstable. Their energy was wobbling like a top out of balance.

Jaguar watched with the pride of a father, as each of Gaia's children entered this group's essence. It was akin to watching the birth of an atomic reaction: Akira's loving sacrifice bringing their essence together; the explosive loving truth from Celeste wanting to discharge and rip at the darkness; Star and Jake filling the union with the understanding of eons of unrelenting love; while Alek's great strength, combined with Cápac's ageless wisdom held the unstable union together, from the center. Each unique elemental soul coursed around Alek's being–as the nucleus–like the electrons, protons and neutrons around an atom. Perspiration beaded on his forehead as Alek strained to keep their combined pulsating energy from spinning out of control. Sweat rolled from his brow stinging his eyes–he wasn't sure how long he could hold them together.

* * *

After the shot rang out during their escape, Walter realized that there was something horribly wrong with this Jump–the space around Walter and Yaozu shook violently, as red droplets swirled around them causing a faint, musty metallic smell in the air. Walter landed hard from the unexpected Jump, and tumbled across the patio at the Falls. Yaozu flopped through a second later landing heavily on top of Walter. "What..." horrified words stuck in Walter's throat as he realized Yaozu wasn't moving, and a wet warmth spread across Walter from beneath Yaozu's limp body.

Jaguar and Rico rushed to their friends and rolled Yaozu off of the stunned Walter, gently laying him on the ground. Jaguar immediately started a healing weave, as Rico cradled Yaozu's head. Suddenly a wavering impression of Yaozu appeared next to them and announced, "Jaguar, Rico, my good friends, I appreciate your healing effort, but please do not. It is time I join Jaguar in his new dimension, I will no longer need that vessel–" indicating his still body laying next to Walter.

A vacant feeling spread through the immediate group, but the urgency of the situation did not allow the group to celebrate his life. Their attentions were immediately drawn back to the raging battle.

As Walter painfully gained his feet, he saw Steele standing with Isis and Maya, staring at his wife. Celeste was standing in a group with a strong bluish-white light coursing around them, emitting a radiance that lit the surrounding area. Before Walter could question what he saw, Fajah rushed to Walter's side. She looked in awe, mixed with a heavy dose of fear, watching Alek struggle to hold Akira-Celeste-Star and Jake's energy together. Louise stepped next to Fajah, "Good to see you, Walter. We will all take time to rejoice in Yaozu's life, after we have pushed this darkness from our home."

"And to see you, m'lady," Walter returned her greeting with a fainthearted bow and a look of confusion mixed with tears.

"I will explain later," Louise said, then took Fajah's and Linda's hands in hers. Lightning streaked above in the black sky. "Do not be afraid, little

258

ones," Louise consoled the two girls. Torrential weather whipped around the group, creating such a loud hum that it became impossible to hear. Yet a comforting voice was clear in Fajah's mind, and she nodded a reassuring okay to Linda.

Louise's unruffled calm was conveyed through her telepathy as she spoke to Fajah. "Remember the courage and love you used against the General when he was going to hurt you before? You possess a mighty strength, and you do not need to be afraid of it. The General is among the negative forces threatening our world. You are an important element to this union. Tell Linda to stay with Walter and be safe here. Then release yourself into the group's oneness. Use Akira's loving bridge to join the others."

Fajah looked into Louise's knowing eyes and understood, then her fear melted away. She spoke quickly with Linda, and hugged a goodbye as Walter joined them. Then she kissed Walter on the cheek and turned to join the group. She made a connection from her heart to Akira, and felt the swift passage toward the others. Taking a deep breath, like she used to, before jumping into the ocean with her Tata, she took a leap of faith.

Immediately she began to swirl around with the group, becoming one with them—yet remaining herself somehow at the same time. Joining their flow seemed like it should be nauseating, but it wasn't. It was tranquil, with a tactile sense of unity and purpose. This is her family, Akira-Alek-Star-Jake-Celeste and herself. This is her life, this is her. It was wonderful, having such a sense of belonging, and being whole at the same time. Her addition to the others brought a symmetry, and the wobble that had threatened to tear apart the group's union stopped.

They were now a united group of six. After settling into a symbiotic balance, they concentrated their combined energy toward the advancing forces. Louise watched the valley below as the darkness lessened, and the Jump platoons slowed their advance, confused by the sudden weakening in their bodies. But they did NOT stop!

There was something missing. Alek concentrated the group's energy again, with no more success than before. He could feel a tremendous energy build-up within his own body. The blood veins in his neck were ready to explode. His inner body felt ready to burst. He was filled past capacity, though the tremendous energy overload would not fully release. What was he going to do? What would Cápac do? All of that pent-up strength had to be released somehow to prevent total disaster.

As the focused pressure of the six pulled more and more energy through Alek, they all watched in confusion at the darkness slashing its way up the valley. Hordes of advancing troops lashed Laser Whips at the perplexed people of Gaia. This once peaceful home of gentle souls, living in harmony with Gaia, was being decimated. Each person touched immediately dropped from their dimension, with their energy becoming heavier as they fell to Earth. The veil between dimensions was so contaminated, that returning to their home in the higher dimension of Gaia was impossible.

Holding their group together was more than Alek could manage. His panic began to spread through the group when Louise received his thoughts of apprehension and cry for help. 'I can't hold our energy any longer. What are we going to do?!'

Darkness continued its march, driven by the hate and anger pushed before Gholam and his men. The General appeared, he was in his element. He used his dead comrade Gregory's favored knife, and channeled his demonic lust for violence, slashing at every perceived enemy that moved. More armed forces entered, two and three at a time, through several Portal openings created by the newly created Wands. Each arrival expanded the damaging effects against the environment. Negativity was being magnified, growing ten-fold for every greedy, hateful, angry emotion entering Gaia. This growth of devouring mayhem was overwhelming.

The Falls' last hope was unraveling. The once blazing bluish-white light that orbited around the group slowed its rotation, convulsed uncontrollably, and dwindled to a small flicker. In the waning light, Alek could hardly see Star standing next to him—he had never seen her beautiful expression so hollow and despondent—she had obviously been drained by the uncontrollable energy running wildly through the group. She babbled something incoherent before he looked away. He personally had nothing left within himself to even console her. He had failed, and even all of their efforts combined had not been able to stop the negative forces. Alek slumped to the ground, tucked his chin to his chest and covered his head with his arms. He couldn't take any more. But the group stayed connected around him, attempting with their last breaths to protect him.

Their treasured valley was completely engulfed by darkness as the battle raged throughout the rocky canyon below, filling it with fear, chaos, death and crying children. "This is from our vision!—A vale of tears,"

Jasmine exclaimed. She held Kristen tight and they cried together for their son and brother. Alek, her friends and her glorious new home were being torn apart and swallowed by this repressive battle.

"Louise, protect Kristen," Jasmine pleaded, then rushed to help her son.

Jaguar stopped her, "It is far too dangerous to intervene while the group's souls are interwoven. We must gently help them to separate, before getting involved with any single person." Jasmine cried out in helpless desperation, "Alek!"

The cancerous swell of hundreds surged again against the Falls. Jaguar put an arm around Jasmine and Louise while Kristen clung to her mother's leg, and they watched men just below their feet claw and crawl up the sandstone rock, more animal-like than human. Others appeared through Portals just yards away, in groups of two and three, ready for blood. Their full onslaught was only seconds away from consuming the young group of crushed champions. Isis and Maya crouched beside the group, hair on their backs standing as they emitted defensive growls. Steele and Walter desperately fought with every ounce of their strength to protect Linda.

Jaguar, the once proud patriarch, pushed Jasmine and Kristen away from a Whip that barely missed its target, "Run, hide in the caves– protect your daughter," he exclaimed, then dove into the battle. He struggled in this dimension to throw energy bursts that knock the closest forces unconscious. Louise scanned the horrific battle scene in the distance, then focused on pushing away those climbing over the top of the rocky cliff at her feet, with her own weaves of air and water. Their beautiful home was being choked beneath this wicked darkness. All was on the verge of being lost in the encompassing blackness.

Being without a physical form in this dimension, Jaguar was less effective to fight the advancing troops, so he did something he never thought his morality was capable of. A young man lay at Jaguar's feet, fatally wounded, struggling to take his last breath. Jaguar knelt and whispered some encouraging words as the man's soul departed the body. Jaguar surrounded the discarded body with light and slid into the vacant host, reanimating the physical form. He jumped to his feet and focused his tremendous energy to weave elements of earth, water and air–then hurled the mix at the advancing troops. He had intentionally not used a weave with fire, as he did not intend to kill the opposition, only disable them. Louise quickly joined him, and they fought side by side, pushing away the darkness with everything they had. But the overall mass attacking their stronghold was too much. The horde swarmed over them, catching Jaguar with a Whip. Louise watched horrified as the young man's body vanished with Jaguar's essence. She retreated moments before she was overcome, and ran for the young group–friendly spirits and mortal friends, who were all now crouched around Alek in a protective huddle.

Suddenly the Earth stopped quaking. An eerie silence took hold of everything...and everyone.

Silence would normally be a welcome relief from the war raging throughout the valley. But this was different–more than silence. This was a lack of substance–a void that seemed to extend forever. This was a negative space without existence–cut off from the divine universal source of Spirit.

This was Nothingness.

❭ ❭ ❭

CHAPTER 26
Genesis

Deep within the encompassing Nothing, Alek's body lay twisted into a fetal position with his arms folded over his head. Their united family was contorted in a spiritual manifestation reflecting his physical form—lost in their united mix of fear. All sense of time was gone. They were not sure if they'd been lost in this void for hours, days—or could it have been weeks or longer?

Commander Gholam's personally-delivered report of victory hung like honey in Speaker Bodner's mind. They had won!

"Let us visit our adversaries and demand their surrender," Director Rebel crowed, rubbing his hands together. "We will secure the area, then return to take you there, sir," Rebel said, and the Speaker nodded his assent.

Then Rebel ordered the Commander to bring Ian and the three of them vanished in the now familiar light, and appeared at the top of the Falls, close to the cowering group of hopeful heroes. They were followed by Agent Duncan with James, locked in cuffs behind his back.

Nearby, Louise stood frozen—trapped by the void encompassing all the higher energy of Gaia. As if in a different universe, Petty Officers Kent and Landell moved silently around her—undisturbed! The Officers struck flares and threw them around the area for light. The Bishop, walk out of a cave, that moments before imprisoned him behind a semi-transparent barrier, that had just vanished. All Louise could do was stand tall and watch her attackers move freely around her, disfigured by the red glow of flares in the darkness. James and Ian watched in confusion and horror, unable to understand the soundless, eerie, demonic scene the red light bathed everything in.

The area was secure to the Director's satisfaction, so he Jumped away—returning moments later with Speaker Bodner. They had come to take prisoners, and gloat over their captives. Bodner wanted to be there first hand to witness the end of this rebellion and watch them grovel.

* * *

... 'what was that'... something drifted through the collective mind of the unified Gaia group...there it was again...

....a warm, soothing thought again tickled their unified mind from within the abyss... 'Relax...Breathe...'

There was something familiar about that notion, that reached deep into the terror-stricken group's mind, gently touching Alek's hopeless perception of reality. He recognized the source of the warm calming thought. 'Louise!'

Alek peeked out from between his fingers, and saw blurred movement in the crimson darkness. He fought back a chill running down his spine, and took a slow breath. Then he uncovered his head and stood, willing their united group to relax and take a deep united breath. And they did! Then another, it felt good to breathe again, they had all but forgotten how to do something as simple as take a breath.

Kent and Landell rushed Alek, but were stopped by an invisible wave of thick air. Fajah smiled at her contribution of protecting the group, remembering her encounter with the General. Funny Kent and Landell had the same startled appearance of confusion as the General had in that horrible little room in DC. Only now, she no longer felt helpless.

At that moment Isis stopped growling, walked into the group and rubbed against Akira's leg, then bumped her snout into Akira's hand, demanding her attention. Akira looked into Isis' fathomless eyes, and saw a deep inner light, radiating a pure emotion that reached for their united psyche. She sensed Isis held the missing ingredient from their matrix. The group having gained their feet, stood proudly. Then a spark arced through Akira as Isis moved her essence into the united group, creating a regularity. A warm, calming sensation spread through everyone simultaneously, emanating from the union of Isis with the medley. Her essence pulsated through the would-be group of heroes revealing the true nature of complete unconditional LOVE.

That was it...the missing element! When this universal truth became part of the group, the universe took an all-encompassing breath through them— the life-giving breath of Prana coming from everything good around them, absorbing through every pore in their being, leaving a single thought— — —

'Let there be light.'

This universal truth became part of their united psyche. And deep from within the once oppressive blackness a tiny spark ignited, barely visible within the abyss. This flicker of a united unconditional spark became tinder for a flame-less fire which sprang to an inferno and spread through the valley. The heat-less flame burned away the insurmountable inky-blackness without scorching a single leaf or blade of grass. The darkness buckled, then folded in on itself, revealing a glorious radiance, which exploded and filled the valley with the light of UNCONDITIONAL LOVE.

This purifying wave of tenderness, warmth, intimacy, attachment, endearment, and connectedness grew exponentially, increasing as it moved outward from the singular strength of the united seven, dissolving the torrent of terror that moments before had consumed the valley. The atrocious malignant memories from lifetimes were re-lived in seconds by every person touched by the light. Those feelings were cleaned away, leaving the pure heart of a newborn.

As the wave passed, the faction of violent men that had been filled with anger and hate, one after the other dropped their weapons and fell to their knees crying. The emotional state created from the horrors that had been directed at them, and-in-turn, that they had conducted against others, became instantly cleansed by the pure vibration that flowed from the universe through their innermost being. Their hearts had been so suddenly expanded, that they struggled to catch their breaths.

The unconditional radiance washed through them, stripping away their transgressions, leaving their hearts completely open. The sudden awakening caused Bodner to collapse. He lay on the ground staring blankly at the now radiant sun, unable to blink. His jaw had gone slack and drool seeped from the corners of his mouth. His respiratory system was so stunned that his body's automatic response to breathe didn't function—he was suffocating from the lack of taking a breath.

Agent Duncan came to his senses, after running through a broad range of emotions that took him on a journey from hysterical depression to joyful laughter. He realized Bodner wasn't breathing and started efforts to revive him.

The rock-hard shell that Rebel had built around his heart shattered, leaving him to relive lifetimes of horrors and revealed seraphic memories from his all-but-forgotten pure heart. He stood frozen, unable to do anything but watch Duncan from a trance-like coma.

After seeing his troubled life, tears ran down the General's face and he turned to Commander Gholam, gave him a hug and kissed him on the mouth. "My name is Francise, I have always loved you." The Commander smiled and responded, "Very nice to meet you," then he rested his head on Francise's shoulder and cried like a baby.

Ian picked up a Wand that had been dropped near him and saw that the Horologe chip had melted from the tremendous unconditional power that had permeated everything in the area. He was happy and saddened to know that this technology was gone.

Louise's smile filled Jasmine with understanding as they sat hand-in-hand experiencing the endless stream of emotions coming from the valley full of open hearts generating a prodigious sense of love that permeated the entire area. An understanding was filling everyone at the Falls, spreading through the valley touching every heart. Without any doubt they all came to understand–

There was no such thing as death. Life itself had no beginning and no end, it just is.

In the clearing at the base of the Falls, once again lush and green, stood an elephant and lamb, drinking from a shimmering, crystal clear pool of water. The animals watched calmly as a mountain lion named Maverick, along with Benard the bear joined them for a casual drink. Everything in the valley was once again living in harmony with the universe.

* * *

Jaguar's incorporeal being hovered high above the Falls. His thoughts filled everyone: 'Many in this valley today have witnessed and done many detestable things. Put that life behind you, return to your homes now, refreshed and renewed, and spread the love and understanding you received today. But before you go, I will share with you something Star and I explained to Louise twenty years ago through her Journals'...

"Life's Primary Lesson:
Conjugate one verb,
to Love,
All Wisdom therein."

Every uninvited person in Gaia then vanished. One-by-one, those from Gaia who had been displaced began to return to their peaceful home. Everyone on the patio smiled.

There was much to rebuild and repair, but for the first time in a long while there was once again hope.

Of course there is no end...

About the Author

RB Anderson was born in New Mexico and raised in a family of artists and authors, giving him a uniquely imaginative view of the world.

An entrepreneur, he established and successfully ran art and design studios in San Francisco during the 1970's, and in Arizona until early 2000's.

Shaping the next chapter in his life as an author, he lives in Arizona with his wife/soul mate. He was inspired to be a writer by a series of notebooks written by his grandmother documenting her process of dying, where she met guiding angels. So he pulled from the creative writing in his background to fashion this moving novel. RB is currently working on a sequel.